Fair Margaret

by F. Marion Crawford

CHAPTER I

'I am a realist,' said Mr. Edmund Lushington, as if that explained everything. 'We could hardly expect to agree,' he added.

It sounded very much as if he had said: 'As you are not a realist, my poor young lady, I can of course hardly expect you to know anything.'

Margaret Donne looked at him quietly and smiled. She was not very sensitive to other people's opinions; few idealists are, for they generally think more of their ideas than of themselves. Mr. Lushington had said that he could not agree with her, that was all, and she was quite indifferent. She had known that he would not share her opinion, when the discussion had begun, for he never did, and she was glad of it. She also knew that her smile irritated him, for he did not resemble her in the very least. He was slightly aggressive, as shy persons often are: and yet, like a good many men who profess 'realism,' brutal frankness and a sweeping disbelief of everything not 'scientifically' true, Mr. Lushington was almost morbidly sensitive to the opinion of others. Criticism hurt him; indifference wounded him to the quick; ridicule made him writhe.

He was a fair man with a healthy skin, and his eyes were blue; but they had a particularly disagreeable trick of looking at one suddenly for an instant, with a little pinching of the lids, and a slight glitter, turning away again in a displeased way, as if he had expected to be insulted, and was sure that the speaker was slighting him, at the very least. He often blushed when he said something sharp. He wished he were dark, because dark men could say biting things without blushing, and pale, because he felt that it was not interesting to be pink and white. His hair, too, was smoother and softer than he could have wished it. He had tried experiments with his beard and moustache, and had finally made up his mind to let both grow, but he still looked hopelessly neat. When he pushed his hair back from his forehead with a devastating gesture it simply became untidy, as if he had forgotten to brush it. At last he had accepted his fate, and he resigned himself to what he considered his physical disadvantages, but no one would ever know how he had studied the photographs of the big men in the front of things, trying to detect in them some single feature to which his own bore a faint resemblance. Hitherto he had failed.

Yet he was 'somebody,' and perhaps it means more to be

somebody nowadays, in the howling fight for place and acknowledgment, than it meant in the latter part of the nineteenth century. How easy life was in the early eighties, compared with this, how mild were the ways of nations, how primitive, pure and upright the dealings of financiers in that day of pristine virtue and pastoral simplicity! It was all very well to be an idealist then, Mr. Lushington sometimes said to Margaret; the world was young, then; there was time for everything, then; there was room for everybody, then; even the seasons were different, then! At least, all old people say so, and it can hardly be supposed that all persons over fifty years of age belong to a secret and powerful association of liars, organised and banded together to deceive the young.

Mr. Lushington was somebody, even at the beginning of this truthful little tale, and that was some time ago; and if anything about him could have really irritated Margaret Donne, it was that she could not understand the reason of his undeniable importance. The people who succeed in life, and in the arts and professions, are not always the pleasantest people, nor even the nicest. Miss Donne had found this out before she was twenty, and she was two years older now. She had learned a good many other things more or less connected with human nature, and more or less useful to a young woman in her position.

She remembered two or three of those comparatively recent discoveries as she smiled at Mr. Lushington and observed that her smile annoyed him. Not that Margaret was cruel or fond of giving pain for the sake of seeing suffering; but she could be both when she was roused to defend her beliefs, her ideals, or even her tastes. The cool ferocity of some young women is awful. Judith, Jael, Delilah, and Athaliah were not mythical. Is there a man who has not wakened from dreams, to find that the woman he trusted has stolen his strength or is just about to hammer the great nail home through his temples?

Margaret Donne was not actually cruel to her fellow-creatures. She was not one of those modern persons who feel sick at the sight of a half-starved horse dragging a heavy load, but will turn a man's life into a temporary hell without changing colour. Such as these give women a bad name among men. Margaret was merely defending herself, for Mr. Lushington sometimes drove her to extremities; his very shyness was so aggressive, that she could not pity him, even when she saw him blush painfully, and noticed the slight dew which an attack of social timidity brought to his smooth forehead.

She had excellent nerves, and was not at all timid; if anything, she thought herself a little too self-possessed, and was slightly ashamed of it, fancying it unwomanly. She had a great fear of ever being that, and with Mr. Lushington, who seemed to take it for granted that she ought to think as men do, and was to be blamed for thinking otherwise, she took especial pains to claim a woman's privileges at every turn.

'I cannot imagine,' he said presently, 'how any intelligent person can really believe in such arrant mythology.'

'But I make no pretension of "intelligence",' murmured Margaret Donne.

'That is absurd,' retorted Mr. Lushington, with a half-furtive, half-angry glance. 'You know you are clever.'

Margaret knew it, of course, and she smiled again. The young man did not need to see her to be sure how she looked at that moment, for he knew her face well. It had fixed itself in the front of his memories some time ago, and he had not succeeded in bringing any other image there to drive it away. Perhaps he had not tried as hard as he supposed.

It was not such a very striking face either, at first sight. The features were not perfect, by any means, and they were certainly not Greek. Anacreon would not have compared Margaret's complexion to roses mixed with milk, but he might have thought of cream tinged with peach-bloom, and it would have been called a beautiful skin anywhere. Margaret had rather light brown eyes, but when she was interested in anything the pupils widened so much as to make them look very dark. Then the lids would stay quite motionless for a long time, and the colour would fade a little from her whole face; but sometimes, just then, she would bite her lower lip, and that spoiled what some people would have called the intenseness of her expression. It is true that her teeth were beyond criticism and her lips were fresh and creamy red--but Mr. Lushington wished she would not do it. The muses are never represented 'biting their lips'; and in his moments of enthusiasm he liked to think that Margaret was his muse. She had thick brown hair that waved naturally, but made no little curls and baby ringlets, such as some young women have, or make. The line of her hair along her forehead and temples, though curved, was rather severe. She had been fair when a little girl, but had grown darker after she was fifteen.

When she thought of it, she rather liked her own face, for she was not everlastingly trying to be some one else. It was a satisfactory face, on the whole, she thought, perfectly natural and frank, and healthy.

No doubt it would have been nice to be as beautiful as a Madame de Villeneuve, or a Comtesse de Castiglione, but as that was quite impossible, it was easy to be satisfied with what she had in the way of looks and not to envy the insolent radiance of the fair beauties, or the tragic splendour of the dark ones. Besides, great beauty has disadvantages; it attracts attention at the wrong moment, it makes travelling troublesome, it is obtrusive and hinders a woman from doing exactly what she pleases. It is celebrity, and therefore a target for every photographing tourist and newspaper man.

And then, to lose it, as one must, is a kind of suffering which no male can quite understand. Every great beauty feels that she is to be unjustly condemned to death between forty and fifty, and that every day of her life brings her nearer to ignominious public execution; and though beauties manage to last longer, yet is their strength but sorrow and weakness, depending largely on the hairdresser, the dentist, the dressmaker and other functions of the unknown quantities x and y, as the mathematicians say.

The Emperor Tiberius is reported to have said that if a man does not know what is good for him when he is forty years old, he must be either a fool or a physician. Similarly, a woman who does not know her own good points at twenty is either very foolish, or a raving beauty--or a saint. Perhaps women can be all three; it is not safe to assert anything positively about them. Margaret Donne was clever, she was a good girl but not a saint, and she was a little more than fairly good-looking. That was all, and she knew her good points. If she was not perpetually showing them to advantage, she at least realised what they were and that she might some day have to make the most of them. They were her complexion, her mouth and her figure; and she was clever, if cleverness be a 'point' in a human being, which is doubtful. It is not considered one in a puppy.

Mr. Lushington discouraged the familiarity of men who called him plain 'Lushington.' When they were older than he, he felt that they were patronising him; if they were younger, he thought them distinctly cheeky. Occasionally he fell in with a relation, or an old schoolfellow, who addressed him as 'Ned,' or even as 'Eddie,' This made him utterly miserable; in the language of Johnson, when Mr. Lushington was called 'Eddie,' he was convolved with agony-- especially if a third person chanced to be present. Margaret sometimes wondered whether she should ever be in a position to use that weapon.

There was a possibility of it, depending on her own choice. In fact, there were two possibilities, for she could marry him if she pleased, or she could make an intimate friend of him, and they might then call each other by their Christian names. At the present time she knew him so well that she avoided using his name altogether, and he called her 'Miss Margaret' when he was pleased, and 'Miss Donne' when he was not.

'It is a pity you think me clever,' she said demurely, after a little pause.

'Why?' he inquired severely.

'The idea makes you so uncomfortable,' Margaret answered. 'If I were just a nice dull girl, you would only have to lay down the law, and I should have to accept it. Or else you would not feel obliged to talk to me at all, which would be simpler.'

'Much,' said Lushington, with some acerbity.

'So much simpler, that I wonder why you do not follow the line of least resistance!'

A short silence came after this suggestion, and Margaret turned over the pages of her book as if making up her mind where to begin reading. This was not quite a pretence, for Lushington had told her that it was a book she ought to read, which it was her intellectual duty to read, and which would develop her reasoning faculties. By way of encouragement he had added that she would probably not like it. On that point she agreed with him readily. To people who read much, every new book has a personality, features and an expression, attractive, dull, or repulsive, like most human beings one meets for the first time. This particular book had a particularly priggish expression, like Lushington's yellow shoes, which were too good and too new, and which he was examining with apparent earnestness. To tell the truth he did not see them, for he was wondering whether the blush of annoyance he felt was unusually visible. The result of thinking about it was that it deepened to scarlet at once.

'You look hot,' observed Margaret, with an exasperating smile.

'Not at all,' answered Lushington, feeling as if she had rubbed his cheeks with red pepper. 'I suppose I am sunburnt.'

Tiny beads of perspiration were gathering on his forehead, and he knew by her smile that she saw them. It would have been delightful to walk into the pond just then, yellow shoes and all.

He told himself that he was Edmund Lushington, the distinguished critic and reviewer, before whom authors trembled and were afraid. It was absurd that he should feel too hot because a mere girl had said something smart and disagreeable. In fact, what she had said was little short of an impertinence, in his opinion.

The fool who does not know that he looks a fool is happy. The fool who is conscious of looking one undergoes real pain. But of all the miserable victims of shyness, the one most to be pitied is the sensitive, gifted man who is perfectly aware that he looks silly while rightly conscious that he is not. Margaret Donne watched Lushington, and knew that she was amply revenged. He would call her 'Miss Donne' presently, and say something about the weather, as if they had never met before. She paid no more attention to him for some time, and began to read bits of the new book, here and there, where one page looked a little less dull than the rest.

Meanwhile Lushington smoked thoughtfully, and the unwelcome blush subsided. He glanced sideways at Margaret's face two or three times, as if he were going to speak, but said nothing, and sent a small cloud straight out before him, with a rather vicious blowing, as if he were trying to make the smoke express his feelings. Margaret knew that trick of his very well. Lushington was an aggressive smoker, and with every puff he seemed to say: 'There! Take that! I told you so!'

Margaret did not look up from her book, for she knew that he would speak before long; and so it happened.

'Miss Donne,' he began, with unnecessary coldness, and then stopped short.

'Yes?' Margaret answered, with mild interrogation.

'Oh!' ejaculated Mr. Lushington, as if surprised that she should reply at all. 'I thought you were reading.'

'I was.' She let the new book shut itself, as she lifted her hand from the open pages.

'I did not mean to interrupt you,' said the young man stiffly.

No answer occurred to Margaret at once, so she waited, gently drumming on the closed book with her loosely gloved fingers.

'I suppose you think I'm an awful idiot,' observed Mr. Lushington, with unexpected and quite unnecessary energy.

'Dear me! This is so very sudden! Awful--idiot? Let me see.'

Her absurd gravity was even more exasperating than her smile. Lushington threw away his cigarette angrily.

'You know what I mean,' he cried, getting red again. 'Don't be horrid!'

'Then don't be silly,' retorted Margaret.

'There! I knew you thought so!'

'Perhaps I do, sometimes,' the girl answered, more seriously. 'But I don't mind it at all. If you care to know, I think you are often much more human when you are--well--"silly," than when you are being clever.'

'And I suppose you would like me better if I were always silly?'

Margaret shook her head and laughed softly, but said nothing. She was thinking that it was good to be alive, and that it was the spring, and that the life was stirring in her, as it stirred amongst the young leaves overhead and in the shooting grasses and budding flowers, and in the hearts of the nesting birds in the oaks and elms. Just then it mattered very little to Margaret whether the man who was talking to her made himself out to be silly or clever. She felt herself much nearer to the simple breathing and growing of all nature than to the silliness or cleverness of any fellow-creature.

Her lips parted a little and she drew in the air again and again, slowly and quietly, as if she could drink it, and live on its sweet taste, and never want food or other drink again, though she was not an ethereal young person, but only a perfectly healthy and natural girl. She was not tired, yet somehow she felt that she was resting body, soul and heart, for a little while, after growing up and before beginning what was to be her life.

Lushington was perfectly healthy, too, but he was not simple, and was often not quite natural. He had real troubles and artificial ways of treating them. He had also been in the thick of the big fight for several years, he had tasted the wine of success and the vinegar of failure, the sticky honey of flattery and some nasty little pills prepared with malignant art by brother critics. With his faults and weaknesses and absurd sensitiveness, he had in him the stuff that wins battles with glory, or loses them with honour, promising to fight again. He was complex. He was rarely quite sure what he felt, though he could express with precision whatever he thought he was feeling at any moment.

'How complicated you are!' he exclaimed, when Margaret laughed.

'I was just thinking how simple I am compared with you,' she answered serenely; 'I mean, when you talk,' she added.

'Thank you for the distinction! "Oliver Goldsmith, for shortness called Noll, Who writes like an angel but talks like poor Poll." That sort of thing, I suppose?'

'I did not say that you write like an angel,' answered Margaret, in a tone of reflection.

'You do not talk like one,' observed Mr. Lushington bitterly. 'Are you going to Paris to-day?' he inquired after a pause; and he looked at his watch.

'No. I had my lesson yesterday. But I am going in to-morrow.'

Lushington knew that she had only two lessons a week, and wondered why she was going to Paris on the following day. But he was offended and would not ask questions; moreover he did not at all approve of her studying singing as a profession, and she knew that he did not.

His disapproval did not disturb her, though she should have liked him to admire her voice because he was really a good judge, and praise from him would be worth having. He often said sharp things that he did not mean, but on the other hand, when he said that anything was good, he always meant that it was first-rate. She wondered where he had learned so much about music.

After all, she knew very little of his life, and as he never said anything about his family she was inclined to think that he had no relations and that he came of people anything but aristocratic. He had worked his way to the front by sheer talent and energy, and she had the good sense to think better of him for that, and not less well of him for his reticence.

Mrs. Rushmore knew no more about Lushington's family than Margaret. The latter was spending the spring in Versailles with the elderly American widow, and the successful young writer had been asked to stop a week with them. Mrs. Rushmore did not care a straw about the family connections of celebrities, and she knew by experience that it was generally better not to ask questions about them, as the answers might place one in an awkward position. She had always acted on the principle that a real lion needs no pedigree, and belongs by right to the higher animals. Lushington was a real lion, though he was a young one. His roar was a passport, and his bite was dangerous. Why make unnecessary inquiries about his parents? They were probably dead, and, socially, they had never been alive, since Society had never heard of them. It was quite possible, Mrs. Rushmore said, that his name was not his own, for she had met two or three celebrities who had deliberately taken names to which they did not pretend any legal claim, but which sounded better than their own.

He had been at Versailles to stay a few days during the previous spring, and Margaret had seen him several times in the interval, and they had occasionally exchanged letters. She was quite well aware that he was in love with her, and she liked him enough not to discourage him. To marry him would be quite another question, though she did not look upon it as impossible. Before all, she intended to wait until her own position was clearly defined.

For the present she did not know whether she had inherited a large fortune, or was practically a penniless orphan living on the charity of her friend Mrs. Rushmore; and several months might pass before this vital question was solved. Mrs. Rushmore believed that Margaret would get the money, or a large part of it; Margaret did not, and in the meantime she was doing her best to cultivate her voice in order to support herself by singing.

Her father had been English, a distinguished student and critical scholar, holding a professorship of which the income, together with what he received from writing learned articles in the serious reviews, had sufficed for himself, his wife and his only child. At his death he had left little except his books, his highly honourable reputation and a small life insurance.

He had married an American whose father had been rich at the time, but had subsequently lost all he possessed by an unfortunate investment, depending upon an invention, which had afterwards become enormously valuable. Finding himself driven to extremities and on the verge of failure, he had been glad to make over his whole interest to a distant relative, who assumed his liabilities as well as his chances of success. Utterly ruined, save in reputation, he had bravely accepted a salaried post, had worked himself to death in eighteen months and had died universally respected by his friends and as poor as Job.

His daughter, Mrs. Donne, had felt her position keenly. She was a sensitive woman, she had married a poor man for love, expecting to make him rich; and instead, she was now far poorer than he. He, on his part, never bestowed a thought on the matter. He was simple and unselfish and he loved her simply and unselfishly. She died of a fever at forty-two and her death killed him. Two years later, Margaret Donne was alone in the world.

Mrs. Rushmore had known Margaret's American grandmother and had been Mrs. Donne's best friend. She had grave doubts as to the conditions on which the whole interest in the invention had been ceded to old Alvah Moon, the Californian millionaire, and, after consulting her own lawyers in New York, she had insisted upon bringing suit against him, in Margaret Donne's name, but at her own risk, for the recovery of an equitable share of the fortune. A tenth part of it would have made the girl rich, but there were great difficulties in the way of obtaining evidence as to an implied agreement, and Alvah Moon was as hard as bedrock.

While the suit was going on, Mrs. Rushmore insisted that Margaret should live with her, and Margaret was glad to accept her protection and hospitality, for she felt that the obligation was not all on her own side. Mrs. Rushmore was childless, a widow and very dependent on companionship for such enjoyment as she could get out of her existence. She had few resources as she grew older, for she did not read much and had no especial tastes. The presence of such a girl as Margaret was a godsend in many ways, and she looked forward with something like terror to the not distant time when she should be left alone again, unless she could induce one of her nieces to live with her. But that would not be easy; they did not want her money, nor anything she could give them, and they thought her dull. Her life would be very empty and sad, then. She had never been vain, and she was well aware that such people as Mr. Edmund Lushington could not be easily induced to come and spend a fortnight with her if Margaret were not in the house. Besides, she loved the girl for her own sake. It was very pleasant to delude herself with the idea that Margaret was almost her daughter, and she wished she could adopt her; but Margaret was far too independent to accept such an arrangement, and Mrs. Rushmore had the common-sense to guess that if the girl were bound to her in any way a sort of restraint would follow which would be disagreeable to both in the end. If there could be a bond, it must be one which Margaret should not feel, nor even guess, and such a relation as that seemed to be an impossibility. Margaret was not the sort of girl to accept anything from an unknown giver, and if the suit failed it would be out of the question to make her believe that she had inherited property from an unsuspected source. Mrs. Rushmore, in her generosity, would have liked to practise some such affectionate deception, and she would try almost anything, however hopeless, rather than let Margaret be a professional singer.

The American woman was not puritanical; she had lived too much in Europe for that and had met many clever people, not to say men of much more than mere talent, who had made big marks on their times. But she had been brought up in the narrow life of old New York, when old New York still survived, as a tradition if not as a fact, in a score or two of families; and one of the prejudices she had inherited early was that there is a mysterious immorality in the practice of the fine arts, whereas an equally mysterious morality is inherent in business. Painters and sculptors, great actors and great singers without end, had sat at her table and she was always interested in their talk and often attracted by their personalities; yet in her heart she knew that she connected them all vaguely with undefined wickedness, just as she associated the idea of virtuous uprightness with all American and English business men. Next to a clergyman, she unconsciously looked upon an American banker as the most strictly moral type of man; and though her hair was grey and she knew a vast deal about this wicked world, she still felt a painful little shock when her favourite newspaper informed her that a banker or a clergyman had turned aside out of the paths of righteousness, as they occasionally do, just like human beings. She felt a similar disagreeable thrill when she thought of Margaret singing in public to earn a living. Prejudices are moral corns; anything that touches one makes it ache more or less, but the pain is always of the same kind. You cannot get a pleasurable sensation out of a corn.

Yet Margaret was working at her music, with persevering regularity, quite convinced that she must soon support herself unhelped and quite sure that her voice was her only means to that end. Singing was her only accomplishment, and she therefore supposed that the gift, such as it was, must be her only talent.

She was modest about it, for the very reason that she believed it was what she did best, and she was patient because she knew that she must do it well before she could hope to live by it. Most successful singers had appeared in public before reaching her age, yet she was only two and twenty, and a year or two could make no great difference. Nevertheless, she was more anxious than she would have admitted, and she had persuaded her teacher to let her sing to Madame Bonanni, the celebrated lyric soprano, whose opinion would be worth having, and perhaps final. The great singer had the reputation of being very good-natured in such cases and was on friendly terms with Margaret's teacher, the latter being a retired prima donna. Margaret felt sure of a fair hearing, therefore, and it was for this trial that she was going to the city on the following morning.

Neither she nor Lushington spoke for a long time after she had given him the information. She took up her book again, but she read without paying any attention to the words, for the recollection of what was coming had brought back all her anxiety about her future life. It would be a dreadful thing if Madame Bonanni should tell her frankly that she had no real talent and had better give it up. The great artist would say what she thought, without wasting time or sympathy; that was why Margaret was going to her. Women do not flatter women unless they have something to gain, whereas men often flatter them for the mere pleasure of seeing them smile, which is an innocent pastime in itself, though the consequences are sometimes disastrous.

Edmund Lushington had at first been wondering why Margaret was going to Paris the next day, then he had inwardly framed several ingenious questions which he might ask her; and then, as he thought of her, he had forgotten himself at last, and had momentarily escaped from the terrible and morbid obligation of putting his thoughts into unspoken words, which is one of the torments that pursue men of letters when they are tired, or annoyed, or distressed. He had forgotten his troubles, too, whatever they were, and could listen to the music spring was making in the trees, without feeling that he might be forced to describe it.

Just then Margaret raised her eyes from her book and saw his face, and he did not know that she was looking at him. For the first time since she had met him she understood a little of his real nature, and guessed the reason why he could write so well. He was a man of heart. She knew it now, in spite of his faults, his shyness, his ridiculous over-sensitiveness, his detestable way of blurting out cutting speeches, his icy criticism of things he did not like. It was a revelation. She wondered what he would say if he spoke just then.

But at that moment Mrs. Rushmore appeared on the lawn, an imposing and rather formal figure in black and violet, against the curtain of honeysuckle that hung down over the verandah.

CHAPTER II

Margaret went alone to the house of the famous singer, for her teacher knew by experience that it was better not to be present on such occasions. Margaret had not even a maid with her, for except in some queer neighbourhoods Paris is as safe as any city in the world, and it never occurred to her that she could need protection at her age. If she should ever have any annoyance she could call a policeman, but she had a firm and well-founded conviction that if a young woman looked straight before her and held her head up as if she could take care of herself, no one would ever molest her, from London to Pekin.

It was not very far from her teacher's rooms in the Boulevard Malesherbes to the pretty little house Madame Bonanni had built for herself in the Avenue Hoche; so Margaret walked. It is the pleasantest way of getting about Paris on a May morning, when one has not to go a long distance. Paris has changed terribly of late years, but there are moments when all her old brilliancy comes back, when the air is again full of the intoxicating effervescence of life, when the well-remembered conviction comes over one that in Paris the main object of every man's and every woman's existence is to make love, to amuse and to be amused. Terrible things have happened, it is true; blood has run like rain through the streets; and great works are created, great books are written, and Art has here her workshop and her temple, her craftsmen and her high priests. The Parisians have a right to take themselves seriously; but we cannot--we graver, grimmer men of rougher race. Do what they will, we can never quite believe that genius can really hew and toil all day and laugh all night; we can never get rid of the idea that there must be some vast delusion about Paris, some great stage trick, some hugely clever deception by which a quicksand is made to seem like bedrock, and a stone pavement like a river of quicksilver.

The great cities all have faces. If all the people who live in each city could be photographed exactly one over the other, the result would be the general expression of that city's face. New York would be discontented and eager; London would be stolidly glum and healthy, with a little surliness; Berlin would be supercilious, overbearing; Rome would be gravely resentful; and so on; but Paris would be gay, incredulous, frivolous, pretty and impudent. The reality may be gone, or may have changed, but the look is in her face still when the light of a May morning shines on it.

What should we get, if we could blend into one picture the English descriptions of Paris left us by Thackeray, Sala, Du Maurier? Would it not show us that face as it is still, when we see it in spring? And drawn by loving hands too, obeying the eyes of genius. An empty square in Berlin suggests a possible regimental parade, in London a mass meeting; in Paris it is a playground waiting for the Parisians to come out and enjoy themselves after their manner, like pretty moths and dragon-flies in the sun.

But there is another side to it. More than any city in the world, Paris has a dual nature. Like Janus, she has two faces; like Endymion, half her life is spent with the gods, half with the powers of darkness. She has her sweet May mornings, but she has her hideous nights when the north wind blows and the streets are of glass. She has her life of art and beauty, and taste and delight, but she has her fevers of blood and fury, her awful reactions of raw brutality, her hidden sores of strange crime. Of all cities, Paris is the most refined, the most progressive in the highest way, the most delicately sensitive; of all cities, too, when the spasm is on her, she is the most mediæval in her violence, her lust for blood, her horrible 'inhumanity to man'--Burns might have written those unforgettable lines of her.

Margaret was not thinking of these things as she took her way through the Parc Monceau, not because it was nearer but because she loved the old trees, and the contrast between the green peace within its gates and the intense life outside. She was nearer than she had perhaps ever been to fright, just then, and yet would not for the world have turned back, nor even slackened her pace. In five minutes she would be ringing the bell at Madame Bonanni's door.

She had heard the prima donna several times but had never met her. She knew that she was no longer young, though her great voice was marvellously fresh and elastic. There were men, of that unpleasant type that is quite sure of everything, who recalled her first appearance and said that she could not be less than fifty years old. As a matter of fact, she was just forty-eight, and made no secret of it. Margaret had learned this from her own singing teacher, but that was all she knew about Madame Bonanni, when she stopped at the closed door of the carriage entrance and rang the bell. She did not know whether she was to meet a Juliet, an Elsa, a Marguerite or a Tosca. She remembered a large woman with heavy arms, in various magnificent costumes and a variety of superb wigs, with a lime-light complexion that was always the same. The rest was music. That, with a choice selection of absurdly impossible anecdotes, is as much as most people ever know about a great singer or a great actress. Margaret had been spared the anecdotes, because most of them were not fit for her to hear, but she had more than once heard fastidious ladies speak of Madame Bonanni as 'that dreadful woman.' No one, however, denied that she was a great artist, and that was the only consideration in Margaret's present need.

She rang the bell and glanced at the big window over the entrance. It had a complicated arrangement of folding green blinds, which were half open, and a grey awning with a red border. She wondered whether it was the window of the singer's own especial room.

The house was different from those next it, though she could hardly tell where the difference lay. She thought that if she had not known the number she should have instinctively picked out this house, amongst all the others in that part of the Avenue Hoche, as the one in which the prima donna or an actress must be living; and as she stood waiting, a very simple and well-bred figure of a young lady, she felt that on the other side of the door there was a whole world of which she knew nothing, which was not at all like her own world, which was going to offend something in her, and which it was nevertheless her duty to enter. She was in that state of mind in which a nun breathes an ejaculatory prayer against the wiles of Satan, and a delicately nurtured girl thinks of her mother. Her heart hardly beat any faster than usual, though she was sure that one of the great moments of her life was at hand; but she drew her skirt round her a little closer, and pursed her lips together a little more tightly, and was very glad to feel that nobody could mistake her for anything but a lady.

CHAPTER III

The servant who opened the door smiled. He was a man of thirty-five, or thereabouts, with cheerful blue eyes, a brown moustache and pink cheeks. He wore a blue cotton apron and had a feather duster in his hand; and he smiled very pleasantly.

'Madame Bonanni said she would see me this morning,' Margaret explained.

'What name, if you please?' the man asked, contemplating her with approval.

'Miss Donne.'

'Very well. But Madame is in her bath,' observed the servant, showing no inclination to let Margaret pass. 'Mademoiselle would do better to come another day.'

'But Madame Bonanni has given me an appointment.'

'It is possible,' the man replied, still smiling calmly.

'I have come to sing to her,' Margaret said, with a little impatience.

'Ah--then it is different!' He positively beamed. 'Then Mademoiselle is a musician? Who would have thought it?'

Margaret was not quite sure who would have thought it, but she thought the servant decidedly familiar. At that moment he stood aside for her to pass, shut the front door after her and led the way to the short flight of steps that gave access to the house from the carriage entrance.

'This way, Mademoiselle. If Mademoiselle will be good enough to wait, I will inform Madame.'

'Please don't disturb her! You said she was in her bath.'

'Oh, that has no importance!' the man cried cheerfully, and disappeared at once.

Margaret looked about her, but if she had been blind she would have been aware that she was in a place quite unlike any she had ever been in before. The air had an indescribable odour that was almost a taste; it smelt of Houbigant, Greek tobacco, Persian carpets, women's clothes, liqueur and late hours; and it was not good to breathe-- except, perhaps, for people used to the air of the theatre. Margaret at first saw nothing particular to sit upon, and stood still.

It was a big room, with two very large windows on one side, a massive chimney-piece at the end opposite the door, and facing the windows the most enormous divan Margaret had ever seen. Over this a great canopy was stretched, a sort of silk awning of which the corners were stretched out and held up by more or less mediæval lances. The divan itself was so high that an ordinary person would have to climb upon it, and it was completely covered by a wild confusion of cushions of all colours, thrown upon it and piled up, and tumbling off, as if a Homeric pillow fight had just been fought upon it by several scores of vigorous school-girls.

The room was plethoric with artistic objects, some good, some bad, some atrocious, but all recalling the singer's past triumphs, and all jumbled together, on tables, easels, pedestals, brackets and shelves with much less taste than an average dealer in antiquities would have shown in arranging his wares. There was not even light enough to see them distinctly, for the terrifically heavy and expensive Genoa velvet curtains produced a sort of dingy twilight. Moreover the Persian carpet was so extremely thick that Margaret almost turned her ankle as she made a step upon it.

As she knew that she must probably wait some time she looked for a seat. There were a few light chairs here and there, but they were occupied by various objects; on one a framed oil-painting was waiting till a place could be found for it, on another there was a bandbox, on a third lay some sort of garment that might be an opera-cloak or a tea-gown, or a theatrical dress, a little silver tray with the remains of black coffee and an empty liqueur glass stood upon a fourth chair, and Margaret's searching eye discovered a fifth, with nothing on it, pushed away in a corner.

She took hold of it by the back, to bring it forward a little, and the gilt cross-bar came off in her hand. She stuck the piece on again as well as she could, and as she did not like to disturb any of the things she stood still, in the middle of the room, wondering vaguely whether Madame Bonanni's visitors usually sat down, and if so, on what.

Suddenly her eyes fell upon a piano, standing behind several easels that almost completely hid it. A piano usually has a stool, and Margaret made her way between the easels and the little oriental tables, and the plants, and the general confusion, towards the keyboard. She was not disappointed; there was a stool, and she sat down at last.

The air was oppressive and she wished herself out in the Pare Monceau, in the May morning. The time seemed endless. By sheer force of habit she slowly turned on the revolving stool and touched the keys; then she struck a few chords softly, and the sound of the perfect instrument gave her pleasure. She played something, trying to make as little noise as possible so long as she remembered where she was, but presently she forgot herself, her lips parted and she was singing, as people do who sing naturally.

She sang the waltz song in the first act of Gounod's Romeo and Juliet, and after the first few bars she had altogether forgotten that she was not at home, with her own piano, or else standing behind her teacher's shoulder in the Boulevard Malesherbes.

Now there are not many singers living who can sing the waltz song and accompany themselves without making a terrible mess of the music; but Margaret did it well, and much more than well, for she was not only a singer with a beautiful voice but a true musician. There was not a quaver or hesitation in her singing from beginning to end, nor a false note in the accompaniment.

When she had finished, her lips closed and she went on playing the music of the scene that follows. She had not gone on a dozen bars, however, when a head appeared suddenly round the corner of a picture on an easel.

'Ah, bah!' exclaimed the head, in an accent of great surprise.

Its thick dark-brown hair was all towzled and standing on end, its brown eyes were opened very wide in astonishment, and it was showing magnificently strong teeth, a little discoloured.

Margaret sprang to her feet with an apology for having forgotten herself, but the head laughed and came forward, bringing with it a large body wrapped in an enormous gown of white Turkish towelling, evidently held together by the invisible hands within. Margaret thought of the statue of Balzac.

[Illustration: "Margaret sprang to her feet with an apology."]

'I thought it was Caravita,' said Madame Bonanni. 'We are great friends you know. I sometimes find her waiting for me. But who in the world are you?'

'Margaret Donne.'

'Ah, bah!' exclaimed the great singer again, the two syllables being apparently her only means of expressing surprise.

'But I told your servant----' Margaret began.

'Why have you not made your début?' cried Madame Bonanni, interrupting her, and shaking her disordered locks as if in protest. 'You have millions in your throat! Why do you come here? To ask advice? To let me hear you sing? Let the public hear you! What are you waiting for? To-morrow you will be old! And all singers are young. How old do you think I am? Forty-five, perhaps, because it is printed so! Not a bit of it! A prima donna is never over thirty, never, never, never! Imagine Juliet over thirty, or Lucia! Pah! The idea is horrible! Fortunately, all tenors are fat. A Juliet of thirty may love a fat Romeo, but at forty it would be disgusting, positively disgusting! I am sick at the mere thought.'

Margaret stood up, resting one hand on the corner of the piano and smiling at the torrent of speech. Yet all the time, while Madame Bonanni was saying things that sounded absurd enough, the young girl was conscious that the handsome brown eyes were studying her quietly and perhaps not unwisely.

'I am twenty-two,' she said by way of answer.

'I made my début when I was twenty,' answered the prima donna. 'But then,' she added, as if in explanation, 'I was married before I was seventeen.'

'Indeed!' Margaret exclaimed politely.

'Yes. He died. Let us sing! I always want to sing when I come out of my bath. Do you know the duo at the beginning of the fourth act? Yes? Good. I will sing Romeo. Oh yes, I can sing the tenor part--it is very high for a man. Sit down. Imagine that you admire me and that the lark is trying to imitate the nightingale so that we need not part. We have not heard it yet. The man is beginning to turn up the dawn outside the window behind us, but we do not see it. We are perfectly happy. Now, begin!'

The chords sounded softly, the two voices blended, rose and fell and died away. The elder woman's rich lower tones imitated a tenor voice well enough to give Margaret the little illusion she needed, and her overflowing happiness did the rest. She sang as she had not sung before.

'I wish to embrace you!' cried Madame Bonanni, when they had finished.

And forthwith Margaret felt herself enveloped in the Turkish bath-gown, and entangled in the towzled hair and held by a pair of tremendously strong white arms; and being thus helpless, she experienced a kindly but portentous kiss on each cheek; after which she was set at liberty.

'You are a real musician, too!' Madame Bonanni said with genuine admiration. 'You can play anything, as well as sing. I hope you will never hear me play. It is awful. I could empty any theatre instantly, if there were a fire, merely by playing a little!'

She laughed heartily at her little joke, for like many great singers she was half a child and half a genius, and endowed with the huge vitality that alone makes an opera singer's life possible.

'I would give my playing to have your voice,' Margaret said.

'You would be cheated in your bargain,' observed Madame Bonanni. 'Let me look at you. Have you a big chest and a thick throat? What are your arms like? If you have a voice and talent, strength is every thing! Young girls come and sing to me so prettily, so sweetly! They want to be singers! Singers, my dear, with chests like paper dolls and throats like plucked spring chickens! Bah! They are good for nothing, they catch cold, they give a little croak and they die. Strength is everything. Let me see your throat! No! You will never croak! You will never die. And your arms? Look at mine. Yes, yours will be like mine, some day.'

Margaret hoped not, for Madame Bonanni seemed to be a very big woman, though she still managed to look human as Juliet. Perhaps that was because the tenors were all fat.

Again a hand emerged from the thick white folds and grasped Margaret's arm firmly above the elbow, as a trainer feels an athlete's biceps.

'Good, good! Very good!' cried Madame Bonanni approvingly. 'It is a pity you are a lady! You are a lady, aren't you?'

Margaret smiled.

'I am a peasant,' the singer answered without the least affectation. 'I always say that it takes five generations of life in the fields to make a voice. But you are English, I suppose. Yes? All English live out of doors. If they had a proper climate they would all sing, but they have to keep their mouths shut all the time, to keep out the rain, and the fog, and the smoke of their chimneys. It is incredible, how little they open their mouths! Come and sit down. We will have a little talk.'

Margaret thought her new friend had managed to talk a good deal already. Madame Bonanni slipped between the easels and pedestals with surprising ease and lightness, and made for the divan. Margaret now saw that a stool was half concealed by a fallen pillow, so that the singer used it in order to climb up. In a moment she had settled herself comfortably, supported on all sides by the huge cushions. Margaret fancied she looked like a big snowball with a human head.

'Why don t you sit down, my dear?' inquired Madame Bonanni blandly.

'Yes, but where?' asked Margaret with a little laugh.

'Here! Climb up beside me on the divan.'

'I'm not used to it!' Margaret laughed. 'It looks awfully hot.'

'Then take a chair. Oh, the things? Throw them on the floor. Somebody will pick them up. People are always sending me perfectly useless things. Look at that picture! Did you ever see such a daub? I'll burn it! No. I'll give it to the missionaries. They take everything one gives them, for the African babies. Ah!'

Madame Bonanni shrieked suddenly, seized a big cushion and held it up as a screen before her. She looked towards the door, and Margaret, looking in the same direction, saw an over-dressed man of thirty-five standing on the threshold.

'Go away!' screamed Madame Bonanni. 'Logotheti! Go away, I say! Don't you see that I'm not dressed?'

'I see nothing but cushions,' answered the new-comer, showing very white teeth and speaking with a thick accent Margaret had never heard.

'Ah! So much the better!' returned Madame Bonanni with sudden calm. 'What do you want?'

'You did me the honour to ask me to breakfast,' said Logotheti, coming forward a few steps.

'To breakfast! Never! You are dreaming!' She paused an instant. 'Yes, I believe I did. What difference does it make? Go and get your breakfast somewhere else!'

'Oh no!' protested the visitor, who had been examining Margaret's face and figure. 'I can wait any length of time, but I shall keep you to your bargain, dear lady.'

'You are detestable! Well, then you must go and look out of the window while I get down.'

'With pleasure,' Logotheti answered, meaning exactly what he said, and turning his back after a deliberate look at Margaret.

Madame Bonanni worked herself to the edge of the divan, with a curious sidelong movement, got one of her feet upon the stool and slipped down, till she stood on the floor. Then she gathered the folds of her bathing-gown to her and ran to the door with astonishing agility, for so large a person.

Margaret was not sure what she should do, and began to follow her, hoping to exchange a few words with her before going away. At the door, Madame Bonanni suddenly draped herself in the dark velvet curtain, stuck her head out and looked back.

'Of course you will stay to breakfast, my dear!' she called out,

'Logotheti! I present you to Miss--Miss--oh, the name doesn't matter! I present you!'

'I'm afraid I cannot----' Margaret began to say, not knowing how long she might be left alone with Logotheti.

But Madame Bonanni had already unfurled the curtain and fled. Logotheti bowed gravely to Margaret, cleared the things off one of the chairs and offered it to her. His manner was as respectful with her as it had been familiar with the singer, and she felt at once that he understood her position.

'Thank you,' she said quietly, as she seated herself.

He cleared another chair and sat down at a little distance. She glanced at him furtively and saw that he was a very dark man of rather long features; that his eyes were almond-shaped, like those of many orientals; that he had a heavy jaw and a large mouth with lips that were broad rather than thick, and hardly at all concealed by a small black moustache which was trained to lie very flat to his face, and turned up at the ends; that his short hair was worn brush fashion, without a parting; that he had olive brown hands with strong fingers, on one of which he wore an enormous turquoise in a ring; that his clothes were evidently the result of English workmanship misguided by a very un-English taste; and finally that he was well-built and looked strong. She wondered very much what his nationality might be, for his accent had told her that he was not French.

After a little pause he turned his head quietly and spoke to her.

'Our friend's introduction was a little vague,' he said. 'My name is Constantine Logotheti. I am a Greek of Constantinople by birth, or what we call a Fanariote there. I live in Paris and I occupy myself with what we call "finance" here. In other words, I spend an hour or two every day at the Bourse. If I had anything to recommend me, I should say so at once, but I believe there is nothing.'

'Thank you!' Margaret laughed a little at the words. 'You are very frank. Madame Bonanni could not remember my name, as she has never seen me before to-day. I am Miss Donne; I am studying to be an opera-singer, and I came here for advice. I am English. I believe that is all.'

They looked at each other and smiled. Margaret was certainly not prepossessed in the man's favour at first sight. She detested over-dressed men, men who wore turquoise rings, and men who had oily voices; but it was perfectly clear to her that Logotheti was a man of the world, who knew a lady when he met one, no matter where, and meant to behave with her precisely as if he had been introduced to her in Mrs. Rushmore's drawing-room.

'It is my turn to thank you,' he said, acknowledging with a little bow the favour she had conferred in telling him who she was. 'I fancy you have not yet seen much of theatrical people, off the stage. Have you?'

No,' answered Margaret. 'Why do you ask?'

'I wonder whether you will like them when you do,' said Logotheti.

'I never thought of it. Is Madame Bonanni a good type of them?'

'No,' Logotheti answered, after a moment's reflection. 'I don't think she is. None of the great ones are. They all have something original, personal, dominating, about them. That is the reason why they are great. I was thinking of the average singer you will have to do with if you really sing in opera. As for Madame Bonanni, she has a heart of pure gold. We are old friends, and I know her well.'

'I can quite believe that she is kind-hearted,' Margaret answered. But don't you think, perhaps, that she is just a little too much so?'

'How do you mean?'

'That she might be too kind to tell a beginner just what she really thinks?'

'No, indeed.' Logotheti laughed at the idea. 'You would not think so if you knew how many poor girls she sends away in tears because she tells them the honest truth, that they have neither voice nor talent, and will fail miserably if they go on. That is real kindness after all! Have you sung to her?'

'Yes,' answered Margaret.

'May I ask what she said? I know her so well that I can perhaps be of use to you. Sometimes, for instance, she says nothing at all. That means that there may be a chance of success but that she herself is not sure.'

'She kissed me on both cheeks,' Margaret said with a laugh, 'and she talked about my début.'

'Then I should advise you to make your début at once,' Logotheti answered. 'She means that you will have a very great success.'

'Do you really think so?' asked Margaret, much pleased.

'I know it,' he replied with conviction. 'That woman is utterly incapable of saying anything she does not think, but she sometimes gives her opinion with horrible brutality.'

'I rather like that.'

'Do you?'

'Yes. It is good medicine.'

'Then you have only been a spectator, and never the patient!' Logotheti laughed.

'Perhaps. Tell me all about Madame Bonanni.'

'All about her?' Logotheti smiled oddly. 'Well, she is a great artist, perhaps the greatest living soprano, though she is getting old. You can see that. Let me see, what else? She is very frank, I have told you that. And she is charitable. She gives away a great deal. She has a great many friends, of whom I call myself one, and we are all sincerely attached to her. I cannot think of anything else to tell you about her.'

'She said she was born a peasant,' observed Margaret who wished to hear more.

'Oh yes!' Logotheti laughed. 'There is no doubt of that! Besides, she is proud of it.'

'She was married at seventeen, too.'

'They all marry,' answered Logotheti vaguely, 'and their husbands disappear, by some law of nature we do not understand--absorbed into the elements, evaporated, drawn up into the clouds like moisture. One might write an interesting essay on the husbands of prima donnas and great actresses. What becomes of them? We know whence they come, for they are often impecunious gentlemen, but where do they go? There must be a limbo for them, somewhere, a place of departed husbands. Possibly they are all in lunatic asylums. The greater the singer, or the actress, the more certain it is that she has been married and that her husband has disappeared! It is very mysterious.'

'Very!' Margaret was rather amused by his talk.

'Have you lived long in Paris?' he asked, suddenly changing the subject.

'We live in Versailles. I come in for my lessons.'

Without asking many direct questions Logotheti managed to find out a good deal about Margaret during the next quarter of an hour. She was not suspicious of a man who showed no inclination to be familiar or to make blatant compliments to her, and she told him that her father and mother were dead and that she lived with Mrs. Rushmore and saw many interesting people, most of whom he seemed to know. He, on his part, told her many things about Versailles which she did not know, and she soon saw that he was a man of varied tastes and wide information. She wondered why he wore such a big turquoise ring and why he had such a wonderful waistcoat, such a superlative tie, such an amazing shirt and such a frightfully expensive pin. But it was not the first time in her life that she had met an otherwise intelligent man who made the mistake of over-dressing, and her first prejudice against him began to disappear. She even admitted to herself that he had a certain charm of manner which she liked, a mingling of reserve and frankness, or repose and strength, the qualities which appeal so strongly to most women. If only his voice had not that disagreeable oiliness! After all, that was what she liked least. He spoke French with wonderful fluency, but he abstained from making the tiresome compliments which so many Frenchmen reel off even at first acquaintance. He had really beautiful almond-shaped eyes, but he never once turned them to her with that languishing look which young men with almond eyes seem to think quite irresistible. Surely, all this was in his favour.

After being gone about half an hour, Madame Bonanni came back, her Juno-like figure clad in a very pale green tea-gown, very open at the throat, and her thick hair was smoothed in great curved surfaces which were certainly supported by cushions underneath them. Her solid arms were bare to the elbows, and the green sleeves hung almost to her feet. Her face was rouged and there were artificial shadows under her eyes. Round her neck she wore a single string of pearls as big as olives, and her fingers were covered with all sorts of rings.

'Now you may look at me,' she said, with a gay laugh.

'I see a star of the first magnitude,' Logotheti answered gravely.

Margaret bit her lip to keep from laughing, but Madame Bonanni laughed herself, very good-naturedly, though she understood.

'I detest this man!' she cried, turning to Margaret. 'I don't know why I ask him to breakfast.'

'Because you cannot live without me, I suppose,' suggested Logotheti.

'I hate Greeks!' screamed the prima donna, still laughing. 'Why are you a Greek?'

'Doubtless by a mistake of my father's, dear lady; quite unpardonable since you are displeased! If he had lived, he certainly would have rectified it to please you, but the Turks killed him when I was a baby in arms; and that was before you were born.'

'Of course it was,' answered Madame Bonanni, who must have been just about to be married at that time. 'But that is no reason why we should stand here starving to death while you chatter.'

Thereupon she put her arm through Margaret's and led her away at a brisk pace, Logotheti following at a little distance and contemplating the young girl's moving figure with the satisfaction that only an Oriental feels in youthful womanly beauty. It was long since he had seen any sight that pleased him as well, for his artistic sense was fastidious in the highest degree where the things of daily life were not concerned. He might indeed wear waistcoats that inspired terror and jewellery that dazzled the ordinary eye, but there were few men in Paris who were better judges of a picture, a statue, an intaglio, or a woman.

In a few moments the three were seated at a carved and polished table overloaded with silver and cut glass, one on each side of Madame Bonanni. Three other places were set, but no one appeared to fill them. The cheerful servant with the moustache was arrayed in a neat frock coat and a white satin tie, and he smiled perpetually.

'I adore plover's eggs!' cried Madame Bonanni, as he set a plate before her containing three tiny porcelain bowls, in each of which a little boiled plover's egg lay buried in jelly.

It was evident that she was speaking the truth, for they disappeared in an instant, and were followed by a bisque of shrimps of the most creamy composition.

'It is my passion!' she said.

She took her spoon in her hand, but appeared to hesitate, for she glanced first at Margaret, then down at her green tea-gown, and then at Margaret again. At last she seemed to make up her mind, and quickly unfolding the damask napkin she tied it round her neck in a solid knot. The stiff points stood out on each side behind her ears. She emitted a sigh of satisfaction and went to work at the soup. Margaret pretended to see nothing and made an indifferent remark to Logotheti.

Madame Bonanni made a good deal of noise, finally tipping up her plate and scraping out the contents to the last drop.

'Ah!' she exclaimed with immense satisfaction. 'That was good!'

'Perfect,' assented Logotheti, who ate delicately and noiselessly, as Orientals do.

'Delicious! said Margaret, who was hungry.

'I taught my cook the real way to make it,' Madame Bonanni said. 'I am a good cook, a very good cook! I always did the cooking at home before I came to Paris to study, because my mother was not able to stand long. One of the farm horses had kicked her and broken her leg and she was always lame after that. Well?' she asked suddenly turning to the cheerful servant. 'Is that all we are to have to-day? I am dying of hunger!'

A marvellous salmon trout made its appearance a moment later.

'Oh yes!' exclaimed the prima donna. 'I am fond of eating! You may laugh at me if you like, Logotheti. I am perfectly indifferent!'

And she was. She did all sorts of things that surprised Margaret, and when a dish of ortolans with a rich brown sauce was put before her, she deliberately discarded her knife and fork altogether and ate with her hands. By way of terminating the operation, she stuck every finger of each hand into her mouth as far as it would go, licked all ten thoroughly, and then looked at them critically before drying them on her napkin. By this time Margaret was past being surprised at anything.

'Logotheti says that in the East they all eat with their fingers,' the singer observed.

'It is much cleaner,' Logotheti answered imperturbably.

Margaret uttered an involuntary exclamation of surprise.

'Of course it is!' he exclaimed. 'I know who washes my fingers. I don't know who washes the forks, nor who used them last. If one stopped to think about it, one would never use a fork or a spoon that was not one's own or washed by oneself. I am sure that every sort of disease is caught from other people's forks and spoons.'

'What a horrible idea!' exclaimed Margaret with disgust. 'I shall never want to eat at a hotel or a restaurant again.'

'You will forget it,' replied Logotheti reassuringly. 'Civilisation makes us forget a great many little things of the sort, I assure you!'

'But is there no way of protecting oneself?' Margaret asked.

'It is absurd!' cried Madame Bonanni. 'I don't believe in germs and microbes and such silly things! If they exist we are full of them, and I have no doubt they do us good.'

'It would be just as easy to boil the forks and spoons for ten minutes in clean water, after they are washed,' observed Logotheti. 'But after all, fingers are safer.'

'Things taste better with fingers,' said Madame Bonanni thoughtfully.

'In the East,' Logotheti answered, 'people pour water on their hands after each course. Why don't you try that?'

'I wash my hands afterwards; it is less trouble.'

Logotheti laughed, but Margaret was disgusted, and did not even smile. Madame Bonanni's proceedings had made an impression on her which it would be hard to forget, and she sat silent for a while, not tasting what followed.

'Logotheti,' said Madame Bonanni later, with her mouth full of strawberries and cream, 'you must do something for me.'

'An investment, dear lady? I suppose you want some of the bonds of the new electric road, don't you? They are not to be had, but of course you shall have them at once. Or else you have decided to give your whole fortune to an eccentric charity. Is that it?'

'No,' answered the singer, swallowing. 'This charming young lady--what is your name, my dear? I have forgotten it twenty times this morning!'

'Donne. Margaret Donne.'

'This charming Miss Donne sings, Logotheti.'

'So I gathered while we were talking.'

'No, you didn't! You gathered no such thing! She told you that she took lessons, perhaps. But I tell you that she sings. It is quite different.'

Madame Bonanni pushed away her plate, planted her large white elbows on the table and looked thoughtfully at Margaret. Logotheti looked at the young girl, too, for he knew very well what his old friend meant by the simple statement, slightly emphasised.

'Ah!' he ejaculated. 'I understand. I am at your service.'

'What is it?' asked Margaret, blushing a little and turning from one to the other.

'Logotheti knows everybody,' answered Madame Bonanni. 'He is rich, immensely rich, fabulously rich, my dear. He is in the "high finance," in fact. It is disgusting, how rich he is, but it is sometimes useful. He wants a theatre, a newspaper; he buys it and does what he likes with it. It makes no difference to him, for he always sells it again for more than he gave for it, and besides, it amuses him. You would not think it, but Logotheti is often dreadfully bored.'

'Very often,' assented the Greek, 'but never when I am with you.'

'Ah, bah! You say that! But why should I care? You always do what I want.'

'Invariably.'

'And out of pure friendship, too.'

'The purest!' Logotheti uttered the two words with profound conviction.

'I never could induce this creature to make love to me,' cried Madame Bonanni, turning to Margaret with a laugh. 'It is incredible! And yet I love him--almost as well as plover's eggs! It is true that if he made love to me, I should have him turned out of the house. But that makes no difference. It is one of the disappointments of my life that he doesn't!'

'What I admire next to your genius, is your logic, dear lady,' said Logotheti.

'Precisely. Now before you have your coffee you will give me your word of honour that Miss Donne shall have a triumph and an ovation at her début, and an engagement to sing next season at the Opéra.'

'Really----' Margaret tried to protest.

'You know nothing about business,' interrupted Madame Bonanni. 'You are nothing but a child! These things are done in this way. Logotheti, give me your word of honour.'

'Are you sure of the voice?' asked the Greek quietly.

'As sure as I am of my own.'

'Very well. I give you my word. It is done.'

'Good. I hate you, Logotheti, because you are so cautious, but you always do what you promise. You may have your coffee now! What name are you going to take, my dear?' she asked, turning to Margaret, who felt very uncomfortable. 'The name is very important, you know, even when one has your genius.'

'My genius!' exclaimed the young girl in confusion.

'I know what I am talking about,' answered Madame Bonanni in a matter-of-fact tone. 'You will get up on the morning of your début as little Miss Donne, nobody! You will go to bed as the great new soprano, famous! That is what you will do. Now don't talk, but let me give you a name, and we will drink your health to it in a drop of that old white Chartreuse. You like that old white Chartreuse, Logotheti. You shall have none till you have found a name for Miss Donne.'

'May I not keep my own?' Margaret asked timidly.

'No. It is an absurd name for the stage, my dear. All the people would make jokes about it. Of course you must be either Italian, or French, or German, or Hungarian, or Spanish. There is no great Italian soprano just now. I advise you to be an Italian. You are Signorina--Signorina what? Logotheti, do make haste! You know Italian.'

'May I ask where you were born, Miss Donne?' inquired Logotheti.

'In Oxford. But what has that to do with it?'

'Translate into Italian: ox, "bove," ford, "guado." No, that won't do'

'Certainly not!' cried Madame Bonanni. 'Guado--guano! Fancy!

Try again. Think of a pretty Italian name. It must be very easy! Take an historical name, the name of a great family. Those people never object.'

'Cordova is a fine name,' observed Logotheti. 'She may just as well be Spanish, after all. Margarita da Cordova. That sounds rather well.'

'Yes. Do you like it, my dear?' asked Madame Bonanni.

'But I don't know a word of Spanish——'

'What in the world has that to do with it? It is a good name. You may have your Chartreuse, Logotheti. Margarita da Cordova, the great Spanish soprano! Your health! You were born in the little town of Boveguado in Andalusia.'

'Your father was the famous contrabandier Ramon da Cordova, who sang like an angel and played the guitar better than any one in Spain.'

'Was there ever such a man?'

'No, of course not! And besides, he was stabbed in a love affair when you were a baby, so that it does not matter. You ought to be able to make something out of that for the papers, Logotheti. Carmen, don't you know? Heavens, how romantic!'

Margaret had a vague idea that she was dreaming, that Madame Bonanni and Logotheti were not real people, and that she was going to waken in a few minutes. The heavy, middle-aged woman with the good-natured face and the painted cheeks could not possibly be the tragic Juliet, the terrible Tosca, the poor, mad, fluttering Lucia, whose marvellous voice had so often thrilled the young girl to the heart, in Paris and in London. It was either a dream or a cruel deception. Her own words sounded far away and unsteady when she was at last allowed to speak.

'I am sure I cannot sing in public in less than a year,' she said. 'You are very kind, but you are exaggerating my talent. I could never get through the whole opera well enough.'

Madame Bonanni looked at her curiously for a moment, not at all certain that she was in earnest; but she saw that Margaret meant what she said. There was no mistaking the troubled look in the girl's eyes.

'I suppose you are not afraid to come here and sing before an impresario and three or four musicians, are you?' inquired the singer.

'No!' cried Margaret. 'But that is different.'

'Did you think that any manager would engage you, even for one night, merely on my word, my child? You will have to show what you can do. But I can tell you one thing, little Miss Donne!' A great, good-natured laugh rolled out before Madame Bonanni proceeded to state the one thing she could tell. 'When you have sung the waltz song in Romeo and Juliet, and the duo in the fifth act, to four or five of the men who make a living out of us artists, you will be surprised at what happens afterwards! Those people will not risk their money for your handsome eyes, my dear! And they know their business, don't they, Logotheti?'

He answered by speaking directly to Margaret.

'I think,' he said quietly, 'that you can have confidence in Madame Bonanni's opinion.'

'Listen to me,' said the prima donna--suddenly, and for some unknown reason, rubbing all the rouge off her right cheek with the corner of her napkin and then inspecting curiously the colour that adhered to the linen--'listen to me! I sing day after to-morrow, for the last time before going to London. Come to my dressing-room after the second act. I will have Schreiermeyer there, and we will make an appointment for the next day, and settle the matter at once. It's understood, isn't it?'

Margaret was delighted, for Logotheti's quiet words had reassured her a little. Madame Bonanni rose suddenly, untying her napkin from her neck as she got up, and throwing it on the floor behind her. Before she had reached the door she yawned portentously.

'I always go to sleep when I have eaten,' she said. 'Find a cab for little Miss Donne, Logotheti--for the famous Señorita da Cordova!' She laughed sleepily, and waved her hand to Margaret.

'I don't know how to thank you,' the young girl began, but before she got any further Madame Bonanni had disappeared.

A few moments later Margaret and Logotheti were in the street. The noonday air was warm and bright and she drew in deep breaths of it, as she had done in the morning. Logotheti looked at her from under the brim of his Panama hat.

'We shall find a cab in a minute,' he said, in an indifferent tone.

'Yes.'

They walked a few steps in silence.

'I hope you don't really mean to do what Madame Bonanni asked of you,' Margaret said, rather awkwardly. 'I mean, about my début, if it really comes off.'

Logotheti laughed lightly.

'She always talks in that way,' he said. 'She thinks I can do anything, but as a matter of fact I have no influence to speak of, and money has nothing to do with an artist's success. I shall certainly be there on your first night, and you will not object to my splitting my gloves in applauding you?'

'Oh no!' Margaret laughed, too. 'You are welcome to do that! There is a cab.'

She held up her parasol to attract the driver's attention, and Logotheti made a few steps forward and called him.

'Where shall I tell the man to take you?' Logotheti asked, as she got in.

'To the Saint Lazare station, please. Thank you very much!'

She smiled pleasantly and nodded as she drove away. He stood still a moment on the pavement, looking after her, and then turned in the opposite direction, lighting a cigarette as he walked.

He was a Greek, and an educated one, and as he sauntered along on the shady side of the Avenue Hoche, the cigarette twitched oddly in his mouth, as if he were talking to himself. From four and twenty centuries away, in the most modern city of the world, broken lines of an ode of Anacreon came ringing to his ears, and his lips formed the words noiselessly:

'I wish I were the zone that lies Warm to thy breast, and feels its sighs ... Oh, anything that touches thee! Nay, sandals for those fairy feet ...'

That, at least, is the English for it, according to Thomas Moore.

CHAPTER IV

Margaret was not quite sure how she could find her way to Madame Bonanni's dressing-room at the Opéra, but she had no intention of missing the appointment. The most natural and easy way of managing matters would be to ask her teacher to go with her, and she could then spend the night at the latter's house. She accordingly stopped there before she went to the station.

The elderly artist burst into tears on hearing the result of the interview with Madame Bonanni, and fell upon Margaret's neck.

'I knew it,' she said. 'I was sure of it, but I did not dare to tell you so!'

Margaret was very happy, but she was a little nervous about her frock and wondered whether tears stained, as sea water does. The old singer was of a very different type from Madame Bonanni, and had never enjoyed such supremacy as the latter, even for a few months. But she had been admired for her perfect method, her good acting, and her agreeable voice, and for having made the most of what nature had given her; and when she had retired from the stage comparatively young, as the wife of the excellent Monsieur Durand, she had already acquired a great reputation as a model for young singers, and she soon consented to give lessons. Unfortunately, Monsieur Durand had made ducks and drakes of her earnings in a few years, by carefully mis-investing every penny she possessed; but as he had then lost no time in destroying himself by the over-use of antidotes to despair, such as absinthe, his widow had soon re-established the equilibrium of her finances by hard work and was at the present time one of the most famous teachers of singers for the stage. Madame Durand was a Neapolitan by birth and had been known to modest fame on the stage as Signora De Rosa, that being her real name; for Italian singers seem to be the only ones who do not care for high-sounding pseudonyms. She was a voluble little person, over-flowing with easy feeling which made her momentarily intensely happy, miserable, or angry, as the case might be. Whichever it might be, she generally shed abundant tears.

Margaret went back to Versailles feeling very happy, but determined to say nothing of what had happened except to Mrs. Rushmore, who need only know that Madame Bonanni had spoken in an encouraging way and wished to see her at the theatre. For the girl herself found it hard to believe half of what the prima donna had told her, and was far from believing that she was on the eve of signing her first engagement.

Madame Bonanni had breakfasted at half-past eleven, but Mrs. Rushmore lunched at half-past one, and Margaret found her at table with Lushington and three or four other people who had dropped in. There was an English officer who had got his Victoria Cross in South Africa and was on his way to India, with a few days to spare by the way; there was a middle-aged French portrait-painter who had caressing ways and an immense reputation; there was a woman of the world whose husband was an Austrian and was in the diplomatic service; and there was a young archæologist just from Crete, who foregathered with Lushington.

They were at the end of luncheon when Margaret came in, they were sipping fine wine from very thin glasses, they were all saying their second-best things, because each one was afraid that if he said his very best before dinner one of the others would steal it; and Mrs. Rushmore was in her element.

Margaret came in with her hat on and sat down in her place, which was opposite Mrs. Rushmore. The men subsided again into their chairs and looked at her. Lushington was next to her, but she smiled at the others first, nodding quietly and answering their greetings.

'You seem pleased,' Lushington said, when he saw that she would hear him.

'Do I?' She smiled again.

'That sort of answer always means a secret,' Lushington replied. 'Happiness for one, don't you know?'

'By the way,' asked the English officer on her other side, 'was not your father the famous army coach?'

'No,' Margaret replied. 'I'm often asked that.'

'What is an army coach?' inquired the French painter, who spoke some English. 'Is it not an ambulance? But I do not understand.'

Mrs. Rushmore began to explain in an undertone.

'Miss Donne's father was an Oxford don,' observed Lushington, rather stiffly.

At this quite unintentional pun the French painter laughed so much that every one turned and looked at him. He had once painted a famous man in Oxford, and knew what a don was.

'Make the next one in Greek,' said Margaret to Lushington, with a smile.

'There are some very bad puns in Aristophanes,' observed the archæologist thoughtfully. 'Why don't you go to Crete?' he inquired very suddenly of Mrs. Rushmore.

Mrs. Rushmore, who did not happen to have heard of the recent discoveries yet, felt a little as if the young man had asked her why she did not go to Jericho. But she concealed her feelings, being quite sure that no offence to her dignity was meant.

'It is so far,' she answered with a vague smile.

'It's a beastly hole,' observed the soldier. 'I was there when that row was going on.'

'The discoveries have all been made since then,' answered the archæologist, who could think of nothing else. 'You have no idea what those paintings are,' he continued, talking to the table. 'I have been there several weeks and I'm going back next month. Logotheti is going to take a party of us in his big yacht.'

'Who is Logotheti?' inquired Margaret, with great calm.

'A financier,' put in Lushington.

'A millionaire,' said the artist. 'I have painted his portrait.'

'He seems to be interested in discoveries,' Margaret said to the archæologist. 'I suppose you know him very well?'

'Oh yes! He is a most interesting person, a Greek of Constantinople by birth, but a real Greek at heart, who knows his own literature, and loves his country, and spends immense sums in helping archæology. He really cares for nothing but art! Finance amuses him now and then for a while, and he has been tremendously lucky. They consider him one of the important men in the money market, don't they?'

The question was directed to the French artist.

'Certainly they do!' replied the latter, with alacrity. 'I have painted his portrait.'

'I should like to know him,' said Mrs. Rushmore.

'He is quite delightful,' the woman of the world chimed in. 'Quite the most amusing man I know!'

'You know him, too?' Mrs. Rushmore asked.

'Everybody knows Logotheti!' answered the other.

'You must really bring him,' said Mrs. Rushmore, in a general way, to everybody.

'I am sure he will be enchanted!' cried the archæologist. 'I am dining with him to-night, and if you will allow me I'll bring him to-morrow afternoon.'

'You seem very sure that he will come,' Margaret said.

'But why should he not? Every one is glad to come to Mrs. Rushmore's house.'

This was an unanswerable form of complimentary argument. Margaret reflected on that strange law by which, when we have just heard for the first time of a fact or a person, we are sure to come across it, or him, again, within the next twenty-four hours. She did not believe that Logotheti could be found at short notice and introduced to new acquaintances so easily as the young scholar seemed to think; but she made up her mind, if he came at all, that she would prevent him from talking about their meeting at Madame Bonanni's, which she wished to avoid mentioning for the present. That would be easy enough, for a man of his tact would understand the slightest sign, and behave as if he had not met her before.

In the afternoon she was alone with Lushington again. He was not at all in an aggressive mood; indeed, he seemed rather depressed. They walked slowly under the oaks and elms.

'What is the matter?' Margaret asked gently, after a silence.

'I have been thinking a great deal about you,' he answered.

'The thought seems to make you sad!' Margaret laughed, for she was very happy.

'Yes. It does,' he answered, with a sigh that certainly was not affected.

'But why?' she asked, growing grave at once.

'There is no reason why I should not tell you. After all, we know each other too well to apologise for saying what we think. Don't we?'

'I hope so,' Margaret answered, wondering what he was going to say.

'But then,' said Lushington disconsolately, 'I am perfectly sure that nothing I can say can have the slightest effect.'

'Who knows?' The young girl's lids drooped a little and then opened again.

'You know.' He spoke gravely and with regret.

She tried to laugh.

'I wish I did! But what is it? There can be no harm in saying it!'

'You have made up your mind to be an opera-singer,' Lushington answered. 'You have a beautiful voice, you have talent, you have been well taught. You will succeed.'

He had never said as much as that about her singing, and she was pleased. After many months of patient work, the acknowledgment of it seemed to be all coming in one day.

'You talk as if you were quite sure.'

'Yes. You will succeed. But there is another side to it. Shall you think me priggish and call me disagreeable if I tell you that it is no life for a woman brought up like you?'

Margaret had just acquired some insight into the existence of the class she meant to join, though by no means into the worst phase of it. She was sure that if she closed her eyes she should see Madame Bonanni vividly before her, and hear her talking to Logotheti, and smell the heavy air of the big room. She felt that she could not call Lushington a prig.

'I think I know what you mean,' she answered. 'But surely, an artist can lead her own life, especially if she is successful.'

'No,' Lushington answered, 'she cannot. That's just it.'

'How do you know?' Margaret asked, incredulously.

'I do know,' he said with emphasis. 'I assure you that I know. I have seen a great deal of operatic people. A few, and they are not generally the great ones, try to lead their own lives, as you put it, but they either don't succeed at all or else they make themselves so disagreeable to their fellow artists that life becomes a burden.'

'If they don't succeed, it's because they have no strength of character,' Margaret answered, 'and if they make themselves disagreeable, it's because they have no tact!'

'That settles it!' Lushington laughed drily. 'I had better not say anything more.'

'I did not mean to cut you short. I beg your pardon. Please go on, please!'

She turned to him as she said the last words, and there was in the word 'please' that one tone of hers which he could never resist. It is said that even lifeless things, like bridges and towers, are subject by nature to the vibration of a sympathetic note, and that the greatest buildings in the world would tremble, and shake, and rock and fall in ruins if that single musical sound were steadily produced near to them. We men cannot pretend to be harder of hearing and feeling than stocks and stones. The woman who loves, whether she herself knows it or not, has her call, that we answer as the wood-bird answers his mate, her sympathetic word and note at which we vibrate to our heart's core.

When Margaret said 'please' in a certain way, Lushington's free will seemed to retire from him suddenly, to contemplate his weakness from a little distance. When she said 'please go on,' he went on, and not only said what he had meant to say but a great deal more, too.

'It would bore you to know all about my existence,' he began, 'but as a critic and otherwise I happen to have been often in contact with theatrical people, especially opera-singers. I have at least one--er--one very dear friend amongst them.'

'A man?' suggested Margaret.

'No. A woman--of a certain age. As I see her very often, I naturally see other singers, especially as she is very much liked by them. I only tell you that to explain why I know so much about them; and if I want to explain at all, it's only because I like you so much, and because I suppose that what I like most about you, next to yourself, is just that something which my dear old friend can never have. Do you understand?'

Lushington was certainly very shy as a rule, and most people would have said that he was very cold; but Margaret suddenly felt that there was a true and deep emotion behind his plain speech.

'You have been very fond of her,' she said gently.

He flushed almost before she had finished speaking; but he could not have been angry, for he smiled.

'Yes, I have always been very fond of her,' he answered, after a scarcely perceptible pause, 'and I always shall be. But she is old enough to be my mother.'

'I'm glad if it's really a friendship,' said Margaret; 'and only a friendship,' she added.

He turned his eyes to her rather slowly.

'I believe you really are glad,' he answered. 'Thank you. I'm very fond of you. I can't help it. I suppose I love you, and I have no business to--and sometimes you say things that touch me. That's all.

After this rather inexplicable speech he relapsed into silence. But there are silences of all sorts, as there is speech of all sorts. There are silences that set one's teeth on edge--it is always a relief to break them; and there are silences that are gentler, kinder, sweeter, more loving, more eloquent than any words, and which it is always a wrench to interrupt. Of these was the pause that followed now; but Margaret was asking herself what he meant by saying that he had no right to love her.

'Do you know what the hardest thing in my life is?' Lushington asked, suddenly rousing himself. 'It is the certainty that my friend can never have been and never can be at all like you in everything that appeals to me most. But it would be still worse--oh, infinitely worse!--to see you grow like her, by living amongst the same people. You will suffer if you do, and you will suffer if you cannot. That is why I dread the idea of your going on the stage.'

'But I really think I shall not change so much as you think, if I do,' Margaret said.

'You don't know the life,' Lushington answered rather sadly. 'All I can do is to tell you that it is not fit for you, or that you are not fit for it, because you are not by nature what most of them are, and please God you never will be.'

He spoke very earnestly, and another little silence followed, during which the two walked on.

'Please notice that I have not called you a prig for saying that,' said Margaret at last. 'And I have not thought you one either,' she added, before he could answer.

'You re very nice!' Lushington tried to laugh, but it was rather a failure.

'But of course you've no business to think me nice, have you?'

'None whatever.'

'Why not?'

It was not even curiosity, nor an idle inclination to flirt that made Margaret ask the question at last. She had never felt so strongly drawn to him as now.

He looked at her quietly, and answered without the least hesitation or shyness.

'I've no business to be in love with you, because I'm a fraud,' he said.

'A fraud! You? What in the world do you mean?'

Margaret was thoroughly surprised. This gifted, shy, youthful man who had fought his way to the front by his own talent and hard work, was of all people she knew the one with whom she least connected any idea of deception. He only nodded and looked at her.

'A fraud!' she exclaimed again. 'I suppose it's some sort of false modesty that makes you say that! You know that you are a very successful writer and that you have earned your success. Why do you try to make out----'

'I'm not trying to make out anything. I tell you the plain truth. I'm a fraud.'

'Nonsense!' Margaret was almost angry at his persistence.

'I would not tell you, if I did not care for you so much,' he answered. 'But as I do, and as you seem to like me a little, I should be an awful cad if I kept you in the dark any longer. You won't publish it on the housetops. I'm not Edmund Lushington at all.'

'You are not Edmund Lushington, the critic?' Margaret's mouth opened in surprise.

'I'm the critic all right,' he answered, with a faint smile. 'I'm the man that writes, the man you've heard of. But I'm not Lushington. It's an assumed name.'

'Oh!' Margaret seemed relieved. 'Is that all? Many people who write take other names.'

'But they are not generally known by them to their friends,' Lushington observed. 'That's where the fraud comes in, in my case. A man may sign his book Judas Iscariot or Peter the Great if he likes, provided he's known as Mr. Smith at home, if that's his real name.'

'Is your real name Smith?' Margaret asked. 'Is that why you changed it?'

Lushington could not help smiling.

'No. If I had been called Smith, I would have stuck to it. Smith is a very good, honest name. Most of the people who originally came by it made armour and were more or less artists. No! I wish I were a Smith, indeed I do! The name is frequent, not common, that's all.'

Margaret was puzzled, and looked at his face, as if she were thinking out the problem.

'No,' she said suddenly, and with decision. 'You are not a Jew. That's impossible!'

'I'm not a Jew.' He laughed this time. 'But I know several very interesting Jews, and I don't dislike them at all. I really should not mind being called Solomon Isaacs! I would not have changed the name either.'

'You might have been called Isidore Guggenheimer,' Margaret suggested, smiling.

'Well--that! For purposes of literature, it would not be practical.'

'You forget that you have not told me your real name yet. You see, if I should ever happen to think of you again, I'd rather not think of you under a pseudonym, unless it were in connection with your books.'

'That's the only way in which you are likely to think of me,' he answered. 'But if you really want to know, my first name is Thomas, diminutive Tom--plain Tom.'

'I like that much better than Edmund,' said Margaret, who had simple tastes. 'Is the other one as nice?'

'I don't know what you might think of it,' Lushington answered. 'It is neither common nor uncommon, and not at all striking, but I cannot tell you what it is. I'm sorry to make a mystery of it, for my father was nobody in particular, and I was nobody in particular until I was heard of as Lushington, the critic. And I've been Lushington so long that I'm used to it. I was called so at school and at Oxford.'

'As long ago as that!' Margaret again seemed relieved.

'Yes. Oh, I've done nothing disgraceful, nor my father either! It's not that. I cannot possibly explain, but it's the reason why I'm a fraud--as far as you are concerned.'

'Only as far as I am concerned?'

'Nobody else happens to matter. Mrs. Rushmore receives all sorts of interesting people, many of whom have played tricks with their names. Why should she care? Why should anybody care? We have all done the things we are known for, and we are not in love with Mrs. Rushmore, though she is a very agreeable woman! She wouldn't care to call me Tom, would she?'

'I don't know,' Margaret answered with a laugh. 'She might!'

'At all events, it's not necessary to tell her,' said Lushington.

'No. But suppose that I should not care to call you Tom either, and yet should wish to call you something, don't you know? That might happen.'

Lushington did not answer at once, and Margaret was a little displeased, for she had said more than she had ever meant to say to show him what she was beginning to feel. She held her head rather high as they walked on under the great trees, and her eyes sparkled coldly now and then.

She had known for a long time that he loved her, and to-day he had told her so, almost roughly; and for some time, also, she had understood that she was growing fond of him. But now that she held out her hand, metaphorically, he would not take it.

'I don't want to know your secret, if it is as important as that,' she said at last. 'A man who hides his real name so carefully must have some very good reason for doing it.'

She emphasised the words almost cruelly and looked straight before her, and her eyes sparkled again. His lips parted to make a quick retort, but he checked himself, and then spoke quietly.

'I have never done anything I am ashamed of,' he said.

'I don't think it's very nice to do what you are doing now,' Margaret retorted, coolly. 'It doesn't inspire confidence, you know.'

'Can't we part without quarrelling?'

'Oh, certainly! Do you mean to go away?'

'You leave me no choice. Shall we turn back to the house? It will sooner be over. I can leave before dinner. It will be easy to find an excuse.'

'Yes! Those proofs you have been talking of lately--your publishers--anything will do!'

Margaret was thoroughly angry with him and with herself by this time, and he was deeply hurt, and they turned and walked stiffly, with their noses in the air, as if they never meant to speak to each other again.

'It's very odd!' Margaret observed at last, as if she had made a discovery.

'What is very odd?'

'I never liked you as much as I did a quarter of an hour ago, and I never disliked you as much as I do now! Do you understand that?'

'Yes. You make it very clear. I never heard any thing put more plainly.'

'I'm glad of that. But it's very funny. I detest you just now, and yet, if you go away at once, I know I shall be sorry. On the whole, do you know?--you had better not leave to-night.'

Lushington turned sharply on her.

'Are you playing with me?' he asked, in an angry tone.

'No,' she answered with exasperating coolness, 'I don't think I am. Only, you are two people, you see. It confuses me. You are Mr. Lushington, and then, the next minute, you're--Tom. I hate Mr. Lushington. I believe I always did. I wish I might never see him again.'

'Oh indeed! How about Tom?'

'Tom is rather bearable than otherwise,' Margaret answered, laughing again. 'He knows that I think so, too, and it's no reason why he should be always trying to keep out of the way!'

'He has no right to be in the way.'

'Then he ought never to have come here. But since he has, I would rather have him stay.'

When she had thus explained herself with perfect frankness and made known her wishes, Margaret seemed to think that there was nothing more to be said. But Lushington thought otherwise.

'Why do you hate Mr. Lushington?' he asked.

'Because he is a fraud,' Margaret answered. 'As you have just told me that he is, you cannot possibly deny it, and you can't quarrel with me for not liking him. So there!'

All her good-humour had come back, the cold sparkle in her eyes had turned into afternoon sunshine, and she swung her closed parasol gently on one finger by its hook as she walked, nodding her head just perceptibly as if keeping time with it. She expected an answer, a laugh perhaps, or a retort; but nothing came. She glanced sideways at Lushington, thinking to meet his eyes, but they were watching the ground as he walked, a yard before his feet. She turned her head and looked at his face, and she realised that it was a little drawn, and had grown suddenly pale, and that there were dark shadows under his eyes which she had never seen before. The healthy, shy, rather too youthful mask was gone, and in its place she saw the features of a mature man who was quietly suffering a great deal. She fancied that he must often look as he did now, when he was alone.

'Could any one do anything to make it easier for you?' she asked softly, after a moment.

He looked up quickly in surprise, and then shook his head, without speaking.

'Because, if I could help you, I would,' she added.

'Thank you. I know you would,' He spoke with real gratitude, and the colour began to come back to his face. You see, it's not a thing that can be changed, or helped, or bettered. It's a condition from which I cannot escape, and I've got to live in it. It would have been easier if I had never met you, my dear Miss Donne!'

He straightened himself and put on something of the formality that had become a habit with him, as it easily does with shy men who feel much.

'Please don't call me Miss Donne,' Margaret said, very low.

'Margaret----' he paused on the syllables, as he almost whispered them. 'No!' he said, suddenly, as if angry with himself. 'That's silly! Don't make me do such things, please, or I shall hate myself! Nothing in the world can ever change what is, and I shall never have the right to put out my hand and ask you to marry me. The best we can do is to say good-bye, and I'll try to keep out of your way. Help me to do that, for it's the only help you can ever give me!'

'I don't believe it,' Margaret answered. 'We can always be friends, if we cannot be anything else.'

Lushington shook his head incredulously, but said nothing.

'Why not?' Margaret asked, clinging to her idea. 'Why can't we like each other, be very, very fond of each other, and meet often, and each help the other in life? I don't want to know your secret. I won't even call you Tom, as I want to, and you shall be as stiff and formal with me as you please. What do such things matter, if we really care? If we really trust one another, and know it? The main thing is to know, to be absolutely sure. Why do you wish to go away, just when I've found out how much I want you to stay? It's not right, and it's not kind! Indeed it's not!'

They had been walking very slowly, and now she stood still and faced him, waiting for his answer.

He looked steadily into her eyes as he spoke.

'I don't think I can stay,' he said slowly. 'You can't tear love up by the roots and plant it in a pot and call it friendship. If you try, something will happen. Excuse me if the simile sounds lyric, but I don't happen to think of a better one, on the spur of the moment. I'll behave all right before the others, but I had better go away to-morrow morning. The thing will only get worse if I keep on seeing you.'

Margaret heard the short, awkward sentences and knew what they cost him. She looked down and stuck the bright metal tip of her parasol into the thin dry mud of the macadamised road, grinding it in slowly, half round and half back, with both hands, and unconsciously wondering what made the earth so hard just in that place.

'I wish I were a man!' she said all at once, and the parasol bent dangerously as she gave it a particularly vicious twist, leaning upon it at the same time.

'It would certainly simplify matters for me, if you were,' said Lushington coldly.

She looked up with a hurt expression.

'Oh, please don't go back to that way of talking!' she said. 'It's bad enough, as it is! Don't you see how hard I am trying?'

'I'm sorry,' Lushington said. 'Don't pay any attention to what I say. I'm all over the place.'

He mumbled the words and turned away from her as he stood. She watched him, and desisted from digging holes in the ground. Then, as he did not look at her again she put out one hand rather shyly and touched his sleeve.

'Look at me,' she said. 'What is this for? What are we making ourselves miserable about? We care for each other a great deal, much more than I had any idea of this morning. Why should we say good-bye? I don't believe it's at all necessary, after all. You have got some silly, quixotic idea into your head, I'm sure. Tell me what it is, and let me judge for myself!'

'I can't,' he answered, in evident distress. 'You may find out what it is some day, but I cannot tell you. It's the one thing I couldn't say to anybody alive. If I did, I should deserve to be kicked out of decent society for ever!'

She saw the look of suffering in his face again, and she felt as if she were going to cry, out of sympathy.

'Of course,' she faltered, 'if it would be--what you call dishonourable--to tell----'

'Yes. It would be dishonourable to tell.'

There was a little silence.

'All I can hope,' he continued presently, 'is that you won't believe it's anything I've done myself.'

'Indeed, indeed I don't. I never could!'

She held out her hand and he took it gladly, and kept it in his for a moment; then he dropped it of his own accord, before she had made the least motion to take it back.

They walked on without speaking again for a long time, and without wishing to speak. When they were in sight of Mrs. Rushmore's gate Margaret broke the silence at last.

'Do you mean to take an early train to-morrow morning?' she asked.

'Nine o'clock, I think,' he answered.

There was another little pause, and again Margaret spoke, but very low, this time.

'I shall be in the garden at half-past eight--to say good-bye.'

'Yes,' Lushington answered. 'Thank you,' he added after a moment.

They were side by side, very near together as they walked, and her left hand hung down close to his right. He caught her fingers suddenly, and they pressed his, and parted from them instantly.

CHAPTER V

Little Madame Durand-De Rosa took Margaret behind the scenes just before the second act of Romeo and Juliet was over. The famous teacher of singing was a privileged person at the Opéra, and the man who kept the side door of communication between the house and the stage bowed low as he opened for her and Margaret. Things are well managed in the great opera-houses nowadays, and it is not easy to get behind when anything is going on.

The young girl felt a new sensation of awe and excitement. It was the first time she had ever found herself on the working side of the vast machinery of artistic pleasure, and her first impression was that she had been torn from an artificial paradise and was being dragged through an artificial inferno. Huge and unfamiliar objects loomed about her in the deep shadows; men with pale faces, in working clothes, stood motionless at their posts, listening and watching; others lurked in corners, dressed in mediæval costumes that glittered in the dark. Between the flies, Margaret caught glimpses of the darkened stage, and the sound of the orchestra reached her as if muffled, while the tenor's voice sounded very loud, though he was singing softly. On a rough bit of platform six feet above the stage, stood Madame Bonanni in white satin, apparently laced to a point between life and death, her hands holding the two sides of the latticed door that opened upon the balcony. In a loft on the stage left a man was working a lime-light moon behind a sheet of blue glass in a frame; the chorus of old retainers in grey stood huddled together in semi-darkness by a fly, listening to the tenor and waiting to hear Madame Bonanni's note when she should come out.

[Illustration: "The young girl felt a new sensation of awe and excitement."]

Margaret would have waited too, but her teacher hurried her along, holding her by the hand and checking her when they came to any obstacle which the girl's unpractised eyes might not have seen in time. To the older woman it was all as familiar as her own sitting-room, for her life had been spent in the midst of it; to Margaret it was all strange, and awe-inspiring, and a little frightening. It was to be her own life, too, before long. In a few months, or perhaps a few weeks, she, too, would be standing on a platform, like Madame Bonanni, waiting to go out into the lime-light, waiting to be heard by two thousand people. She wondered whether she should be frightened, whether by any possibility her voice would stick in her throat at the great moment and suddenly croak out a hideous false note, and end her career then and there. Her heart beat fast at the thought, even now, and she pressed her teacher's guiding hand nervously; and yet, as the music reached her ears, she longed to be standing in Madame Bonanni's place with only a latticed balcony door between her and the great public. She was not thinking of Lushington now, though she had thought all day of his face when she had met him for one moment under the trees, yesterday morning, and had felt that something was gone from her life which she was to miss for a long time. That was all forgotten in what she felt at the present moment, in the wild quivering longing to be in front, the centre of the great illusion, singing as she knew that she could sing, as she had never sung before.

Madame De Rosa led her quickly down a dark corridor and a moment later she found herself in a dazzling blaze of light, in the prima donna's dressing-room.

The ceiling was low, the walls were white, and innumerable electric lamps, with no shades, filled the place with a blinding glare. It all looked bare and uncomfortable, and very untidy. There was a toilet-table, covered with little pots of grease and paint, and well-worn pads and hare's-feet, and vast stores of hairpins, besides a quantity of rings and jewels of great value, all lying together in bowls in the midst of the confusion. A tall mirror stood on one side, with wing mirrors on hinges, and bunches of lamps that could be moved about. On one of the walls half-a-dozen theatrical gowns and cloaks hung limply from pegs. Two large trunks were open and empty not far from the door. The air was hot and hard to breathe, and smelt of many things.

There were three people in the room when the two visitors entered; there was a very tall maid with an appallingly cadaverous face and shiny black hair, and there was a short fat maid who grinned and showed good teeth at Madame De Rosa. Both wore black and had white aprons, and both were perspiring profusely. The third person was an elderly man in evening dress, who rose and shook hands with the retired singer, and bowed to Margaret. He seemed to be a very quiet, unobtrusive man, who was nevertheless perfectly at his ease, and he somehow conveyed the impression that he must be always dressed for the evening, in a perfectly new coat, a brand-new shirt, a white waistcoat never worn before, and a made tie. Perhaps it was the made tie that introduced a certain disquieting element in his otherwise highly correct appearance. He wore his faded fair hair very short, and his greyish yellow beard was trimmed in a point. His fat hands were incased in tight white gloves. His pale eyes looked quietly through his glasses and made one think of the eyes of a big fish in an aquarium when it swims up and pushes its nose against the plate-glass front of the tank to look at visitors.

The eyes examined Margaret attentively.

'Monsieur Schreiermeyer, this is Miss Donne, my pupil,' said Madame De Rosa.

'Enchanted,' mumbled the manager.

He continued to scrutinise the young girl's face, and he looked so much like a doctor that she felt as if he were going to feel her pulse and tell her to put out her tongue. At the thought, she smiled pleasantly.

'Hum!' Schreiermeyer grunted softly, almost musically, in fact.

Perhaps this was a good sign, for little Madame De Rosa beamed. Margaret looked about for an empty chair, but there never seemed to be any in a room used by Madame Bonanni. There was one indeed, but Schreiermeyer had appropriated it, and sat down upon it again with perfect calm.

'Sit down,' he said, as he did so himself.

'Yes,' answered Margaret sweetly, and remained standing.

Suddenly he seemed to realise that she could not, and that the maids were not inclined to offer her a seat. His face and figure were transfigured in an instant, one fat, gloved hand shot out with extended forefinger in a gesture of command and his pale eyes flashed through his glasses, and glared furiously at the maids.

'Clear two chairs!' he shouted in a voice of thunder.

Margaret started in surprise and protest.

'But the things are all ready----' objected the cadaverous maid.

'Damn the things!' yelled Schreiermeyer. 'Clear two chairs at once!'

He seemed, on the verge of a white apoplexy, though he did not move from his seat. The cadaverous maid lifted an embroidered bodice from one of the chairs and laid it in one of the black trunks; she looked like a female undertaker laying a dead baby in its coffin. The fat maid showed all her teeth and laughed at Schreiermeyer and cleared the other chair, and brought up both together for the two ladies.

'Give yourselves the trouble to be seated,' said Schreiermeyer, in a tone so soft that it would not have disturbed a sleeping child.

As soon as he was obeyed he became quite quiet and unobtrusive again, the furious glare faded from his eyes, and the white kid hand returned to rest upon its fellow.

'How good you are!' cried Madame De Rosa gratefully, as she sat down on the cane chair.

'Hum!' grunted Schreiermeyer, musically, as if he agreed with her.

'Miss Donne has a good soprano,' the teacher ventured to say after a time.

'Ah?' ejaculated the manager in a tone of very indifferent interrogation.

There was a little pause.

'Lyric,' observed Madame De Rosa, breaking the silence.

Another pause. Schreiermeyer seemed not to have heard, and neither moved nor looked at the two.

'Lyric?' he inquired, suddenly, but with extreme softness.

'Lyric,' repeated Madame De Rosa, leaning forward a little, and fanning herself violently.

Another pause.

'Thank God!' exclaimed Schreiermeyer, without moving, but so very devoutly that Margaret stared at him in surprise.

Madame De Rosa knew that this also was an excellent sign; she looked at Margaret and nodded energetically. Whatever Schreiermeyer might mean by returning devout thanks to his Maker at that moment, the retired singer was perfectly sure that he knew his business. He was probably in need of a lyric soprano for the next season, and that might lead to an immediate engagement for Margaret.

'How hot it is!' the latter complained, in an undertone. 'There is no air at all here!'

The maids were mopping their faces with their handkerchiefs, and Madame De Rosa's fan was positively whirring. Schreiermeyer seemed quite indifferent to the temperature.

He must nevertheless have been reflecting on Margaret's last remark when he slowly turned to her after a silence of nearly a minute.

'Have you a good action of the heart?' he inquired, precisely as a doctor might have done.

'I don't know.' Margaret smiled. 'I don't know anything about my heart.'

'Then it is good,' said the manager. 'It ought to be, for you have a magnificent skin. Do you eat well and sleep well, always?'

'Perfectly. May I ask if you are a doctor?'

Madame De Rosa made furious signs to Margaret. A very faint smile flitted over the manager's quiet face.

'Some people call me an executioner,' he answered, 'because I kill the weak ones.'

'I am not afraid of work.' Margaret laughed.

'No. You will grow fat if you sing. You will grow very fat.' He spoke thoughtfully. 'After you are forty,' he added, as if by way of consolation.

'I hope not!' cried the young girl.

'Yes, you will. It is the outward sign of success in the profession. Singers who grow thin lose their voices.'

'I never grew very fat,' said Madame De Rosa, in a tone of regret.

'Precisely, my darling,' answered Schreiermeyer. 'Therefore you retired.'

Margaret was a little surprised that he should call her teacher 'my darling,' and that the good lady should seem to think it quite natural, but her reflections on obesity and the manners of theatrical people were interrupted, though not by any means arrested for the night, by the clattering sound of high-heeled shoes in the corridor. The act was over, and Madame Bonanni was coming back from the stage. In a moment she was in the doorway, and as she entered the room she unmasked a third maid who followed her with a cloak.

She saw Margaret first, as the latter rose to meet her. Margaret felt as if the world itself were putting huge arms round her and kissing her on both cheeks. The embrace was of terrific power, and a certain amount of grease paint came off.

'Little Miss Donne,' cried the prima donna, relaxing her hold on Margaret's waist but instantly seizing her by the wrist and turning her round sharply, like a dressmaker's doll on a pivot, 'that is Schreiermeyer! The great Schreiermeyer! The terrible Schreiermeyer! You see him before you, my child! Tremble! Every one trembles before Schreiermeyer!'

The manager had risen, but was perfectly imperturbable and silent. He did not even grunt. Madame Bonanni dropped Margaret's wrist and shrugged her Juno-like shoulders.

'Schreiermeyer,' she said, as if she had forgotten all about Margaret, 'if that lime-light man plays the moon in my eyes again I shall come out on the balcony with blue goggles. You shall hear the public then! It is perfectly outrageous! I am probably blind for life!'

She winked her big painted eyelids vigorously as if trying whether she could see at all. Margaret was looking at her, not sure that it was not all a dream, and wondering how it was possible that such a face and figure could still produce illusions of youth and grace when seen from the other side of the footlights. Yet Margaret herself had felt the illusion only a quarter of an hour ago. The paint on Madame Bonanni's face was a thick mask of grease, pigments and powder; the wig was the most evident wig that ever was; the figure seemed of gigantic girth compared with the woman's height, though that was by no means small; the eye lids were positively unwieldy with paint and the lashes looked like very thick black horsehairs stuck in with glue, in rows.

She shook her solid fist at Schreiermeyer and blinked violently again.

'It is outrageous!' she cried again. 'Do you understand?'

'Perfectly.'

'Schreiermeyer!' screamed Madame Bonanni. 'If you take no more notice of my complaints than that I refuse to finish the opera. I will not sing the rest of it! Find somebody else to go on. I am going home! Undress me!' she cried, turning to the three perspiring maids, not one of whom moved an inch at her summons. 'Oh, you won't? You are afraid of him? Ah, bah! I am not. Schreiermeyer, I refuse to go on; I absolutely refuse. Go away! I am going to undress.'

Thereupon she tore off her brown wig with a single movement and threw it across the room. It struck the wall with a thud and fell upon the floor, a limp and shapeless mass. The cadaverous maid instantly picked it up and began smoothing it. Madame Bonanni's own dark hair stood on end, giving her a decidedly wild look.

Schreiermeyer smiled perceptibly.

'Miss Donne will go on and sing the rest of the opera with pleasure, I have no doubt,' he said, gently, looking at Margaret.

The girl's heart stood still for an instant at this sudden proposal, before she realised that the manager was not in earnest.

'Of course she can sing it!' chimed in Madame De Rosa, understanding perfectly. 'But our dear friend is much too kind to disappoint the Parisian public,' she added, turning to the prima donna and speaking soothingly.

'Nothing can move that man!' cried Madame Bonanni, in a helpless tone.

'Nothing but the sound of your marvellous voice, my angel artist,' said Schreiermeyer. 'That always makes me weep, especially in the last act of this opera.'

Margaret could not fancy the manager blubbering, though she had more than once seen people in front with their handkerchiefs to their eyes during the scene in the tomb.

'Put my wig on,' said Madame Bonanni to the cadaverous maid, and she sat down in front of the toilet-table. 'We must talk business at once,' she continued, suddenly speaking with the utmost calm. 'The appointment is at my house, at ten o'clock to-morrow morning, Schreiermeyer. Miss Donne will sing for us. Bring a pianist and the Minister of Fine Arts if you can get him.'

'I have not the Minister of Fine Arts in my pocket, dearest lady,' observed the manager, 'but I will try. Why do you name such a very early hour?'

'Because I breakfast at eleven. Tell the Minister that the King is coming too. That will bring him. All Ministers are snobs.'

'The King?' repeated Margaret in surprise, and somewhat aghast.

'He is in Paris,' explained Madame Bonanni carelessly. 'He's an old friend of mine, and we dined together last night. I told him about you and he said he would come if he could but you never can count on those people.'

Margaret was too timid to ask what king Madame Bonanni was talking of, but she supposed her teacher would tell her in due time; and, after all, he might not come. Margaret hoped that he would, however, for she had never spoken to a royalty in her life and thought it would be very amusing to see a real, live king in the prima donna's eccentric surroundings.

'I shall turn you all out when you have heard her sing,' continued Madame Bonanni. You and I will lunch quite alone, my dear, and talk things over. There is one good point in Schreiermeyer's character. He never flatters unless he wants something. If he tells you that you sing well, it means an engagement next year. If he says you sing divinely, your début will be next week, or as soon as you can rehearse with a company.'

She touched up her cheeks with a hare's-foot while she talked.

'So that is settled,' she said, turning sharp round on the stool, which creaked loudly. 'Go home and go to bed, my children, unless you want to hear poor old Bonanni sing the rest of this stupid opera!'

She laughed, at herself perhaps; but suddenly in the tones

Margaret heard a far-off suggestion of sadness that went to her heart very strangely. The singer turned her back again and seemed to pay no more attention to her visitors. Margaret came close to her, to say goodbye, and to thank her for all she was doing. The great artist looked up quietly into the young girl's eyes for a moment, and laid a hand on hers very kindly.

'Good-night, little Miss Donne,' she said, so low that the others could not hear distinctly. 'It is the setting sun that bids you good-night, child--you, the dawn and the sun of to-morrow!'

Margaret pressed the kind hand, and a moment later her teacher was hurrying her back through the dark wilderness of the stage to the brilliant house beyond. Schreiermeyer had already disappeared without so much as a word.

CHAPTER VI

Mrs. Rushmore had not been at all surprised at Lushington's sudden departure. She was accustomed to the habits of lions and was well aware that they must be allowed to come and go exactly as they please if you wish them to eat out of your hand from time to time; and when the eminent young critic announced rather suddenly that he must leave early the next morning the good lady only said that she was sorry, and that she hoped he would come back soon. Sham lions love to talk about themselves, and to excite curiosity, but real ones resent questions about their doings as they would resent a direct insult. Mrs. Rushmore knew that, too.

She was really sorry to lose him, however, and had counted on his staying at least a week longer. She liked him herself, and she saw that Margaret liked him very much; and it was more moral in a nice girl to like an Englishman than a foreigner, just as it would be still more moral of her to prefer an American to an Englishman, according to Mrs. Rushmore's scale of nationalities. Next to what was moral, she was fond of lions, who are often persons without any morals whatsoever. But Lushington seemed to fill both requirements. He was a highly moral lion. She was quite sure that he did not drink, did not gamble, and did not secretly worship Ashtaroth; and he never told her naughty stories. Therefore she was very sorry when he was gone.

At the present juncture, however, she was in considerable anxiety about Margaret. She did not know one note from another, but she had heard all the greatest singers of the last thirty years, in all the greatest opera-houses from Bayreuth to New York, and it horrified her to be obliged to admit that Margaret's singing sounded dreadfully like the best. The girl meant to sing in opera, and if she could really do it well it would be quite impossible to hinder her, as she had no means of support and could not be blamed for refusing to live on charity. Everything was combining to make an artist of her, for the chances of winning the suit brought on her behalf were growing as slender as the seven lean kine.

It was characteristic of Margaret that she had kept to herself most of what Madame Bonanni had told her, but Mrs. Rushmore knew the girl well, and guessed from her face that there was much more behind. The appointment at the theatre confirmed this surmise, and when Margaret telegraphed the next day that she was going to stay in town until the afternoon, with Madame De Rosa, there was no longer any room for doubt.

As for poor Lushington, Margaret had told him nothing at all, and her visit to Madame Bonanni had been a secret between herself and Mrs. Rushmore. Logotheti had not made his appearance after all, but the young archæologist had brought assurances that the financier would be honoured, charmed and otherwise delighted to be presented to Mrs. Rushmore within a day or two, if convenient to her. So it happened that Logotheti made his first visit after Lushington had left Versailles.

The latter went away in a very disconsolate frame of mind, and disappeared into Paris. It is not always wise to follow a discouraged man into the retirement of a shabby room in a quiet hotel on the left bank of the Seine, and it is never amusing. Psychology in fiction seems to mean the rather fruitless study of what the novelist himself thinks he might feel if he ever got himself into one of those dreadful scrapes which it is a part of his art to invent outright, or to steal from the lives of men and women he has known or heard of. People who can analyse their own feelings are never feeling enough to hurt them much; a medical student could not take his scalpel and calmly dissect out his own nerves. You may try to analyse pain and pleasure when they are past, but nothing is more strangely and hopelessly undefined than the memory of a great grief, and no analysis of pleasure can lead to anything but the desire for more. The only real psychologists have been the great lyric poets, before they have emerged from the gloom of youth.

The outward signs of Lushington's condition were few and not such as would have seemed dramatic to an acquaintance. When he was in his room at the hotel in the Rue des Saints Pères, he got an old briar pipe out of his bag, filled it and lit it, and stood for nearly a quarter of an hour at the window, smoking thoughtfully with his hands in his pockets. The subtle analyst, observing that the street is narrow and dull and presents nothing of interest, jumps to the conclusion that Lushington is thinking while he looks out of the window. Perhaps he is. The next thing to be done is to unpack his bag and place his dressing things in order on the toilet-table. They are simple things, but mostly made expressly for him, of oxidised silver, with his initials in plain block letters; and each object has a neat sole leather case of its own, so that they can be thrown pell-mell into a bag and jumbled up together without being scratched. But Lushington takes them out of their cases and disposes them on the table with mathematical precision, smoking vigorously all the time. This done, he unpacks his valise, his shirt-case and other belongings, in the most systematic way possible, looks through the things he left in the room when he went to Versailles, to see that everything is in order, and at last rings for the servant to take away the clothes and shoes that need cleaning. The subtle analyst would argue from all this that Lushington was one of those painfully orderly persons, who are made positively nervous by the sight of a hair-brush lying askew, or a tie dropped on the floor.

It was at most true that he had acquired a set of artificially precise habits to which he clung most tenaciously, and which certainly harmonised with the natural appearance of neatness that had formerly been his despair. Why he had taken so much trouble to become orderly was his own business. Possibly he had got tired of that state of life in which it is impossible to find anything in less than half an hour when one wants it in half a minute. At all events, he had taken pains to acquire orderliness, and, for reasons which will appear hereafter, it is worth while to note the fact.

When everything was arranged to his satisfaction, he sat down in the most comfortable chair in the room, filled another of the three wooden pipes that now lay side by side on the writing-table, and continued to smoke as if his welfare depended on consuming a certain quantity of tobacco in a given time. He must have had a sound heart and a strong head, for he did not desist from his occupation for many hours, though he had not eaten anything particular at breakfast, at Mrs. Rushmore's, and nothing at all since.

The afternoon was wearing on when he knocked the ashes out of his pipe very carefully, laid it in its place, rose from his seat and uttered a single profane ejaculation.

'Damn!'

Having said this, he said no more, for indeed, if taken literally, there could be nothing more to be said. The malediction, however, was directed against nothing particular, and certainly against no person living or dead; it only applied to the aggregate of the awkward circumstances in which he found himself, and as he was alone he felt quite sure of not being misunderstood.

He did not even take a servant with him when he travelled, though he had an excellent Scotchman for a valet, who could do a great variety of useful things, besides holding his tongue, which is one of the finest qualities in the world, in man or dog. And he also had a dog in London, a particularly rough Irish terrier called Tim; but as Tim would have been quarantined every time he came home it was practically impossible to bring him to the Continent. It will be seen, therefore, that Lushington was really quite alone in the quiet hotel in the Rue des Saints Pères.

He might have had company enough if he had wanted it, for he knew many men of letters in Paris and was himself known to them, which is another thing. They liked him, too, in their own peculiar way of liking their foreign colleagues. Most of them, without affectation and in perfect good faith, are convinced that there never was, is not, and never can be any literature equal to the French except that of Edgar Poe; but they feel that it would be rude and tactless of them to let us know that they think so. They are the most agreeable men in the world, as a whole, and considering what they really think of us--rightly or wrongly, but honestly--the courtesy and consideration they show us are worthy of true gentlemen. The most modest among ourselves seem a little arrogant and self-asserting in comparison with them. They praise us, sometimes, and not faintly either; but their criticism of us compares us with each other, not with them. The very highest eulogy they can bestow on anything we do is to say that it is 'truly French,' but they never quite believe it and they cannot understand why that is perhaps the very compliment that pleases us least, though we may have the greatest admiration for their national genius. With all our vanity, should we ever expect to please a French writer by telling him that his work was 'truly English'?

Lushington liked a good many of his French colleagues in literature, and had at least one friend among them, a young man of vast learning and exquisite taste, who was almost an invalid. For a moment, he thought of going to see this particular one amongst them all, but he realised all at once that he did not wish to see any one at all that day. He went out and wandered towards the Quai Voltaire, and smelt the Seine and nosed an old book here and there at the stalls. Later he went and ate something in an eating-house on the outskirts of the Latin Quarter, and then went back to his hotel, smoked several more pipes by the open window, and went to bed.

That was the first day, and the second was very like it, so that it is not necessary to describe it in detail in order to produce an impression of profound dulness in the reader's mind. Lushington's hair continued to be as preternaturally smooth as before, his beard was as glossy and his complexion as blooming and child-like, and yet the look of pain that Margaret had seen in his face was there most of the time during those two days.

But in the evening he crossed the river and went to hear Romeo and Juliet, for he knew that it was the last night on which Madame Bonanni would sing before she left for the London season. He sat in the second row of the orchestra stalls, and never moved from his seat during the long performance. No secret intuition told him that Margaret was in the house, and that if he stood up and looked round after the second act he might see her and Madame De Rosa going out and coming back again and sitting at the end of a back row. He did not want to see any one he knew, and the surest way of avoiding acquaintances was to sit perfectly still while most people went out between the acts. His face only betrayed that the music pleased him, by turning a shade paler now and then; at the places he liked best, he shut his eyes, as if he did not care to see Madame Bonanni or the fat tenor.

She sang very beautifully that night, especially after the second act, and Lushington thought he had hardly ever heard so much real feeling in her marvellous voice. Afterwards he walked home, and he heard it all the way, and for an hour after he had gone to bed, when he fell asleep at last, and dreamt that he himself had turned into a very fat tenor and was singing Romeo, but the Juliet was Margaret Donne instead of Madame Bonanni, and though she sang like an angel, she was evidently disgusted by his looks; which was very painful indeed, and made him sing quite out of tune and perspire terribly.

'You look hot,' said Margaret-Juliet, with cruel distinctness, just as he was trying to throw the most intense pathos into the words, "tis not the lark, it is the nightingale!'

Perhaps dreaming nonsense is also a subject for the inquiries of psychology. At the moment the poor man's imaginary sufferings were positively frightful, and he awoke with a gasp. He had always secretly dreaded growing fat, he had always felt a horror of anything like singing or speaking in public, and the only thing in the world he really feared was the possibility of being ridiculous in Margaret's eyes. Of course the ingenious demon of his dreams found a way of applying all these three torments at once, and it was like being saved from sudden death to wake up in the dark and smell the stale smoke of the pipe he had enjoyed before putting out his light.

Then he fell asleep again and did not awake till morning, being naturally a very good sleeper. It was raining when he got up, and he looked out disconsolately upon the dull street. It seemed to him that if it was going to rain in Paris he might as well go back to London, where he had plenty to do, and he began to consider which train he should take, revolving the advantages and disadvantages of reaching London early in the evening or late at night. He knew the different time-tables by heart.

But it stopped raining while he was dressing, and the sun came out, and a bird began to sing somewhere at a window high above the street, and it was suddenly spring again. It was a great thing to be alone in spring. If he went back to London he must see people he knew, and dine with people he hardly knew at all, and be asked out by others whom he had not even met, because he was the distinguished critic, flattered and feared and asked to dinner by everybody who had a seventh cousin in danger of literary judgment. He belonged to the flock of dramatic lions and must herd with them, eat with them and roar with them, for the greater glory of London society and his native country generally. Under ordinary circumstances such an existence was bearable and at times delightful, but just now he wanted to roar in the wilderness and assert his leonine right of roaming in desolate places not less than two geographical degrees east of Pall Mall.

He went out at last and strolled towards the bridge, and across it and much farther, but not aimlessly, for though he did not always take the shortest way, he kept mainly in the same direction till he came to the Avenue Hoche.

At the end of the street he stopped and looked at his watch. It was five minutes to eleven. Looking along the pavement in front of him his eye was attracted by the striped awning that distinguished Madame Bonanni's house from the others on the same side, and he noticed an extremely smart brougham that stood just before the door. The handsome black horse stood perfectly motionless in the morning sunshine, the stony-faced English coachman sat perfectly motionless on the box, looking straight between the horse's ears; he wore a plain black livery that fitted to perfection and there was no cockade on his polished hat. No turnout could have been simpler and yet none could have looked more overpoweringly smart.

Lushington suddenly turned on his heel and walked off in the opposite direction, as if he were not pleased, but he had not gone fifty yards when he heard the brougham behind him, and in a few seconds it passed him at a sharp pace. He caught sight of the elderly man inside--a tremendous profile over a huge fair beard that was half grey, one large and rather watery blue eye behind a single eyeglass with a broad black ribbon, a gardenia in the button-hole of a smart grey coat, a cloud of cigarette smoke, one very large and aristocratic hand, with a plain gold ring, holding the cigarette and resting on the edge of the window. He smelt the smoke after the brougham had passed, and he recognised the fact that it was superlatively fragrant.

He turned back again in a few moments and saw that three men were just coming out of Madame Bonanni s house. One was Schreiermeyer, whom he knew, and one looked like a poor musician. The third was the Minister of Fine Arts, whom he did not know but recognised. The Minister and the pianist walked one on each side of Schreiermeyer, and were talking excitedly, but the manager looked at neither of them and never turned his head. They went down the Avenue Hoche away from Lushington, who walked very slowly and looked at his watch twice before he reached Madame Bonanni's door. There he stopped, rang and was admitted without question, as if he were in the habit of coming and going as he pleased. He apparently took it for granted that the prima donna must be alone and already at her late breakfast, but he was stopped by the smiling servant who came out of the dining-room, arrayed as usual in a frock coat and a white satin tie.

'I will inform Madame,' he said.

'Is there any one there?' asked Lushington, evidently not pleased.

The servant shrugged his shoulders in a deprecatory way, and his smile became rather compassionate.

'One young person to breakfast,' he said, 'a musician'.

'Oh, very well.' Lushington's brow cleared.

The servant left him and went in again. A screen was so placed as to mask the interior of the dining-room when the door was open. Within, Madame Bonanni and Margaret were seated at table. Encouraged by circumstances the prima donna had on this occasion tied her napkin round her neck as soon as she had sat down; the inevitable plovers' eggs had already been demolished, and she was at work on a creamy purée soup of the most exquisite pale green colour. It was clear that she had not lost a moment in getting to her meal after the men had left. Margaret was eating too, but though there was fresh colour in her cheeks her eyes had a startled look each time she looked up, as if something very unusual had happened.

The servant whispered something in Madame Bonanni's ear. She seemed to hesitate a moment, and glanced at Margaret before making up her mind. Then she nodded to the man without saying a word, and went on eating her soup.

A few seconds later Lushington entered. Margaret faced the door and their eyes met. Madame Bonanni dropped her spoon into her plate with a clang and uttered a scream of delight, as if she had not known perfectly well that Lushington was coming.

'What luck!' she cried. 'Little Miss Donne, this is my son!'

Margaret's jaw dropped in sheer amazement.

'Your son? Mr. Lushington is your son?'

'Yes. Ah, my child!' she cried, springing up and kissing Lushington on both cheeks with resounding affection. 'What a joy it is to see you!'

Lushington was rather pale as he laid his hand quietly on Madame Bonanni's.

'I have the pleasure of knowing Miss Donne already, mother,' he said steadily, 'but she did not know that I was your son. She is a little surprised.'

'Yes,' answered Margaret, faintly, 'a little.'

'Ah, you know each other?' Madame Bonanni seemed delighted. 'So much the better! Miss Donne will keep our little secret, I am sure. Besides she has another name, too. She is Señorita Margarita da Cordova from to-day. Sit down, my darling child! You are starving! I know you are starving! Angelo!' she screamed at the smiling servant, 'why do you stand there staring like a stuffed codfish? Bring more plovers' eggs!'

Angelo smiled as sweetly as ever and disappeared for an instant. Madame Bonanni took Lushington by the shoulders, as if he had been a little boy, made him sit down in the vacant place beside her, unfolded the napkin herself, spread it upon his knees, patted both his cheeks and kissed the top of his head, precisely as she had done when he was six years old. Margaret looked on in dumb surprise, and poor Lushington turned red to the roots of his hair.

'You have no idea what a dear child he is,' she said to Margaret, as she sat herself down in her own chair again. 'He has been my passion ever since he was born! My dear, you never saw such a beautiful baby as he was! He was all pink and white, like a little sugar angel, and he had dimples everywhere--everywhere, my dear!' she repeated with suggestive emphasis.

'I don't doubt it,' said Margaret, biting her lips and looking at her plate.

By this time the plovers' eggs had come for Lushington and he was glad of anything to do with his hands.

'My mother can never believe that I am grown up,' he said, with much more self-possession than Margaret had expected; and suddenly he raised his eyes and looked steadily and quietly at her across the table.

It must have cost him something of an effort, for his colour came and went quickly. Margaret knew what he was suffering and her respect for him increased a hundredfold in those few minutes, because he did not betray the least irritation in his tone or manner. His mother evidently worshipped him, but her way of showing it was such as must be horribly uncomfortable to a man of his retiring character and sensitive taste. He might easily have been forgiven if he had shown that it hurt him, as well it might. Whatever reason he and Madame Bonanni might have had for changing his name, he was brave enough not to be falsely ashamed of her, in the presence of the woman he loved.

'You see,' Margaret said, looking at him, but speaking to the prima donna, 'Mr. Lushington has been stopping with us at Versailles for a good while, but I did not tell him that I had been to see you, and he never even said that he know you, though he often spoke of your singing.'

'Did he?' asked Madame Bonanni with intense anxiety. 'What did he say? Did he say that I was growing old and ought to give up the stage?'

'Mother!' exclaimed Lushington reproachfully.

'He never said anything of the kind!' cried Margaret, taking his part with energy.

'Because he always says just what he thinks,' explained Madame Bonanni, who seemed relieved. 'And the worst part of it is that he knows,' she added, thoughtfully. 'I do not pretend to understand what he writes, but I would take his opinion about music rather than any one's. You wretched little boy!' she cried, turning on Lushington suddenly. 'How you frightened me!'

'I frightened you? How?'

'I was sure that you had told everybody that I was growing old! How could you? My darling child, how could you be so unkind? Oh, you have no heart!'

'But he never said so!' cried Margaret vehemently and feeling as if she were in a madhouse. 'He has told me again and again that you are still the greatest lyric soprano living----'

'Angelo,' said Madame Bonanni, with perfect calm, 'change my plate.'

Margaret glanced at Lushington, who seemed to think it all quite natural. He was eating little bits of thin toast thoughtfully, and from time to time he looked at his mother with a gentle expression. But he did not meet Margaret's glance.

'You never sang better in your life than you did last night, mother,' he observed.

The prima donna's face glowed with pleasure, and as she turned her big eyes to his Margaret saw in them a look of such loving tenderness as she had rarely seen in her life.

'I saw you, my dear,' said Madame Bonanni to her son. 'You were in the second row of the stalls. I sang for you last night, for I thought you looked sad and lonely.'

Lushington laid his hand on hers for a moment.

'Thank you,' he said simply.

There was a short silence, which was unusual when the prima donna was present. Margaret had recovered from her first surprise, and had understood that Madame Bonanni adored her son and that he felt real affection for her, though he suffered a good deal from the manner in which hers showed itself. If Lushington had fancied that he might fall in Margaret's estimation through her discovery of his birth, he was much mistaken. His patience and perfect simplicity did more to make her love him than anything he had done before. She had learned his secret, or a great part of it, and she understood him now, and the reason why he had changed his name, and she felt that he had behaved very well to her in going away, though she wished that he had boldly taken her into his confidence before leaving Mrs. Rushmore's. But she did not know all, though she was neither too young nor too innocent to guess a part of the truth. Few young women of twenty-two years are. Madame Bonanni's career as an artist had been a long series of triumphs, but her past as a woman had been variegated, of the sort for which the French have invented a number of picturesquely descriptive expressions, such as 'leading the life of Punch,' 'throwing one's cap over the windmills,' and other much less elegant phrases. Margaret saw that Lushington was not ashamed of his mother, as his mother; but she knew instinctively that his mother's past was a shame which he felt always and to the quick.

Madame Bonanni ate a good deal before she spoke again, feeling, perhaps, that she had lost time.

'Schreiermeyer says she sings divinely,' she said at last, looking at Lushington and then nodding at Margaret. 'You know what that means.'

'London?' inquired Lushington, who knew the manager.

'London next year, and an appearance this season if any one breaks down. Meanwhile he signs for her début in Belgium and a three months' tour. Twenty-four performances in three operas, fifty thousand francs.'

'I congratulate you,' said Lushington, looking at Margaret and trying to seem pleased.

'You seem to think it is too little,' observed Madame Bonanni.

'Little?' cried Margaret. 'It's a fortune!'

'You may talk of a fortune when you get three hundred pounds a night,' said Lushington. 'But it is a good beginning. I wonder that Schreiermeyer agreed to it so easily.'

'Easily!' Madame Bonanni laughed. 'I wish you had been there, my dear boy! He kicked and screamed, and we called him bad names. The King told him he was a dirty little Jew, which he is not, poor man, but it had a very good effect.'

'Oh!' Lushington did not seem surprised at the royal personage's reported language. 'Then it was the King who passed me in that smart brougham? I thought so.'

'Yes,' answered Madame Bonanni rather brusquely, and she became very busy with some little birds.

'It's funny,' Margaret said to Lushington. 'One always imagines a king with a crown and a sort of ermine dressing-gown, and a sceptre like the Lord Mayor's mace! Of course it s perfectly ridiculous, isn't it?'

'I believe His Majesty possesses those things,' answered Lushington, as if he did not like the subject.

'He looked and talked much more like an old friend than anything else,' Margaret went on, remembering that Madame Bonanni had used the same expression before Schreiermeyer.

To her surprise and sudden discomfiture neither of the two paid the least attention to her remark.

'What train shall you take, mother?' asked Lushington so abruptly upon Margaret's speech that she understood her mistake.

Though she had guessed something, it had somehow not occurred to her to connect the royal personage with Madame Bonanni's past; but now she scarcely dared to glance at Lushington. When she did, he seemed to be avoiding her eyes again, and she saw the old look of pain in his face, though he was talking about the timetables and the turbine channel-boat.

'You must come over to London and see me before your début, my dear,' Madame Bonanni said, breaking off the discussion of trains and turning to Margaret. 'That is, if Schreiermeyer will let you,' she added. 'You will have to do exactly what he tells you, now, and he is always right. He will be a father to you, now that he is going to make money out of you.'

'Will he call me his "darling"?' inquired Margaret, with a shade of anxiety.

'Of course he will! And when you sing well he will kiss you on both cheeks.'

'Indeed he won't!' cried Margaret, turning red.

Madame Bonanni laughed heartily, but Lushington looked annoyed.

'My dear, why not?' asked the prima donna. 'Everybody kisses us artists, when we have a triumph, and we kiss everybody! The author, the manager, the dressmaker and the stage carpenter, besides all our old friends! What difference can it make? It means nothing.'

'But it's such an unpleasant idea!' Margaret objected.

'Of course,' returned Madame Bonanni, licking her fingers between the words, 'there are artists who ride the high horse and insist on being treated like duchesses. The other artists hate them, and real society laughs at them. It is far better to be simple, and kiss everybody. It costs so little and it gives them so much pleasure, as Rachel said of her lovers!'

'It was Sophie Arnould,' said Lushington, correcting her mistake.

'Was it? I don't care. I say it, and that is enough. Besides I hate children who are always setting their parents right! It's my own fault, because I was so anxious to have you well educated. If I had brought you up as I was brought up, you would never have left me! As it is'-- she turned to Margaret with suddenly flashing eyes--'do you know, my dear? that atrocious little wretch will never take a penny from me, from me, his own mother! Ah, it is villainous! He is perfectly heartless! He denies me the only pleasure I wish for. Even when he was at school, at Eton, my dear, at the great English school, you know, he worked like a poor boy and won scholarships--money! Is it not disgusting? And at Oxford he lived on that money and won more! And then he worked, and worked at those terrible books, and wrote for the abominable press, and never would let me give him anything. Ah, you ungrateful little boy!

She seemed perfectly furious with him and shook her fist in his face; but the next moment she laughed and patted his cheek with her fat hand.

'And to say that I am proud of him!' she said, beaming with motherly smiles. 'Proud of him, my dear, you don't know! He is beating them all, as he always did! At the school, at the university, he was always the best! He used to get what they call firsts and double firsts every week!'

Margaret could not help laughing, and even Lushington smiled in his agony.

'It was splendid,' said the young girl, looking at him. 'Did you really get a double first?'

Lushington nodded.

'One?' screamed Madame Bonanni. 'Twenty, I tell you! A hundred----'

'No, no, mother,' interrupted Lushington. No one can get more than one.'

'Ah, did I not tell you?' cried the prima donna, triumphantly. There is only one, and he got it! What did I tell you? How can you expect me not to be proud of him?'

'You ought to be,' answered Margaret, very much in earnest, and for the first time Lushington saw in her eyes the light of absolutely unreserved admiration.

It was not for the double first at Oxford that she gave it. There had been a moment when it had hurt her to think that he probably accepted a good deal of luxury in his existence out of his mother's abundant fortune, but it was gone now. Even as a schoolboy he had guessed whence at least a part of that wealth really came, and had refused to touch a penny of it. But Lushington felt as if he were being combed with red-hot needles from head to foot, and the perspiration stood on his forehead. It would have filled him with shame to mop it with his handkerchief and yet he felt that in another moment it would run down. The awful circumstances of his dream came vividly back to him, and he could positively hear Margaret telling him that he looked hot, so loud that the whole house could understand what she said. But at this point something almost worse happened.

Madame Bonanni's motherly but eagle eye detected the tiny beads on his brow. With a cry of distress she sprang to her feet and began to wipe them away with the corner of her napkin that was tied round her neck, talking all the time.

'My darling!' she cried. 'I always forget that you feel hot when I feel cold! Angelo, open everything--the windows, the doors! Why do you stand there like a dressed-up doll in a tailor's window? Don't you see that he is going to have a fit?'

'Mother, mother! Please don't!' protested the unfortunate Lushington, who was now as red as a beet.

But Madame Bonanni took the lower end of her napkin by the corners, as if it had been an apron, and fanned him furiously, though he put up his hands and cried for mercy.

'He is always too hot,' she said, suddenly desisting and sitting down again. 'He always was, even when he was a baby.' She was now at work on a very complicated salad. 'But then,' she went on, speaking between mouthfuls, 'I used to lay him down in the middle of my big bed, with nothing on but his little shirt, and he would kick and crow until he was quite cool.'

Again Margaret bit her lip, but this time it was of no use, and after a conscientious effort to be quiet she broke into irrepressible laughter. In a moment Lushington laughed too, and presently he felt quite cool and comfortable again, feeling that after all he had been ridiculous only when he was a baby.

'We used to call him Tommy,' said Madame Bonanni, putting away her plate and laying her knife and fork upon it crosswise. 'Poor little Tommy! How long ago that was! After his father died I changed his name, you know, and then it seemed as if little Tommy were dead too.'

There was visible moisture in the big dark eyes for an instant. Margaret felt sorry for the strange, contradictory creature, half child, half genius, and all mother.

'My husband's name was Goodyear,' continued the prima donna thoughtfully. 'You will find it in all biographies of me.'

'Goodyear,' Margaret repeated, looking at Lushington. 'What a nice name! I like it.'

'You understand,' Madame Bonanni went on, explaining. '"Goodyear," "buon anno," "bonanno," "Bonanni"; that is how it is made up. It's a good name for the stage, is it not?'

'Yes. But why did you change it at all for your son?'

Madame Bonanni shrugged her large shoulders, glanced furtively at Lushington, and then looked at Margaret.

'It was better,' she said. 'Fruit, Angelo!'

'Can I be of any use to you in getting off, mother?' asked Lushington.

Margaret felt that she had made another mistake, and looked at her plate.

'No, my angel,' said Madame Bonanni, answering her son's question, and eating hothouse grapes; 'you cannot help me in the least, my sweet. I know you would if you could, dear child! But you will come and dine with me quietly at the Carlton on Sunday at half-past eight, just you and I. I promise you that no one shall be there, not even Logotheti--though you do not mind him so much.'

'Not in the least,' Lushington answered, with a smile which Margaret thought a little contemptuous. 'All the same, I would much rather be alone with you.'

'Do you wonder that I love him?' asked Madame Bonanni, turning to Margaret.

'No, I don't wonder in the least,' answered the young girl, with such decision that Lushington looked up suddenly, as if to thank her.

The ordeal was over at last, and the prima donna rose with a yawn of satisfaction.

'I am going to turn you out,' she said. 'You know I cannot live without my nap.'

She kissed Margaret first, and then her son, each on both cheeks, but it was clear that she could hardly keep her eyes open, and she left Margaret and Lushington standing together, exactly as she had left the young girl with Logotheti on the first occasion.

Their eyes met for an instant and then Lushington got his hat and stick and opened the door for Margaret to go out.

'Shall I call a cab for you?' he asked.

'No, thank you. I'll walk a little way first, and then drive to the station.'

When they were in the street, Lushington stood still.

'You believe that it was an accident, don't you?' he asked. 'I mean my coming to-day.'

'Of course! Shall we walk on?'

He could not refuse, and he felt that he was not standing by his resolution; yet the circumstances were changed, since she now knew his secret, and was warned.

They had gone twenty steps before she spoke.

'You might have trusted me,' she said.

'I should think you would understand why I did not tell you,' he answered rather bitterly.

She opened her parasol so impatiently that it made an ominous little noise as if it were cracking.

'I do understand,' she said, almost harshly, as she held it up against the sun.

'And yet you complain because I did not tell you,' said Lushington in a puzzled tone.

'It's you who don't understand!' Margaret retorted.

'No. I don't.'

'I'm sorry.'

They went on a little way in silence, walking rather slowly. She was angry with herself for being irritated by him, just when she admired him more than ever before, and perhaps loved him better; though love has nothing to do with admiration except to kindle it sometimes, just when it is least deserved. Now it takes generous people longer to recover from a fit of anger against themselves than against their neighbours, and in a few moments Margaret began to feel very unhappy, though all her original irritation against Lushington had subsided. She now wished, in her contrition, that he would say something disagreeable; but he did not. He merely changed the subject, speaking quite naturally.

'So it is all decided,' he said, 'and you are to make your début.'

'Yes,' she answered, with a sort of eagerness to be friendly again. 'I'm a professional from to-day, with a stage name, a prey to critics, reporters and photographers--just like your mother, except that she is a very great artist and I am a very little one.'

It was not very skilfully done, but Lushington was grateful for what she meant by it, and for saying 'your mother' instead of 'Madame Bonanni.'

'I think you will be great, too,' he said, 'and before very long. There is no young soprano on the stage now, who has half your voice or half your talent.'

Margaret coloured with pleasure, though she could not quite believe what he told her. But he glanced at her and felt sure that he was right. She had voice and talent, he knew, but even with both some singers fail; she had the splendid vitality, the boundless health and the look of irresistible success, which only the great ones have. She was not a classic beauty, but she would be magnificent on the stage.

There was a short silence, before she spoke.

'Two days ago,' she said, 'I did not think we would meet again so soon.'

'Part again so soon, you ought to say,' he answered. 'It is nothing but that, after all.'

She bit her lip.

'Must we?' she asked, almost unconsciously.

'Yes. Don't make it harder than it is. Let's get it over. There's a cab.'

He held up his stick and signalled to the cabman, who touched his horse and moved towards them. Margaret stood still, with a half-frightened look, and spoke in a low voice.

'Tom, if you leave me, I won't answer for myself!'

'I will. Good-bye--God bless you!'

The cab stopped beside them, as he held out his hand. She took it silently and he made her get in. A moment later she was driving away at a smart pace, sitting bolt upright and looking straight before her, her lips pressed tight together, while Lushington walked briskly in the opposite direction. It had all happened in a moment, in a sort of despairing hurry.

CHAPTER VII

Constantine Logotheti had at least two reasons for not going out to Versailles as soon as Mrs. Rushmore signified her desire to know him. In the first place he was 'somebody,' and an important part of being 'somebody' is to keep the fact well before the eyes of other people. He was altogether too great a personage to be at the beck and call of every one who wanted to know him. Secondly, he did not wish Margaret to think that he was running after her, for the very good reason that he meant to do so with the least possible delay.

Lushington, who was really both sensitive and imaginative, used to tell Margaret that he was a realist. Logotheti, who was by nature, talent and education a thorough materialist, loved to believe that he possessed both a rich imagination and the gift of true sentiment.

Margaret had delighted him at first sight, though he was hard to please, and though she was not a great beauty. She appealed directly to that love of life for its own sake which was always the strength, the genius and the snare of the Greek people, and which is not extinct in their modern descendants. Logotheti certainly had plenty of it, and his first impression, when he had met Margaret Donne, was that he had met his natural mate. There was nothing in the very least psychological about the sensation, and yet it was not the result of a purely physical attraction. It brought with it a satisfaction of artistic taste that was an unmarred pleasure in itself.

True art has gone much further in deifying humanity than in humanising divinity. The Hermes of Olympia is a man made into a god; no Christian artist has ever done a tenth as well in presenting the image of God made Man. When imagination soars towards an invisible world it loses love of life as it flies higher, till it ends in glorifying death as the only means of reaching heaven; and in doing that it has often descended to a gross realism that would have revolted the Greeks--to the materialism of anatomical preparations that make one think of the dissecting-room, if one has ever been there.

Love of genuine art is the best sort of love of life, and the really great artists have always been tremendously vital creatures. So-called artistic people who are sickly or merely under-vitalised generally go astray after strange gods; or, at the best, they admire works of art for the sake of certain pleasing, or sad, or even unhealthy associations which these call up.

Logotheti came of a race which, through being temporarily isolated from modern progress, has not grown old with it. For it seems pretty sure that progress means, with many other things, the survival of the unfit and the transmission of unfitness to a generation of old babies; but where men are not disinfected, sterilised, fed on preserved carrion and treated with hypodermics from the cradle to the grave, the good old law of nature holds its own and the weak ones die young, while the strong fight for life and are very much alive while they live.

Such people, when transplanted from what we call a half-barbarous state to live amongst us, never feel as we do, and when they are roused to action their deeds are not of the sort which our wives, our mothers-in-law and the clergy expect us to approve. It does not follow that they are villains, though they may occasionally kill some one in a fit of anger, or carry off by force the women they fall in love with; for such doings probably seem quite natural in their own country, and after all they cannot be expected to know more about right and wrong than their papas and mammas taught them when they were little things.

The object of this long-winded digression is not to excite sympathy on behalf of Logotheti, but to forestall surprise at some of the things he did when he had convinced himself that of all the women he had ever met, Margaret Donne was the one that suited him best, and that she must be his at any cost and at any risk.

The conviction was almost formed at the first meeting, and took full possession of him when he met her again, and she seemed glad to see him. By this time she had no reason for concealing from Mrs. Rushmore that she had seen him at Madame Bonanni's, and she held out her hand with a frank smile. It was on a Sunday afternoon and there were a number of lions on the lawn, and half a dozen women of the world. Logotheti seemed to know more than half the people present, which is rather unusual in Paris, and most of them treated him with the rather fawning deference accorded by society to the superior claims of wealth over good blood.

The Greek smiled pleasantly and reflected that the nobility of the Fanar, which goes back to the Byzantine Empire, is as good as any in France, and even less virtuous. He by no means despised his wealth, and he continually employed his excellent faculties in multiplying it; but in his semi-barbarous heart he was an aristocrat and was quietly amused when people whose real names seemed to have been selected from a list of Rhine wines took titles which emanated from the

Vatican, or when plain Monsieur Dubois turned himself into 'le comte du Bois de Vincennes'. Yet since few people seemed to know anything about Leo the Isaurian, under whom his direct ancestor had held office as treasurer and had eventually had his eyes put out for his pains, Logotheti was quite willing to be treated with deference for the sake of the more tangible advantages of present fortune. In Mrs. Rushmore's garden of celebrities, he at once took his place as a rare bird.

He crossed the lawn beside Margaret, indeed, with the air and assurance of a magnificent peacock. He was perhaps a shade less overdressed than when she had seen him last, but there was an astonishing lustre about everything he wore, and even his almond-shaped eyes were bright almost to vulgarity; but though he tired the sight, as a peacock does in the sun, it was impossible not to watch him.

'What a handsome man Logotheti is!' exclaimed a Roumanian poetess, who was there.

'What an awful cad!' observed a fastidious young American to the English officer who was still on his way to India, and was very comfortable at Mrs. Rushmore's.

The Englishman looked at Logotheti attentively for nearly half a minute before he answered.

'No,' he said quietly. 'That man is not a cad, he is simply a rich Oriental, dressed up in European clothes. I've met that sort before, and they are sometimes nasty customers. That fellow is as strong as a horse and as quick as a cat.'

Meanwhile the Greek and Margaret reached a seat near the little pond and sat down. She did not know that he had watched every one of her movements with as much delight as if Psyche, made whole and alive, had been walking beside him. He had not seemed to look at her at all, and he did not begin the conversation by making her compliments.

'I should have left a card on Mrs. Rushmore the day after I met you,' he began in a rather apologetic tone, 'but I was not quite sure that she knew about your visit to our friend, and she might have asked who I was and where you had met me. Besides, as she is an American, she would have thought I was trying to scrape acquaintance.'

'Hardly that. But you did quite right,' Margaret answered. 'Thank you.'

He was tactful. She leaned back a little in the corner of the seat and looked at him with an air of curiosity, wondering why everything he had said and done so far had pleased her so much better than his appearance. She was always expecting him to say something blatant or to do something vulgar, mainly because he wore such phenomenal ties and such gorgeous pins. To-day he displayed a ruby of astonishing size and startling colour. She was sure that it must be real, because he was so rich, but she had never known that rubies could be so big except in a fairy story. The tie was knitted of the palest mauve, shot with green and gold threads.

'I have seen Schreiermeyer,' he said. 'Is there to be any secret about your début?'

'None whatever! But I have said nothing about it, and none of the people here seem to have found it out yet.'

'So much the better. In everything connected with the theatre I believe it is a mistake to try and excite interest before the event. What is said beforehand is rarely said afterwards. You can be sure that Schreiermeyer will say nothing till the time comes, and if Madame Bonanni talks about you to her friends in London, nobody will believe she is in earnest.'

'But she is so outspoken,' Margaret objected.

'Yes, but no one could possibly understand that a prima donna just on the edge of decline could possibly wish to advertise a rising light. It is hardly human!'

'I think she is the most good-natured woman I ever knew,' said Margaret with conviction.

'She has a heart of gold. Her only trouble in life is that she has too much of it! There is enough for everybody. She has always had far too much for one.'

Logotheti smiled at his own expression.

'Perhaps that is better than having no heart at all,' Margaret answered, not quite realising how the words might have been misunderstood.

'The heart is a convenient and elastic organ,' observed Logotheti. 'It does almost everything. It sinks, it swells, it falls, it leaps, it stands still, it quivers, it gets into one's throat and it breaks; but it goes on beating all the time with more or less regularity, just as the violin clown scrapes his fiddle while he turns somersaults, sticks out his tongue, sits down with frightful suddenness and tumbles in and out of his white hat.'

He talked to amuse her and occupy her while he looked at her, studying her lines, as a yacht expert studies those of a new and beautiful model; yet he knew so well how to glance and look away, and glance again, that she was not at all aware of what he was really doing. She laughed a little at what he said.

'Where did you learn to speak English so well?' she asked.

'Languages do not count nowadays,' he answered carelessly. 'Any Levantine in Smyrna can speak a dozen, like a native. Have you never been in the East?'

'No.'

'Should you like to go to Greece?'

'Of course I should.'

'Then come! I am going to take a party in my yacht next month. It will give me the greatest pleasure if you and Mrs. Rushmore will come with us.'

Margaret laughed.

'You forget that I am a real artist, with a real engagement!' she answered.

'Yes, I forgot that. I wanted to! I can make Schreiermeyer forget it, too, if you will come. I'll hypnotise him. Will you authorise me?'

He smiled pleasantly but his long eyes were quite grave. Margaret supposed that it would be absurd to suspect anything but chaff in his proposal, and yet she felt an odd conviction that he meant what he said. Only vain women are easily mistaken about such things. Margaret turned the point with another little laugh.

'If you put him to sleep he will hibernate, like a dormouse,' she said. 'It will take a whole year to wake him up!'

'I don't think so, but what if it did?'

'I should be a year older, and I am not too young as it is! I'm twenty-two.'

'It's only in Constantinople that they are so particular about age,' laughed the Greek. 'After seventeen the price goes down very fast.'

'Really?' Margaret was amused. 'What do you suppose I should be worth in Turkey?'

Logotheti looked at her gravely and seemed to be estimating her value.

'If you were seventeen, you would be worth a good thousand pounds,' he said presently, 'and at least three hundred more for your singing.'

'Is that all, for my voice?' She could not help laughing. 'And at twenty-two, what should I sell for?'

'I doubt whether any one would give much more than eight

hundred for you,' answered Logotheti with perfect gravity. 'That's a big price, you know. In Persia they give less. I knew a Persian ambassador, for instance, who got a very handsome wife for four hundred and fifty.'

'Are you in earnest?' asked Margaret. 'Do you mean to say that you could just go out and buy yourself a wife in the market in Constantinople?'

'I could not, because I am a Christian. The market exists in a quiet place where Europeans never find it. You see all the Circassians in Turkey live by stealing horses and selling their daughters. They are a noble race, the Circassians! The girls are brought up with the idea, and they rarely dislike it at all.'

'I never heard of such things!'

'No. The East is very interesting. Will you come? I'll take you wherever you like. We will leave the archæologists in Crete and go on to Constantinople. It will be the most beautiful season on the Bosphorus, you know, and after that we will go along the southern shore of the Black Sea to Samsoun, and Kerasund, and Trebizond, and round by the Crimea. There are wonderful towns on the shores of the Black Sea which hardly any European ever sees. I'm sure you would like them, just as I do.'

'I am sure I should.'

'You love beautiful things, don't you?'

'Yes--though I don't pretend to be a judge.'

'I do. And when I see anything that really pleases me, I always try to get it; and if I succeed, nothing in the world will induce me to part with it. I'm a miser about the things I like. I keep them in safe places, and it gives me pleasure to look at them when I'm alone.'

'That's not very generous. You might give others a little pleasure, too, now and then.'

'So few people know what is good! Some of us Greeks have the instinct in our blood still, and we recognise it in a few men and women we meet--you are one, for instance. As soon as I saw you the first time, I was quite sure that we should think alike about a great many things. Do you mind my saying as much as that, at a second meeting?'

'Not if you think it is true,' she answered with a smile. 'Why should I?'

'It might sound as if I were trying to make out that we have some natural bond of sympathy,' said Logotheti. 'That's a favourite way of opening the game, you know. "Do you like carrots? So do I"--a bond, at once! "Do you go in, when it rains? I always do"--second bond. "We must be sympathetic to each other! Do you smile when you are pleased? Of course! We are exactly alike, and our hearts beat in unison!" That's the sort of thing.'

He amused her; perhaps she was easily amused now, because she had been feeling rather depressed all the morning. Women are subject to such harmless self-contradictions.

'I love to be out in the rain, and I don't like carrots!' she answered. 'There are evidently things about which our hearts don't beat in unison at all!'

'If people agreed about everything, what would become of conversation, lawyers and standing armies? But I meant to suggest that we might possibly like each other if we met often.'

'I daresay.'

'I have begun,' said Logotheti lightly, but again his long eyes were grave.

'Begun what?'

'I have begun by liking you. You don't object, do you?'

'Oh no! I like to be liked--by everybody!' Margaret laughed again, and watched him.

'It only remains for you to like everybody yourself. Will you kindly include me?'

'Yes, in a general way, as a neighbour, in the biblical sense, you know. Are you English enough to understand that expression?'

'I happen to have read the story of the Good Samaritan in Greek,' Logotheti answered. 'Since you are willing that we should be neighbours, "in the biblical sense," you cannot blame me for saying that I love my neighbour as myself.'

Once more her instinct told her that the words were meant less carelessly than they were spoken, though she could not possibly seem to take them in earnest. Yet her curiosity was aroused, as he intended that it should be.

'I remember that the Samaritan loved his neighbour, "in the biblical sense," at first sight,' he said, with a quick glance.

'But those were biblical times, you know!'

'Men have not changed much since then. We can still love at first sight, I assure you, even after we have seen a good deal of the world. It depends on meeting the right woman, and on nothing else. Do you suppose that if the Naples Psyche, or the Syracuse Venus, or the

Venus of Milo, or the Victory of Samothrace suddenly appeared in Paris or London, all the men would not lose their heads about her--at first sight? Of course they would!'

'If you expect to have such neighbours as those--"in the biblical sense"----'

'I have one,' said Logotheti, 'and that's enough.'

Margaret had received many compliments of a more or less complicated nature, but she did not remember that any one had yet compared her to two Venuses, the Psyche and the Samothrace Nikê in a single breath.

'That's nonsense!' she exclaimed, blushing a little, and not at all indignant.

'No,' Logotheti answered, imperturbably. 'Besides, neither the Victory nor the Venus of Syracuse has a head, so I am at liberty to suppose yours on their shoulders. Take the Victory. You move exactly as she seems to be moving, for she is not flying at all, you know, though she has wings. The wings are only a symbol. The Greeks knew perfectly well that a winged human being could not fly straight without a feathered tail two or three yards long!'

'How absurd!'

'That you should move like the Victory? Not at all. The reason why I love my neighbour as myself is that my neighbour is the most absolutely satisfactory being, from an artistic point of view. I don't often make compliments.'

'They are astonishing when you do!'

'Perhaps. But I was going on to say that what satisfies my love of the beautiful, can only be what satisfies my love of life itself, which is enormous.'

'In other words,' said Margaret, wondering how he would go on, 'I am your ideal!'

'Do you know what an "ideal" is?'

'Yes--well--no!' She hesitated. 'Perhaps I could not define it exactly.'

'A man's ideal is what he wants, and nothing else in the world.'

Margaret was not sure whether she should resent the speech a little, or let it pass. For an instant they looked at each other in silence. Then she made up her mind to laugh.

'Do you know that you are going ahead at a frightful pace?' she asked.

'Why should I waste time? My time is my life. It's all I have. Any fool can make money when he has wasted it and really wants more, but no power in heaven or earth can give me back an hour thrown away, an hour of what might have been.'

'I'm sure you must have learnt that in an English Sunday school! It's a highly moral and practical sentiment! But what becomes of the imagination?'

'Oh, that's the other side,' Logotheti answered, laughing. 'Never do to-day what you can put off till to-morrow, for if you do you'll lose all the pleasure of anticipating it! And the anticipation is much more delightful than the reality, so you must never realise your dream, if you mean to be happy--and all that sort of thing! But if reality knocks at my door while I am asleep and dreaming, and if I don't wake up to let it in, it may never take the trouble to knock again, you know, and I shall be left dreaming. I don't know about the Sunday school maxim being moral in all cases, but it's certainly very practical. I wish you would follow it and come with me to the East--you and Mrs. Rushmore.'

'You mean that if I don't, you'll never ask me again, I suppose?'

'No. That was not what I meant.' He looked steadily into her eyes till she turned her head away. 'What I meant was that you might be induced to give up the idea of the stage.'

'And as an inducement to throw up my engagement and sacrifice a career that may turn out well--you have told me so!--you offer me a trip to Constantinople!'

'You shall keep the yacht as a memento of the cruise. She's not a bad vessel.'

'What should I do with a steam yacht?'

'Oh, you would have to take the owner with her,' Logotheti answered airily.

'Eh?' Margaret stared at him in amazement.

'Yes. Don't be surprised. I'm quite in earnest. I never lose time, you know.'

'I should think not! Do you know that this is only our second meeting?'

'Exactly,' replied the Greek coolly. 'Of course, I might have asked you the first time we met, when we were standing together on the pavement outside Madame Bonanni's door. I thought of it, but I was afraid it might strike you as sudden.'

'A little!'

'Yes. But a second meeting is different. You must admit that I have had plenty of time to think it over and to know my own mind.'

'In two meetings?'

'Yes. Surely you know that in France young people are often engaged to be married when they have never seen each other at all.'

'That is arranged for them by their parents,' objected Margaret.

'Whereas we can arrange the matter for ourselves,' Logotheti said. 'It's more dignified, and far more independent. Isn't it?'

'I suppose so--I hardly know.'

'Oh yes, it is! You cannot deny it. Besides we have no parents and we are not children. You may think me hasty, but you cannot possibly be offended.'

'I'm not, but I think you are quite mad--unless you are joking.'

'Mad, because I love you?' asked Logotheti, lowering his voice and looking at her.

'But how is it possible? We hardly know each other!' Margaret was beginning to feel uncomfortable.

'Never mind; it is possible, since it is so. Of course, I cannot expect you to feel as I do, so soon, but I want to be before any one else.'

Margaret was silent, and her expression changed as she listened to his low and earnest tones.

'I don't want to believe there is any one else,' he went on. 'I don't believe it, not even if you tell me there is. But you would not tell me, I suppose.'

She turned her eyes full upon him and spoke as low as he, but a little unsteadily.

'There is some one else,' she said slowly.

Logotheti's lips moved, but she could not hear what he said, and almost as soon as she had spoken he looked down at the grass. There was no visible change in his face, and though she watched him for a few seconds, she did not think his hold tightened on his stick or that his brows contracted. She was somewhat relieved at this, for she was inclined to conclude that he had not been in earnest at all, and had idly asked her to marry him just to see whether he could surprise her into saying anything foolish. Yet this idea did not please her either. If there is anything a woman resents, it is that a man should pretend to be in love with her, in order to laugh at her in his sleeve. Margaret rose during the silence that followed. Logotheti sat still for a moment, as if he had not noticed her, and then he got up suddenly, and glanced at her with a careless smile.

'I wish you good luck,' he said lightly.

'Thank you,' she answered. 'One can never have too much of it!'

'Never. Get a talisman, a charm, a "jadoo." You will need something of the sort in your career. A black opal is the best, but if you choose that you must get it yourself, you must buy it, find it, or steal it. Otherwise it will have no effect!'

They moved away from the place where they had sat, and they joined the others. But after they had separated Margaret looked more than once at Logotheti, as if her eyes were drawn to him against her will, and she was annoyed to find that he was watching her.

She had thought of Lushington often that day, and now she wished with all her heart that he were beside her, standing between her and something she could not define but which she dreaded just because she could not imagine what it was, though it was certainly connected with Logotheti and with what he had said. She changed her mind about the Greek half-a-dozen times in an hour, but after each change the conviction grew on her that he had meant not only what he had said, but much more. His eyes were not like other men's eyes at all, when they looked at her, though they were so very quiet and steady; they were the eyes of another race which she did not know, and they saw the world as her own people did not see it, nor as Frenchmen, nor as Italians, nor Germans, nor as any people she had met. They had seen sights she could never see, in countries where the law, if there was any, took it for granted that men would risk their lives for what they wanted. She, who was not easily frightened, suddenly felt the fear of the unknown, and the unknown was somehow embodied in Logotheti.

She did not show what she felt when he strolled up to her to say good-bye, but through her glove she felt that his hand was stone cold, and as he said the half-dozen conventional words that were necessary she was sure that he smiled strangely, even mysteriously, as if such phrases as 'I hope to see you again before long,' and 'such a heavenly afternoon,' would cloak the deadly purposes of a diabolical design.

Margaret was alone with Mrs. Rushmore for a few minutes before dinner.

'Well?'

Mrs. Rushmore uttered the single word in an ejaculatory and interrogative tone, as only a certain number of old-fashioned Americans can. Spoken in that peculiar way it can mean a good deal, for it can convey suspicion, or approval or disapproval and any degree of acquaintance with the circumstances concerned, from almost total ignorance to the knowledge of everything except the result of the latest development.

On the present occasion Mrs. Rushmore meant that she had watched Margaret and Logotheti and had guessed approximately what had passed--that she thought the matter decidedly interesting, and wished to know all about it.

But Margaret was not anxious to understand, if indeed her English ear detected all the hidden meaning of the monosyllable.

'There were a good many people, weren't there?' she observed with a sort of query, meant to lead the conversation in that direction.

Mrs. Rushmore would not be thrown off the scent.

'My dear,' she said severely, 'he proposed to you on that bench. Don't deny it.'

'Good gracious!' exclaimed Margaret, taken by surprise.

'Don't deny it,' repeated Mrs. Rushmore.

'I had only met him once before to-day,' said Margaret.

'It's all the same,' retorted Mrs. Rushmore with an approach to asperity. 'He proposed to you. Don't deny it. I say, don't deny it.'

'I haven't denied it,' answered Margaret. 'I only hoped that you had not noticed anything. He must be perfectly mad. Why in the world should he want to marry me?'

'All Greeks,' said Mrs. Rushmore, 'are very designing.'

Margaret smiled at the expression.

'I should have said that Monsieur Logotheti was hasty,' she answered.

'My dear,' said Mrs. Rushmore with conviction, 'this man is an adventurer. You may say what you like, he is an adventurer. I am sure that ruby he wears is worth at least twenty thousand dollars. You may say what you like; I am sure of it.'

'But I don't say anything,' Margaret protested. 'I daresay it is.'

'I know it is,' retorted Mrs. Rushmore with cold emphasis. 'What business has a man to wear such jewellery? He's an adventurer, and nothing else.'

'He's one of the richest men in Paris for all that,' observed Margaret.

'There!' exclaimed Mrs. Rushmore. 'Now you're defending him! I told you so!'

'I don't quite see----'

'Of course not. You're much too young to understand such things. The wretch has designs on you. I don't care what you say, my dear, he has designs.'

In Mrs. Rushmore's estimation she could say nothing worse of any human being than that.

'What sort of "designs"?' inquired Margaret, somewhat amused.

'In the first place, he wants to marry you. You admit that he does. My dear Margaret, it's bad enough that you should talk in your cold-blooded way of going on the stage, but that you should ever marry a Greek! Good heavens, child! What do you think I am made of? And then you ask me what designs the man has. It's not to be believed!'

'I must be very dull,' said Margaret in a patient tone, 'but I don't understand.'

'I do,' retorted Mrs. Rushmore with severity, 'and that's enough! Wasn't I your dear mother's best friend? Haven't I been a good friend to you?'

'Indeed you have!' cried Margaret very gratefully.

'Well then,' explained Mrs. Rushmore, 'I don't see that there is anything more to be said. It follows that the man is either an agent of that wicked old Alvah Moon----'

'Why?' asked Margaret, opening her eyes.

'Or else,' continued Mrs. Rushmore with crushing logic, 'he means to live on you when you've made your fortune by singing. It must be one or the other, and if it isn't the one, it's certainly the other. Certainly it is! You may say what you like. So that's settled, and I've warned you. You can't afford to despise your old friend's warning, Margaret--indeed you can't.'

'But I've no idea of marrying the man,' said Margaret helplessly.

'Of course not! But I should like to say, my child, that whatever you do, I won't leave you to your fate. You may be sure of that. If nothing else would serve I'd go on the stage myself! I owe it to your mother.'

Margaret wondered in what capacity Mrs. Rushmore would exhibit herself to the astounded public if she carried out her threat.

CHAPTER VIII

If Mrs. Rushmore's logic was faulty and the language of her argument vague, her instinct was keen enough and had not altogether misled her. Logotheti was neither a secret agent of the wicked Alvah Moon who had robbed Margaret of her fortune, nor had he the remotest idea of making Margaret support him in luxurious idleness in case she made a success. But if, when a young and not over-scrupulous Oriental has been refused by an English girl, he does not abandon the idea of marrying her, but calmly considers the possibilities of making her marry him against her will, he may be described as having 'designs' upon her, then Logotheti was undeniably a very 'designing' person, and Mrs. Rushmore was not nearly so far wrong as Margaret thought her. Whether it was at all likely that he might succeed, was another matter, but he possessed both the qualities and the weapons which sometimes ensure success in the most unpromising undertakings.

He was tenacious, astute and cool, he was very rich, he was very much in love and he had no scruples worth mentioning; moreover, if he failed, he belonged to a country from which it is extremely hard to obtain the extradition of persons who have elsewhere taken the name of the law in vain. It is with a feeling of national pride and security that the true-born Greek takes sanctuary beneath the shadow of the Acropolis.

He had played his first card boldly, but not recklessly, to find out how matters stood. He had been the target of too many matrimonial aims not to know that even such a girl as Margaret Donne might be suddenly dazzled and tempted by the offer of his hand and fortune, and might throw over the possibilities of a stage career for the certainties of an enormously rich marriage. But he had not counted on that at all, and had really set Margaret much higher in his estimation than to suppose that she would marry him out of hand for his money; he had reckoned only on finding out whether he had a rival, and in this he had succeeded, to an extent which he had not anticipated, and the result was not very promising. There had been no possibility of mistaking Margaret's tone and manner when she had confessed that there was 'some one else.'

On reflection he had to admit that Margaret had not been dazzled by his offer, though she had seemed surprised. She had either been accustomed to the idea of unlimited money, because Mrs. Rushmore was rich, or else she did not know its value. It came to the same thing in the end. Orientals very generally act on the perfectly simple theory that nine people out of ten are to be imposed upon by the mere display of what money can buy, and that if you show them the real thing they will be tempted by it. It is not pleasant to think how often they are right; and though Logotheti had made no impression on Margaret with his magnificent ruby and his casual offer of a yacht as a present, he did not reproach himself with having made a mistake. He had simply tried what he considered the usual method of influencing a woman, and as it had failed he had eliminated it from the arsenal of his weapons. That was all. He had found out at once that it was of no use, and as he hated to waste time he was not dissatisfied with the result of his day's work.

Like most men who have lived much in Paris he cared nothing at all for the ordinary round of dissipated amusement which carries foreigners and even young Frenchmen off their feet like a cyclone, depositing them afterwards in strange places and in a damaged condition. It was long since he had dined 'in joyous company,' frequented the lobby of the ballet or found himself at dawn among the survivors of an indiscriminate orgy. Men who know Paris well may not have improved upon their original selves as to moral character, but they have almost always acquired the priceless art of refined enjoyment; and this is even more true now than in the noisy days of the Second Empire. In Paris senseless dissipation is mostly the pursuit of the young, who know no better, or of much older men who have never risen above the animal state, and who sink with age into half-idiotic bestiality. Logotheti had never been counted amongst the former, and was in no danger of ending his days in the ranks of the latter. He was much too fond of real enjoyment to be dissipated. Most Orientals are.

He spent the evening alone in an inner room to which no mere acquaintance and very few of his friends had ever been admitted. His rule was that when he was there he was not to be disturbed on any account.

'But if the house should take fire?' a new man-servant inquired on receiving these instructions.

'The fire-engines will put it out,' Logotheti answered. 'It is none of my business. I will not be disturbed.'

'Very good, sir. But if the house should burn down before they come?'

'Then I should advise you to go away. But be careful not to disturb me.'

'Very good, sir. And if'--the man's voice took a confidential tone--'if any lady should ask for you, sir?'

'Tell her that to the best of your knowledge I am dead. If she faints, call a cab.'

'Very good, sir.'

Thereupon the new man-servant had entered upon his functions, satisfied that his master was an original character, if not quite mad. But there was no secret about the room itself, as far as could be seen, and it was regularly swept and dusted like other rooms. The door was never locked except when Logotheti was within, and the room contained no hidden treasures, nor any piece of furniture in which such things might have been concealed. There was nothing peculiar about the construction of the place, except that the three windows were high above the ground like those of a painter's studio, and could be opened or shut, or shaded, by means of cords and chains. There were also heavy curtains, such as are never seen in studios, which could be drawn completely across the windows.

In a less civilised country Logotheti's servants might have supposed that he retired to this solitude to practise necromancy or study astrology, or to celebrate the Black Mass. But his matter-of-fact Frenchmen merely said that he was 'an original'; they even said so with a certain pride, as if there might be bad copies of him extant somewhere, which they despised. One man, who had an epileptic aunt, suggested that Logotheti probably had fits, and disappeared into the inner room in order to have them alone; but this theory did not find favour, though it was supported, as the man pointed out, by the fact that the double doors of the room were heavily padded, and that the whole place seemed to be sound-proof, as indeed it was. On the other hand there was nothing about the furniture within that could give colour to the supposition, which was consequently laughed at in the servants' hall. Monsieur was simply 'an original'; that was enough to explain everything, and his order as to being left undisturbed was the more strictly obeyed because it would apparently be impossible to disturb him with anything less than artillery.

It is a curious fact that when servants have decided that their masters are eccentric they soon cease to take any notice of their doings, except to laugh at them now and then when more eccentric than usual. It being once established that Logotheti was an original he might have kept his private room full of Bengal tigers for all the servants hall would have cared, provided the beasts did not get about the house. It was a 'good place,' for he was generous, and there were perquisites; therefore he might do anything he pleased, so long as he paid--as indeed most of us might in this modern world, if we were able and willing to pay the price.

On this particular evening Logotheti dined at home alone, chiefly on a very simple Greek pilaff, Turkish preserved rose leaves and cream cheese, which might strike a Parisian as strange fare, unless he were a gourmet of the very highest order. Having sipped a couple of small glasses of very old Samos wine, Logotheti ordered lights and coffee in his private room, told the servants not to disturb him, went in and locked the outer door.

Then he gave a sigh of satisfaction and sat down, as if he had reached the end of a day's journey. He tasted his coffee, and kicked off first one of his gleaming patent leather slippers and then the other, and drew up his feet under him on the broad leather seat, and drank more coffee, and lit a big cigarette; after which he sat almost motionless for at least half an hour, looking most of the time at a statue which occupied the principal place in the middle of the room. Now and then he half closed his eyes, and then opened them again suddenly, with an evident sense of pleasure. He had the air of a man completely satisfied with his surroundings, his sensations and his thoughts. There was something almost Buddha-like in his attitude, in his perfect calm, in the expression of his quiet almond eyes; even the European clothes he wore did not greatly hinder the illusion. Just then he did not look at all the sort of person to do anything sudden or violent, to pitch order to the dogs and tear the law to pieces, to kill anything that stood in his way as coolly as he would kill a mosquito, or to lay violent hands on what he wanted if he was hindered from taking it peacefully. Neither does a wild-cat look very dangerous when it is dozing.

On the rare occasions when he allowed any one but his servants to enter that room, he said that the statue was a copy, which he had caused to be very carefully made after an original found in Lesbos and secretly carried off by a high Turkish official, who kept it in his house and never spoke of it. This accounted for its being quite unknown to the artistic world. He called attention to the fact that it was really a facsimile, rather than a copy, and he seemed pleased at the perfect reproduction of the injured points, which were few, and of the stains, which were faint and not unpleasing. But he never showed it to an artist or an expert critic.

'A mere copy,' he would say, with a shrug of his shoulders. 'Nothing that would interest any one who really knows about such things.'

A very perfect copy, a very marvellous copy, surely; one that might stand in the Vatican, with the Torso, or in the Louvre, beside the Venus of Milo, or in the British Museum, opposite the Pericles, or in Olympia itself, facing the Hermes, the greatest of all, and yet never be taken for anything but the work of a supreme master's own hands. But Constantine Logotheti shrugged his shoulders and said it was a mere copy, nothing but a clever facsimile, carved and chipped and stained by a couple of Italian marble-cutters, whose business it was to manufacture antiquities for the American market and whom any one could engage to work in any part of the world for twenty francs a day and their expenses. Yes, those Italian workmen were clever fellows, Logotheti admitted. But everything could be counterfeited now, as everybody knew, and his only merit lay in having ordered this particular counterfeit instead of having been deceived by it.

As Logotheti sat there in the quiet light, looking at it, the word 'copy' sounded in his memory, as he had often spoken it, and a peaceful smile played upon his broad Oriental lips. The 'copy' had cost human lives, and he had almost paid for it with his own, in his haste to have it for himself, and only for himself.

His eyes were half-closed again, and he saw outlines of strong ragged men staggering down to a lonely cove at night, with their marble burden, and he heard the autumn gale howling among the rocks, and the soft thud of the baled statue as it was laid in the bottom of the little fishing craft; and then, because the men feared the weather, he was in the boat himself, shaming them by his courage, loosing the sail, bending furiously to one of the long sweeps, yelling, cheering, cursing, promising endless gold, then baling with mad energy as the water swirled up and poured over the canvas bulwark that Greek boats carry, and still wildly urging the fishermen to keep her up; and then, the end, a sweep broken and foul of the next, a rower falling headlong on the man in front of him, confusion in the dark, the crazy boat broached to in the breaking sea, filling, fuller, now quite full and sinking, the raging hell of men fighting for their lives amongst broken oars, and tangled rigging and floating bottom-boards; one voice less, two less, a smashing sea and then no voices at all, no boat, no men, no anything but the howling wind and the driving spray, and he himself, Logotheti, gripping a spar, one of those long booms the fishermen carry for running, half-drowned again and again, but gripping still, and drifting with the storm past the awful death of sharp black rocks and pounding seas, into the calm lee beyond.

And then, a week later, on a still October night, his great yacht lying where the boat had sunk, with diver and crane and hoisting gear, and submarine light; and at last, the thing itself brought up from ten fathoms deep with noise of chain and steam winch, and swung in on deck, the water-worn baling dropping from it and soon torn off, to show the precious marble perfect still. And then--'full speed ahead' and west by north, straight for the Malta channel.

Logotheti's personal reminiscences were not exactly dull, and the vivid recollection of struggles and danger and visible death made the peace of his solitude more profound; the priceless thing he had fought for was alive in the stillness with the supernatural life of the ever beautiful; his fingers pressed an ebony key in the table beside him and the marble turned very slowly and steadily and noiselessly on the low base, seeming to let her shadowy eyes linger on him as she looked back over the curve of her shoulder. Again his fingers moved, and the motion ceased, obedient to the hidden mechanism; and so, as he sat still, the goddess moved this way and that, facing him at his will, or looking back, or turning quite away, as if ashamed to meet his gaze, being clothed only in warm light and dreamy shadows, then once more confronting him in the pride of a beauty too faultless to fear a man's bold eyes.

He leaned against his cushions, and sipped his coffee now and then, and let the thin blue smoke make clouds of lace between him and the very slowly moving marble, for he knew what little things help great illusions, or destroy them. Nothing was lacking. The dark blue pavement, combed like rippling water and shot with silver that cast back broken reflections, was the sea itself; snowy gauze wrapped loosely round the base was breaking foam; the tinted walls, the morning sky of Greece; the goddess, Aphrodite, sea-born, too human to be quite divine, too heavenly to be only a living woman.

And she was his; his not only for the dangers he had faced to have her, but his because he was a Greek, because his heart beat with a strain of the ancient sculptor's blood; because his treasure was the goddess of his far forefathers, who had made her in the image of the loveliness they adored; because he worshipped her himself, more than half heathenly; but doubly his now, because his imagination had found her likeness in the outer world, clothed, breathing and alive, and created for him only.

He leaned against his cushions, and lines of the old poetry rose to his lips, and the words came aloud. He loved the sound when he was alone, the vital rush of it, and the voluptuous pause and the soft, lingering cadence before it rose again. In the music of each separate verse there was the whole episode of man's love and woman's, the illusion and the image, the image and the maddening, leaping, all-satisfying, softly-subsiding reality.

It was no wonder that he would not allow anything to disturb him in that inner sanctuary of rare delight. His bodily nature, his imagination, his deep knowledge and love of his own Hellenic poets, his almost adoration of the beautiful, all that was his real self, placed him far outside the pale that confines the world of common men as the sheepfold pens in the flock.

It was late in the night when he rose from his seat at last, extinguished the lights himself and left the room, with a regretful look on his face; for, after his manner, he had been very happy in his solitude, if indeed he had been alone where his treasure reigned.

He went downstairs, for the sanctuary was high up in the house, and he found his man dozing in a chair in the vestibule at the door of his dressing-room. The valet rose to his feet instantly, took a little salver from the small table beside him, and held it out to Logotheti.

'A telegram, sir,' he said.

Logotheti carelessly tore the end off the blue cover and glanced at the contents.

Can buy moon. Cable offer and limit.

Logotheti looked at his watch and made a short calculation which convinced him that no time would really be lost in buying the moon if he did not answer the telegram till the next morning. Then he went to bed and read himself to sleep with Musurus' Greek translation of Dante's Inferno.

CHAPTER IX

On the following day Margaret received a note from Schreiermeyer informing her in the briefest terms and in doubtful French that he had concluded the arrangements for her to make her début in the part of Marguerite, in a Belgian city, in exactly a month, and requiring that she should attend the next rehearsal of Faust at the Opéra in Paris, where Faust is almost a perpetual performance and yet seems to need rehearsing from time to time.

She showed the letter to Mrs. Rushmore, who sighed wearily after reading it, and said nothing. But there was a little more colour in Margaret's cheek, and her eyes sparkled at the prospect of making a beginning at last. Mrs. Rushmore took up her newspaper again with an air of sorrowful disapproval, but presently she started uncomfortably and looked at Margaret.

'Oh!' she exclaimed, and sighed once more.

'What is it?' asked the young girl.

'It must be true, for it's in the Herald.'

'What?'

Mrs. Rushmore read the following paragraph:--

We hear on the best authority that a new star is about to dazzle the operatic stage. Monsieur Schreiermeyer has announced to a select circle of friends that it will be visible in the theatrical heaven on the night of June 21, in the character of Marguerite and in the person of a surprisingly beautiful young Spanish soprano, the Señorita Margarita da Cordova, whose romantic story as daughter to a contrabandista of Andalusia and granddaughter to the celebrated bullfighter Ramon and----

'Oh, my dear! This is too shameful! I told you so!'

Mrs. Rushmore's elderly cheeks were positively scarlet as she stared at the print. Margaret observed the unwonted phenomenon with surprise.

'I don't see anything so appallingly improper in that,' she observed.

'You don't see! No, my child, you don't! I trust you never may. Indeed if I can prevent it, you never shall. Disgusting! Vile!'

And the good lady read the rest of the paragraph to herself, holding up the paper so as to hide her modest blushes.

'My dear, what a story!' she cried at last. 'It positively makes me creep!'

'This is very tantalising,' said Margaret. 'I suppose it has to do with my imaginary ancestry in Andalusia.'

'I should think it had! Where do they get such things, I wonder? A bishop, my dear--oh no, really! it would make a pirate blush! Can you tell me what good this kind of thing can do?'

'Advertisement,' Margaret answered coolly. 'It's intended to excite interest in me before I appear, you know. Don't they do it in America?'

'Never!' cried Mrs. Rushmore with solemn emphasis. 'Apart from its being all a perfectly gratuitous falsehood.'

'Gratuitous? Perhaps Schreiermeyer paid to have it put in.'

'Then I never wish to see him, Margaret, never! Do you understand! I think I shall bring an action against him. At all events I shall take legal advice. This cannot be allowed to go uncontradicted. If I were you, I would sit down and write to the paper this very minute, and tell the editor that you are a respectable English girl. You are, I'm sure!'

'I hope so! But what has respectability to do with art?'

'A great deal, my dear,' answered Mrs. Rushmore wisely. 'You may say what you like, there is a vast difference between being respectable and disreputable--perfectly vast! It's of no use to deny it, because you can't.'

'Nobody can.'

'There now, I told you so! I must say, child, you are getting some very strange ideas from your new acquaintances. If these are the principles you mean to adopt, I am sorry for you, very sorry!'

Margaret did not seem very sorry for herself, however, for she went off at this point, singing the 'jewel song' in Faust at the top of her voice, and wishing with all her heart that she were already behind the footlights with the orchestra at her feet.

Two days later, Mrs. Rushmore received a cable message from New York which surprised her almost as much as the paragraph about Margaret had.

Alvah Moon has sold invention for cash to anonymous New York syndicate who offer to compromise suit. Cable instructions naming sum you will accept, if disposed to deal.

Now Mrs. Rushmore was a wise woman, as well as a good one, though her ability to express her thoughts in concise language was insignificant. She had long known that the issue of the suit she had brought was doubtful, and that as it was one which could be appealed to the Supreme Court of the United States, it might drag on for a long time; so that the possibility of a compromise was very welcome, and she at once remembered that half a loaf is better than no bread, especially when the loaf is of hearty dimensions and easily divided. What she could not understand was that any one should have been willing to pay Alvah Moon the sum he must have asked, while his interest was still in litigation, and that, after buying that interest, the purchasers should propose a compromise when they might have prolonged the suit for some time, with a fair chance of winning it in the end. But that did not matter. More than once since Mrs. Rushmore had taken up the case her lawyers had advised her to drop it and submit to losing what she had already spent on the suit, and of late her own misgivings had increased. The prospect of obtaining a considerable sum for Margaret, at the very moment when the girl had made up her mind to support herself as a singer, was in itself very tempting; and as it presented itself just when the horrors of an artistic career had been brought clearly before Mrs. Rushmore's mind by the newspaper paragraph, she did not hesitate a moment.

Margaret was in Paris that morning, at her first rehearsal, and could not come back till the afternoon; but after all it would be of no use to consult her, as she was so infatuated with the idea of singing in public that she would very probably be almost disappointed by her good fortune. Mrs. Rushmore read the message three times, and then went out under the trees to consider her answer, carrying the bit of paper in her hand as if she did not know by heart the words written on it. For once, she had no guests, and for the first time she was glad of it. She walked slowly up and down, and as it was a warm morning, still and overcast, she fanned herself with the telegram in a very futile way, and watched the flies skimming over the water of the little pond, and repeated her inward question to herself many times.

Mrs. Rushmore never thought anything out. When she was in doubt, she asked herself the same question, 'What had I better do?' or, 'What will he or she do next?' over and over again, with a frantic determination to be logical. And suddenly, sooner or later, the answer flashed upon her in a sort of accidental way as if it were not looking for her, and so completely outran all power of expression that she could not put it into words at all, though she could act upon it well enough. The odd part of it all was that these accidental revelations rarely misled her. They were like fragments of a former world of excellent common-sense that had gone to pieces, which she now and then encountered like meteors in her own orbit.

When she had walked up and down for a quarter of an hour one of these aeroliths of reason shot across the field of her mental sight, and she understood that one of two things must have occurred. Either Alvah Moon had lost confidence in his chances and had sold the invention to some greenhorn for anything he could get; or else some one else had been so deeply interested in the affair as to risk a great deal of money in it. Mrs. Rushmore's gleam of intelligence was a comet; but her comet had two tails, which was very confusing.

Her meditations were disturbed by the noise of a big motor car, approaching the house from a distance, and heralding its advance with a steadily rising whizz and a series of most unearthly toots. Motor cars often passed the house and ran down the Boulevard St. Antoine at frightful speed, for the beautiful road is generally clear; but something, perhaps a small meteor again, warned her that this one was going to stop at the gate and demand admittance for itself.

Thereupon Mrs. Rushmore looked at her fingers; for she kept up an extensive correspondence, in the course of which she often inked them. For forty years she had asked herself why she, who prided herself on her fastidious neatness, should have been predestined and condemned to have inky fingers like an untidy school-girl, and she had spent time and money in search of an ink that would wash off easily and completely, without the necessity of flaying her hands with pumice stone and chemicals. When suddenly aware of the approach of an unexpected visitor, she always looked at her fingers.

The thing came nearer, roared, sputtered, tooted and was silent. In the silence Mrs. Rushmore heard the tinkle of the gate bell and in a few moments she saw Logotheti coming towards her across the lawn. She was not particularly pleased to see him.

'I am afraid,' she said rather stiffly, 'that Miss Donne is out.'

In a not altogether well-spent life Logotheti had seen many things; but he was not accustomed to American chaperons, whose amazing humility always takes it for granted that no man under forty can possibly call upon them except for the sake of seeing the young woman in their charge. Logotheti looked vaguely surprised.

'Indeed?' he answered, with a little interrogation as though he found it hard to be astonished, but wished to be obliging. 'That is rather fortunate,' he continued, 'for I was hoping to find you alone.'

'Me?' Mrs. Rushmore unbent a little and smiled rather grimly.

'Yes. If I had not been so anxious to see you at once, I should have written or telegraphed to ask for a few minutes alone with you. But I could not afford to waste time.'

He spoke so gravely that she immediately suspected him of dark designs. Perhaps he was going to propose to her, since Margaret had refused him. She remembered instances of adventurers who had actually married widows of sixty for their money. She compressed her lips. She would be firm with him; he should have a piece of her mind.

'I am alone,' she said severely, a little as if warning him not to take liberties.

'My errand concerns a matter in which we have common interests at stake,' he said.

Mrs. Rushmore sat down on a garden chair, and pointed to the bench, on which he took his seat.

'I cannot imagine what interests you mean,' she said, with dignity. 'Pray explain. If you refer to Miss Donne, I may as well inform you with perfect frankness that it is of no use.'

Logotheti smiled and shook his head gently, keeping his eyes on Mrs. Rushmore's face, all of which she took to mean incredulity on his part.

'You may say what you like,' she said. 'It's of no use.'

When Mrs. Rushmore declared that you might say what you liked, she was in earnest, but her visitor was not familiar with the expression.

'Nevertheless,' he said, in a soothing way, 'my errand concerns Miss Donne.'

'Well then,' said Mrs. Rushmore, 'don't! That's all I have to say, and it's my last word. She doesn't care for you. I don't want to be unkind, but I daresay you have made yourself think all sorts of things.'

She felt that this was a great concession, to a Greek and an adventurer.

'Excuse me,' said Logotheti quietly, 'but we are talking at cross purposes. What I have to say concerns Miss Donne's financial interests--her fortune, if you like to call it so.'

Mrs. Rushmore's suspicions were immediately confirmed.

'She has none,' said she, with a snap as if she were shutting up a safe with a spring lock.

'That depends on what you call a fortune,' answered the Greek coolly. 'In Paris most people would think it quite enough. It is true that it is in litigation.'

'I really cannot see how that can interest you,' said Mrs. Rushmore in an offended tone.

'It interests me a good deal. I have come to see you in order to propose that you should compromise the suit about that invention.'

Mrs. Rushmore drew herself up against the straight back of the garden chair and glared at him in polite wrath.

'You will pardon my saying that I consider your interferences very much out of place, sir,' she said.

'But you will forgive me, dear madam, for differing with you,' said Logotheti with the utmost blandness. 'This business concerns me quite as much as Miss Donne.'

'You?' Mrs. Rushmore was amazed.

'I fancy you have heard that Mr. Alvah Moon has sold the invention to a New York syndicate.'

'Yes--but----'

'I am the syndicate.'

'You!' The good lady was breathless with astonishment. 'I cannot believe it,' she gasped.

Logotheti's hand went to his inner breast pocket.

'Should you like to see the telegrams?' he asked quietly. 'Here they are. My agent's cable to me, my instructions to him, his acknowledgment, his cable saying that the affair is closed and the money paid. They are all here. Pray look at them.'

Mrs. Rushmore looked at the papers, for she was cautious, even when surprised. There was no denying the evidence he showed her. Her hands fell upon her knees and she stared at him.

'So you have got control of all that Margaret can ever hope to have of her own,' she said blankly, at last. 'Why have you done it?'

Logotheti smiled as he put the flimsy bits of paper into his pocket again.

'Purely as a matter of business,' he answered. 'I shall make money by it, though I have paid Mr. Moon a large sum, and expect to make a heavy payment to you if we agree to compromise the old suit, which, as you have seen by the telegrams, I have assumed with my eyes open. Now, my dear Mrs. Rushmore, shall we talk business? I am very anxious to oblige you, and I am not fond of bargaining. I propose to pay a lump sum on condition that you withdraw the suit at once. You pay your lawyers and I pay those employed by Mr. Moon. Now, what sum do you think would be fair? That is the question. Please understand that it is you who will be doing me a favour, not I who offer to do you a service. As I understand it, you never claimed of Mr. Moon the whole value of the invention. It was a suit in equity brought on the ground that Mr. Moon had paid a derisory price for what he got, in other words--but is Mr. Moon a personal friend of yours, apart from his business?'

'A friend!' cried Mrs. Rushmore in horror. 'Goodness gracious, no!'

'Very well,' continued Logotheti. 'Then we will say that he cheated Miss Donne's maternal grandfather--is that the relationship? Yes. Very good. I propose to hand over to you the sum out of which Miss Donne's maternal grandfather was cheated. If you will tell me just how much it was, allowing a fair interest, I will write you a cheque. I think I have a blank one here.'

He produced a miniature card-case of pale blue morocco, which exactly matched his tie, and drew from it a blank cheque carefully folded to about the size of two postage stamps.

'Dear me!' exclaimed Mrs. Rushmore. 'Dear me! This is very sudden!'

'You must have made up your mind a long time ago as to what Miss Donne's share should be worth,' suggested Logotheti, smoothing the cheque on his knee.

Mrs. Rushmore hesitated.

'But you have already paid much more to Senator Moon,' she said.

'That is my affair,' answered the Greek. 'I have my own views about the value of the invention, and I have no time to lose. What shall we say, Mrs. Rushmore.'

'I wish Margaret were here,' said the good lady vaguely.

'I'm very glad she is not. Now, tell me what I am to write, please.'

He produced a fountain pen and was already writing the date. The pen was evidently one specially made to suit his tastes, for it was of gold, the elaborate chasing was picked out with small rubies and a large brilliant was set in the end of the cap. Mrs. Rushmore could not help looking at it, and in her prim way she wondered how any man who was not an adventurer or a sort of glorified commercial traveller could carry such a thing. There was an unpleasant fascination in the mere look of it, and she watched it move instead of answering.

'Yes?' said Logotheti, looking up interrogatively. 'What shall we say?'

'I--I honestly don't know what to say,' Mrs. Rushmore answered, really confused by the suddenness of the man's proposal. I suppose--no--you must let me consult my lawyer.'

'I am sorry,' said Logotheti, 'but I cannot afford to waste so much time. Allow me to be your man of business. How much were you suing Mr. Moon for?'

'Half a million dollars,' answered Mrs. Rushmore.

'Have you been paying your lawyer, or was he to get a percentage on the sum recovered?'

'I have paid him about seventeen thousand, so far.'

'For doing nothing. I should like to be your lawyer! I suppose three thousand more will satisfy him? Yes, that will make it a round twenty thousand. That leaves your claim worth four hundred and eighty thousand dollars, does it not?'

'Yes, certainly.'

'Which at four-eighty-four is--' he looked at the ceiling for ten seconds--'ninety-nine thousand one hundred and eleven pounds, two shillings and twopence halfpenny--within a fraction. Is that it? My mental arithmetic is generally pretty fair.'

'I've no doubt that the calculation is correct,' said Mrs. Rushmore, 'only it seems to me--let me see--I'm a little confused--but it seems to me that if I had won the suit for half a million, the lawyer's expenses would have come out of that.'

'They do come out of it,' answered Logotheti blandly. 'That is why you don't get half a million.'

'Yes,' insisted Mrs. Rushmore, who was not easily misled about money, 'certainly. But as it is, after I have received the four hundred and eighty thousand, I shall still have to deduct the twenty thousand for the lawyers before handing it over to Margaret, who would only get four hundred and sixty. Excuse me, perhaps you don't understand.'

'Yes, yes! I do.' Logotheti smiled pleasantly. 'It was very stupid of me, wasn't it? I'm always doing things like that!'

As indeed financiers are, for arithmetical obliquity about money is caused by having too much or too little of it, and the people who lose to both sides are generally the comparatively honest ones who have enough. It certainly did not occur to Logotheti that he had tried to do Margaret Donne out of four thousand pounds; he would have been only too delighted to give her ten times the sum if she would have accepted it, and so far as profit went the whole transaction was for her benefit, and he might lose heavily by it. But in actual dealing he was constitutionally unable to resist the impulse to get the better of the person with whom he dealt. And on her side, Mrs. Rushmore, though generous to a fault, was by nature incapable of allowing money to slip through her fingers without reason. So the two were well matched, being both born financiers, and Logotheti respected Mrs. Rushmore for detecting his little 'mistake,' and she recognised in him a real 'man of business' because he had made it.

'Let us call it a half million dollars, then,' he said, with a smile. 'At four-eighty-four, that is'--again he looked at the ceiling for ten seconds--'that is one hundred and three thousand three hundred and five pounds fifteen shillings fivepence halfpenny, nearly. Is that it? Shall we say that, Mrs. Rushmore.'

'How quickly you do it!' exclaimed the lady in admiration. 'I wish I could do that! Oh yes, I have no doubt it is quite correct. You couldn't do it on paper, could you? You see it doesn't matter so much about the halfpenny, but if there were a little slip in the thousands, you know--it would make quite a difference----'

She paused significantly. Logotheti quietly pulled his cuff over his hand, produced a pencil instead of his fountain pen, and proceeded to divide five hundred thousand by four hundred and eighty-four to three places of decimals.

'Fifteen and fivepence halfpenny,' he said, when he had turned the fraction into shillings and pence, 'and the pounds are just what I said.'

'Do you mean to say that you did all that in your head in ten seconds?' asked Mrs. Rushmore, with renewed admiration.

'Oh no,' he answered. 'We have much shorter ways of reckoning money in the East, but you could not understand that. You are quite satisfied that this is right?'

'Oh, certainly!'

Mrs. Rushmore could no more have divided five hundred thousand by four hundred and eighty-four to three places of decimals than she could have composed Parsifal, but her doubts were satisfied by its having been done 'on paper.'

Logotheti put away his jewelled pencil, took out his jewelled fountain pen again, spread the cheque on the seat of the bench beside him and filled it in for the amount, including the halfpenny. He handed it to her, holding it by the corner.

'It's wet,' he observed. 'It's drawn on the Bank of England. It will be necessary for you to sign a statement to the effect that you withdraw the suit and that Miss Donne's claim is fully satisfied. She will have to sign that too. I'll send you the paper. If you have any doubts,' he smiled, 'you need not return it until the cheque has been cashed.'

That was precisely what Mrs. Rushmore intended to do, but she protested politely that she had no doubt whatever on the score of the cheque, looking all the time at the big figures written out in Logotheti's remarkably clear handwriting. Only the signature was perfectly illegible. He noticed her curiosity about it.

'I always sign my cheques in Greek,' he observed 'It is not so easy to imitate.'

He rose and held out his hand.

'I suppose I ought to thank you on Margaret's behalf,' said Mrs. Rushmore, as she took it. 'She will be so sorry not to have seen you.'

'It was much easier to do business without her. And as for that, there is no reason for telling her anything about the transaction. You need only say that a syndicate has bought out Alvah Moon and has compromised the old suit by a cash payment. I am not at all anxious to have her know that I have had a hand in the matter--in fact, I had rather that she shouldn't, if you don't object.'

Mrs. Rushmore looked hard at him. She had not even thought of refusing his offer, which would save Margaret a considerable fortune by a stroke of a pen; but she had taken it for granted that what might easily be made to pass for an act of magnificent liberality was intended to produce a profound impression on Margaret's feelings. The elder woman was shrewd enough to guess that the Greek would not lose money in the end, but she went much too far in suspecting him of anything so vulgar as playing on the girl's gratitude. She looked at him keenly.

'Do you mean that?' she asked, almost incredulously.

His quiet almond eyes gazed into hers with the trustful simplicity of a child's.

'Yes,' he answered. 'This is purely a matter of business, in which I am consulting nothing but my own interests. I should have acted precisely in the same way if I had never had the pleasure of knowing either of you. If it chances that I have been of service to Miss Donne, so much the better, but there is no reason why she should ever know it, so far as I am concerned. I would rather she should not. She might fancy that I had acted from other motives.'

'Very well,' Mrs. Rushmore answered; 'then I shall not tell her.'

Nevertheless, when the motor car had tooted and puffed itself away to Paris and Mrs. Rushmore still sat in her straight-backed garden chair holding the cheque in her hand, she thought it all very strange and unaccountable; and the only explanation that occurred to her was that the invention must be worth far more than she had supposed. This was not altogether a pleasant reflection either, as it made her inclined to reproach herself for not having driven a hard bargain with Logotheti.

'But after all,' she said to herself, 'if half a million is not a fortune, it's a competence, even nowadays, and I suppose the man isn't an adventurer after all--at least, not if his cheque is good.'

In her complicated frame of mind she felt a distinct sense of disappointment at the thought that her judgment had been at fault, and that the Greek was not a blackleg, as she had decided that he ought to be.

CHAPTER X

Logotheti's motor car was built to combine the greatest comfort and the greatest speed which can be made compatible. It was not meant for sport, though it could easily beat most things on the road, for though the Greek lived a good deal among sporting men and often did what they did, he was not one himself. It was not in his nature to regard any sport as an object to be pursued for its own sake. Only the English take that view naturally, and, of late years, some Frenchmen. All other Europeans look upon sport as pastime which is very well when there is nothing else to do, but not at all comparable with love-making, or gambling, for the amusement it affords. They take the view of the late Shah of Persia, who explained why he would not go to the Derby by saying that he had always known that one horse could run faster than another, but that it was a matter of perfect indifference to him which that one horse might be. In the same way Logotheti did not care to possess the fastest motor car in Europe, provided that he could be comfortable in one which was a great deal faster than the majority. Moreover, though he was by no means timid, he never went in search of danger merely for the sake of its pleasant excitement. Possibly he was too natural and too primitive to think useless danger attractive; but if danger stood between him and anything he wanted very much, he could be as reckless as an Irishman or a Cossack-- which is saying all there is to be said.

The motor tooted and whizzed itself from Mrs. Rushmore's gate to the stage entrance of the Opéra in something like thirty minutes without the slightest strain, and could have covered the distance in much less time if necessary.

Logotheti found Schreiermeyer sitting alone in the dusk, in the stalls. Half the footlights and one row of border lights illuminated the stage, and a fat man in very light grey clothes, a vast white waistcoat and a pot hat was singing 'Salut demeure' in a nasal half-voice to the tail of the Commendatore's white horse, from Don Juan. The monumental animal had apparently stopped to investigate an Egyptian palm tree which happened to grow near the spot usually occupied by Marguerite's cottage. The tenor had his hands in his pockets, his hat was rather on the back of his head, and he looked extremely bored.

So did Schreiermeyer when Logotheti sat down beside him. He

turned his round glasses to the newcomer with a slight expression of recognition which was not perceptible at all in the gloom, and then he looked at the stage again, without a word. The tenor had heard somebody moving in the house, and he stuck a single glass in his eye and peered over the footlights into the abyss, thinking the last comer might be a woman, in which case he would perhaps have condescended to sing a little louder and better. A number of people were loafing on the stage, standing up or sitting on the wooden steps of somebody's enchanted palace, but Logotheti could not see Margaret amongst them.

The conductor of the orchestra rapped sharply on his desk, the music ceased suddenly and he glared down at an unseen offender.

'D sharp!' he said, as if he were swearing at the man.

'I believe they hire their band from the deaf and dumb asylum,' observed the tenor very audibly, but looking vaguely at the plaster tail of the horse.

Some of the young women at the back of the stage giggled obsequiously at this piece of graceful wit, but the orchestra manifested its indignation by hissing. Thereupon the director rapped on his desk more noisily than ever.

'Da capo,' he said, and the bows began to scrape and quiver again.

The tenor only hummed his part now, picking bits of straw out of the plaster tail and examining them with evident interest.

'Is Miss Donne here?' Logotheti inquired of Schreiermeyer.

The impresario nodded indifferently, without looking round.

'I wish you had chosen Rigoletto for her début,' said the Greek. 'The part of Gilda is much better suited to her voice, take my word for it.'

'What do you know about it?' asked Schreiermeyer, smiling faintly, just enough to save the rude question from being almost insulting.

'When Gounod began Faust he was in love with a lady with a deep voice,' answered Logotheti, 'but when he was near the end he was in love with one who had a high voice. The consequence is that Marguerite's part ranges over nearly three octaves, and is frightfully trying, particularly for a beginner.'

'Bosh!' ejaculated the impresario, though he knew it was quite true.

He looked at the stage again, as if Logotheti did not exist.

'Oh, very well,' said the latter carelessly. 'It probably won't matter much, as they say that Miss Donne is going to throw up her engagement, and give up going on the stage.'

He had produced an effect at last, for Schreiermeyer's jaw dropped as he turned quickly.

'Eh? What? Who says she is not going to sing? What?'

'I dare say it is nothing but gossip,' Logotheti answered coolly. 'You seem excited.'

'Excited? Eh? Some one has heard her sing and has offered her more! You shall tell me who it is!' He gripped Logotheti's arm with fingers that felt like talons. 'Tell me quickly!' he cried. 'I will offer her more, more than anybody can! Tell me quickly.'

'Take care, you are spoiling my cuff,' said Logotheti. 'I know nothing about it, beyond that piece of gossip. Of course you are aware that she is a lady. Somebody may have left her a fortune, you know. Her only reason for singing was that she was poor.'

'Nonsense!' cried Schreiermeyer, with a sort of suppressed yell. 'It is all bosh! Somebody has offered her more money, and you know who it is! You shall tell me!' He was in a violent passion by this time, or seemed to be. 'You come here, suggesting and interfering with my prima donnas! You are in league, damn you! Damn you, you are a conspiracy!'

His face was as white as paper, his queer eyes blazed through his glasses, and his features were disfigured with rage. He showed his teeth and hissed like a wildcat; his nervous fingers fastened themselves upon Logotheti's arm.

But Logotheti gazed at him with a look of amusement in his quiet eyes, and laughed softly.

'If I were conspiring against you, you would not guess it, my friend,' he observed in a gentle tone. 'And you will never get anything out of me by threatening, you know.'

Schreiermeyer's face relaxed instantly into an expression of disappointment, and he looked wearily at the stage again.

'No, it is of no use,' he answered in a melancholy tone. 'You are phlegmatic.'

'Perfectly,' Logotheti assented. 'If I were you, I would put her on in Rigoletto.'

'Does she know the part?' Schreiermeyer asked, as calmly as if nothing had happened.

'Ask Madame De Rosa,' suggested the Greek. 'I see her on the stage.'

'I will. There is truth in what you say about Faust. The part is trying.'

'You told me it was bosh,' Logotheti observed with a smile.

'I had forgotten that you are such a phlegmatic man, when I said that,' answered Schreiermeyer with the frankness of a conjurer who admits that his trick has been guessed.

They had been talking as if nothing were going on, but now the conductor turned to them, and gave a signal for silence, which was taken up by all the people on the stage.

'Sh--sh--sh--sh--' it came from all directions.

'Here comes Cordova,' observed Schreiermeyer in a low tone.

Margaret appeared, wearing an extremely becoming hat, and poked her head round the white horse's tail, which represented the door of her cottage as to position.

The tenor, who had nothing to do and was supposed to be off, at once turned himself into a stage Faust, so far as expression went, but his white waistcoat and pot hat hindered the illusion so much that Margaret smiled.

She sang the 'King of Thule,' and every one listened in profound silence. When she had finished, Schreiermeyer and Logotheti turned their heads slowly, by a common instinct, looked at each other a moment and nodded gravely. Then Logotheti rose rather suddenly.

'What's the matter?' asked the impresario.

But the Greek had disappeared in the gloom of the house and Schreiermeyer merely shrugged his shoulders when he saw that his question had not been heard. It would have been perfectly impossible for him to understand that Logotheti, who was so 'phlegmatic,' could not bear the disturbing sight of the white waistcoat and the hat while Margaret was singing the lovely music and looking, Logotheti thought, as she had never looked before.

He went behind, and sat down in a corner where he could hear without seeing what was going on; he lent himself altogether to the delight of Margaret's voice, and dreamt that she was singing only for him in some vast and remote place where they were quite alone together.

The rehearsal went on by fits and starts; some scenes were repeated, others were left out; at intervals the conductor rapped his desk nervously and abused somebody, or spoke with great affability to Margaret, or with the familiarity of long acquaintance to one of the other singers. Logotheti did not notice these interruptions, for his sensitiveness was not of the sort that suffers by anything which must be and therefore should be; it was only the unnecessary that disturbed him--the tenor's white waistcoat and dangling gold chain. While Margaret was singing, the illusion was perfect; the rest was a blank, provided that nothing offended his eyes.

The end was almost reached at last. There was a pause.

'Will you try the trio to-day?' inquired the conductor of Margaret. 'Or are you tired?'

'Tired?' Margaret laughed. 'Go on, please.'

Now Marguerite's part in the trio, where she sings 'Anges pures,' repeating the refrain three times and each time in a higher key, is one of the most sustained high pieces ever written for a woman's voice; and Logotheti, listening, suddenly shut out his illusions and turned himself into a musical critic, or at least into a judge of singing.

Not a note quavered, from first to last; there was not one sound that was not as true as pure gold, to the very end, not one tone that was forced, either, in spite of the almost fantastic pitch of the last passage.

It is not often that everybody applauds a singer at a rehearsal of Faust, which has been sung to death for five-and-forty years; but as the trio ended, and the drums rolled the long knell, there was a shout of genuine enthusiasm from the little company on the stage.

'Vive la Cordova! Vive la Diva!' yelled the tenor, and he threw up his pot hat almost to the border lights, quite forgetting to be indifferent.

'Brava, la Cordova!' boomed the bass, with a tremendous roar.

'Brava, brava, brava!' shouted all the lesser people at the back of the stage.

Little Madame De Rosa was in hysterics of joy, and embraced everybody and everything in her way till she came to Margaret and reached the climax of embracing in a perfect storm of tears. By this time the tenor and bass were kissing Margaret's gloved hands with fervour and every one was pressing round her.

Logotheti had come forward and stood a little aloof, waiting for the excitement to subside. Margaret, surrounded as she was, did not see him at once, and he watched her quietly. She was the least bit pale and her eyes were very bright indeed. She was smiling rather vaguely, he thought, though she was trying to thank everybody for being so pleased, and Logotheti fancied she was looking for somebody who was not there, probably for the mysterious 'some one else,' whose existence she had confessed a few days earlier.

Presently she seemed to feel that he was looking at her, for she turned her head to him and met his eyes. He came forward at once, and the others made way for him a little, for most of them knew him by sight as the famous financier, though he rarely condescended to come behind the scenes at a rehearsal, or indeed at any other time.

Margaret held out her hand, and Logotheti had just begun to say a few rather conventional words of congratulation when Schreiermeyer rushed up with his hat on, pushing everybody aside without ceremony till he seized Margaret's wrist and would apparently have dragged her away by main force if she had not gone with him willingly.

'Ill-mannered brute!' exclaimed Logotheti in such a tone that Schreiermeyer must certainly have heard the words, though he did not even turn his head.

'I must speak to you at once,' he was saying to Margaret, very hurriedly, as he led her away. 'It is all bosh, nonsense, stupid stuff, I tell you! Rubbish!'

'What is rubbish?' asked Margaret in surprise, just as they reached the other side of the stage. 'My singing?'

'Stuff! You sing well enough. You know it too, you know it quite well! Good. Are you satisfied with the contract we signed?'

'Perfectly,' answered Margaret, more and more surprised at his manner.

'Ah, very good. Because, I tell you, if you are not pleased, it is just the same. I will make you stick to it, whether you like it or not. Understand?'

Margaret drew herself up, and looked at him coldly.

'If I carry out my contract,' she said, 'it will be because I signed my name to it, not because you can force me to do anything against my will.'

Schreiermeyer turned a little pale and glared through his glasses.

'Ah, you are proud, eh? You say to yourself, "First I am a lady, and then I am a singer that is going to be a prima donna." But the law is on my side. The law will give me heavy damages, enormous damages, if you fail to appear according to contract. You think because you have money in your throat somebody will pay me my damages if you go to somebody else. You don't know the law, my lady! I can get an injunction to prevent you from singing anywhere in Europe, pending suit. The other man will have to pay me before you can open your beautiful mouth to let the money out! Just remember that! You take my advice. You be an artist first and a lady afterwards when you have plenty of time, and you stick to old Schreiermeyer, and he'll stick to you. No nonsense, now, no stupid stuff! Eh?'

'I haven't the slightest idea what you are driving at,' said Margaret. 'I have made an agreement with you, and unless I lose my voice during the next month I shall sing wherever you expect me to.'

'All right, because if you don't, I'll make you dance from here to Jerusalem,' answered Schreiermeyer, glaring again.

'Do you know that you are quite the rudest and most brutal person I ever met?' inquired Margaret, raising her eyebrows.

But Schreiermeyer now smiled in the most pleasant manner possible, ceased glaring, spread out his palms and put his head on one side as he answered her, apparently much pleased by her estimate of him.

'Ah, you are not phlegmatic, like Logotheti! We shall be good friends. I shall be rude to you when I am in a rage, and tell you the truth, and you shall call me many bad names. Then we shall be perfectly good friends. You will say, "Bah! it is only old Schreiermeyer!" and I shall say, "Pshaw! Cordova may call me a brute, but she is the greatest soprano in the world, what does it matter?" Do you see? We are going to be good friends!'

It was impossible not to laugh at his way of putting it; impossible, too, not to feel that behind his strange manner, his brutal speeches and his serio-comic rage there was the character of a man who would keep his word and who expected others to do the same. There might even be lurking somewhere in him a streak of generosity.

'Good friends?' he repeated, with an interrogation.

'Yes, good friends,' Margaret answered, taking his hand frankly and still smiling.

'I like you,' said Schreiermeyer, looking at her with sudden thoughtfulness, as if he had just discovered something.

And then without a word he turned on his heel and disappeared as quickly as he had come, his head sinking between his shoulders till the collar of the snuff-coloured overcoat he wore in spite of the warm weather was almost up to the brim of his hat behind.

Logotheti and little Madame De Rosa came up to Margaret at once. The other singers were already filing out, eager to get into the fresh air.

'The Signora,' said Logotheti, 'says she will come and lunch with me. Will you come too? I daresay we shall find something ready, and then, if you like, I'll run you out to Mrs. Rushmore's in the motor car.'

Margaret hesitated a moment, and looked from one to the other.

She was very hungry, and the prospect of a luxurious luncheon was much more alluring than that of the rather scrappy sort of meal she had expected to get at a Bouillon Duval. As 'Miss Donne,' a fortnight ago, she would certainly not have thought of going to Logotheti's house, except with Mrs. Rushmore; but as the proposal tempted her she found it easy to tell herself that since she was a real artist she could go where she pleased, that people would gossip about her wherever she went, and that what she did was nobody's business. And surely, for an artist, Madame De Rosa was a chaperon of sufficient weight. Moreover, Margaret was curious to see the place where the man lived. He interested her in spite of herself, and since Lushington had insisted on going off, though she had begged him to stay, she felt just a little reckless.

'Do come!' said Logotheti.

The two words were spoken in just the right tone, neither as if his life depended on her answer, nor as if he were asking her to do something just a little risky, which would be amusing; but quite naturally, as if he would be really glad should she accept, but by no means overwhelmed with despair if she refused.

'Thank you,' she answered. 'It's very nice of you to ask us. I'll come.'

Logotheti smiled pleasantly, but looked away, perhaps not caring that she should see his eyes, even in the uncertain light. The three hastened to leave the theatre, for the stage was already full of workmen, the Egyptian palm was moving in one direction, the Commendatore's white horse was joggling away uneasily in another, and the steps of somebody's enchanted palace were being dragged forward into place. All was noise, dust and apparent confusion.

Margaret expected that Logotheti's house would somehow correspond with his own outward appearance and would be architecturally over-dressed, inside and out, but in this she was greatly mistaken. It was evidently a new house, in a quarter where many houses were new and where some were not in the most perfect taste, though none were monstrosities. It was not exceptionally big, and was certainly not showy; on the whole, it had the unmistakable air of having been built by a good architect, of the very best materials and in a way to last as long as hewn stone can. Such beauty as it had lay in its proportions and not in any sort of ornament, for it was in fact rather plainer than most of its neighbours in the Boulevard Péreire.

The big door opened noiselessly just as the car came up, but

Logotheti, who drove himself, did not turn in.

'It's rather a tight fit,' he explained, as he stopped by the curbstone.

He gave his hand to Margaret to get down. As her foot touched the pavement a man who was walking very fast, with his head down, made a step to one side, to get out of the way, and then, recognising her and the Greek, lifted his hat hastily and would have passed on. She started with an exclamation of surprise, for it was Lushington, whom she had supposed to be in London. Logotheti spoke first, calling to him in English.

'Hollo! Lushington--I say!'

Lushington stopped instantly and turned half round, with an exclamation intended to express an imaginary surprise, for he had recognised all three at first sight.

'Oh!' he exclaimed coldly. 'Is that you? How are you?'

Margaret offered her hand as he did not put out his. She was a little surprised to see that he did not change colour when he took it, as he always used to do when they met; he did not seem in the least shy, now, and there was a hard look in his eyes.

'All right?' he said, with a cool interrogation, and he turned to Logotheti before Margaret could give any answer.

'Come in and lunch, my dear fellow,' said the Greek affably.

'I never lunch--thanks all the same.' He moved to go on, nodding a good-bye.

'Are you here for long?' asked Margaret, forcing him to stop again.

'That depends on what you call long. I leave this evening.'

'I should call that a very short time!' Margaret tried to laugh a little, with a lingering hope that he might unbend.

'It's quite long enough for me, thank you,' he answered roughly. 'Good-bye!'

He lifted his hat again and walked off very fast. Margaret's face fell, and Logotheti saw the change of expression.

'He's an awfully good fellow in spite of his shyness,' he said quietly. 'I wish we could have made him stay.'

'Yes,' Margaret answered, in a preoccupied tone.

She was wondering whether Logotheti had guessed that there had been anything between her and Lushington. Logotheti ushered his guests in under the main entrance.

'Do you know Mr. Lushington well?' she asked.

'Yes, in a way. I once published a little book, and he wrote a very nice article about it in a London Review. You did not know I was a man of letters, did you?' Logotheti laughed quietly. 'My book was not very long--only about a hundred pages, I think. But Lushington made out that it wasn't all rubbish, and I was always grateful to him.'

'What was your book about?' asked Margaret, as they entered the house.

'Oh, nothing that would interest you--the pronunciation of Greek. Will you take off your hat?'

At every step, at every turn, Margaret realised how much she had been mistaken in thinking that anything in Logotheti's house could be in bad taste. There was perfect harmony everywhere, and a great deal of simplicity. The man alone offended her eye a little, the man himself, with his resplendent tie, his jewellery and his patent leather shoes; and even so, it was only the outward man, in so far as she could not help seeing him and contrasting his appearance with his surroundings. For he was as tactful and quiet, and as modest about himself as ever; he did not exhibit the conquering air which many men would have found it impossible not to assume under the circumstances; he showed himself just as anxious to please little Madame De Rosa as Margaret herself, and talked to both indiscriminately. If Margaret at first felt that she was doing something a little eccentric, not to say compromising, in accepting the invitation, the sensation had completely worn off before luncheon was half over, and she was as much at her ease as she could have been in Mrs. Rushmore's own house. She felt as if she had known Logotheti all her life, as if she understood him thoroughly and was not displeased that he should understand her.

They went into the next room for coffee.

'You used to like my Zara maraschino,' said Logotheti to Madame De Rosa.

He took a decanter from a large case, filled a good-sized liqueur glass for her and set it beside her cup.

'It is the most delicious thing in the world,' cried the little woman, sipping it eagerly.

'May I not have some, too?' asked Margaret.

'Not on any account,' answered Logotheti, putting the decanter back on the other side. 'It's very bad for the voice, you know.'

'I never heard that,' said Madame De Rosa, laughing. 'I adore it! But as my singing days are over it does not matter at all. Oh, how good it is!'

She sipped it again and again, with all sorts of little cries and sighs of satisfaction.

Logotheti and Margaret looked on, smiling at her childish delight.

'Do you think I might have a little more?' she asked, presently. 'Only half a glass!'

Logotheti filled the glass again, though she laughingly protested that half a glass was all she wanted. But he took none himself.

Margaret saw a picture at the other end of the room which attracted her attention, and she rose to go and look at it. Logotheti followed her, but Madame De Rosa, who had established her small person in the most comfortable arm-chair in the room, was too much interested in the maraschino to move. Margaret stood in silence before the painting for a few moments, and Logotheti waited for her to speak, watching her as he always did when she was not looking.

'What is it?' she asked, at last. 'It's quite beautiful, but I don't understand it.'

'Nor do I, in the least,' answered Logotheti. 'I found it in Italy two years ago. It's what they call an encaustic painting, like the Muse of Cortona, probably of the time of Tiberius. It is painted on a slab of slate three inches thick, and burnt in by a process that is lost. You might put it into the fire and leave it there without doing it any harm. That much I know, for I found it built into a baker's oven. But I can tell you no more about it. I have some pretty good things here, but this is quite my best picture. It is very like somebody, too--uncommonly like! Do you see the resemblance?'

'No. I suppose I don't know the person.'

Logotheti laughed and took up a little mirror set in an old Spanish frame.

'Look at yourself,' he said. 'The picture is the image of you.'

'Of me?' Margaret took the glass, and her cheek flushed a little as she looked at herself and then at the picture, and realised that the likeness was not imaginary.

'In future,' said Logotheti, 'I shall tell people that it is a portrait of you.'

'Of me? Oh please, no!' cried Margaret anxiously, and blushing deeper. 'Don't!'

Logotheti laughed.

'Did you think I was in earnest?' he asked.

The painting represented the head and shoulders of a woman--perhaps of a goddess, though it had that strangely living look about the eyes and mouth which belongs to all good portraits that are like the originals. The woman's head was thrown back, her deep-set eyes were looking up with an expression of strange longing, the rich hair flowed down over her bare neck, where one beautiful hand caught it and seemed to press the tangled locks upon her heart.

The picture's beauty was the beauty of life, for the features were not technically faultless. The lips glowed with burning breath, the twining hair was alive and elastic, the after-light of a profound and secret pleasure lingered in the liquid eyes, blending with the shadow of pain just past but passionately desired again.

Margaret gazed at the painting a few seconds, for it fascinated her against her will. Then she laid down the small looking-glass and turned away rather abruptly.

'I don't like to look at it,' she said, avoiding Logotheti's eyes. 'I think it must be time to be going,' she added. 'Mrs. Rushmore will be wondering where I am.'

She went back across the room a little way with Logotheti by her side. Suddenly he stopped and laughed softly.

'By Jove!' he exclaimed under his breath, pointing to the arm-chair in which Madame De Rosa was sitting. 'She's fast asleep!'

She was sleeping as peacefully as a cat after a meal, half curled up in the big chair, her head turned to one side and her cheek buried in a cushion of Rhodes tapestry. Margaret stood and looked at her with curiosity and some amusement.

'She's not generally a very sleepy person,' said the young girl.

'The emotions of your first rehearsal have tired her out,' said Logotheti. 'They don't seem to have affected you at all,' he added. 'Shall we wake her?'

Margaret hesitated, and then bent down and touched the sleeping woman's arm gently, and called her by name in a low tone; but without the slightest result.

'She must be very tired,' Margaret said in a tone of sympathy. 'After all, it's not so very late. We had better let her sleep a few minutes longer, poor thing.'

Logotheti bent his head gravely.

'We'll make up the time with the motor in going to Versailles,' he said.

By unspoken consent, they moved away and sat down at some distance from Madame De Rosa's chair, at the end of the room opposite to the picture. Logotheti did not speak at once, but sat leaning forward, his wrists resting on his knees, his hands hanging down limply, his eyes bent on the carpet. As she sat, Margaret could see the top of his head; there was a sort of fascination about his preternaturally glossy black hair, and the faultless parting made it look like the wig on a barber's doll. She thought of Lushington and idly wondered whether she was always to be admired by men with phenomenally smooth hair.

'What are you thinking of?' Logotheti asked, looking up suddenly and smiling as he met her eyes.

She laughed low.

'I was wondering how you kept your hair so smooth!' she answered.

'I should look like a savage if I did not,' he said. 'My only chance of seeming civilised is to overdo the outward fashions of civilisation. If I wore rough clothes like an Englishman, and did not smooth my hair and let my man do all sorts of things to my moustache to keep it flat, I should look like a pirate. And if I looked like a Greek pirate you would have hesitated about coming to lunch with me to-day. Do you see? There is a method in my bad taste.'

Margaret looked at him a moment and then laughed again.

'So that's it, is it? How ingenious! Do you know that I have wondered at the way you dress, ever since I met you?'

'I'm flattered. But think a moment. I daresay you wonder why I wear a lot of jewellery, too. Of course it's in bad taste. I quite agree with you. But the world is often nearer to first principles than you realise. A man who wears a ruby in his tie worth ten thousand pounds is not suspected of wanting to get other people's money as soon as he makes acquaintance. On the contrary, they are much more likely to try to get his, and are rather inclined to think him a fool for showing that he has so much. It is always an advantage to be thought a fool when one is not. If one is clever it is much better to have it believed that one is merely lucky. In business everybody likes lucky people, but every one avoids a clever man. It is one of the elements of success to remember that!'

'You won't easily persuade any one that you are a foolish person,' said Margaret.

'It would be much harder if I did not take pains,' he answered gravely. 'Now you know my secret, but don't betray me.'

'Not for worlds!'

They both laughed a little, and their eyes met.

'But just now, I'm in a very awkward position about that,' Logotheti continued. I cannot afford to sacrifice my reputation as a lucky fool, and yet I want you to think me a marvel of cleverness, good taste and perfection in every way.'

'Is that all?' asked Margaret, more and more amused.

'Almost all. You see I know perfectly well that I cannot surprise you into falling in love with me---- Yes, she's sound asleep! The ideal chaperon, isn't she?'

'I don't know,' Margaret answered lightly, and she glanced at Madame De Rosa, as if she thought of waking her.

'Excuse me, you do; for if I were "some one else" you would be delighted that she should be asleep. But that's not the question. As I cannot surprise you into--there's no harm in saying it!--into loving me, I'm driven to use what they call the "arts of persuasion"! But in order to persuade, it's necessary to inspire confidence. Do you understand?'

'Vaguely!'

'Have I succeeded at all?' His voice changed suddenly as he asked the question.

'I don't know why I should distrust you, I'm sure,' Margaret answered gravely. 'You are certainly very outspoken,' she continued more lightly, as if wishing to keep the conversation from growing serious. 'In fact, I never knew anything like your frankness!'

'I'm in earnest, and I don't wish to leave the least doubt in your mind. You are the first woman I have ever met whom I wanted to marry, and you are likely to be the last. I'm not a boy and I know the world as you can never know it, even if you insist upon going on the stage. I'm not amazingly young, for I'm five-and-thirty, and I suppose I have had as large a share of what the world holds as most rich men. That is my position. Until I met you, I thought I had really had everything. When I knew you I found that I had never had the only thing worth having at all.'

He spoke quietly, without the least affectation of feeling, or the smallest apparent attempt to make an impression upon her; but it was impossible not to believe that he was speaking the truth. Margaret was silent, and looked steadily at an imaginary point in the distance.

'So far,' he said, in the same tone, 'I have always got what I wanted. I don't mean to say,' he continued quickly, as she made a movement, 'that I expected you to accept me when I asked you to marry me, at our second meeting. I was sure you would not. I merely put in a claim--that was all.'

Margaret turned a little and rested her elbow on the back of her chair, facing him.

'And I told you there was some one else. Do you understand clearly? I am frank, too. I love another man, and he loves me.'

'And you are going to be married, I suppose?' said Logotheti, his lids contracting a very little.

'I hope so. Some day.'

'Ah! There is an obstacle. I see. A question of fortune, I daresay?'

'No.' Her tone was meant to discourage further questioning, and she moved in her seat and looked away again.

'That man does not love you,' Logotheti said. 'If he did, nothing could hinder your marriage, since he knows that you are willing.'

'There may be a reason you don't understand,' Margaret answered reluctantly.

'A man who loves does not reason. A man who wants a certain woman wants nothing else, any more than a man who is dying of thirst can want anything but drink. He must have it or die, and nothing can keep him from it if he sees it.'

There was a shade of more energy in his tone now, though he still spoke quietly enough. Margaret was silent again, possibly because the same thought had crossed her own mind during the last few days, and even an hour ago, when she had met Lushington at the door. Since she was willing to marry him, in spite of his birth, could he be in earnest as long as he hesitated?

She wished that he might have said what Logotheti was saying now, instead of reasoning with her about a point of honour.

'When people think themselves in love and hesitate,' Logotheti continued, almost speaking her own thoughts aloud, 'it is because something else in them is stronger than love, or quite as strong.'

'There may be honour,' said Margaret, defending Lushington in her mind, out of sheer loyalty.

'There ought to be, sometimes, but it is more in the nature of real love to tear honour to pieces than to be torn in pieces for it. I'm not defending such things, I'm only stating a fact. More men have betrayed their country for love than have sacrificed love to save their country!'

'That's not a very noble view of love!'

'If you were passionately in love with a man, should you like him to sacrifice you in order to save his country, especially if his country were not yours? If it were your own, you might be as patriotic as he and you would associate yourself with him in the salvation of your own people. But that would not be a fair case. The question is whether, in a matter that concerns him only and not yourself, you would set his honour higher than his love for you and let yourself be sacrificed, without feeling that if he had loved you as you would like to be loved he would forfeit his honour rather than give you up.'

'That's a dreadfully hard question to answer!' Margaret smiled.

'It is only hard to answer, because you are conscious of a convention called honour which man expects you to set above everything. Very good. A couple of thousand years hence there will be some other convention in its place called by another name; but love will be precisely the same passion that it is now, because it's purely human and not subject to any conventions when it is real--any more than you can make the circulation of your blood conventional or the beating of your heart, or hunger, or thirst, or sleepiness, instead of being natural as they all are.'

'You're a materialist,' said Margaret, finding nothing else to say.

'I don't think so, but whatever I am, I'm in earnest, and I don't pretend to be anything but human.'

He stopped and looked straight into Margaret's eyes; and somehow she did not turn away, for there was nothing in his that she was afraid to meet. Just then she would rather have tried to stare him out of countenance than look for one minute at the woman's face in the picture, which he said was so like her. She did not remember that in all her life anything had so strangely disturbed her as that likeness. She had seen pictures and statues by the score in exhibitions and public places, which should have offended her maiden modesty far more. What was there in that one painting that could offend at all? A woman's head thrown back, a woman's hand pressing her hair to her breast--it ended there, and that was all; and what was that, compared with the acres of raw nudity that crowd the walls of the Salon every year.

Logotheti said that he was 'human,' and she felt it was true, in the sense that he was a 'primitive,' or an 'elementary being,' as some people would say. The fact that he had all the profound astuteness of the true Oriental did not conflict with this in the least. The astuteness of the Asiatic, and of the Greek of Asia, is an instinct like that of the wild animal; talent alone is 'human' in any true sense, but instinct is animal, even in men, whether it shows itself in matters of money-getting or matters of taste.

Yet somehow Margaret was beginning to be attracted by the man. He had never shown the least lack of respect, or of what Mrs.

Rushmore would have called 'refinement,' and he had done nothing which even distantly resembled taking a liberty. He spoke quietly, and even gently, and his eyes did not gloat upon her face and figure as some men's eyes did. Even as to the picture, he had not led her to see it, for she had gone up to it herself, drawn to it against her will, and he had only told the truth in saying that it was like her. Yet he was very much in love with her, she was sure, and most of the men she had met would not have behaved as well as he did, under the rather unusual circumstances. For little Madame De Rosa had been sleeping so soundly that she might as well not have been in the room at all. Behind all he did and said, she felt his almost primitive sincerity, and the elementary strength of the passion she had inspired. No woman can feel that and not be flattered, and few, being flattered by a man's love, can resist the temptation to play with it.

Women are more alike than men are; some of the nature of the worst of them is latent in the very best, and in the very worst there are little treasures of gentleness and faith that can ransom the poor soul at last.

'I am in earnest, indeed I am,' Logotheti repeated, looking at Margaret still.

'Yes,' she answered, 'I am sure you are.'

There was something in her tone that acquiesced, that almost approved, and he felt that these were the first words of encouragement she had vouchsafed him.

A portentous yawn from Madame De Rosa made them both turn round. She was stretching herself like a cat when it wakes, and looking about her with blinking eyes, as if trying to remember where she was. Then she saw Margaret, smiled at her spasmodically, and yawned again.

'I must have been asleep,' she said, and she laughed rather foolishly.

'Only for a few minutes,' answered Logotheti in a reassuring tone.

Margaret rose and came up to her, followed by the Greek.

'It's most extraordinary!' cried Madame De Rosa. 'I never go to sleep like that! Do you think it could possibly have been the maraschino?'

'No indeed!' Logotheti laughed carelessly. 'You were tired, after the rehearsal.'

He put the decanter back into the large liqueur case from which he had taken it, shut down the lid, locked it and put the key in his pocket.

Madame De Rosa watched him in silence, but Margaret paid no attention to what he was doing, for she was accustomed to see Mrs. Rushmore do the same thing. The taste of servants for liqueur and cigars is quite irreproachable; they always take the best there is.

A few minutes later the three were on their way to Versailles, and before long Logotheti put Margaret down at Mrs. Rushmore's gate, starting to take Madame De Rosa back to Paris, as soon as the girl had gone in. Neither of them said much on the way, and the motor stopped again in the Boulevard Malesherbes. Madame De Rosa thanked Logotheti, with an odd little smile of intelligence.

'Take care!' she said, as they parted, and her beady little black eyes looked sharply at him.

'Why?' he asked, with perfect calm, but his lids were slightly contracted.

Madame De Rosa shook her finger at him, laughed and ran in, leaving him standing on the pavement.

CHAPTER XI

Great singers and, generally, all good singers, are perfectly healthy animals with solid nerves, in which respect they differ from other artists, with hardly an exception. They have good appetites, they sleep soundly, they are not oppressed by morbid anticipations of failure nor by the horrible reaction that follows a great artistic effort of any kind except singing. Without a large gift of calm physical strength they could not possibly do the physical work required of them, and as they possess the gift they have also the characteristics that go with it and help to preserve it.

It does not follow that they have no feelings; but it does follow that their feelings are natural and healthy, when those of other musicians are apt to be frightfully morbid. A great deal of nonsense has been thought and written about the famous Malibran, because Alfred de Musset was moved to write of her as if she were a consumptive and devoured by the flame of genius. Malibran was a genius, but she was no more consumptive than Hercules. She died of internal injuries caused by a fall from a horse.

Margaret Donne, when she was about to go on the stage as Margarita da Cordova, was a perfectly normal young woman; which does not mean that she felt no anxiety about her approaching début, but only that her actual diffidence as to the result did not keep her awake or spoil her appetite, though it made her rather more quiet and thoughtful than usual, because so very much depended on success.

At least, she had thought so when Logotheti had set her down at the gate. Five minutes later that aspect of the matter had changed. Mrs. Rushmore met her at the door of the morning room and gathered her in with a large embrace.

'My dear child!' cried the good lady. 'My dear child!'

This was indefinite, but Margaret felt that something more was coming, of a nature which Mrs. Rushmore considered fortunate in the extreme, and in a short time she had learned the news, but with no mention of Logotheti's name.

Six months earlier Margaret would have rejoiced at her good fortune. Yesterday she might still have hesitated about keeping the engagement she had signed with Schreiermeyer; but between yesterday and today there was her first rehearsal, there was the echo of that little round of real applause from fellow-artists, there was the sound of her own voice, high and true, singing 'Anges pures'; and there was the smell of the stage, with its indescribable attraction. To have gone back now would have been to gainsay every instinct and every aspiration she felt. She told Mrs. Rushmore this, as quietly as she could.

'You're quite mad,' said Mrs. Rushmore. 'You may say what you please. I maintain that you are quite mad.'

'I can't help it,' Margaret answered without a smile. 'I began by wishing to do it to earn my living, if I could, but as it turns out, I have a great voice. I believe I have one of the great voices of the day. I'm born to sing, and I should sing if you told me I had millions. I feel it now, and I am not boasting in the least. Ask Schreiermeyer, if you like.'

'Who is that person with the queer name?' inquired Mrs. Rushmore severely.

'He's one of the big managers--the one who has engaged me.'

'Engaged fiddlesticks!' commented Mrs. Rushmore, with contempt. 'I say you are quite mad. If not, how do you account for your wishing to go on the stage?'

Margaret was thinking how she could account for it, when Mrs. Rushmore went on.

'I'll have a specialist out this afternoon to look at you,' she said. 'You're not sane. I wonder who the best man is.'

The last sentence was spoken in an undertone of reflection.

'Nonsense!' exclaimed Margaret emphatically, and adding to the emphasis by taking off her hat and throwing her head back, shaking it a little as if she wished her hair were down.

Mrs. Rushmore turned upon her with the moral dignity of five generations of Puritan ancestors.

'Do you mean to say that after all I've done to get you this money, you are going to give me up to be an actress?' she demanded with scorn. 'That you're going to give up your best friends, and your position as a lady, and the chance of making a respectable marriage, not to mention your immortal soul, just for the pleasure of showing yourself every night half-dressed to every commercial traveller in Europe? It's disgraceful. I don't care what you say. You're insane. You shan't do it!'

At this view of the case Margaret's forehead flushed a little.

'You talk as if I were going to be a music-hall singer,' she said.

'That's where you'll end!' retorted Mrs. Rushmore, without the slightest regard for facts. 'That's where they all end! There, or in the divorce courts--or both! It's the same thing!' she concluded triumphantly.

'I never heard a divorce court compared to a music-hall,' observed Margaret.

'You know exactly what I mean,' answered Mrs. Rushmore angrily. 'Don't take me up at every word! Contradicting isn't reasoning. Anybody can contradict.'

'And besides,' continued Margaret, growing cooler as the other grew warm, 'one cannot be divorced till one has been married.'

'Oh, you'll marry soon enough!' cried Mrs. Rushmore, infuriated by her calm. 'You'll marry an adventurer with dyed moustaches and a sham title, who'll steal your money and beat you! And though I am your dear mother's best friend, Margaret, I'm bound to say that it will serve you right. It's useless to deny it. It will serve you right.'

'It would certainly serve me right if I married the individual with the dyed moustaches,' said Margaret, smiling in spite of herself.

'I'm glad you agree with me at last. It shows that you're not so perfectly mad as you seemed. If you had gone on as you were talking at first I should certainly have had a mad doctor to examine you. As it is, I don't believe you're fit to have all that money. You mean well, I daresay. But you have no sense. None at all.'

Margaret laughed and took the opportunity of the lull in the battle to escape to her own room. A moment later Mrs. Rushmore followed her and knocked at the door.

'I'm sure you've had nothing to eat all day,' she called out anxiously, before Margaret could answer.

Margaret opened and put her head out, to explain that she had lunched, but she did not say where.

'Oh, very well!' answered Mrs. Rushmore, unwilling to show that her anger had subsided so soon. 'That's all I wanted to know.'

Like most Anglo-Saxons, she vaguely connected regular meals with morality.

When Margaret was alone she realised that she was more disturbed by Lushington's unexpected appearance at Logotheti's door than she had thought it possible to be. At the time, she had been surprised to see him and a little hurt by his manner, but she had attributed the latter to his natural shyness. Now that she could think quietly about the meeting, she remembered his eyes and the look of cold resentment she had seen in them for the first time since she had known him. He had no right to be angry with her for lunching with Logotheti, she was quite sure. He had parted from her, giving her to understand that they were to meet as little as possible in future. How could he possibly claim to criticise her actions after that? A few days ago, she would have married him, if he had not insisted that it was impossible. She was not sure that she would marry him now, if he came back. He had looked as if he meant to interfere in her life, after refusing to share it. No woman will tolerate that.

Yet she was disturbed, and a little sad, now that the day was over. Logotheti had found words for a thought that had passed through her mind, it was true; if Lushington loved her, how could he make an obstacle of what she had been so ready to overlook? The Greek's direct speeches had appealed to her, while he had been at her side. But now, she wished with all her heart that Lushington would appear to ask her questions, and let her answer them. She had a most unreasonable impression that she had somehow angered him, and wronged herself in his eyes. She would not ask herself whether she loved him still, or whether she had really loved him at all, but she longed to see him. He had said that he was leaving again in the evening, but perhaps he would think better of it and come out to see her. She even thought of writing to him, for she knew his London address. He lived in Bolton Street, Piccadilly, and she remembered his telling her that his windows looked upon a blank brick wall opposite, in which he sought inspiration and sometimes found it. Sometimes, he had said, he saw her face there.

Then she remembered the last hour they had spent together at Madame Bonanni's, and the quiet dignity and courage of his behaviour under circumstances that might almost have driven a sensitive man out of his senses.

She thought of him a great deal that afternoon, and the result of her thoughts was that she resolved not to go to Logotheti's house again, though she had a vague idea that such a resolution should not be connected with Lushington, if she meant to respect her own independence. But when she had reached this complicated state of mind, both Lushington and Logotheti took themselves suddenly out of the sphere of her meditations, and she was standing once more on the half-lighted stage, singing 'Anges pures' into the abyss of the dark and empty house.

The evening post brought Margaret three notes from Paris. One, in bad French, was from Schreiermeyer, to say that he had changed his mind, that she was to make her début in Rigoletto instead of in Faust, and that a rehearsal of the former opera was called for the next day but one at eleven o'clock, at which, by kindness of the director of the Opéra, she would be allowed to sing the part of Gilda.

When she read this, her face fell, and she felt a sharp little disappointment. She had already fancied herself Marguerite, the fair-haired Gretchen, mass-book in hand and eyes cast down, and then at the spinning-wheel, and in the church, and in the prison, and it was an effort of imagination to turn herself into the Italian Duke's Gilda, murdered to save her lover and dragged away in the sack--probably by proxy!

The next note was from Logotheti, who begged her to use his motor car for going in to her rehearsals. The chauffeur would bring it to Mrs. Rushmore's gate, the day after to-morrow, in plenty of time. The note was in French and ended with the assurance of 'most respectful homage.'

When she had read it she stared rather vacantly into the corner of her room for a few seconds, and then tossed the bit of paper into the basket under her writing-table.

The third letter was from Lushington. She had recognised the small scholarly handwriting and had purposely laid it aside to read last. It was rather stiffly worded, and it contained a somewhat unnecessary and not very contrite apology for having seemed rude that morning in answering her question so roughly and in hurrying away. He had not much else to say, except that he was going back at once to his London lodgings in Bolton Street--a hint that if Margaret wished to write to him he was to be found there.

She bit her lip and frowned. The note was useless and tactless as well. If he had wished to please her he might have written a word of greeting, as if nothing had happened, just to say that he wished he could have seen her for a few minutes. It would have been so easy to do that instead of sending a superfluous apology for having been rude on purpose! She read the note again and grew angry over it. It was so gratuitous! If he really meant to avoid her always, he need not have written at all. 'Superfluous' was the word; it was superfluous. She tore the letter into little bits and threw them into the basket; and then, by an afterthought, she fished up Logotheti's note, which she had not torn, and read it again.

At all events, he was a man of the world and could cover two pages of note-paper without saying anything that could irritate a woman.

Like everything he said, what he wrote was just right. He did not protest that he could not use his motor car himself, and he did not apologise for taking the liberty of offering her the use of it; he did not even ask for an answer, as if he were trying to draw her into writing to him. The car would be at the gate, and he would be glad if she could use it; meaning that if she did not want it she could send it away. There was not the least shade of familiarity in the phrases. 'Respectful homage' was certainly not 'familiar.' Just because he did not ask for an answer, he should have one!

She took up her pen and began. When she had written three or four lines to thank him, she found herself going on to say more, and she told him of the change in regard to her début, and asked if he knew why it was made so suddenly. She explained why she preferred Faust to Rigoletto, and all at once she saw that she had filled a sheet and must either break off abruptly or take another. She finished the note hastily and signed her name. When it was done she remembered that she had not told him anything about the money which had unexpectedly come to her, and she hesitated a moment; but she decided that it was none of his business, and almost wondered why she had thought of telling him anything so entirely personal. She sealed the letter, stamped it and sent it to be posted.

Then she sat down at her piano to look over Rigoletto, whistling her part softly while she played, in order to save her voice, and in a few minutes she had forgotten Logotheti, Schreiermeyer and Lushington.

CHAPTER XII

Madame Bonanni sat in the spring sunshine by the closed window of her sitting-room in London; she was thankful that there was any sunshine at all, and by keeping the window shut and wrapping herself in furs she produced the illusion that it was warming her. The room was not very large and a good deal of space was taken up by a grand piano, a good deal more by the big table and the heavy furniture, and the rest by Madame Bonanni herself. Her bulk was considerably increased by the white furs, from which only her head emerged; and as her face was made up for the day with rather more paint than she wore in Paris, on the ground that London is a darker city, the effect of the whole was highly artificial and disconcerting. One might have compared the huge bundle of white to an enormous egg out of which a large and very animated middle-aged fowl was just hatching.

Lushington was seated before the open piano, but had turned half away from it on the stool and was looking quietly at his mother. His face had an expression of listless weariness which was not natural to him. Madame Bonanni moved just then and the outer fur slipped a little from its place. Lushington rose at once and arranged it again.

'Will you have anything else over you, mother?' he asked.

'No, my child. I am warm at last. Your English sun is like stage lime-light. It shines, and shines, and does no good! The man turns it off, and London is pitch dark! Nothing warms one here but eating five times a day and wearing a fur coat all the time. But I am growing old. Why do you say I am not? It is foolish.'

'Your voice is as perfect as ever,' said Lushington.

'My voice, my voice! What did you expect? That it would crack, or that I should sing false? Ungrateful boy! How can you say such things of your mother? But I am growing old. Soon I shall make the effect on the public of a grandmother in baby's clothes. Do you think I am blind? They will say, "Poor old Bonanni, she remembers Thiers!" They might as well say at once that I remember the Second Empire! It is infamous! Have people no heart? But why do I go on singing, my dear? Tell me that! Why do I go on?'

'Because you sing as well as ever,' suggested Lushington gently.

'It is no reason why I should work as hard as ever! Why should I go on earning money, money, money? Yes, I know! They come to hear me, they crowd the house, they pay, they clap their hands when I sing the mad scene in Lucia, or Juliet's waltz song, or the crescendo trills in the Huguenots! But I am old, my dear!'

'Nonsense!' interjected Lushington in an encouraging tone.

'Do you know why I am sure of it? It is this. I do not care any more. It is all the same to me, what they do. I do not care whether they come or not, or whether they applaud, or hiss, or stamp on the floor. Why should I care? I have had it all so often. I have seen the people standing on the seats all over the theatre and yelling, and often in foreign countries they have taken the horses from my carriage and dragged it themselves. I have had everything. Why should I care for it? And I do not want money. I have too much already.'

'You certainly have enough, mother.'

'It is your fault that I have too much,' she said, in sudden anger. 'You have no heart; you are a cruel, ungrateful boy! Is there anything I have not done to make you happy, ever since you were a baby? Look at your position! You are a celebrated writer, a critic! Other writers are green with jealousy and fear of you! And why? Because I made up my mind that you should be a great man, and sent you to school and the university instead of keeping you to myself, at home, always pressed against my heart! Is not that the greatest sacrifice that a mother can make, to send her child to college, to be left alone herself, always wondering whether he is catching cold and is getting enough to eat, and is not being led away by wicked little boys? Ah, you do not know! You can never be a mother!'

This was unanswerable, but Lushington really looked sorry for her, as if it were his fault.

'And what have you given me in return for it all? How have you repaid me for the days of anxiety and nights of fever all the time when you were at those terrible studies? I ask you that! How have you rewarded me? You will not take money from me. I go on making more and more, and you will not spend it. Oh, it is not to be believed! I shall die of grief!'

Madame Bonanni put one fat hand out from under the furs, and pressed a podgy finger to each eyelid in succession by way of stopping the very genuine tears that threatened her rouged cheeks with watery destruction.

'Mother, please don't!' cried Lushington, in helpless distress. 'You know that I can't take money from you!'

'Oh, I know, I know! That is the worst of it--I know! It is not because you are proud of earning your own living, it's because you're ashamed of me!'

Lushington rose again, and began to walk up and down, bending his head and glancing at her now and then.

'Why will you always go back to that question?' he asked, and his tone showed how much he resented it. 'You cannot unlive your life. Don't make me say more than that, for you don't know how it hurts to say that much. Indeed you don't!'

He went to the closed window and looked out, turning away from her. She stretched out her hand and pulled at his coat timidly, as a dog pulls his master's clothes to attract his attention. He turned his head a little.

'I've tried to live differently, Tom,' she said. 'Of late years I've tried.'

Her voice was low and unsteady.

'I know it,' he said just above a whisper, and he turned to the window-pane again.

'Can't you forgive me, Tom?' she asked pitifully. 'Won't you take some of the money--only what I made by singing?'

He shook his head without looking round, for it would have hurt him to see her eyes just then.

'I have enough, mother,' he answered. 'I make as much as I need.'

'You will need much more when you marry.'

'I shall never marry.'

'You will marry little Miss Donne,' said Madame Bonanni, after a moment's pause.

Lushington turned sharply now, and leaned back against the glass.

'No,' he answered, with sudden hardness, 'I can't ask Miss Donne to be my wife. No man in my position could have the right. You understand what I mean, and heaven knows I don't wish to pain you, mother--I'd give anything not to! Why do you talk of these things?'

'Because I feel that you're unhappy, Tom, and I know that I am--and there must be some way out of it. After all, my dear--now don't be angry!--Miss Donne is a good girl--she's all that I wish I had been--but after all, she's going to be an opera-singer. You are the son of an artist and I don't see why any artist should not marry you. The public believes we are all bad, whether we are or not.'

'I'm not thinking of the public,' Lushington answered. 'I don't care a straw what the world says. If I had been offered my choice I would not have changed my name at all.'

'But then, my dear, what in the world are you thinking of?' asked the prima donna, evidently surprised by what he said. 'If the girl loves you, do you suppose she will care what I've done?'

'But I care!' cried Lushington with sudden vehemence. 'I care, for her sake!'

Madame Bonanni's hand had disappeared within the furs again, after she had ascertained that the two tears were not going to run down her cheeks. Her large face wore the expression of a coloured sphinx, and there was something Egyptian about the immobility of her eyes and her painted eyebrows. No one could have guessed from her look whether she were going to cry or laugh the next time she spoke. Lushington walked up and down the room without glancing at her.

'Do you think----' she began, and broke off as he stopped to listen.

'What?' he inquired, standing still.

'Would it make it any better if--if I married again?' She asked the question with hesitation.

'How? I don't understand.'

'They always say that marriage is so respectable,' Madame Bonanni answered, in a matter-of-fact tone. 'I don't know why, I'm sure, but everybody seems to think it is, and if it would help matters--I mean, if Miss Donne would consider that a respectable marriage with a solid, middle-class man would settle the question, I suppose I could manage it. I could always divorce, you know, if it became unbearable!'

'Yes,' Lushington answered. 'Marriage is the first step to the divorce court. For heaven's sake, don't talk in this way! I've made up my mind that I cannot marry, and that ends it. Let it alone. We each know what the other thinks, and we are each trying to make the best of what can't be undone. Talking about it can do no good. Nothing can. It's the inevitable, and so the least said about it, the better. Sometimes you say that I am ungrateful, mother, but I'm not, you don't mean it seriously. If I've made my own way, it is because you started me right, by making me work instead of bringing me up at your apron-strings, to live on your money. You did it so well, too, that you cannot undo it, now that you would like to make me rich. Why aren't you proud of that, mother? It's the best thing you ever did in your life--God bless you! And yet you say I'm ungrateful!'

At this, there was a convulsion of the white furs; Madame Bonanni suddenly emerged, erect, massive and seething with motherly emotion; throwing her arms round her son she pressed him to her with a strength and vehemence that might have suffocated a weaker man. As it was, Lushington was speechless in her embrace for several seconds, while she uttered more or less incoherent cries of joy.

'My child! My own darling Tommy! Oh, you make me so happy!'

Lushington let her print many heavy kisses on his cheeks, and he gently patted her shoulder with his free hand. He was very patient and affectionate, considering the frightful dilemma with regard to her in which he had lived all his life; for, as his mother, he loved her, but as a woman, he knew that he could never respect her, whatever she might do to retrieve her past. He could find excuses for the life she had led, but they were only palliatives that momentarily soothed the rankling sore in his heart, which nothing could heal. In his own world of literature and work and publicity, he had a name of his own, not without honour, and respected by every one. But to himself, to the few trusted persons who knew his secret, above all to Margaret Donne, he was the son of that 'Bonanni woman,' who had been the spoilt plaything of royalty and semi-royalty from London to St. Petersburg, whose lovers had been legion and her caprices as the sand on the seashore. There were times when Lushington could not bear to see her, and kept away from her, or even left the city in which they were together. There were days when the natural bond drew him to her, and when he realised that, with countless faults, she had been to him a far better mother than most men are blessed with.

And now, poor thing, she was grateful to the verge of tears for his one word of blessing that seemed to wipe out all the rest. She wished that when her hour came, she might hear him say again 'God bless you,' and then die.

She let him go, and sat down amongst her furs, with a deep sigh of satisfaction.

'I've made up my mind what to do,' she said, almost as if she were talking to herself. 'I'm tired of it all, Tom, and I'm losing my good looks and my figure. If this goes on, I shall soon be ridiculous. You would not like your mother to be ridiculous, would you?'

'Certainly not!'

'No, my angel! Be good if you can; if you can't be good, be bad; but never be ridiculous! Oh, never, never! I could not bear that. So I shall leave the stage, quietly, without any farewell. I shall cancel my engagements when I have finished singing here. The doctors will swear to anything. What are they for? I was never ill in my life, but they shall say I am ill now. What is it that every one has nowadays-- the appendix? I will have the appendix. The doctors shall swear that I have it well. So I shall leave the stage with a good reason, and pay no forfeit for cancelling the contracts. That is business. Then I will be a nun.'

'Eh?' ejaculated Lushington, staring at her.

'Yes, I will be a nun,' continued Madame Bonanni unmoved. 'I will go into religion. When your mother is a nun, my child, I presume that the Church will protect her, and no one will dare to say anything against her. Then you can marry or not, as you please, but you will no longer be ashamed of your mother! I shall be a blue nun with a white bonnet and a black veil, and I shall call myself Sister Juliet, because that has been my great part, and the name will remind me of old times. Don't you think "Sister Juliet" sounds very well? And dark blue is becoming to me--I always said so.'

'Yes--yes,' answered Lushington in an uncertain tone and biting his lip.

'I cannot do more than that for you, my treasure,' said his mother, a touch of real human sadness in her voice. 'You will not take the miserable money--but perhaps you will take the sacrifice, if I shut myself up in a convent and wear a hair shirt, and feed sick babies, and eat cabbage. How could any one say a word against me then? And you will be happy, Tom. That is all I ask.'

'I shall not be happy, if you make yourself miserable, mother,' said Lushington, smiling.

'Miserable? Ah, well, I daresay there will not be cabbage every day,' answered Madame Bonanni thoughtfully. 'And I like fish. Fortunately, I am fond of fish. The simplest, you know. Only a fried sole with a meunière sauce. Bah! When I talk of eating you never believe I am in earnest. Go away, my beloved child! Go and write to little Miss Donne that she may have all my engagements, because I am entering religion. You shall see! She will marry you in a week. Go over to Paris and talk to her. She is crying her eyes out for you, and that is bad for the voice. It relaxes the vocal cords frightfully. I always have to gargle for half-an-hour if I have been crying and am going to sing.'

Through all her rambling talk, half earnest and half absurd, Lushington detected the signs of a coming change. He did not think she would leave the stage so suddenly as she said she would; he assuredly did not believe that she would ever 'enter religion'; but he saw for the first time that she was tired of the life she had led, that she felt herself growing old and longed for rest and quiet. She had lived as very few live, to satisfy every ambition and satiate every passion to the full, and now, with advancing years, she had not the one great bad passion of old age, which is avarice, as an incentive for prolonging her career. In its place, on the contrary, stood her one redeeming virtue, that abundant generosity which had made her welcome Margaret Donne's great talent with honest enthusiasm, and which had been like a providence to hundreds, perhaps to thousands of unknown men, women and children ever since she had gained the means of helping the poor and distressed. But it had been part of her nature to hide that. Logotheti, who managed most of her business, knew more about her charities than her own son, and the world knew next to nothing at all.

CHAPTER XIII

When Lushington had run over to Paris the day before the conversation just recorded, he had entertained a vague notion of going out to Versailles in the afternoon; for he felt that all had not been said between himself and Margaret and that their last parting in the street had not been really final. The fact was that he merely yielded to the tormenting desire to see her again, if for only a few minutes and in the presence of Mrs. Rushmore.

But the meeting in the Boulevard Péreire had chilled him like a stream of cold water poured down his back; than which homely simile there is none more true. He had fancied her very grave and even a little sad, going quietly to her rehearsals with a maid, or even with Mrs. Rushmore, speaking to no one at the theatre and returning at once to Versailles to reflect on the vicissitudes to which human affections are subject.

He had come upon her suddenly and unawares, in a very smart frock and a superlatively becoming hat, smiling gaily, just stepping out of a magnificent white motor car, resting her hand familiarly on that of the most successful young financier in Paris, whose conquests among women of the world were a byword, and chaperoned by a flighty little Neapolitan teacher of singing. Truly, if some one had deliberately rubbed the back of his neck with a large lump of ice on that warm spring day, the chill could not have been more effectual. Morally speaking, Lushington caught a bad cold, which 'struck in,' as old people used to say.

He might have explained to himself that as he had insisted upon parting from Margaret for ever, and against her will, her subsequent doings were none of his business. But he was half an Englishman by birth and altogether one by bringing up, and he therefore could not admit that she should be apparently enjoying herself, while he was gloomily brooding over the misfortunes that put her beyond his reach. The fable of the Dog in the Manger must have been composed to describe us Anglo-Saxons. It is sufficient that we be hindered from getting what we want, even by our own sense of honour; we are forthwith ready to sacrifice life and limb to prevent any other man from getting it. The magnanimity of our renunciation is only to be compared with our tenacity in asserting our claim to what we have renounced. Even our charities usually have strings to them on which our hold never relaxes, in case we should want them back.

Lushington had never trusted Logotheti, but since his instinct and the force of circumstances had told him that the Greek was making love to Margaret and that Margaret liked his society, he hated the man in a most unchristian manner, and few things would have given the usually peaceable man of letters such unmitigated satisfaction as to see the shining white motor car blow up and scatter his rival's arms and legs to the thirty-two points of the compass.

Logotheti, on the other hand, was as yet unaware that Lushington was the 'some one else' of whom Margaret had spoken twice with evident feeling. The consequence was that when the Englishman began to give himself the bitter satisfaction of watching Logotheti, the latter was very far from suspecting such a thing, and took no pains at all to hide his doings; and Lushington established himself in Paris and watched him, in his coming and going, and nursed his jealousy into hatred and his hatred into action.

He would not have stooped to employ any one in such work, for that would have seemed like an insult to Margaret, and a piece of cowardice into the bargain. The time would come when the astute Greek would discover that he was followed, and Lushington had no intention of putting some one else in his shoes when that time came; on the contrary, he looked forward with all a real Englishman's cool self-confidence to the explanation that must take place some day. But he wished to remain undiscovered as long as possible.

He had gone back to his old rooms in the Hôtel des Saints Pères, but in order to disappear more effectually from his acquaintances he took a lodging, and walked to it, after sending on his belongings. On his way he stopped at a quiet barber's shop and had his beard and moustache shaved off. After that it was not likely that any of his acquaintances would recognise him, but he took further steps towards completing his disguise by making radical and painful changes in his dress. He bought ready-made French clothes, he put on a pair of square kid boots with elastic sides and patent leather tips, he wore a soft silk cravat artificially tied in a bow knot with wide and floating ends, and he purchased a French silk hat with a broad and curving brim. Having satisfied himself that the effect was good, he laid in a stock of similar articles, and further adorned his appearance with a pair of tortoise-shell-rimmed spectacles, and a green umbrella. For possibly cool or rainy weather he provided himself with a coffee-coloured overcoat that had a velvet collar and tails reaching almost to the ground.

When he had been younger Lushington had tried in vain to ruffle his naturally excessive neatness, but he now realised that he had only lacked the courage to make a thorough change. In his present costume he ran no risk of being taken for a smart English lounger, nor for a French dandy. The effect of forgetting to shave, too, was frightful, for in forty-eight hours his fair face was covered with shiny bristles that had a positively metallic look. Though he was so unlike his mother in most ways, he must have inherited a little of the theatrical instinct from her, for he wore his disguise as easily as if he had always been used to it.

He also had the advantage of speaking French like a native, though possibly with a very slight southern accent caught from his mother, who originally came from Provence. As for his name, it was useless to assume another, for Paris is full of Parisians of foreign descent, whose names are English, German, Polish and Italian; and in a really great city no one takes the least notice of a man unless he does something to attract attention. Besides, Lushington had no idea of disappearing from his own world, or of cutting himself off from his regular correspondents.

He had not any fixed plan, for he was not sure what he wanted; he only knew that he hated and distrusted Logotheti, and that while he could not forgive Margaret for liking the Greek's society, he meant, in an undetermined way, to save her from destruction. Probably, if he had attempted to put his thoughts into words, he could have got no further than Mrs. Rushmore, who suspected Logotheti of designs, and at the root of his growing suspicion he would have found the fine old Anglo-Saxon prejudice that a woman might as well trust herself to Don Juan, an Italian Count, or Beelzebub, as to the offspring of Cadmus or Danaus.

Englishmen have indolent minds and active bodies, as a rule, but on the other hand, when they are really roused, no people in the world are capable of greater mental concentration and energy. They are therefore not good detectives as a rule, but there are few better when they are deeply and selfishly interested in the result.

Incidentally, Lushington meant to do his utmost to prevent Margaret from going on the stage, and he would have been much surprised to learn that in this respect he was Logotheti's ally, instead of his enemy, against Margaret's fixed determination. If there was to be a struggle, therefore, it was to be a three-cornered one, in which the two men would be pitted against each other, and both together against the resolution of the woman they both loved. Unfortunately for Lushington, he had begun by withdrawing from Margaret's surroundings and had made way for his adversary.

Meanwhile Logotheti made the running. He had offered Margaret his motor car for coming in to her rehearsals, and a chauffeur appeared with it in good time, masked, coated and gloved in the approved fashion. Margaret supposed that Logotheti meant to ask her to luncheon again with Madame De Rosa, and she made up her mind to refuse, for no particular reason except that she did not wish to seem too willing to do whatever he proposed. Mrs. Rushmore thought it bad enough that she should accept the offer of the motor car, but was beginning to understand that the machine had quite irresistible temptations for all persons under fifty. She was even a little shocked that Margaret should go alone to Paris under the sole protection of the chauffeur, though she would have thought it infinitely worse if Logotheti himself had appeared.

The man held the door open for Margaret to get in, when she came out upon the step with Mrs. Rushmore, who seemed anxious to keep an eye on her as long as possible; as if she could project an influence of propriety, a sort of astral chaperonage, that would follow the girl to the city. She detained her at the last minute, holding her by the elbow. The chauffeur stood impassive with his hand on the door, while she delivered herself of her final opinion in English, which of course he could not understand.

'I must say that your sudden intimacy with this suspicious Greek is most extraordinary,' she said.

'Don't you think there is just a little prejudice in your opinion of him?' asked Margaret sweetly.

'No,' answered Mrs. Rushmore with firmness, 'I don't, and I think it very strange that a clever girl like you should be so easily taken in by a foreigner. Much worse than a foreigner, my dear! A Greek is almost as bad as a Turk, and we all know what Turks are! Fancy a decent young woman trusting herself alone with a Turk! I declare, it's not to be believed! Your dear mother's daughter too! You'll end in a harem, Margaret, mark my word.'

'And be sewn up in a sack and thrown into the Bosphorus,' laughed Margaret, trying to get away.

'Such things have happened before now,' said Mrs. Rushmore gloomily.

'Greeks don't have harems,' Margaret objected.

'Don't catch cold,' said Mrs. Rushmore, by way of refuting Margaret's argument. 'It looks as if it might rain.'

The morning was still and soft and overcast, and the air was full of the scent of the flowers and leaves, and fresh-clipped grass. The small birds chirped rather plaintively from the trees on the lawn, or stood about the edge of the little pond apparently expecting something to happen, hopping down to the water occasionally, looking down at the reflections in it and then hopping back again with a dissatisfied air; and they muffled themselves up in their feathers as if they meant to go to sleep, and then suddenly spread their wings out, without flying, and scraped the grass with them. The elms were quite green already, and the oaks were pushing out thousands of bright emerald leaves. There is a day in every spring when the maiden year reaches full girlhood, and pauses on the verge of woman's estate, to wonder at the mysterious longings that disquiet all her being, and at the unknown music that sings through her waking dreams.

Margaret sat in the motor car wrapped in a wide thin cloak and covering her mouth lest the rush of air should affect her voice; but the quick motion was pleasant, and she felt all the illusion of accomplishing something worth doing, merely because she was spinning along at breakneck speed. Somehow, too, the still air and the smell of the flowers had made her restless that morning before starting, and the rapid movement soothed her. If she had been offered her choice just then, she would perhaps have been on horseback for a gallop across country, but the motor car was certainly the next best thing to that.

For some minutes the chauffeur kept his eyes on the road ahead and both hands on the steering-gear. Then one hand moved, the speed of the car slackened suddenly, and the man turned and spoke over the back of his seat.

'I hope you'll forgive me,' he said in English.

Margaret started and sat up straight, for the voice was Logotheti's. The huge goggles, the protecting curtain over half the face, the wide-visored cap and the turned-up coat collar, had disguised him beyond all recognition. Even his usually smooth black moustache was ruffled out of shape, and hid his characteristic mouth.

Margaret uttered an exclamation of surprise, not quite sure whether she ought to smile or frown.

'I thought Mrs. Rushmore would not like it, if I came for you myself,' he continued, looking at her through his goggles.

'I'm sure she wouldn't,' Margaret assented readily.

'In point of fact,' Logotheti continued, with a grin, 'she expressed her opinion of me with extraordinary directness. Suspicious Greek! Worse than a foreigner! As bad as a Turk! The unprincipled owner of a harem! It's really true that eavesdroppers never hear any good of themselves! I never tried it before, and it served me right.'

'You cannot say that I said anything against you,' laughed Margaret. 'I took your defence.'

'Not with enthusiasm.' Logotheti joined in her laugh.

'You thought there might be just a little prejudice in her opinion and you told her that Greeks don't have harems. Yes--yes--I suppose that might be called defending an absent friend.'

The car was moving very slowly now.

'If I had known it was you, I would have called you all sorts of names,' Margaret answered. 'Should you mind taking that thing off your face for a moment? I don t like talking to a mask, and you may be some one else after all.'

'No,' said Logotheti, 'I'm not "some one else".' He emphasised the words that had become familiar to them both. 'I wish I were! But if I take off my glasses and cap, you will be frightened, for my hair is not smooth and I'm sure I look like a Greek pirate!'

'I should like to see one, and I shall not be frightened.'

He pulled off his cap and glasses, and faced her. She stared at him in surprise, for she was not sure that she should have recognised him. His thick black hair stuck up all over his head like a crest, his heavy eyebrows were as bushy as an animal's fur and his rough and bristling moustache lent his large mouth and massive jaws a look approaching to ferocity. The whole effect was rather startling, and Margaret opened her eyes wide in astonishment. Logotheti smiled.

'Now you understand why I smooth my hair and dress like a tailor's manikin,' he said quietly. 'It's enough to cow a mob, isn't it?'

'Do you know, I'm not sure that I don't like you better so. You're more natural!'

'You're evidently not timid,' he answered, amused. 'But you can fancy the effect on Mrs. Rushmore's nerves, if she had seen me.'

'I should not have dared to come with you. As it is----' She hesitated.

'Oh, as it is, you cannot help yourself,' Logotheti said. 'You can't get out and walk.'

'I could get out when you have to stop at the petrol station; and I assure you that I can refuse to come with you again!'

'Of course you can. But you won't.'

'Why not?'

'Because you're much too sensible. Have I offended you, or frightened you? What have I done to displease you?'

'Nothing--but----' She laughed and shook her head as she broke off.

'I haven't even asked you to marry me to-day! I should think that I was taking an unfair advantage, if I did, since I could easily carry you off just now. The car will run sixty miles at a stretch without any trouble at all, and I don't suppose you would risk your neck to jump, merely for the sake of getting away from me, would you?'

'Not if you behaved properly,' Margaret answered.

'And then,' Logotheti continued, 'I could put her at full speed and say, "If you won't swear to marry me, I'll give myself the satisfaction of being killed with you at the very next bridge we come to!" Most women would rather marry a man than be smashed to atoms with him, even if he looks like a pirate.'

'Possibly!'

'But that would be unfair. Besides, an oath taken under compulsion is not binding. I should have to find some other way.'

'Shall we go on?' Margaret asked. 'I shall be late for the rehearsal.'

'Give it up,' suggested Logotheti calmly. 'We'll spend the morning at St. Cloud. Much pleasanter than tiring yourself out in that wretched theatre! I want to talk to you.'

'You can talk to me when I am not singing.'

'No. Singing will distract your attention, and you won't listen to what I tell you. You have no idea what delightful things I can say when I try!'

'I wonder!' Margaret laughed lightly. 'You might begin trying while you take me to Paris. We haven't run a mile in the last ten minutes, and it's getting late.'

'Unless you are always a little late nobody will respect you. I'll go a little faster, just to prove to you that you can do anything you like with me, even against my judgment. Let me put on my glasses first.'

At that moment a man met them on a bicycle, and passed at a leisurely pace. There was not much traffic on the Versailles road at that hour, and Margaret let her eyes rest idly on the man, who merely glanced at her and looked ahead again. Logotheti had taken off his cap in order to adjust his goggles and shield. When the bicycle had gone by he laughed.

'There goes a typical French bookworm, bicycling to get an appetite,' he observed. 'I wonder why a certain type of Frenchman always wears kid boots with square patent leather toes, and a Lavallière tie, and spectacles with tortoise-shell rims!'

'If he could see you as you generally are,' answered Margaret, 'he would probably wonder why a certain type of foreigner plasters his hair down and covers himself with diamonds and rubies! Do go a little faster, it's getting later every moment.'

'It always does.'

'Especially when one doesn't wish it to! Please go on!'

'Say at once that I've bored you to death.' He put the car at half-speed.

'No. You don't bore me at all, but I want to get to the theatre.'

'To please you, I am going there--for no other reason. I'll do anything in the world to give you pleasure. I only wish you would do the smallest thing for me!'

'What, for instance? Perhaps I may do some very little thing. You'll get nothing if you don't ask for it!'

'Some people take without asking. Greek pirates always do, you know! But I can't drive at this rate and talk over my shoulder.'

The way was clear and for several minutes he ran at full speed, keeping his eyes on the road. Margaret turned sideways and kept behind him as much as possible, shielding her face and mouth from the tremendous draught.

She had told the truth when she had said that he did not bore her. The whole thing had a savour of adventure in it, and it amused her to think how shocked Mrs. Rushmore would have been if she had guessed that the chauffeur was Logotheti himself. There was something in the man's coolness that attracted her very much, for though there was no danger on the present occasion, she felt that if there had been any, he would have been just as indifferent to it if it stood in the way of his seeing her alone. Poor Lushington had always been so intensely proper, so morbidly afraid of compromising her, and above all, so deadly in earnest!

She did not quite like to admit that the Greek was altogether in earnest, too, and that she was just a little afraid of him; still less that her unacknowledged fear gave her rather a pleasant sensation. But it was quite true that she had liked him better than before, from the moment when he had pulled off his cap and glasses and shown his face as nature had made it. However he might appear hereafter when she met him, she would always think of him as she had seen him then.

Most women are much more influenced by strength in a man than by anything which can reasonably be called beauty. Actually and metaphorically every woman would rather be roughly carried off her feet by something she cannot resist than be abjectly worshipped and flattered; yet worship and flattery, though second-best, are much better than the terribly superior and instructive affection which the born prig bestows upon his idol with the air of granting a favour on moral grounds.

Men, on the other hand, detest being carried away, almost as much as being led. The woman who lets a man guess that she is trying to influence him is lost, and generally forfeits for ever any real influence she may have had. The only sort of cleverness which is distinctly womanly is that which leads a man to do with energy, enthusiasm and devotion the very thing which he has always assured everybody that he will not think of doing. The old-fashioned way of making a pig go to market is to pull his tail steadily in the opposite direction. If you do that, nothing can save him from his fate; for he will drag you off your feet in his effort to do what he does not want to do at all; and there is more 'psychology' in that plain fact than in volumes of subtle analysis.

CHAPTER XIV

Lushington's first discovery was not calculated to soothe his feelings. It had come about simply enough. He had bicycled in the Boulevard Péreire, keeping an eye on Logotheti's house from a distance, and had seen the motor car waiting before the door, in charge of the chauffeur. A man had come out, dressed precisely like the latter, had got in and had gone off, apparently in no hurry, while the original chauffeur went into the house, presumably to wait. It had been easy enough to keep the machine in sight till it was fairly out on the road to Versailles, after which Lushington had felt tolerably sure that by going slowly he should meet it coming back and probably bringing Margaret. As has been seen, this was what happened, and, as chance favoured him, he passed the motor before Logotheti had covered his face again. He was not likely to forget that face either, and it had done more to reveal to him his adversary's true character than any number of meetings in society. For once he had seen the real Logotheti, as Margaret had. He had ridden on till they were out of sight and had then turned back, in no very amiable frame of mind.

He understood very well that Logotheti had made great progress in a few days; he even took it for granted that Margaret had expected him that morning, and approved of the disguise; for it was nothing else, after all. If the world, and therefore Mrs. Rushmore, had been meant to know that Logotheti was acting as his own chauffeur, Margaret would have been sitting beside him in front. Instead, she was behind him, in the body of the car, and had evidently been talking with him over the back of the seat. The big machine, too, was moving at a snail's pace, clearly in order that they might talk at leisure. In other words, Logotheti had arranged a secret meeting with Margaret, with her consent; and that could only mean one thing. The Greek had gained enough influence over her to make her do almost anything he liked.

It was not a pleasant discovery, but it was an important one, and Lushington thought over the best means of following it up. He almost choked with anger as he reflected that if matters went on at this rate, Margaret would soon be going to Logotheti's house without even the nominal protection afforded by little Madame De Rosa. He rode back by the way he had taken outward and passed the Greek's house. The motor car was not there, which was a relief, on the whole.

He went on as far as the Opéra, for he knew from his mother that Margaret's rehearsals were taking place there, by the kindness of the director, who was on very friendly terms with Schreiermeyer. But the motor was not to be seen. Logotheti, who could hardly have entered disguised as his own chauffeur, and who would not leave the machine unguarded in the street, had possibly left Margaret at the door and gone away. Lushington got off his bicycle and went in under the covered way to the stage door.

In answer to his questions, the keeper told him that Mademoiselle da Cordova was rehearsing, and would probably not come out for at least two hours. Lushington asked the man whether he had seen Logotheti. No, he had not; he knew Monsieur Logotheti very well; he knew all the subscribers, and particularly all those who were members of the 'high finance.' Besides, every one in Paris knew Monsieur Logotheti by sight; every one knew him as well as the column in the Place Vendôme. He had not been seen that morning. The door-keeper, who had absolutely nothing to do just at that hour, was willing to talk; but he had nothing of importance to say. Monsieur Logotheti came sometimes to rehearsals. A few days ago he and Mademoiselle da Cordova had left the theatre together. The keeper smiled, and ventured to suppose that Mademoiselle da Cordova was 'protected' by the 'financier.' Lushington flushed angrily and went away.

It had come already, then; what the man had said this morning, he would say to-morrow and the next day, to any one who cared to listen, including the second-class reporters who go to underlings for information; Margaret's name was already coupled with that of a millionaire who was supposed to protect her. Ten days ago, she had been unassailable, a 'lady'--Lushington did not particularly like the word--a young English girl of honourable birth, protected by no less a personage than Mrs. Rushmore, and defended from calumny by that very powerful organisation for mutual defence under all circumstances, which calls itself society, which wields most of the capital of the world, rewards its humble friends with its patronage and generally kills or ruins its enemies. That was ten days ago. Now, the 'lady' had become an 'artist,' and was public property. The stage doorkeeper of a theatre could smilingly suggest that she was the property of a financier, and no one had a right to hit him between the eyes for saying so. Lushington had been strongly tempted to do that, but he had instantly foreseen the consequences; he would have been arrested for an unprovoked assault, the man would have told his story, the papers would have repeated it with lively comments, and Margaret's name would have been dragged through the mud of a newspaper scandal. So Lushington put his hands in his pockets and went away, which was by far the wisest thing he could do.

He set himself resolutely to think out a plan of action, but like many men of tolerably fertile imagination he was at a loss for any expedient in the presence of urgent need. He could watch Logotheti and Margaret, and they would not easily recognise him, but he was fain to admit that he had nothing to gain by spying on them. He had seen enough and heard enough already to convince him that Margaret had allowed herself to be led into a situation very dangerous for her good name, to say the least. It did not occur to him that Logotheti wished to marry her, still less that he meant to hinder her from singing in public. He could not help thinking of the very worst motives, and he attributed them all to the Greek.

The mild English man of letters was momentarily turned into an avenging demon, breathing wrath and destruction upon his adversary. The most extravagant and reckless crimes looked comparatively easy just then, and very tempting. He thought of getting into Logotheti's cellar with enough dynamite to blow the house, its owner and himself to atoms, not to speak of half the Boulevard Péreire. He fancied himself pounding Logotheti's face quite out of shape with his fists, riddling him with revolver bullets, running him through in all directions with duelling swords, tearing him in pieces with wild horses and hanging him out of his own front window. These vivacious actions all looked possible and delightful to Lushington as he walked up and down his little sitting-room. Then came the cold shower-bath of returning common-sense. He sat down, filled a pipe and lit it.

'I'm an awful ass,' he said aloud to himself, in a reproachful tone.

He wished that some spirit voice would contradict him, but in the absence of any supernatural intervention the statement remained unrefuted. The worst of it was that he had always thought himself clever, and in his critical writings he had sneered in a superior way at the inventions of contemporary novelists. Just then, he would have given his reputation for the talents of the hero in a common detective story. But his mind refused to work in that way, and he watched with growing discouragement the little clouds of smoke that floated upwards to the whitewashed ceiling without leaving the least shadow of a serviceable idea behind them.

He looked disconsolately at the square patent leather toes of his shoes, very dusty from bicycling, and he sadly passed his hand over his smooth-shaven chin; the curious creases in his ready-made trousers, so conspicuously in the wrong place, depressed him still further, and the sight of his broad-brimmed hat, lying on the table, enhanced the melancholy of his reflections. The disguise was admirable, undoubtedly, but it had only helped him to see with his eyes what he had already seen in imagination, and so far as he could guess, it was not likely to help him one step further. At that very moment Margaret was probably seated at Logotheti's table, without even Madame De Rosa to chaperon her, and Logotheti's men-servants were exchanging opinions about her outside the door. Lushington nearly bit through the mouthpiece of his pipe as he thought of that, knowing that he was powerless to interfere. The same thing might go on for a month, and he could not stop it; then Margaret would make her début, and the case would be more hopeless than ever.

The truth was that after launching himself as a disguised detective, he found himself barred from going any further than merely watching his enemy, simply because he was incapable of stooping to a detective's methods of work. He would as soon have lost his hand as have written an anonymous letter or deliberately inveigled Logotheti into a trap, and while he was so carefully concealing himself he longed in reality for open fight, and felt that he had made himself ridiculous in his own eyes. Yet he hesitated to put on his own English clothes and go about as usual, for he had to pass the porter's window on the stairs every time he went out or came in, and such a sudden change in his appearance would certainly make the porter suspect that he was engaged in some nefarious business. Porters are powerful personages in Parisian lodging-houses, and this one would probably inform the police that he had a suspicious lodger; after which Lushington would be watched in his turn and would very probably have trouble. These reflections made him feel more ridiculous than ever.

Now it very often happens that when a man, even of considerable intelligence, has made up his mind to do something which at first seemed very clever, but which, by degrees, turns out to be quite useless, if not altogether foolish, he perseveres in his course with mule-like obstinacy. He has taken endless trouble to prepare the means, he has thought it all out so nicely, only omitting to reach the conclusion! It would be a pity to go back, it would be useless to desist, since everything has been so well prepared. Something is sure to come of it, if he only sticks to his original plan, and any result must be better than allowing events to go their way.

Therefore, when the clouds that curled up from Lushington's pipe failed to shape themselves into a vision both wise and prophetic, and left absolutely no new idea behind when they vanished, he came to the conclusion that his first scheme was a very good one after all, and that he had better abide by the square-toed, spring-side boots and the rest of his admirable disguise, until something happened. Then he would seize the opportunity and act decisively; he was not at all sure how he should act, but he secretly hoped that the action in question might be of the nature of a fight with something or somebody. There are many quiet and shy men who would really rather fight than do anything else, though they will rarely admit it, even to themselves.

Returning to his plan of watching Logotheti, Lushington argued rightly that the trip in the motor car would be repeated the very next time that Margaret had a rehearsal, and that the car would therefore leave the house in the Boulevard Péreire at about the same time, every two or three days, but never on two days consecutively. When there was no rehearsal, Margaret would not come into town. When that was the case it would be easy to watch the house in Versailles. Lushington was not quite sure what he expected to see, but he would watch it all the same. Perhaps, on those days, Logotheti would appear undisguised and call. But what Lushington was most anxious to find out was whether Margaret had been to the house again. He wished he had waited near the Opéra to see where she went when she came out, or in the Boulevard Péreire, instead of coming back to his lodgings in a bad temper after his interview with the stage doorkeeper.

He looked out of the window and saw that it was raining. That made it sure that Margaret would not go back to Versailles in the motor car, but in the meantime she might very possibly be at Logotheti's, at luncheon.

He glanced at his watch, and a few minutes later he was on his bicycle again, an outlandish figure in his long-tailed, coffee-coloured overcoat and soft student's hat. He hitched up the tails as well as he could and sat on them, to keep them out of the mud, and he pulled the hat well down to keep the rain off his big spectacles and his nose. His own mother would certainly not have recognised him.

He spent a melancholy hour, riding up and down in the wet between the Place Péreire and the Place Wagram, till he wished with all his heart that he might never again set eyes on the statue of Alphonse de Neuville. Half the time, too, he was obliged to look back every moment in order to watch Logotheti's door, lest he should miss what he was waiting so patiently to see. The rain was cold, too, and persistent as it can be in Paris, even in spring. His gloves were pulpy and jellified, his spring-side kid boots felt as if he were taking a foot bath of cold glue, and some insidious drops of cold water were trickling down his back. The broad street was almost deserted, and when he met any one he wished it were altogether so. Yet he wondered why a man as rich as Logotheti should have built his house there.

At last his patience was rewarded. A brougham drove up past him at a smart pace, stopped before the door and waited. He turned back and wheeled round, crossing and re-crossing the street, so as to keep behind the carriage. As it was impossible to continue this singular exercise without attracting the attention of a policeman who came in sight just then, he rode on towards the Batignolles station. Just then, when his back was turned, he heard the door of the brougham sharply shut, and as he quickly turned again he saw the carriage driving off in the opposite direction. It was driving fast, but he overtook it in a couple of minutes and passed close to the window, which was half up, against the rain. He almost looked in as he went by, and suddenly he met Logotheti's almond eyes, looking straight at him, with an air of recognition. He bent his head, swerved away from the brougham and took the first turning out of the wide street. But he had seen that the Greek was alone in his carriage. Margaret had not lunched at the house in the Boulevard Péreire.

During the next few days Lushington did not lead a life of idle repose; in fact, he did not remember that he had ever taken so much exercise since his Oxford days. On an average he must have bicycled twenty or thirty miles between breakfast and dinner, which is not bad work for a literary man accustomed to spend most of his time at his writing-table and the rest in society. Unknown to himself, he was fast becoming one of the sights on the Versailles road, and the men at the octroi station grinned when he went by, and called him the crazy professor.

More than once he met the motor, bringing Margaret to town or taking her back, and though he did not again chance upon it when Logotheti was without his glasses and shield, he felt tolerably sure that he was the chauffeur, and Margaret was always alone in the body of the car. Twice he was quite certain that the two were talking when he saw them in the distance coming towards him, but when they passed him Margaret was leaning back quietly in her place, and the chauffeur merely glanced at him and then kept his eyes on the road. Margaret looked at him and smiled faintly, as if in spite of herself, most probably at his appearance.

He ascertained also that after one more rehearsal at the Opéra, Margaret did not go there again. The newspapers informed him very soon that Schreiermeyer had got his own company together and had borrowed the stage of an obscure theatre in the outskirts of Paris for the purpose of rehearsing. It had been an advantage for the young prima donna to sing two or three times with the great orchestra of the Opéra, but the arrangement could of course not continue. Margaret's début was to take place in July in a Belgian town.

Lushington was certain that Margaret had been at least once again to Logotheti's house with Madame De Rosa, but he did not believe that she had stayed to luncheon, for she had not remained in the house much over half-an-hour.

During all this time he made no attempt to communicate with her, and was uncomfortably aware that Logotheti was having it all his own way. He yielded to a morbid impulse in watching the two, since no good could come of it for himself or Margaret. Almost every time he went out on the Versailles road he knew that he should see them together before he came back, and he knew equally well that he could do nothing to separate them. He wondered what it was that attracted such a woman as Margaret Donne to such a man, and with a humility which his friends and enemies would have been far from suspecting in him he honestly tried to compare himself with Logotheti, and to define the points in which the latter had the advantage of him.

Very naturally, he failed to discover them. In spite of what philosophers tell us, most of us know ourselves pretty well. The conclusive and irrefutable proof of this is that we always know when we are not telling, or showing, the truth about ourselves, as, for instance, when we are boasting or attributing to ourselves some gift, some knowledge, or some power which we really do not possess. We also know perfectly well when our impulses are good and when they are bad, and can guess approximately how much courage we have in reserve for doing the one, and how far our natural cowardice will incline us to do the other. But we know very little indeed about other people, and almost always judge them by ourselves, because we have no other convenient standard. A great many men are influenced in the same general way by the big things in life, but one scarcely ever finds two men who are similarly affected by the little things from which all great results proceed. Mark Antony lost the world for a woman, but it was for a woman that Tallien overthrew Robespierre and saved France.

So Lushington's comparison came to nothing at all, and he was no nearer to a solution of his problem than before.

Then came the unexpected, and it furnished him with a surprisingly simple means of comparing himself with his rival in the eyes of Margaret herself.

There are several roads from Paris to Versailles, as every one knows, leaving the city on opposite sides of the Seine. Hitherto Logotheti had always taken the one that leads to the right bank, along the Avenue de Versailles to the Porte St. Cloud. Another follows the left bank by Bas Meudon, but the most pleasant road goes through the woods Fausses Reposes.

One morning, when he knew that there was to be a rehearsal, Lushington bicycled out by the usual way without meeting the motor car. It naturally occurred to him that Logotheti must have returned by another road. Whether he would bring Margaret out again by the same way or not, was of course uncertain, but Lushington resolved to try the Fausses Reposes on the chance of meeting the car, after waiting in Versailles as long as he thought the rehearsal might last.

He set out again about half-past one. The road is in parts much more lonely than the others, especially in the woods, and is much less straight; there are sharp turns to the right and left in several places. Lushington did not know the road very well and hesitated more than once, going slowly and fast by turns, and at the end of half-an-hour he felt almost sure that he had either lost his way or that Logotheti was coming back by another route.

CHAPTER XV

Margaret knew by this time that Logotheti was really very much in love; she was equally sure that she was not, and that when she encouraged him she was yielding to a rather complicated temptation that presented elements of amusement and of mild danger. In plain English, she was playing with the man, though she guessed that he was not the kind of man who would allow himself to be played with very long.

There are not many young women who could resist such a temptation under the circumstances, and small blame to them. Margaret had done nothing to attract the Greek and was too unsophisticated to understand the nature of her involuntary influence over him. He was still young, he was unlike other men and he was enormously rich; a little familiarity with him had taught her that there was nothing vulgar about him below the surface, and he treated her with all the respect she could exact when she chose to put herself in his power. The consequence was that as she felt nothing herself she sometimes could not resist making little experiments, just to see how far he would run on the chain by which she held him. Besides, she was flattered by his devotion.

It was not a noble game that she was playing with him, but in real life very few young men and women of two-and-twenty are 'noble' all the time. A good many never are at all; and Margaret had at least the excuse that the victim of her charms was no simple sensitive soul with morbid instincts of suicide, like the poor youth who cut his throat for Lady Clara Vere de Vere, but a healthy millionaire of five-and-thirty who enjoyed the reputation of having seen everything and done most things in a not particularly well-spent life.

Besides, she ran a risk, and knew it. The victim might turn at any moment, and perhaps rend her. Sometimes there was a quick glance in the almond-shaped eyes which sent a little thrill of not altogether unpleasant fear through her. She had seen a woman put her head into a wild beast's mouth, and she knew that the woman was never quite sure of getting it out again. That was part of the game, and the woman probably enjoyed the sensation and the doubt, since playing for one s life is much more exciting than playing for one's money. Margaret began to understand the lion-tamer's sensations, and not being timid she almost wished that her lion would show his teeth. She gave herself the luxury of wondering what form his wrath would take when he was tired of being played with.

He was already approaching that point, on the day when Lushington was looking out for him on the road through the Fausses Reposes woods. When they were well away from the city, he slackened his speed as usual and began to talk.

'I wish,' he said, 'that you would sometimes be in earnest. Won't you try?'

'You might not like it,' Margaret answered, carelessly. 'For my part, I sometimes wish that you were not quite so much in earnest yourself!'

'Do I bore you?'

'No. You never bore me, but you make me feel wicked, and that is very disagreeable. It is inconsiderate of you to give me the impression that I am a sort of Lorelei, coolly luring you to your destruction! Besides, you would not be so easily destroyed, after all. You are able to take care of yourself, I fancy.'

'Yes. I think my heart will be the last of me to break.' He laughed and looked at her. 'But that is no reason why you should try to twist my arms and legs off, as boys do to beetles.'

'I wish I could catch a boy doing it!'

'You may catch a woman at it any day. They do to men what boys do to insects. Cruelty to insects or animals? Abominable! Shocking! There is the society, there are fines, there is prison, to punish it! Cruelty to human beings? Bah! They have souls! What does it matter, if they suffer? Suffering purifies the spirit for a better life!'

'Nonsense!'

'That is easily said. But it was on that principle that Philip burned the Jews, and they did not think it was nonsense. The beetles don't think it funny to be pulled to pieces, either. I don't. A large class of us don't, and yet you women have been doing it ever since Eve made a fool and a sinner of the only man who happened to be in the world just then. He was her husband, which was an excuse, but that's of no consequence to the argument.'

'Perhaps not, but the argument, as you call it, doesn't prove anything in particular, except that you are calling me names!' Margaret laughed again. 'After all,' she went on, 'I do the best I can to be--what shall I say?--the contrary of disagreeable! You ask me to let you take me to my rehearsals, and I come day after day, risking something, because you are disguised. I don't risk much, perhaps-- Mrs. Rushmore's disapproval. But that is something, for she has been very, very good to me and I wouldn't lose her good opinion for a great deal. And you ask me to lunch with you, and I come--at least, I've been twice to your house, and I've lunched once. Really, if you are not satisfied, you're hard to please! We've hardly known each other a month.'

'During which time I've never had but one idea. Don't raise your beautiful eyebrows as if you didn't understand!' He spoke very gently and smiled, though she could not see that.

'You've no idea how funny that is!' laughed Margaret.

'What?'

'If you could see yourself, and hear yourself at the same time! With those goggles, and your leather cap and all the rest, you look like the Frog Footman in Little Alice--or the dragon in Siegfried! It does very well as long as you are disagreeable, but when you speak softly and throw intense expression into your voice'--she mimicked his tone--'it's really too funny, you know! It's just as if Fafnir were to begin singing "Una furtiva lacrima" in a voice like Caruso's! Siegfried would go into convulsions of laughter, instead of slitting the dragon's throat.'

'I wasn't trying to be picturesque just then,' answered Logotheti, quite unmoved by the chaff. 'I was only expressing my idea. I've known you about a month. The second time we met, I asked you to marry me, and I've asked you several times since. As you can't attribute any interested motive to my determination----'

'Eh?'

'I said, to my determination----'

'Determination? How that sounds!'

'It sounds very like what I mean,' answered Logotheti, in an indifferent tone.

'But really, how can you "determine" to marry me, if I won't agree?'

'I'll make you,' he replied with perfect calm.

'That sounds like a threat,' said Margaret, her voice hardening a little, though she tried to speak lightly.

'A threat implies that the thing to be done to the person threatened is painful or at least disagreeable. Doesn't it? I'm only a Greek, of course, and I don't pretend to know English well! I wish you would sometimes correct my mistakes. It would be so kind of you!'

'You know English quite as well as I do,' Margaret answered. 'Your definition is perfect.'

'Oh! Then would it be painful, or disagreeable to you, to marry me?'

Margaret laughed, but hesitated a moment.

'It's always disagreeable to be made to do anything against one's will,' she answered.

'I'm sorry,' said Logotheti coolly, 'but it can't be helped.'

She was not quite sure how it would be best to meet this uncompromising statement, and she thought it wiser to laugh again, though she felt quite sure that at the moment there was that quick gleam in his eyes, behind the goggles, which had more than once frightened her a little. But he was looking at the road again, and a moment later he had put the car at full speed along a level stretch. That meant that the conversation was at an end for a little while. Then an accident happened.

A straight rush up an easy incline towards a turning ahead, and the deep note of the horn; round the corner to the right, close in; the flash of a bicycle coming down on the wrong side, and swerving desperately; a little brittle smashing of steel; then a man sprawling on his face in the road as the motor car flew on.

Logotheti kept his eyes on the road, one hand went down to the levers and the machine sprang forward at forty miles an hour.

'Stop!' cried Margaret. 'Stop! you've killed him!'

Full speed. Fifty miles an hour now, on another level stretch beyond the turn. No sign of intelligence from Logotheti. Both hands on the wheel.

'Stop, I say!' Margaret's voice rang out clear and furious.

Logotheti's hands did not move. Margaret knew what to do. She had often been in motor cars and had driven a little herself. She was strong and perfectly fearless. Before Logotheti saw what she was going to do, she was beside him, she had thrown herself across him and had got at the brake and levers. He was too much surprised to make any resistance; he probably would not have tried to hinder her in any case, as he could not have done so without using his strength. The car was stopped in a few seconds; he had intuitively steered it until it stood still.

'How ridiculous!' he exclaimed. 'As if one ever stopped for such a thing!'

Margaret's eyes flashed angrily and her answer came short and sharp.

'Turn back at once,' she said, and she sat down beside him on the front seat.

He obeyed, for he could do nothing else. In running away from the accident, he had simply done what most chauffeurs do under the circumstances. His experience told him that the man was not killed, though he had lain motionless in the road for a few moments. Logotheti had seen perfectly well that the car had struck the hind wheel of the bicycle without touching the man's body. Moreover, the man had been on the wrong side of the road, and it was his fault that he had been run into. Logotheti had not meant to give him a chance to make out a case.

But now he turned back, obedient to Margaret's command. Before she had stopped the car it had run nearly a mile from the scene of the accident. When it reached the spot again, coming back at a more moderate pace, nearly five minutes had elapsed. She found the man leaning against the rail fence that followed the outer curve of the turning. It was the man they had so often met on the other road, in his square-toed kid boots and ill-fitting clothes; it was Edmund Lushington, with his soft student's hat off, and his face a good deal scratched by the smashing of his tortoise-shell-rimmed spectacles. They had been tied behind with a black string, and the rims of them, broken in two, hung from his ears. His nose was bleeding profusely, as he leaned against the fence, holding his head down. He was covered with mud, his clothes were torn, and he was as miserable, damaged and undignified a piece of man as ever dreaded being taken at disadvantage by the idol of his affections. He would have made a pact with the powers of evil for a friendly wall or a clump of trees when he saw the car coming back. There was nothing but the fence.

The car stopped close beside him. He held his handkerchief to his nose, covering half his face as he looked up.

'Are you hurt, Monsieur?' Margaret asked anxiously in French.

'On the contrary, Mademoiselle,' Lushington answered through the handkerchief, and it sounded as if he had a bad cold in the head.

'I am afraid----' Margaret began, and then stopped suddenly, staring at him.

'You were on the wrong side of the road, Monsieur,' said Logotheti in an assertive tone.

'Perfectly,' assented Lushington, holding his nose and turning half away.

'Then it was your fault,' observed Logotheti.

'Precisely,' admitted the other. 'Pray don't stop. It's of no consequence!'

But he had betrayed himself unconsciously, in the most natural way. His spectacles were gone, and by covering the lower part of his face with his handkerchief he had entirely concealed the very great change made by shaving his beard and moustache. While he and Logotheti had been speaking, Margaret had scrutinised his features and had made sure of the truth. Then she believed that she would have recognised him by his voice alone. Between the emotion that followed the accident and the extreme anxiety his position caused him, the perspiration stood in beads on his forehead. Margaret smiled maliciously, for she remembered how often they had passed him on the road, and realised in an instant that he had disguised himself to watch her doings. He should pay for that.

'You look hot,' she observed in English, fixing her eyes on him severely.

He blushed to the roots of his hair, though he had been rather pale. Logotheti, whose only preoccupation hitherto had been to get away as soon as possible, now stared at him, too. Margaret's tone and her sudden change to the use of English did the rest. He recognised Lushington, but remembered that he himself was completely disguised in his chauffeur's dress and mask; so he said nothing.

Lushington writhed under Margaret's eyes for a moment; but then his English courage and coolness suddenly returned, the colour subsided from his face and his expression hardened, as far as the necessary handkerchief permitted her to see it.

'Yes,' he said, 'I'm Lushington. I can only repeat that the accident happened by my fault. I'm used to taking the left side in England and I lost my head. Monsieur Logotheti need not have run away, for it would never have occurred to me to make a complaint.'

He looked straight at Logotheti's goggles as he spoke, and Margaret began to feel uncomfortable.

'I supposed that you had recognised me,' observed the Greek coldly. 'That is, no doubt, why you have taken the trouble to disguise yourself and watch me of late.'

'That was the reason,' answered Lushington, facing his adversary, but conscious that the necessity for holding his nose put him at a disadvantage as to his dignity.

'It was very well done,' said the Greek with gravity. 'I should never have known you.'

'Your own disguise is admirable,' answered the Englishman, with cool politeness. 'If I had not seen you without your mask the other day

I should not have recognised you.'

'Shall we go on?' inquired Logotheti, turning to Margaret.

'No,' she answered, rather sharply. 'Are you hurt?' she inquired, looking at Lushington again.

He was busy with his nose, which he had neglected for a few moments. He shook his head.

'I won't leave him here in this state,' Margaret said to Logotheti.

The Greek made a gesture of indifference, but said nothing. Meanwhile Lushington got so far as to be able to speak again.

'Please go on,' he said. 'I can take care of myself, thank you. There are no bones broken.'

Logotheti inwardly regretted that his adversary had not broken his neck, but he had tact enough to see that he must take Margaret's side or risk losing favour in her eyes.

'I really don't see how we can leave you here,' he said to Lushington. 'Your bicycle is smashed. I had not realised that. I'll put what's left of it into the car.'

He jumped out as he spoke, and before Lushington could hinder him he had hold of the broken wheel. But Lushington followed quickly, and while he held his nose with his left hand, he grabbed the bicycle with the other. It looked as if the two were going to try which could pull harder.

'Let it alone, please,' said Lushington, speaking with difficulty.

'No, no'! protested Logotheti politely, for he wished to please Margaret. 'You must really let me put it in.'

'Not at all!' retorted Lushington. 'I'll walk it to Chaville.'

'But I assure you, you can't!' retorted the Greek. 'Your hind wheel is broken to bits! It won't go round. You would have to carry it!'

And he gently pulled with both hands.

'Then I'll throw the beastly thing away!' answered Lushington, who did not relinquish his hold. 'It's of no consequence!'

'On the contrary,' objected Logotheti, still pulling, 'I know about those things. It can be made a very good bicycle again for next to nothing.'

'All the better for the beggar who finds it!' cried the Englishman. 'Throw it over the fence!'

'You English are so extravagant,' said the Greek in a tone of polite reproach, but not relinquishing his hold.

'Possibly, but it's my own bicycle, and I prefer to throw it away.'

Margaret had watched the contest in silence. She now stepped out of the car, came up to the two men and laid her hands on the object of contention. Logotheti let go instantly, but Lushington did not.

'This is ridiculous,' said Margaret. 'Give it to me!'

Lushington had no choice, and besides, he needed his right hand for his nose, which was getting the better of him again. He let go, and Margaret lifted the bicycle into the body of the car herself, though Logotheti tried to help her.

'Now, get in,' she said to Lushington. 'We'll take you as far at the Chaville station.'

'Thank you,' he answered. 'I am quite able to walk.'

He presented such a lamentable appearance that he would have hesitated to get into the car with Margaret even if they had been on good terms. He was in that state of mind in which a man wishes that he might vanish into the earth like Korah and his company, or at least take to his heels without ceremony and run away. Logotheti had put up his glasses and shield, over the visor of his cap, and was watching his rival's discomfiture with a polite smile of pity. Lushington mentally compared him to Judas Iscariot.

'Let me point out,' said the Greek, that if you won't accept a seat with us, we, on our part, are much too anxious for your safety to leave you here in the road. You must have been badly shaken, besides being cut. If you insist upon walking, we'll keep beside you in the car. Then if you faint, we can pick you up.'

'Yes,' assented Margaret, with a touch of malice, 'that is very sensible.'

Lushington was almost choking.

'Do let me give you another handkerchief,' said Logotheti, sympathetically. 'I always carry a supply when I'm motoring--they are so useful. Yours is quite spoilt.'

A forcible expression rose to Lushington's lips, but he checked it, and at the same time he wondered whether anybody he knew had ever been caught in such a detestable situation. But Anglo-Saxons generally perform their greatest feats of arms when they are driven into a corner or have launched themselves in some perfectly hopeless undertaking. It takes a Lucknow or a Balaclava to show what they are really made of. Lushington was in a corner now; his temper rose and he turned upon his tormentors. At the same time, perhaps under the influence of his emotion, his nose stopped bleeding. It was scratched and purple from the fall, but he found another handkerchief of his own and did what he could to improve his appearance. His shoulders and his jaw squared themselves as he began to speak and his eyes were rather hard and bright.

'Look here,' he said, facing Logotheti, 'we don't owe each other anything, I think, so this sort of thing had better stop. You've been going about in disguise with Miss Donne, and I have been making myself look like some one else in order to watch you. We've found each other out and I don t fancy that we're likely to be very friendly after this. So the best thing we can do is to part quietly and go in opposite directions. Don't you think so?'

The last question was addressed to Margaret. But instead of answering at once she looked down and pushed some little lumps of dry mud about with the toe of her shoe, as if she were trying to place them in a symmetrical figure. It is a trick some young women have when they are in doubt. Lushington turned to Logotheti again and waited for an answer.

Now Logotheti did not care a straw for Lushington, and cared very little, on the whole, whether the latter watched him or not; but he was extremely anxious to please Margaret and play the part of generosity in her eyes.

'I'm very sorry if anything I've said has offended you,' he said in a smooth tone, answering Lushington. 'The fact is, it's all rather funny, isn't it? Yes, just so! I'm making the best apology I can for having been a little amused. I hope we part good friends, Mr. Lushington? That is, if you still insist on walking.'

Margaret looked up while he was speaking and nodded her approbation of the speech, which was very well conceived and left Lushington no loophole through which to spy offence. But he responded coldly to the advance.

'There is no reason whatever for apologising,' he said. 'It's the instinct of humanity to laugh at a man who tumbles down in the street. The object of our artificial modern civilisation is, however, to cloak that sort of instinct as far as possible. Good morning.'

After delivering this Parthian shot he turned away with the evident intention of going off on foot.

None of the three had noticed the sound of horses' feet and a light carriage approaching from the direction of Versailles. A phaeton came along at a smart pace and drew up beside the motor. Margaret uttered an exclamation of surprise, and the two men stared with something approaching to horror. It was Mrs. Rushmore, who had presumably taken a fancy for an airing as the day had turned out very fine. The coachman and groom had both seen Margaret and supposed that something had happened to the car.

Before the carriage had stopped Mrs. Rushmore had recognised Margaret too, and was leaning out sideways, uttering loud exclamations of anxiety.

'My dear child!' she cried. 'Good heavens! An accident! These dreadful automobiles! I knew it would happen!'

Portly though she was, she was standing beside Margaret in an instant, clasping her in a motherly embrace and panting for breath. It was evidently too late for Logotheti to draw his glasses and shield over his face, or for Lushington to escape. Each stood stock-still, wondering how long it would be before Mrs. Rushmore recognised him, and trying to think what she would say when she did. For one moment, it seemed as if nothing were going to happen, for Mrs. Rushmore was too much preoccupied on Margaret's account to take the slightest notice of either of the others.

'Are you quite sure you're not hurt?' she inquired anxiously, while she scrutinised Margaret's blushing face. 'Get into the carriage with me at once, my dear, and we'll drive home. You must go to bed at once! There's nothing so exhausting as a shock to the nerves! Camomile tea, my dear! Good old-fashioned camomile tea, you know! There's nothing like it! Clotilde makes it to perfection, and she shall rub you thoroughly! Get in, child! Get in!'

Quick to see the advantage of such a sudden escape, Margaret was actually getting into the carriage, when Mrs. Rushmore, who was kindness itself, remembered the two men and turned to Logotheti.

'I will leave you my groom to help,' she said, in her stiff French.

Then her eyes fell on Lushington's blood-stained face, and in the same instant it flashed upon her that the other man was Logotheti. Her jaw dropped in astonishment.

'Why--good gracious--how's this? Why--it's Monsieur Logotheti himself! But you'--she turned to Lushington again 'you can't be Mr. Lushington--good Lord--yes, you are, and in those clothes, too. And--what have you done to your face?'

As her surprise increased she became speechless, while the two men bowed and smiled as pleasantly as they could under the circumstances.

'Yes, I'm Lushington,' said the Englishman. 'I used to wear a beard.'

'My chauffeur was taken ill suddenly,' said the Greek without a blush, 'and as Miss Donne was anxious to get home I thought there would be no great harm if I drove the car out myself. I had hoped to find you in so that I might explain how it had happened, for, of course, Miss Donne was a little--what shall I say?--a little----'

He hesitated, having hoped that Margaret would help him out. After waiting two or three seconds, Mrs. Rushmore turned on her.

'Margaret, what were you?' she asked with severity. 'I insist upon knowing what you were.'

'I'm sure I don't know,' Margaret answered, trying to speak easily, as if it did not matter much. 'It was very kind of Monsieur Logotheti, at all events, and I'm much obliged to him.'

'Oh, and pray, what has happened to Mr. Lushington?' inquired Mrs. Rushmore.

'I was on the wrong side of the road, and the car knocked me off my bicycle,' added Lushington. 'They kindly stopped to pick me up. They thought I was hurt.'

'Well--you are,' said Mrs. Rushmore. 'Why don't you get into the automobile and let Monsieur Logotheti take you home?'

As it was not easy to explain why he preferred walking in his battered condition, Lushington said nothing. Mrs. Rushmore turned to her groom, who was English.

'William,' she said, 'you must have a clothes-brush.'

William had one concealed in some mysterious place under the box.

'Clean Mr. Lushington, William,' said the good lady.

[Illustration: "'Clean Mr. Lushington, William,' said the good lady."]

'Oh, thank you--no--thanks very much,' protested Lushington.

But William, having been told to clean him, proceeded to do so, gently and systematically, beginning at his neck and proceeding thence with bold curving strokes of the brush, as if he were grooming a horse.

Instinctively Lushington turned slowly round on his heels, while he submitted to the operation, and the others looked on. They had ample time to note the singular cut of his clothes.

'He used to be always so well dressed!' said Mrs. Rushmore to Margaret in an audible whisper.

Lushington winced visibly, but as he was not supposed to hear the words he said nothing. William had worked down to the knees of his trousers, which he grasped firmly in one hand while he vigorously brushed the cloth with the other.

'That will do, thank you,' said Lushington, trying to draw back one captive leg.

But William was inexorable and there was no escape from his hold. He was an Englishman, and was therefore thorough; he was a servant, and he therefore thoroughly enjoyed the humour of seeing his betters in a pickle.

'And now, my dear,' said Mrs. Rushmore to Margaret, 'get in and I'll take you home. You can explain everything on the way. That's enough, William. Put away your brush.'

Margaret had no choice, since fate had intervened.

'I'm very much obliged to you,' she said, nodding to Logotheti; 'and I hope you'll be none the worse,' she added, smiling at Lushington.

Mrs. Rushmore bent her head with dignified disapproval, first to one and then to the other, and got into the carriage as if she were mounting the steps of a throne. She further manifested her displeasure at the whole affair by looking straight before her at the buttons on the back of the coachman's coat after she had taken her seat. Margaret got in lightly after her and she scarcely glanced at Logotheti as the carriage turned; but her eyes lingered a little with an expression that was almost sad as she met Lushington's. She was conscious of a reaction of feeling; she was sorry that she had helped to make him suffer, that she had been amused by his damaged condition and by his general discomfiture. He had made her respect him in spite of herself, just when she had thought that she could never respect him again; and suddenly the deep sympathy for him welled up, which she had taken for love, and which was as near to love as anything her heart had yet felt for a man.

She knew, too, that it was really her heart, and nothing else, where he was concerned. She was human, she was young, she was more alive than ordinary women, as great singers generally are, and Logotheti's ruthless masculine vitality stirred her and drew her to him in a way she did not quite like. His presence disturbed her oddly and she was a little ashamed of liking the sensation, for she knew quite well that such feelings had nothing to do with what she called her real self. She might have hated him and even despised him, but she could never have been indifferent when he was close to her. Sometimes the mere touch of his hand at meeting or parting thrilled her and made her feel as if she were going to blush. But she was never really in sympathy with him as she was with Lushington.

'And now, Margaret,' said Mrs. Rushmore after a silence that had lasted a full minute, 'I insist on knowing what all this means.'

Margaret inwardly admitted that Mrs. Rushmore had some right to insist, but she was a little doubtful herself about the meaning of what had happened. If it meant anything, it meant that she had been flirting rather rashly and had got into a scrape. She wondered what the two men were saying now that they were alone together, and she turned her head to look over the back of the phaeton, but a turn of the road already hid the motor car from view.

Meanwhile Mrs. Rushmore's face showed that she still insisted, and Margaret had to say something. As she was a truthful person it was not easy to decide what to say, and while she was hesitating Mrs. Rushmore expressed herself again.

'Margaret,' said she, 'I'm surprised at you. It makes no difference what you say. I'm surprised.'

The words were spoken with a slow and melancholy intonation that might have indicated anything but astonishment.

'Yes,' Margaret remarked rather desperately, 'I don't wonder. I suppose I've been flirting outrageously with them both. But I really could not foresee that one would run over the other and that you would appear just at that moment, could I? I'm helpless. I've nothing to say. You must have flirted when you were young. Try to remember what it was like, and make allowance for human weakness!'

She laughed nervously and glanced nervously at her companion, but Mrs. Rushmore's face was like iron.

'Mr. Rushmore,' said the latter, alluding to her departed husband, 'would not have understood such conduct.'

Margaret thought this was very probable, judging from the likenesses of the late Ransom Rushmore which she had seen. There was one in particular, an engraving of him when he had been president of some big company, which had always filled her with a vague uneasiness. In her thoughts she called him the 'commercial missionary,' and was glad for his sake and her own that he was safe in heaven, with no present prospect of getting out.

'I'm sorry,' she said, without much contrition. 'I mean,' she went on, correcting herself, and with more feeling, 'I'm sorry I've done anything that you don't like, for you've been ever so good to me.'

'So have other people,' answered the elder woman with an air of mystery and reproof.

'Oh yes! I know! Everybody has been very kind--especially

Madame Bonanni.'

'Should you be surprised to hear that the individual who bought out Mr. Moon and made you independent, did it from purely personal motives?'

Margaret turned to her quickly in great surprise.

'What do you mean? I thought it was a company. You said so.'

'In business, one man can be a company, if he owns all the stock,' said Mrs. Rushmore, sententiously.

'I don't understand those things,' Margaret answered, impatient to know the truth. 'Who was it?'

'I hardly think I ought to tell you, my dear. I promised not to. But I will allow you to guess. That's quite different from telling, and I think you ought to know, because you are under great obligations to him.'

'You don't mean to say----' Margaret stopped, and the blood rose slowly in her face.

'You may ask me if it was one of those two gentlemen we have just left in the road,' said Mrs. Rushmore. 'But mind, I'm not telling you!'

'Monsieur Logotheti!' Margaret leaned back and bit her lip.

'You've made the discovery yourself, Margaret. Remember that I've told you nothing. I promised not to, but I thought you ought to know.'

'It's an outrage!' cried Margaret, breaking out. 'How did you dare to take money from him for me?'

Mrs. Rushmore seemed really surprised now, though she did not say she was.

'My dear!' she exclaimed, 'you would not have had me refuse, would you? Money is money, you know.'

The good lady's inherited respect for the stuff was discernible in her tone.

'Money!' Margaret repeated the word with profound contempt and a good deal of anger.

'Yes, my dear,' retorted Mrs. Rushmore severely. 'Yes, money. It is because your father and mother spoke of it in that silly, contemptuous way that they died so poor. And now that you've got it, take my advice and don't turn up your nose at it.'

'Do you suppose I'll keep it, now that I know where it comes from? I'll give it back to him to-day!'

'No, you won't,' answered Mrs. Rushmore, with the conviction of certainty.

'I tell you I will!' Margaret cried. 'I could not sleep to-night if I knew that I had money in my possession that was given me--given me like a gift--by a man who wants to marry me! Ugh! It's disgusting!'

'Margaret, this is ridiculous. Monsieur Logotheti came to see me and explained the whole matter. He said that he had made a very good bargain and expected to realise a large sum by the transaction. Do you suppose that such a good man of business would think of making any one a present of a hundred thousand pounds? You must be mad! A hundred thousand pounds is a great deal of money, Margaret. Remember that.'

'So much the better for him! I shall give it back to him at once!'

Mrs. Rushmore smiled.

'You can't,' she said. 'You've never even asked me where it is, and while you are out of your mind, I shall certainly not tell you. You seem to forget that when I undertook to bring suit against Alvah Moon you gave me a general power of attorney to manage your affairs. I shall do whatever is best for you.'

'I don't understand business,' Margaret answered, 'but I'm sure you have no power to force Monsieur Logotheti's money upon me. I won't take it.'

'You have taken it and I have given a receipt for it, my dear, so it's of no use to talk nonsense. The best thing you can do is to give up this silly idea of going on the stage, and just live like a lady, on your income.'

'And marry my benefactor, I suppose!' Margaret's eyes flashed. 'That's what he wants--what you all want--to keep me from singing! He thought that if he made me independent, I would give it up, and you encouraged him! I see it now. As for the money itself, until I really have it in my hands it's not mine; but just as soon as it is I'll give it back to him, and I'll tell him so to-day.'

The carriage rolled through the pretty woods of Fausses Reposes, and the sweet spring breeze fanned Margaret's cheeks in the shade. But she felt fever in her blood and her heart beat fast and angrily as if it were a conscious creature imprisoned in a cage. She was angry with herself and with every one else, with Logotheti, with Mrs. Rushmore, with poor Lushington for making such a fool of himself just when she was prepared to like him better than ever. She was sure that she had good cause to hate every one, and she hated accordingly, with a good will. She wished that she might never spend another hour under Mrs. Rushmore's roof, that she might never see Logotheti again, that she were launched in her artistic career, free at last and responsible to no one for her actions, her words or her thoughts.

But Mrs. Rushmore began to think that she had made a mistake in letting her know too soon who had bought out Alvah Moon, and she wondered vaguely why she had betrayed the secret, trying to account for her action on the ground of some reasonably thought-out argument, which was quite impossible, of course. So they both maintained a rather hostile silence during the rest of the homeward drive.

CHAPTER XVI

Until the carriage was out of sight, Logotheti and Lushington stood still where Margaret had left them. Then Lushington looked at his adversary coolly for about four seconds, stuck his hands into his pockets, turned his back and deliberately walked off without a word. Logotheti was so little prepared for such an abrupt closure that he stood looking after the Englishman in surprise till the latter had made a dozen steps.

'I say!' said the Greek, calling after him then and affecting an exceedingly English tone. 'I say, you know! This won't do.'

Lushington stopped, turned on his heel and faced him from a distance.

'What won't do?' he asked coolly.

Seeing that he came no nearer, Logotheti went forward a little.

'You admitted just now that you had been playing the spy,' said the Greek, whose temper was getting beyond his control, now that the women were gone.

'Yes,' said Lushington, 'I've been watching you.'

'I said spying,' answered Logotheti; 'I used the word "spy." Do you understand?'

'Perfectly.'

'You don't seem to. I'm insulting you. I mean to insult you.'

'Oh!' A faint smile crossed the Englishman's face. 'You want me to send you a couple of friends and fight a duel with you? I won't do anything so silly. As I told you before Miss Donne, we don't owe each other anything to speak of, so we may as well part without calling each other bad names.'

'If that is your view of it, you had better keep out of my way in future.' He laid his hand on the car to get in as he spoke.

Lushington's face hardened.

'I shall not take any pains to do that,' he answered. 'On the contrary, if you go on doing what you have been doing of late, you'll find me very much in your way.'

Logotheti turned upon him savagely.

'Do you want to marry Miss Donne yourself?' he asked.

Lushington, who was perfectly cool now that no woman was present, was struck by the words, which contained a fair question, though the tone was angry and aggressive.

'No,' he answered quietly. 'Do you?'

Logotheti stared at him.

'What the devil did you dare to think that I meant?' he asked. 'It would give me the greatest satisfaction to break your bones for asking that!'

Lushington came a step nearer, his hands in his pockets, though his eyes were rather bright.

'You may try if you like,' he said. 'But I've something more to say, and I don't think we need fall to fisticuffs on the highroad like a couple of bargees. I've misunderstood you. If you are going to marry Miss Donne, I shall keep out of your way altogether. I made a mistake, because you haven't the reputation of a saint, and when a man of your fortune runs after a young singer it's not usually with the idea of marrying her. I'm glad I was wrong.'

Logotheti was too good a judge of men to fancy that Lushington was in the least afraid of him, or that he spoke from any motive but a fair and firm conviction; and the Greek himself, with many faults, was too brave not to be generous. He turned again to get into the car.

'I believe you English take it for granted that every foreigner is a born scoundrel,' he said with something like a laugh.

'To tell the truth,' Lushington answered, 'I believe we do. But we are willing to admit that we can be mistaken. Good morning.'

He walked away, and this time Logotheti did not stop him, but got in and started the car in the opposite direction without looking back. He was conscious of wishing that he might kill the cool Englishman, and though his expression betrayed nothing but annoyance a little colour rose and settled on his cheek-bones; and that bodes no good in the faces of dark men when they are naturally pale. He reached home, and it was there still; he changed his clothes, and yet it was not gone; he drank a cup of coffee and smoked a big cigar, and the faint red spots were still there, though he seemed absorbed in the book he was reading.

It was not his short interview with Lushington which had so much moved him, though it had been the first disturbing cause. In men whose nature, physical and moral, harks back to the savage ancestor, to the pirate of northern or southern seas, to the Bedouin of the desert, to the Tartar of Bokhara or the Suliote of Albania, the least bit of a quarrel stirs up all the blood at once, and the mere thought of a fight rouses every masculine passion. The silent Scotchman, the stately Arab, the courtly Turk are far nearer to the fanatic than the quick-tempered Frenchman or the fiery Italian.

For a long time Constantine Logotheti had been playing at civilisation, at civilised living and especially at the more or less gentle diversion of civilised love-making; but he was suddenly tired of it all, because it had never been quite natural to him, and he grew bodily hungry and thirsty for what he wanted. The round flushed spots on his cheeks were the outward signs of something very like a fever which had seized him within the last two hours. Until then he would hardly have believed that his magnificent artificial calm could break down, and that he could wish to get his hands on another man's throat, or take by force the woman he loved, and drag her away to his own lawless East. He wondered now why he had not fallen upon Lushington and tried to kill him in the road. He wondered why, when Margaret had been safe in the motor car, he had not put the machine at full speed for Havre, where his yacht was lying. His artificial civilisation had hindered him of course! It would not check him now, if Lushington were within arm's length, or if Margaret were in his power. It would be very bad for any one to come between him and what he wanted so much, just then, that his throat was dry and he could hear his heart beating as he sat in his chair. He sat there a long time because he was not sure what he might do if he allowed himself the liberty of crossing the room. If he did that, he might write a note, or go to the telephone, or ring for his secretary, or do one of fifty little things whereby the train of the inevitable may be started in the doubtful moments of life.

It did not occur to him that he was not the arbiter of his actions in that moment, free to choose between good and evil, which he, perhaps, called by other names just then. He probably could not have remembered a moment in his whole life at which he had not believed himself the master of his own future, with full power to do this, or that, or to leave it undone. And now he was quite sure that he was choosing the part of wisdom in resisting the strong temptation to do something rash, which made it a physical effort to sit still and keep his eyes on his book. He held the volume firmly with both hands as if he were clinging to something fixed which secured him from being made to move against his will.

One of fate's most amusing tricks is to let us work with might and main to help her on, while she makes us believe that we are straining every nerve and muscle to force her back.

If Logotheti had not insisted on sitting still that afternoon nothing might have happened. If he had gone out, or if he had shut himself up with his statue, beyond the reach of visitors, his destiny might have been changed, and one of the most important events of his life might never have come to pass.

But he sat still with his book, firm as a rock, sure of himself, convinced that he was doing the best thing, proud of his strength of mind and his obstinacy, perfectly pharisaical in his contempt of human weakness, persuaded that no power in earth or heaven could force him to do or say anything against his mature judgment. He sat in his deep chair near a window that was half open, his legs stretched straight out before him, his flashing patent leather feet crossed in a manner which showed off the most fantastically over-embroidered silk socks, tightly drawn over his lean but solid ankles.

From the wall behind him the strange face in the encaustic painting watched him with drooping lids and dewy lips that seemed to quiver; the ancient woman, ever young, looked as if she knew that he was thinking of her and that he would not turn round to see her because she was so like Margaret Donne.

His back was to the picture, but his face was to the door. It opened softly, he looked up from his book and Margaret was before him, coming quickly forward. For an instant he did not move, for he was taken unawares. Behind her, by the door, a man-servant gesticulated apologies--the lady had pushed by him before he had been able to announce her. Then another figure appeared, hurrying after Margaret; it was little Madame De Rosa, out of breath.

Logotheti got up now, and when he was on his feet, Margaret was already close to him. She was pale and her eyes were bright, and when she spoke he felt the warmth of her breath in his face. He held out his hand mechanically, but he hardly noticed that she did not take it.

'I want to speak to you alone,' she said.

Madame De Rosa evidently understood that nothing more was expected of her for the present, and she sat down and made herself comfortable.

'Will you come with me?' Logotheti asked, controlling his voice.

Margaret nodded; he led the way and they left the room together. Just outside the door there was a small lift. He turned up the electric light, and Margaret stepped in; then he followed and worked the lift himself. In the narrow space there was barely room for two; Logotheti felt a throbbing in his temples and the red spots on his cheek-bones grew darker. He could hear and almost feel Margaret's slightest movement as she stood close behind him while he faced the shut door of the machine. He did not know why she had come, he did not guess why she wished to be alone with him, but that was what she had asked, and he was taking her where they would really be alone together; and it was not his fault. Why had she come?

When a terrible accident happens to a man, the memory of all his life may pass before his eyes in the interval of a second or two. I once knew a man who fell from the flying trapeze in a circus in Berlin, struck on one of the ropes to which the safety net was laced and broke most of his bones. He told me that he had never before understood the meaning of eternity, but that ever afterwards, for him, it meant the time that had passed after he had missed his hold and before he struck and was unconscious. He could associate nothing else with the word. Logotheti remembered, as long as he lived, the interminable interval between Margaret's request to see him alone, and the noiseless closing of the sound-proof door when they had entered the upper room, where Aphrodite stood in the midst and the soft light fell from high windows that were half-shaded.

Even then, though her anger was hot and her thoughts were chasing one another furiously, Margaret could not repress an exclamation of surprise when she first saw the statue facing her in its bare beauty, like a living thing.

Logotheti laid one hand very lightly upon her arm, and was going to say something, but she sprang back from his touch as if it burnt her. The colour deepened in his dark cheeks and his eyes seemed brighter and nearer together. When a woman comes to a man's house and asks to be alone with him, she need not play horror because the tips of his fingers rest on her sleeve for a moment. Why did she come?

Margaret spoke first.

'How did you dare to settle money on me?' she asked, standing back from him.

Logotheti understood for the first time that she was angry with him, and that her anger had brought her to his house. The fact did not impress him much, though he wished she were in a better temper. The sound of her voice was sweet to him whatever she said.

'Oh?' he ejaculated with a sort of thoughtful interrogation. 'Has she told you? She had agreed to say nothing about it. How very annoying!'

His sudden calm was exasperating, for Margaret did not know him well enough to see that below the surface his blood was boiling. She tapped the blue tiled floor sharply with the toe of her shoe.

'It's outrageous!' she said with energy.

'I quite agree with you. Won't you sit down?' Logotheti looked at the divan. Margaret half sat upon the arm of a big leathern chair.

'Oh, you agree with me? Will you please explain?'

'I mean, it is outrageous that Mrs. Rushmore should have told you----'

'You're quibbling!' Margaret broke in angrily. 'You know very well what I mean. It's an outrage that a man should put a woman under an enormous obligation in spite of herself, without her even knowing it!'

Logotheti had seated himself where he could watch her; the fashion of dress was close-fitting; his eyes followed the graceful lines of her figure. If she had not come to drive him mad, why did she take an attitude which of all others is becoming to well-made women and fatal to all the rest?

'I'm sorry,' said Logotheti, rather absently and as if her anger did not affect him in the least, if he even noticed it. 'I happened to want the invention for a company in which I am interested. You stood in the way of my having the whole thing, so I was obliged to buy you out. I'm very sorry that it happened to be you, and that Mrs. Rushmore could not keep the fact to herself. I knew you wouldn't be pleased if you ever found it out.'

'I don't believe a word of what you are telling me,' Margaret answered.

'Really not?' Logotheti seemed momentarily interested. 'That's generally the way when one speaks the truth,' he added, more carelessly again. 'Nobody believes it.'

His eyes caressed her as he spoke. He was not thinking much of what he said.

'I've come here to make you take back the money,' Margaret said. 'I won't keep it another day.'

'Have you come all the way from Versailles again to say that?' asked Logotheti, laughing.

Again, as she sat on the arm of the big chair, she tapped the dark blue tiles with the toe of her shoe. The slight movement transmitted itself through her whole figure, and for an instant each beautiful line and curve quivered and was very slightly modified. Logotheti saw and drew his breath sharply between his teeth.

'Yes,' Margaret was saying impatiently. 'When Mrs. Rushmore had told me the truth, I walked to the station and took the first train. I only stopped to get Madame De Rosa.'

'She is not a very powerful ally,' observed Logotheti. 'She is probably asleep in her arm-chair in the drawing-room by this time. Are you still angry with me? Yes, I believe you are. Please forgive me. I had not the least idea of offending you, because I trusted that old---- I mean, because I was so sure that Mrs. Rushmore would never tell.'

'Never mind Mrs. Rushmore,' Margaret said. 'What I will not forgive you is that you made me take your money without my knowing it. I've been flirting with you--yes, I confess it! I'm not perfection, and you're rather amusing sometimes----'

'You are adorable!' Logotheti put in, as a sort of murmuring parenthesis.

'Don't talk nonsense,' Margaret answered. 'I mean that whatever I may have said to you I've never given you the right to make me a present of a hundred thousand pounds. It's the most unparalleled piece of impertinence I ever heard of.'

'But I've not made you a present of anything. I bought what was yours without letting you know, that's all.'

'Then give me back what is mine and take your money again.'

'Hm!' Logotheti smiled. 'That would be very like going into a business partnership with me. Do you wish to do that?'

'What do you mean?'

'You see, I'm the whole company at present. But if you come in with a third of the stock to your credit, we shall be partners, to all intents and purposes. We shall have meetings of the board of directors, just you and I, and we shall decide what to do. It will be rather a queer sort of board, for of course I shall always do exactly what you wish, but it's not impossible that we may make money together. Well--on the whole I have no particular objection to selling you exactly the amount of stock I bought from you the other day. That's the shape the transaction takes. I'll do any thing to please you, but I'm quite willing you should know that I am doing you a favour, as business men would look at it.'

'A favour!' Margaret slipped from the arm of the chair as she spoke and stood upright and made a step towards him. 'Do you think I'm a child to believe such nonsense?'

'In matters of business all women are children. With the possible exception of Mrs. Rushmore,' he added in a tone of reflection. 'Besides, this is not nonsense.'

'It is!' cried Margaret. 'It is absurd to try and make me believe that a mere claim set up on the chance of getting something should have turned out to be worth so much. It has cost Mrs. Rushmore I don't know how much in lawsuits, and no one ever really believed in it. She fought for it out of pure kindness of heart, and even the lawyers said she was very foolish to go on----'

'Will you listen to me?' asked Logotheti, interrupting her. 'I've not much to say, but it's rather convincing. You probably admit that the invention is valuable, and that Alvah Moon has made money by it.'

'I should think he had, the old thief!'

'Very well. I happened to want that invention. I've bought several at different times and have founded companies and sold them. That's a part of finance, which is a form of game. You deal yourself a hand and then play it. I made up my mind to play with this particular invention. I know much more about it than you do; in fact, I understand it thoroughly. I cabled to my agent in America to buy it, if he could, and he succeeded. Now please tell me whether you think Mrs. Rushmore, acting for you, would have withdrawn the suit after the property had changed hands, merely because I've dined in her house.'

'No,' Margaret was forced to admit. 'No, she would have gone on.'

'Precisely. Now I don't want property of that kind, about which there is constant litigation. The credit of such property is injured by the talk there always is about lawsuits. So I went to Mrs. Rushmore and asked her what she thought your claim was worth, and she told me, and I gave her a cheque for the money, and she has given me a full release, as your attorney. If it had been her claim, or Madame De Rosa's or any one else's, I should have done exactly the same thing. Will you tell me how I could have acted otherwise in order to get the property into my hands free of all chance of dispute? Was there any other way?'

Margaret was silent, for she could find no answer.

'There was one other way,' Logotheti continued. 'I could have proposed that you should go into partnership with me, which is what you yourself are proposing now. But in the eyes of the world I confess that might look intimate, to say the least of it. Don't you think so too?'

'You're the most plausible person I ever listened to!' Margaret almost laughed, though her anger had not subsided.

'Will you leave things as they are and forget all about this business? What has been done cannot possibly be undone now. Won't you separate me from it in your thoughts? You can, if you try. You know, I'm two people in one. So are you. I'm Logotheti the financier, and I'm Logotheti the man. You are Margaret Donne, and you are Señorita da Cordova, on the very eve of being famous--and then, I think you are some thing else which I don't quite understand, but which is like my fate, for I cannot escape from you, whether I see you, or only dream of you.'

Margaret was silent, and looked at the Aphrodite while she sat on the arm of the big chair. She might have breathed a little faster if she had known that the two doors through which she had entered, and which had closed so silently and surely after her, were as sound-proof as six feet of earth. She would not have been afraid, for she was fearless and confident, but her heart would have beaten a little more quickly at the thought that she was out of hearing of the world, and in the presence of a man whose eyes looked at her strangely and whose cheeks were darkly flushed, who was a good deal nearer to the primitive human animal than most men are, and in whom the main force of nature was awake and hungry.

'I don't want you to make love to me just now,' she said, swinging her foot a little as she sat. 'You've done something that has hurt me very much, and has made me almost wish that I might never see you again after this time. I wish you could find a way of undoing it--I'm sure there is a way.'

Unconsciously wise, she had checked his pulse for a moment, and she looked at him calmly and shook her head. With a sudden and impatient movement he rose, turned away from her and began to walk up and down at a little distance, his head bent and his hands behind him.

Though the air in the high room was pure, it was still and hot, for the late spring afternoon had turned sultry all at once; the fluid of a near storm was fast condensing to the point of explosion.

The man felt the tension more than the woman just then. It acted on his state, and made it almost unbearable. His hands were locked behind him and his fingers twisted each other till they changed colour. He moved with the short, noiseless steps of a young wild animal measuring its cage, up and down, up and down, without pause.

'It's this,' Margaret continued, much more gently than she had meant to speak, 'I don't quite believe you. I'm almost sure you thought that I would give up the stage if I had enough money to live on without my work.'

'Yes, I did.' He stopped as if in anger and the words came sharply; but he was not angry.

'You see!' Margaret answered triumphantly. 'I knew it! What becomes of your story about the company now?'

She rose also and began to walk. The big leathern arm-chair was between them; he leaned his elbows on the back of it and watched her, and compared her hungrily with the Aphrodite.

'All I have told you is true,' he said. 'The business happened to serve two purposes, that's all. At least, I thought it would, and it was a pleasure to help you without your knowing it. Why should I be sorry? That money might as well come to you through me as through anybody else. You're angry with me. Why? Because I'm too fond of you? It cannot reasonably be about the money any more--the wretched money! If you can't keep the filthy stuff--if it won't prevent you from going on the stage after all--why then, give it away! Throw it away! Lose it, if you can. But don't come to me with it, for it's the price of a thing I bought in the way of business and which I won't give up, nor take as a gift from anybody.'

He spoke in such a harsh tone now that she paused in her short walk and met his eyes, to see what he meant, over and above what he was saying. She stood in front of the chair; he was leaning over the back of it, with his hands together; one hand was slowly kneading the closed fist, and the veins stood out on both. His voice was hoarse but rather low, like that of a man who wants water.

The light in the room had a yellowish tinge now, and the window showed a dull glare where there had been blue sky before. The lurid light got into Logotheti's eyes, and was ready to flash while Margaret looked at him. The marble Aphrodite took a creamy, living tint, and the little shadows that modelled her quivered and deepened.

All at once Margaret knew that there was danger. She could not have told how she knew it, nor just what the danger was, but she raised her fair head suddenly, as the stag does when the scent of the hounds comes down the breeze. Watching her, he saw and understood, and his hands left each other and closed tightly upon the back of the chair.

'Will you take me back to Madame De Rosa, please?' Margaret asked, and her voice did not shake.

Before he could answer, a flash of lightning filled the room, vivid as flame, and almost purple; it flared and danced two or three times before it went out.

If Logotheti spoke at all, his words were drowned in the crash that shook the house and rolled away over the city. His eyes never moved from Margaret's face; she felt that his gaze was fastened on her lips, as if he would have drawn them to meet his own. She was not exactly afraid, but she knew that she must get away from him, for he was stronger than she, and he was like a man going mad. That was what she would have called it. And it seemed to her that one of two things was going to happen. Either she would let his lips reach hers, without resisting, or else she would try to kill him when he came near her. She did not know which she should do. She was in herself two people; the one was a human woman, tempted by the mysterious sympathy of flesh and blood; the other self was a startled maiden caught in a trap and at bay, without escape.

With the great peal of thunder the Aphrodite trembled from head to foot, twice, as the vibration ran down the walls of the house to the very foundations and then came up again and died away, like the second shock of an earthquake. The statue trembled as if it were alive and afraid.

With a glance, Margaret measured the distance which separated her from the door, but it was too far. There were half-a-dozen steps, and Logotheti was much nearer to her than that, even allowing that he must get past the chair to reach her.

Now he moved a little and it was too late to try. He was beside the chair instead of behind it; but then he stopped and came no further yet, while he spoke to her.

'Why did you come?' he asked in a low tone. 'You might have guessed that it wasn't quite safe!'

It was almost as if he were speaking to himself. She kept her eyes on him, and tried to back away towards the door so slowly that he should not notice it. But he smiled and his lids drooped.

'You could not open the door if you reached it,' he said. 'You said that you wanted to speak with me alone. We are alone here--quite alone. No one can hear, even if you scream. No one can get in. Why did you say you wanted to be alone with me, if you were not in earnest? Why do you risk playing with a man who is crazy about you, and has everything in the world except you, and would throw it all away to have you? And now that you are here of your own accord, why should I let you go?'

The speech was rough, but there was a sudden caress in his voice with the last words, and he had scarcely spoken them when another flash of lightning filled the room with a maddening purple light.

Before the peal broke, Logotheti held Margaret by the wrists, and spoke close to her face, very fast.

'I will not let you go. I love you, and I will not let you go.'

The thunder burst, and roared and echoed away, while he drew her nearer, looking for the woman in her eyes, too mad to know that she did not feel what he felt. He touched her now; he could feel her breathings, fast and frightened, and the quiver that ran through her limbs. He held her, but without hurting her in the least--she could turn her wrists loosely in the bonds he made of his fingers. Yet she could not get away from him and he drew her closer.

She threw her head back from his face, and tried to speak.

'Please--please, let me go.'

'No. I love you.'

He drew her till she was pressed against him, and he held her hands in his behind her waist. The air was clearing with a furious rush of rain, and her courage was not all gone yet. She looked up to the high windows, as one about to die might look up from the scaffold, and there was a streak of clear blue sky between the driving clouds. It was as if hope looked through, out of heaven, at the girl driven to bay.

Margaret did not try to use her strength, for she knew it was useless against his. But she held her head back and spoke slowly.

'For your mother's sake,' she said, low and clear, her eyes on his.

For one moment his grasp tightened and his white teeth caught his lower lip; but his look was changing slowly.

'For her sake,' Margaret said, 'as you would have kept harm from her----'

His hold relaxed, and he turned away. There was good in him still; he had loved his mother.

He turned deliberately, till he could see neither Margaret nor the Aphrodite, and he leaned heavily on the table, with bent head, resting the weight of his body on the palms of his hands, and remaining quite motionless for some time.

He heard her go towards the door. Without looking round he slowly shook his head.

'Don't be afraid of me,' he said, in a low voice. 'It's all over, now. I'll let you out in a moment.'

'Yes.'

She waited quietly by the door, which she did not understand how to open. Presently he moved a little, and his head sank lower between his shoulders; then he spoke again, but still without turning towards her.

'I'm sorry,' he said. 'I did not know I could be such a brute. Forgive me, will you?'

As usual, when he was very much in earnest, there was something rudely abrupt about his speech.

'It was my fault,' Margaret answered from the door. 'I should not have come.'

Even after her escape, something about him still pleased her. The maiden that had been brought to bay was scarcely safe, before the human woman began to be drawn to him again by that sympathy of flesh and blood that had nearly cost her more than life.

But Margaret revolted against it now, as soon as she knew what it was that made her speak kindly.

'I'm not afraid of you,' she said, almost coldly, 'but I want you to let me out, please.'

He straightened himself and turned slowly to her. The dark red colour was gone from his cheeks, he was suddenly pale and haggard, and if he had not been really young, he would have looked old; as it was, his face was drawn and pinched as if by sharp physical suffering. He drew two or three quick, deep breaths as he came towards her.

He stood beside her a moment, and then without a word, he unfastened the door. It swung inwards and stood open. Margaret saw that it was thickly padded to prevent any sound from passing, and that there was another padded door beyond it which she had not noticed when she had entered. He understood her look of doubt.

'That one is open now,' he said. 'It locks and unlocks itself as I shut or open the inner door.'

He was willing to let her see how completely she had been cut off from the outer world; and she realised the truth and shuddered.

'Good-bye,' she said, abruptly, as if he were not to go downstairs with her, and she made a step to pass him.

He thrust his arm out across the way, resting his head against the door-post. She started, almost nervously, and then stood still again and looked at him.

'No,' he said, 'I shall not try to keep you, and the door is open. But please don't say good-bye like that, as if we were not going to meet soon.'

'It's not good for us to be alone together,' she said.

The words came by instinct, and acknowledged a weakness in

herself. After she had spoken, she was very sorry. His drawn face softened.

'That's why I forgive you,' she said, with sudden frankness, and a blush reddened her cheeks under the fawn-coloured veil she had drawn down again.

He took her hand, against her will and almost violently, but in an instant his own was gentle again.

'Margaret!' His voice had a thrill in it.

'No,' she answered, but not roughly now, and scarcely trying to free herself. 'No. I don't love you in the least. That is why I won't marry you. There's something that draws me to you against my will sometimes--yes, I know that! But I hate it, and I'm afraid of it. It's not what I like in you, it's what I like least. It's something like hypnotism, I'm sure. I'm ashamed of it, because it is what has made me flirt with you. Yes, I have! I've flirted outrageously, except that I've always told you that I never would marry you. I've been truthful in that, at all events.'

'Do you think I reproach you?'

'You might have, this morning. Now we have each something to reproach the other. We will forgive and say good-bye for a while. When we meet again, that something I'm afraid of will be gone--perhaps--then everything will be different. Now, good-bye.'

He had held her hand all the time while she had been speaking. She pressed his now, with an impulse of frank loyalty, and dropped it suddenly.

'Do you mean that I may not even come and see you?' he asked.

'Not till after my début,' answered Margaret in a decided tone, for she felt that she dominated him at last. 'You don't want me to be a singer and I cannot help feeling your opposition. It disturbs me, as the time comes near. Of course I can't hinder you from being there on the first night----'

'No indeed!'

'And when you've heard me, and seen Gilda's head come out of the sack, and when the curtain has gone down on Rigoletto's despair--why, then you may come behind and congratulate me, especially if I've made a failure! Till then I don't want to see you, please!'

'I cannot wait so long. It is nearly three weeks.'

Margaret stood up very straight in the doorway, already past him and free to go out.

'Since I am willing to forgive you for losing your head just now,' she said, 'it's for me to decide whether you may ever see me again, and if so when, and where. I've been very good to you. Now I am going.'

It seemed to him that she had grown all at once in strength and individuality till there was nothing for him to do but to submit. This was an illusion, no doubt; she was just what she had always been, and what he had always judged her, a gifted young woman, rather inclined to flirt and easily guided in any direction, whose exuberant animal vitality might pass for strong character in the eyes of an inexperienced innocent like Lushington, but could not deceive an old hand like Logotheti for a moment. Nevertheless, when she had spoken her last words and was leading the way out of the room, Logotheti felt a little like a small boy who has had his ears boxed for being too cheeky, which is a sensation not at all pleasant or natural to an old hand.

As he took her down in the little lift, he vaguely wondered whether he had ever thought of her till now except as an animated work of art; comparable in beauty with his encaustic painting or his dearly loved Aphrodite; worth more than either of them as a possible possession, as life is worth more than stone, and endowed with a divine voice; but having neither soul, intelligence, nor will to speak of, nor any original power of ruling others, still less of resisting a systematic and prolonged attack.

The change had come quickly. Logotheti thought of beautiful beings of old, disguised as yielding, mortal women, who had visited the men they loved on earth and had by and by revealed themselves as true and puissant goddesses, moving in a sphere of rosy light, and speaking only to command.

Logotheti took her down in the lift and they went back into the big room where they had left Madame De Rosa. They found her looking out of the window. Books did not interest her, nor pictures either, there was no piano in the room and the maraschino was locked up. So there was nothing to do but to look out of the window. As the two came in she turned sharply to them, with her head on one side, as birds do, and her intelligent little eyes sparkled. She was a good little woman herself, and believed in heaven and salvation, but she had no particular belief in man and none at all in woman. On the other hand, she had a very keen scent for the truth in love affairs, and in Logotheti's subdued expression she instantly detected sure signs of discomfiture, which were fully confirmed by Margaret's serene and superior manner. Men sometimes follow women into a room with such an air of submission that one almost looks for the string by which they are led.

Madame De Rosa nodded her approval to Margaret in a rather officious manner, much as if she were congratulating her pupil on having soundly beaten an unruly and dangerous dog.

'Well done,' the nod said. 'Beat him again, the very next time he does it!'

But Margaret either did not understand at all, or did not care for Madame De Rosa's approbation, for she returned no answering glance of intelligence.

'I hope,' she said, 'that I have not kept you too long.'

The former prima donna looked at a tiny watch set in diamonds, the gift of a great tenor whom she had taught.

'Not at all,' she said. 'It's not twenty minutes since we came.'

She put the watch to her ear and listened. Nine women out of ten are generally in doubt as to whether their watches have not just stopped.

'Yes,' she said. 'It is going.'

Logotheti remembered how long the seconds had seemed while he was taking Margaret up in the lift, and it seemed as if hours had passed since then.

'Good-bye,' said Margaret, holding out one hand and passing the other through Madame De Rosa's arm to lead her away.

'Good-bye,' Logotheti answered. 'Of course,' he continued, 'you must please remember that if I can be of any use in making investments for you, you have only to send me your commands. I am at your service for anything connected with the money market.'

'Thank you,' said Margaret, ambiguously, as to the tone in which the words were spoken, but with a quick glance of approval.

He had meant his speech for Madame De Rosa, who had probably been told that Margaret came to see him on a matter of business. But it was quite unnecessary. The little Neapolitan woman could judge of the state of a love affair at any moment with a certainty as unerring as that of a great cook who can tell by a mere glance what stage of development the finest sauce has reached. She supported Logotheti's fiction, however, without a smile.

'Ah, my dear,' she said, 'always consult him, if he will help you! Bonanni owes half her fortune to his judgment, and I could certainly not live as I do if he had not given me his advice and kind assistance.'

'You exaggerate, dear lady,' said Logotheti, opening the door for them, and following them into the hall.

'Not in the least,' laughed Madame De Rosa, 'though I am sure that Cordova is quite able to take care of herself and is much too proud to owe you anything.'

She often called Margaret by her stage name, as artists do among themselves, but it jarred disagreeably on Logotheti's ear.

'You are right in that,' he said, rather coldly, as a footman appeared and opened the outer door. 'Miss Donne'--he emphasised the name a little--'will probably not need any help from me. But if she should, I am her very humble servant.'

'Thank you,' Margaret said, in the same ambiguous tone as before.

Thereupon she and Madame De Rosa nodded to him and left him bowing on his doorstep. They walked away in the direction of the Batignolles station. When they had heard the door of the house shut, Madame De Rosa spoke.

'You are splendid, my dear,' she said with admiration. 'But take care! To play with Logotheti is like balancing a volcano on the tip of your nose while you juggle with the world, the flesh and the devil--you know what I mean--the man who keeps a cannon-ball, an empty bottle and a bit of paper all going at once with one hand. I am afraid Logotheti will do something unexpected, to upset all our plans.'

'He had better not!' answered Margaret, drooping her lids; and her eyes flashed, and her handsome lips pouted a little.

CHAPTER XVII

Margaret, it is sad to relate, was much less concerned about the two men who were in love with her than is considered becoming in a woman of heart. She confessed to herself, without excess of penitence, that she had flirted abominably with them both, she consoled her conscience with the reflection that they were both alive and apparently very well, and she put all her strength, which was great, into preparing for her début.

Men never love so energetically and persuasively as when they are fighting every day for life, honour or fame, and are already on the road to victory; but a woman's passion, though true and lasting, may be momentarily quite overshadowed by the anticipation of a new hat or of a social battle of uncertain issue. How much more, then, by the near approach of such an event as a first appearance on the stage!

Logotheti bribed the doorkeeper at the small theatre where Margaret was rehearsing. Whenever there was a rehearsal he was there before her, quite out of sight in the back of a lower box, and he did not go away until he was quite sure that she had left. He knew women well enough to be certain that if anything could make Margaret wish to see him it would be his own strict observance of her request not to show himself; and in the meantime he enjoyed some moments of keen delight in watching her and listening to her. He felt something of the selfish pleasure which filled that King of Bavaria who had a performance of Lohengrin given for himself alone. But the pleasure was not unmixed, nor was the delight unclouded.

Even Schreiermeyer had given up coming to the rehearsals, for he was now sure of Margaret's success and had passed on to other business. In the dim stalls there appeared only the shabby relations and rather gorgeous friends of the other members of the company. There was the young painter who loved the leading girl of the chorus, there was the wholesale upholsterer who admired the contralto, and a little apart there was the middle-aged great lady who entertained a romantic and expensive passion for the tenor. The tenor was a young Italian, who was something between a third-rate poet and a spoilt child when he was in love and was as cynical as Macchiavelli when he was not, which was the case at present, at least so far as the middle-aged woman of the world was concerned. His friends could always tell the state of his affections by the way he sang in Rigoletto. When he was hopelessly in love himself, he sang 'La donna è mobile' with tears in his voice, as if his heart were breaking; when, on the contrary, he knew that some unhappy female was hopelessly in love with him, he sang it with a sort of laugh that was diabolically irritating. At the present time he seemed to be in an intermediate state, for he sometimes sang it in the one way and sometimes in the other, to the despair of the poor foolish lady in the stalls. The truth was that at irregular intervals he felt that he was in love with Margaret.

Leading singers are very rarely attracted by each other. Perhaps that is because they receive such a vast amount of adulation which pleases them better, and of course there have been famous instances of the contrary, such as Mario and Grisi. As a rule singers do not meet much except at the theatre; it is only during rehearsals that they have a chance of talking, and then, as everybody knows, they show the worst side of themselves and are often in a very bad temper indeed.

Margaret had not reached that stage yet, for she had met with no disappointments and could not complain of her manager, and moreover she was not at all above learning what she could from her fellow-artists. She was therefore popular with them in spite of the fact that she was a lady born. They overlooked that, because she could sing, and the tenor only remembered it when he tried to patronise her a little. He had often sung with Melba, and she did this or that, and he had sung with Bonanni and knew exactly how she sang the difficult passages, and he reeled off the precepts and practice of half-a-dozen other lyric sopranos, giving Margaret to understand that he was willing and able to teach her a good deal. But she only smiled kindly, and did precisely what Madame De Rosa told her to do, seeing that the little Neapolitan had taught most of them what they knew. It was clear that Margaret could not be patronised, and the other members of the company liked her the better for it, because the tenor patronised them all and gave them to understand that they were rather small fry compared with a man who could hold the high C and walk off the stage with it.

From the darkness of his lower box Logotheti looked on and approved of Margaret's behaviour. At the same time he abstracted himself from her life and saw how she lived with respect to other men and women, and a great change began to take place in his feelings, one of those changes which are sometimes salutary because they may hinder an act of folly, but which humiliate a man in his own eyes, in proportion as they are unexpected, and tend to contradict something which he has believed to be beyond all doubt. To many men the loss of a noble illusion feels like a loss of strength in themselves, perhaps because such men can never keep an ideal before them without making an unconscious effort against the material tendency of their natures.

The change in Logotheti during the next three weeks was profound; and it was humiliating because it deprived him all at once of a sort of power over himself which had grown up with his love for Margaret and depended on that for its nourishment and life; a power which had perhaps not been an original force at all, but only a chivalrous willingness to do her will instead of his own. He looked on and did not betray his presence, and she, on her side, began to wonder at his prolonged obedience. More than once she felt a sudden conviction that he must be near, and he saw how she peered into the gloom of the empty house as if looking for some one she expected. It was only natural, and no theory of telepathy was needed to explain it. She had so often seen him there in reality! But he would not show himself now, for he was determined that she should send for him; if she did not, he could wait for her début; and little by little, as he kept to his determination and only saw her from a distance in the frame of the stage, the woman who had dominated him in a moment when he was beside himself with passion, became once more an animated work of art which he unconsciously compared with his Aphrodite and his ancient picture, and which he coveted as a possession.

It did not at first occur to him that Margaret had really changed since he had met her, and not exactly in the way he might have wished. Instead of showing any inclination to give up the stage, as he had hoped that she might, she seemed more and more in love with her future career.

When he had first met her he had made the acquaintance of a strikingly good-looking English girl, born and brought up a lady, full of talent and enthusiasm for her art, but as yet absolutely ignorant of professional artistic life and still in a state of mind in which some sides of it were sure to be disagreeable to her, if not absolutely repulsive.

Hidden in his box, and watching her as well as listening to her, he gradually realised the change, and he remembered many facts which should have prepared him for it. He recollected, for instance, her perfect coolness and self-possession with Madame Bonanni, so absolutely different from the paralysing shyness, the visible fright and the pitiful helplessness at the moment of trial, which he had more than once seen in young girls who came to Madame Bonanni for advice. They had good voices, too, those poor trembling candidates; many of them had talent of a certain order; but it was not the real thing, there was not the real strength behind it, there was not the absolute self-reliance to steady it; above all, there was not the tremendous physical organisation which every great singer possesses.

But Margaret had all that; in other words, she had every gift that makes a first-rate professional on the stage, and as the life became familiar to her, those gifts, suddenly called into play, exerted their influence directly upon her character and manner. She was born to be a professional artist, to face the public and make it applaud her, to believe in her own talent, to help herself, to trust to her nerves and to defend herself with cool courage in moments of danger.

This was assuredly not the girl with whom Logotheti had fallen in love at first sight, whom he, as well as Lushington, had believed far too refined and delicately brought up to be happy in the surroundings of a stage life, and much too sensitive to bear such familiarity as being addressed as 'Cordova,' without any prefix, by an Italian tenor singer whose father had kept a butcher's shop in Turin.

No doubt, the refinement, the sensitiveness, the delicacy of manner were all there still, for such things do not disappear out of a woman in a few days; but they belonged chiefly to one side of a nature that had two very distinct sides. There was the 'lady' side, and there was the 'actress' side; and unfortunately, thought Logotheti, there was now no longer the slightest doubt as to which was the stronger. Margaret Donne was already a memory; the reality was 'Cordova,' who was going to have a fabulous success and would soon be one of the most successful lyric sopranos of her time.

'Cordova' was a splendid creature, she was a good girl, she had a hundred fine qualities not always found together in a great prima donna; but no power in the world could ever make her Margaret Donne again.

Logotheti watched her and once or twice he sighed; for he knew that he no longer wished to marry her. It is not in the nature of Orientals to let their wives exhibit themselves to the public, and in most ways the prejudices of a well-born Greek of Constantinople are just as strong as those of a Mohammedan Turk.

As an artistic possession, 'Cordova' was as desirable as ever in Logotheti's eyes; but she was no longer at all desirable as a wife. The Greek, in spite of the lawless strain in him, was an aristocrat to the marrow of his very solid bones. An aristocrat, doubtless, in the Eastern sense, proud of his own long descent, but perfectly indifferent to any such matter as a noble pedigree in the choice of a wife; quite capable, if he had not chanced to be born a Christian, of taking to himself, even by purchase, the jealously-guarded daughter of a Circassian horse-thief, or of a Georgian cut-throat, a girl brought up in seclusion for sale, like a valuable thoroughbred; but a man who revolted at the thought of marrying a woman who could show herself upon the stage, and for money, who could sing for money, and for the applause of a couple of thousand people, nine-tenths of whom he would never have allowed to enter his house. He was jealous of what he really loved. To him, it would have been a real and keen suffering to see his marble Aphrodite set up in a hall of the Louvre, to be admired in her naked perfection by every passing tourist, criticised and compared with famous living models by loose-talking art students, and furtively examined by prurient and disapproving old maids from distant countries. He prized her, and he had risked his life, not to mention the just anger of a government, to get possession of her. If he could feel so much for a piece of marble, it was not likely that he should feel less keenly where the woman he loved was concerned; and circumstance for circumstance, point for point, it was much worse that Margaret Donne should stand and sing behind the footlights, for money, and disguise herself as a man in the last act of Rigoletto, than that the Aphrodite should go to the Louvre and take her place with the Borghese Gladiator, the Venus of Milo and the Victory of Samothrace. It was true that he would have given much to possess one of those other treasures, too, but even then it would not have been like possessing the Aphrodite. The other statues had been public property and had faced the public gaze for many years; but he had found his treasure for himself, buried safe in the earth since ages ago, and he had brought her thence directly to that upper room where few eyes but his own had ever seen her. Perhaps he was a little mad on this point, for strong natures that hark back to primitive types often seem a little mad to us. But at the root of his madness there was that which no man need be ashamed of, for it has been the very foundation of human society--the right of every husband to keep the mother of his children from the world in his own home. For human society existed before the Ten Commandments, and a large part of it seems tolerably able to survive without them even now; but no nation has ever come to any good or greatness, since the world began, unless its men have kept their wives from other men. Yet nature is not mocked, and woman is a match for man; she first drove him to invent divorce for his self-defence, and see, it is a two-edged sword in her own hands and is turned against him! No strong nation, beginning its life and history, ever questioned the husband's right to kill the unfaithful wife; no old and corrupt race has ever failed to make it easy for a wife to have many husbands--including those of her friends.

Logotheti belonged to the primitives. As he had once laughingly explained to Margaret, his people had dropped out of civilisation during a good many centuries; they had absorbed a good deal of wild blood in that time, and, scientifically speaking, had reverted to their type; and now that he had chosen to mingle in the throng of the moderns, whose fathers had lost no time in the race, while his own had remained stationary, he found himself different from other people, stronger than they, bolder and much more lawless, but also infinitely more responsive to the creations of art and the facts of life, as well as to the finer fictions of his imagination and the simple cravings of his very masculine being.

Men who are especially gifted almost always seem exaggerated to average society, either because, like Logotheti, they feel more, want more and get more than other men, by sheer all-round exuberance of life and energy, or else because, as in many great poets, some one faculty is almost missing, which would have balanced the rest, so that in its absence the others work at incredible speed and tension, wear themselves out in half a lifetime and leave immortal records of their brief activity.

There had been a time when Margaret had appealed only to Logotheti's artistic perceptions; at their second meeting he had asked her to marry him because he felt sure that until he could make her his permanent possession, he could never again know what it was to be satisfied.

There had been a moment when she had risen in his estimation from an artistic treasure to the dignity of an ideal, and had dominated him, even when the human animal in him was most furiously roused.

Again, and lastly, the time had come when, by watching her unseen, instead of spending hours with her every day, by abstracting himself from her life instead of trying to take part in it, he had lost his hold upon his ideal for ever, and had been cruelly robbed of what for a few short days he had held most dear.

Moreover, after the ideal had withered and fallen, there remained something of which the man felt ashamed, though it was what had seemed most natural before the higher thought had sprung up full-grown in a day, and had blossomed, and perished. It was simply this. Margaret was as much as ever the artistic treasure he coveted, and he was tormented by the fear lest some one else should get possession of her before him.

He remembered the sleepless nights he had spent while his marble Aphrodite had lain above ground, before he was ready to carry her off, the unspeakable anxiety lest she should be found and taken from him, the terror of losing her which had driven him to make the attempt in the teeth of weather which his craft had not been fit to face; and he remembered, too, that the short time while she had lain at the bottom of the bay had not passed without real dread lest by a miracle another should find her and steal her.

He felt that same sensation now, as he watched Margaret from a distance; some one would find her, some one would marry her, some one would take her away and own her, body and soul, and cheat him of what had been within his grasp and all but his; and yet he was ashamed, because he no longer wanted her for his wife, but only as a possession--as Achilles wanted Briseis and was wroth when she was taken from him. He felt shame at the thought, because he had already honoured her in his imagination as his wife, and because to dream of her as anything as near, yet less in honour, was a sort of dishonour to himself. Let the subtle analyst make what he can of that; it is the truth. But possibly the truth about a man very unlike his fellow-men is not worth analysing, since it cannot lead to any useful generality; and if analysis is not to be useful, of what use can it possibly be? It would be more to the purpose to analyse the character of Margaret, for instance, who represents a certain class of artists, or of Madame Bonanni who is an arch-type, or of poor Edmund Lushington, a literary Englishman, who was just then very unhappy and very sorry for himself. Margaret and Lushington, and the elderly prima donna, and even Mrs. Rushmore, are all much more like you and me than Constantine Logotheti, the Greek financier of artistic tastes, watching the woman he covets, from the depths of his lower box during rehearsal.

He watched, and he coveted; and presently he fell to thinking of the wonderful things which money can do, when it is skilfully used; and he fell to scheming and plotting, and laying deep plans; and moreover he recalled the days when Margaret had first appeared to him as an animated work of art, and he remembered why he had persuaded Schreiermeyer to change the opera from Faust to Rigoletto. He had regretted the change later, when she had risen to the higher place in his heart, because it required her to wear a man's disguise in the last act; but now that she was again in his eyes what she had been at first, he was glad he had made the suggestion, and that the manager had taken his advice, for there was something in that last act which should serve him when the time came.

CHAPTER XVIII

After the adventure on the Versailles road, Lushington eschewed disguises, changed his lodgings again and appeared in clothes that fitted him. It was a great relief to look like a human being and a gentleman, even at the cost of calling himself an ass for having tried to look like something else. There was but one difficulty in the way of resuming his former appearance, and that lay in the loss of his beard, which would take some time to grow again, while its growth would involve retirement from civilisation during several weeks. But he reflected that it was fashionable to be clean-shaven, and that, in point of appearance, all that is fashionable is right, though Plato would have declared it to be removed in the third degree from truth.

A week after the accident he went out to Versailles in the morning. Mrs. Rushmore had a headache and Margaret received him. She smiled as she took his hand, and she looked hard at his face, as if to be sure that it was he, after all. The absence of the gleaming fair beard made a great difference.

'I think I like you better without it,' she said, at last. 'Your face has more character!'

'It's the inevitable,' answered Lushington, 'so I'm glad you are pleased.'

'Come out,' she said, turning to the door. 'It always seems more natural to talk to you on the lawn, and the bench is still there.'

He felt like an exile come home. Nothing was changed, except that Margaret was gentler and seemed more glad to see him than formerly. He wondered how that could be, seeing that he had made himself so very ridiculous; for he was not experienced enough to know that a woman's sense of humour is very different from that of a man she likes, when she herself has been concerned in the circumstances that have made him an object of ridicule to others. Then her face grows grave, her eyes harden, and her head goes up. 'I cannot see that there is anything to laugh at,' she says very coldly, to the disagreeable people who are poking fun at the poor man. At these signs, the disagreeable people generally desist and retire to whisper in a corner.

Lushington followed Margaret out. As they passed through the hall, she took an old garden hat from the table and fastened it upon her head with the pin that had been left stuck in it. It was done almost with a single motion and without even glancing at the mirror which hung above the hall table. Lushington watched her, but not as Logotheti would have done, in artistic admiration of the graceful movement and perfect balance. The Englishman, who called himself a realist, was admiring the ideal qualities with which he had long ago invested the real woman. As he watched her, his imagination clothed her handsome reality with a semi-divine mantle of glory; for him she could never be anything but Margaret Donne, let her call herself Cordova or anything else, let her sing in Rigoletto or in any other opera.

'It was nice of you to come,' she said, as they reached the bench near the pond. 'I wanted to see you.'

'And I wanted you to see me,' Lushington laughed a little, remembering how she had seen him the last time, after his fall, in very bad clothes and much damaged, particularly as to his nose.

'You certainly look more civilised,' Margaret said.

'Did Logotheti tell you anything about what happened after you left us?' asked Lushington, suddenly.

Margaret's face lost its expression for a moment. It was exactly as if, while sitting in the full sunshine, a little cloud had blown across the sun, taking the golden light out of her face.

'I have not seen Monsieur Logotheti since that day,' she said.

It was not necessary to tell Lushington that she had seen the Greek once again on the same afternoon. Her companion seemed surprised.

'That's strange,' he said. 'I supposed you saw him--no, I beg your pardon, I've no right to suppose anything about you. Please forgive me.'

'What did you suppose?' asked Margaret in a rather imperative tone.

'We are likely to meet so seldom that I may as well tell you what happened,' answered Lushington, with more decision than he had formerly been wont to show. 'I'd just as soon have you know, if you don't mind.'

Margaret leaned back in her seat, and pulled the garden hat over her eyes. It was warm, and she could see the gnats in the strong light reflected from the pond.

'He asked me if I wanted to marry you,' Lushington continued. 'I said that such a thing was impossible. Then he gave me to understand that he did.'

He paused, but as if he had more to say.

'What did you answer?' asked Margaret.

'I said I would keep out of the way, since he was in earnest.'

'Oh!'

Margaret uttered the ejaculation in a tone that might have meant anything, and she watched the gnats darting hither and thither in the sunshine.

'I did right, didn't I?' asked Lushington after a long pause.

'You meant to,' said Margaret almost roughly. 'I suppose it's the same thing. You're always so terribly honourable!'

Her humour changed suddenly, and there was a shade of contempt in her voice. She had been very glad to see him a few moments earlier, but now she wished he would go. She was perhaps just then in the temper to be won, though she did not know it, and she unconsciously wished that Lushington would take hold of her and almost hurt her, as Logotheti had done, instead of being so dreadfully anxious to be told that he had done right a week ago.

'You don't care a straw for Logotheti,' he said, so suddenly that she started a little. 'I don't know why you should,' he added, as she said nothing, 'but I had got the impression that you did.'

'There are days—I mean,' she corrected herself, 'there have been days, when I have liked him very much—more, it seems to me, than I ever liked you, though in quite a different way.'

'There will be more such days,' Lushington answered.

'I hope not.'

Margaret spoke almost as if to herself and very low, turning her head away. Lushington heard the words, however, and was surprised.

'Has anything happened?' he asked quickly, and quite without reflection.

Again she answered in a low tone, unfamiliar to him.

'Yes. Something has happened.'

Then neither spoke for some time. When Margaret broke the silence at last, there was a little defiance in her voice, a touch of recklessness in her manner, as new to Lushington as her low, absent-minded tone had been when she had last spoken.

'It was only natural, I suppose,' she laughed, a little sharply. 'I'm too good for one and not good enough for the other! It would be really interesting to know just how good one ought to be—when one is an artist!'

'What do you mean?' asked Lushington, not understanding at all.

'My dear child!' She laughed again, and both the words and the laugh jarred on Lushington, as being a little unlike her—she had never addressed him in that way before. 'You don't really suppose that I am going to explain, do you? You made up your mind that I was much too fine a lady to marry the son of a singer--much too good for you, in fact--though I would have married you just then!'

'Just then!' Lushington repeated the words sadly.

'Certainly not now,' answered Margaret viciously. 'You would come to your senses in a week with a start, to find your idol in a very shaky and moth-eaten state. I'm horribly human, after all! I admit it!'

'What is the matter with you?' asked Lushington, rather sharply. 'What has become of you?' he asked, as she gave him no answer. 'Where are you, the real you? I saw you when I came, and you brought me out on the lawn, and it was going to be so nice, just as it used to be; and now, on a sudden, you are gone, and there is some one I don't know in your place.'

Margaret laughed, leaned back in her chair and looked at the pond.

'Some one you don't know?' she repeated, with a question.

'Yes.'

'I wonder!' She laughed again. 'It must be that,' she said presently. 'It cannot be anything else.'

'What?'

'It must be "Cordova." Don't you think so? I know just what you mean--I feel it, I hear it in my voice when I speak, I see it in the glass when I look at myself. But not always. It comes and it goes, it has its hours. Sometimes I'm it when I wake up suddenly in the night, and sometimes I'm Margaret Donne, whom you used to like. And I'm sure of something else. Shall I tell you? One of these days Margaret Donne will go away and never come back, and there will be only Cordova left, and then I suppose I shall go to the bad. They all do, you know.'

Lushington did know, and made an odd movement and bent himself, as if something sharp had run into him unawares, and he turned his face away, to hide the look of pain which he could not control. Margaret had hardly spoken the cruel words when she realised what she had done.

'Oh, I'm so sorry!' she cried, in dreadful distress, and the voice came from her heart and was quite her own again.

In her genuine pain for him, she took his hand in both her own, and drew it to her and looked into his eyes.

'It's all right,' he answered. 'You did not mean it. Don't distress yourself.'

There were tears in her eyes now, but they were not going to overflow. She dropped his hands.

'How splendidly good and generous you are!' Margaret cried. 'There's nobody like you, after all!'

Lushington forgot his pain in the pleasure he felt at this outburst.

'But why?' he asked, not very clear as to her reasons for praising him.

'It was the same thing the other day,' she said, 'when we upset you on the Versailles road. You were in a bad way; I don't think I remember ever seeing a man in a worse plight! I couldn't help laughing a little.'

'No,' said Lushington, 'I suppose you couldn't.'

'You had your revenge afterwards, though you did not know it,' Margaret answered.

'What sort of revenge?'

'Monsieur Logotheti was detestable. It would have given me the greatest satisfaction to have stuck hat-pins into him, ever so many of them, as thick as the quills on a porcupine!'

Lushington laughed, in a colourless way.

'As you say, I was revenged,' he answered.

'Oh, that wasn't it!' she laughed, too. 'Not at all! Besides, you knew that! You were perfectly well aware that you had the heroic part, all through.'

'Indeed, I wasn't aware of it at all! I felt most awfully small, I assure you.'

'That's because you're not a woman,' observed Margaret thoughtfully. 'No,' she went on, after a short pause, during which Lushington found nothing to say, 'the revenge you had was much more complete. I don't think I'll tell you what it was. You might think----'

She broke off abruptly, and drew the big garden hat even further over her eyes. Lushington watched her mouth, as he could see so little of the rest of her face, but the lips were shut and motionless, with rather a set look, as if she meant to keep a secret.

'If you don't tell me, I suppose I'm free to think what I please,' Lushington answered. 'I might even think that you were seized with remorse for being so extremely horrid and that you went home and drenched a number of pillows with your tears.'

He laughed lightly. Margaret was silent for a moment, but she slowly nodded and drummed a five-fingered exercise on her knee with her right hand.

'I cried like a baby,' she said suddenly, with a little snort of dissatisfaction.

'Not really?' Lushington was profoundly surprised, before he was flattered.

'Yes. I hope you're satisfied? Was I not right in saying that you were revenged?'

'You have more heart than you like to show,' he answered. 'Thank you for caring so much! It was nice of you.'

'I don't believe it was what you mean by "heart" at all,' said Margaret. 'I don't pretend to have much, and what there is of it is not a bit of the "faithful squaw" kind. I cried that night about you, exactly as I might have cried over a poor lame horse, if somebody had kicked it uphill and I had been brute enough to laugh at its pain!'

'Hm!' ejaculated Lushington. 'Pity, I suppose?'

'Not a bit of it. How rude you are! I should have pitied you at the time, then. But I didn't, not the least bit. I laughed at you. Afterwards I cried because I had been such a beast as to laugh, and I wished that somebody would come and beat me! I assure you, it was entirely out of disgust with myself that I cried, and not in the least out of pity for you!'

'I'm delighted to hear it,' said Lushington. 'In the first place, I should be sorry to have been the direct means of bringing you to tears; secondly, I hate to be pitied; and thirdly, it's a much more difficult thing to make a woman disgusted with herself than it is to excite her compassion by playing lame horse or sick puppy!'

Margaret looked at him from under the brim of her hat, throwing her head far back so as to do so. Then they both laughed a little, and Lushington felt happy for a moment; but Margaret did not know what she felt, if indeed she felt anything at all, beyond a momentary satisfaction in the society of a man she really liked very much, whom she had once believed she loved, and whom she might still have been willing to marry if she had not been at the point of beginning her public career, and if he had asked her, and if--but there were altogether too many conditions, and for the moment matrimony was out of sight.

'I like you very much,' she said, suddenly thoughtful. 'I've seen you act like a hero, and you always act like a gentleman. One cannot say that of many men. If I were not such a wicked flirt, I suppose I should be in love with you, as I was that day when you left here. I'm glad I'm not! Do you know that it's frightfully humiliating to want to marry a man, and to have him object, no matter why?'

Lushington said something, but he felt that again the real Margaret had slipped away out of sight for a while, leaving somebody else in her place.

Whenever it happened, he felt a little painful sensation of choking, like a man who is suddenly deprived of air; until he looked at her and saw that she was outwardly herself. Then he adjusted the halo of ideality upon the artist again, and continued to love Margaret Donne with all his heart.

CHAPTER XIX

There is a certain kind, or perhaps it is only a certain degree, of theatrical reputation, which makes its coming felt in all sorts of ways, like a change in the weather. The rise of literary men to fame is almost always a surprise to themselves, their families, and their former instructors. Especially the latter, who know much more than the young novelist does, but have never been able to do anything with their knowledge, hold up their shrivelled, or podgy, or gouty old hands in sorrow, declaring that the success of a boy who was such a dolt, such a good-for-nothing, such a conceited jackanapes at school, only shows what the judgment of the public is worth, and how very low its standard has fallen. But the great public does not think much of decayed schoolmasters at best, and is never surprised that a young man should succeed, for the very simple reason that if he did not, some other young man certainly would; and to those who do not know the colour of the author's hair and eyes, the difference between Mr. Brown, Mr. Jones, and Mr. Robinson, in private life, must be purely a matter of imagination.

But theatrical reputation is a different matter, and its rise affects the professional barometer beforehand. The people who train great singers and great actors know what they are about and foresee the result, as no publisher can foresee it with regard to a new writer. There is a right way and a wrong way of singing, one must sing in tune unless one sings out of tune, there are standards of comparison in the persons of the great singers who are still at their best. It is not easy to be mistaken, where so much is a matter of certainty and so little depends on chance, and the facts become known very easily. The first-rate second-rate artists, climbing laboriously in the wake of the real first-rates, and wishing that these would die and get out of the way, feel a hopeless sinking at the heart as they hear behind them the rush of another coming genius. The tired critics sleep less soundly in the front row of the stalls, the fine and frivolous ladies who come to the opera to talk the whole evening are told that for once they will have to be silent, the reporters put on little playful airs of mystery to say that they have been allowed to assist at a marvellous rehearsal or have been admitted to see the future diva putting on her cloak after a final interview with Schreiermeyer, whose attitude before her is described as being that of the donor of the picture in an old Italian altar-piece.

And all this is not mere advertisement; much of it is, in fact, nothing of the sort, and is not even suggested by Schreiermeyer, for he knows perfectly well that one performance will place his new star very nearly at her true value before the public, who will flock to hear her and take infinite pains to find out where and when she is going to sing the next time. It is just the outward, healthy stir that goes before certain kinds of theatrical success, and which is quite impossible where most other arts are concerned; perhaps--I suggest it with apologies to all living prima donnas and first tenors--the higher the art, the less can success be predicted. Was ever a great painter, a great sculptor or a great poet 'announced'? On the other hand, was there ever a great singer who was not appreciated till after death?

The public probably did not hear the name of Margaret Donne till much later, and then, with considerable indifference, but long before Margarita da Cordova made her début, her name was repeated, with more or less mistakes and eccentricities of pronunciation, from mouth to mouth, in London and Paris, and was even mentioned in St. Petersburg, Berlin and New York. Every one connected with the musical world, even if only as a regular spectator, felt that something extraordinary was coming.

Madame Bonanni wrote to Margaret that she wished to see her, and would come over to Paris expressly, if Margaret would only telegraph. She would come out to Versailles, she would make the acquaintance of that charming Mrs. Rushmore. Margaret wondered what would happen if the two women met, and what mutual effect they would produce upon each other, but her knowledge of Mrs. Rushmore made her doubt whether such a meeting were desirable. Instead of telegraphing to Madame Bonanni, she wrote her answer, proposing to go to the prima donna's house. But Madame Bonanni was impatient, and as no telegram came when she expected one, she did not wait for a possible letter. To Margaret's dismay and stupefaction, she appeared at Versailles about luncheon time, arrayed with less good taste than the lilies of the field, but yet in a manner to outdo Solomon in all his glory, and she was conveyed in a perfectly new motor car. When Margaret, looking on from beyond the pond, saw her descend from the machine, she could not help thinking of a dreadful fresco she had once seen on the ceiling of an Italian villa, representing a very florid, double-chinned, powerful eighteenth-century Juno apparently in the act of getting down into the room from her car, to the great inconvenience of every one below.

The English servant who opened the door was in distress of mind when he saw her, for since he had served in Mrs. Rushmore's very proper household he had never seen anything like Madame Bonanni as she stood there asking for Miss Donne, and evidently not in a mood to be patient. He was very much inclined to tell her that she had mistaken the house, and to shut the door in her face. There were people coming to luncheon, and it was just possible that she might be one of them; but if she was not, and if the others came and found such a person there, how truly awful it would be! Thus the footman reflected as he stood in the doorway, listening to Madame Bonanni's voluble French speech.

As she paused for a moment, he heard some one on the stairs. It was Mrs. Rushmore herself. He recognised her step and turned sharp round on his heels, still filling the door but exposing his broad back to the visitor.

'Very odd person asking to see Miss Donne, ma'am,' he said in low and hurried tones. 'Shall I say "not at home," ma'am?'

'By all means "not at home," James,' said Mrs. Rushmore.

James had not miscalculated his breadth, as to the door, but his height as compared with that of the odd person outside. She put her head over his shoulder and looked in at Mrs. Rushmore.

'May I please come in?' she asked in comprehensible English. 'I am Bonanni, the singer, and I want to see Miss Donne. I've come from London to--please? Yes?'

'Goodness gracious!' cried Mrs. Rushmore. 'Let the lady in at once, James!'

James disappeared, somehow, and the artist came into the darkened hall, and met Mrs. Rushmore.

The latter did not often meet a woman much bigger than herself, and actually felt small when she held out her hand. Madame Bonanni seemed to fill the little hall of the French cottage, and Mrs. Rushmore felt as if she were in danger of being turned out of it to make room.

'Margaret is in the garden,' she said. 'I am so pleased to meet you, Madame Bonanni! I hope you'll stay to lunch. Do come in, and I'll send for her. James!'

All this was said while the two large hands were mildly shaking one another; Mrs. Rushmore was not easily startled by the sudden appearance of lions--or lionesses--and was conscious of being tolerably consecutive in her speech. It was not Madame Bonanni's greatness that had taken her by surprise, but her size and momentum. The prima donna answered in French.

'You understand? Of course! Thank you! Then I will speak in my own language. I will go out to Miss Donne, if you permit. Luncheon? Ah, if I could! But I have just eaten. I am sure you have so many good things! Little Miss Donne--ah! here she is!'

At this point Margaret came in, pulling off the old garden hat she had worn when Lushington had come to see her. She was surprised that the prima donna did not throw her arms round her and kiss her, but the artist had judged Mrs. Rushmore in a flash and behaved with almost English gravity as she took Margaret's hand.

'I have come to Paris expressly to see you,' she said.

'Let me introduce you to Mrs. Rushmore,' said Margaret.

'It is done,' said Madame Bonanni, making a little stage courtesy at the elder woman. 'I broke into the house like a burglar, and found a charming hostess waiting to arrest me with the kindest invitation to luncheon!'

'What a delightful way of putting it!' cried Mrs. Rushmore, much pleased.

Margaret felt that Madame Bonanni was showing a side of her nature which she had not yet seen. It had never occurred to the girl that the singer could make pretty society speeches. But Madame Bonanni had seen many things in her time.

Margaret carried her off to her own room, after a few words more, for it was clear that her visitor had something private to say, and had come all the way from London to say it, apparently out of pure friendship. Her manner changed again when they were alone. By force of habit the big woman sat down on the piano-stool and turned over the music that was open on the instrument, and she seemed to pay no heed to what Margaret said. Margaret was thanking her for her visit, arranging the blinds, asking her if there was enough air, for the day was hot, inquiring about the weather in London, moving about the room with each little speech, and with the evident desire to start the conversation so as to find out why Madame Bonanni had come. But the singer turned over the pages obstinately, looked up rather coldly at Margaret now and then, and once or twice whistled a few bars of Rigoletto in a way that would have been decidedly rude, had it not been perfectly clear that she did not know what she was doing, and was really trying to make up her mind how to begin. Margaret understood, and presently let her alone, and just sat down on a chair at the corner of the piano with a bit of work, and waited to see what would happen.

'I thought it might help you a little if I ran through the opera with you,' said Madame Bonanni, after a long time. 'I have sung it very often.'

But as she spoke she shut the score on the piano rather sharply, as if she had changed her mind. Margaret looked up quickly in surprise and dropped her work in her lap.

'You did not come all the way from London for that?' she asked, in a voice full of gratitude and wonder.

There was a moment's pause, during which the singer looked uneasy.

'No,' she said, 'I didn't. I never could lie very well--I can't at all to-day! But I would have come, only for that, if I had thought you needed it. That is the truth.'

'How good you are!' Margaret cried.

'Good!'

The singer's hand covered her big eyes for a moment and her elbow rested on the edge of the piano desk. There was a very sad note in the single word she had spoken, a note of despair not far off; but Margaret did not understand.

'What is the matter?' she asked, leaning forward, and laying one hand gently on Madame Bonanni's wrist. 'Why do you speak like that?'

'Do you think you would have been any better, in my place?'

The question came in a harsh tone, suddenly, as if it broke through some opposing medium, the hand dropped from the brow, and the big dark eyes gazed into Margaret's almost fiercely. Still the girl did not understand.

'Better? I? In what way? Tell me what it is, if something is distressing you. Let me help you, if I can. You know I will, with all my heart.'

'Yes, I know.' Madame Bonanni's voice sank again. 'But how can you? The trouble is older than you are. There is one thing--yes--there is one thing, if you could say it truly! It would help me a little if you could say it--and yet--no--I'm not sure--if you did, it would only show that you have more heart than he has.'

'Who?' Margaret vaguely guessed the truth.

'Who? Tom--my son! "Edmund Lushington," who feels that he cannot ask a respectable girl to marry him because his mother has been a wicked woman.'

The big woman shook from head to foot as she spoke.

Margaret was pained and her fingers tightened nervously on the other's wrist.

'Oh, please don't!' she cried. 'Please don't!'

'He's right,' answered Madame Bonanni, hanging her large head and shaking it despairingly. 'Of course, he's right, and it's true! But, oh!--she looked up again, suddenly--'oh, how much more right it must be for a man to forgive his mother, no matter what she has done!'

Margaret's fingers glided from the wrist they held, to the large hand, and pressed it sympathetically, but she could not find anything to say which would do. The friendly pressure, however, evidently meant enough to the distressed woman.

'Thank you, dear,' she said gratefully. 'You re very good to me. I know you mean it, too. Only, you re not placed as he is. If you were my daughter, you would think as he thinks--you would not live under my roof! Perhaps you would not even see me when we met in the street! You would look the other way!'

Margaret could not have told, for her life, what she would have done, but she was far too kind-hearted not to protest.

'Indeed I wouldn't!' she cried, with so much energy that Madame Bonanni believed her.

'No matter what I had done?' asked she pathetically eager for the assurance.

'You'd have been my mother just the same,' answered Margaret softly.

As the girl spoke, she felt a little sharp revolt in her heart against what she had said, at the mere thought of associating the word 'mother' with Madame Bonanni.

There was nothing at all psychological in that, and it would hardly bear analysing even by a professional dissector of character. It was just the natural feeling, in a natural girl, whose mother had been honest and good. But Madame Bonanni only heard the kind words.

'Yes,' she answered, 'I should have been your mother, just the same. But I couldn't have been a better mother to you than I've been to Tom. I couldn't, indeed!'

'No,' Margaret said, in the same gentle tone as before, 'you've been very good to him.'

'Yes! I have! He knows it, and he does not deny it!' Madame Bonanni suddenly sat up quite straight and squeezed Margaret's hands by way of emphasis. 'But he does not care,' she went on, her anger rising a little. 'Not he! He would rather that I should have been any sort of miserable little proper middle-class woman, if I could only have been technically "virtuous"! If I had been that, I might have beaten him to an omelette every day when he was a boy, and tormented him like a gadfly when he was a man! He would have preferred it--oh, by far! That is the logic of men, my dear, their irrefutable logic that they are always talking about and facing us down with! The miserable little animal! I will give up loving him, I will hate him, as he deserves, I will tell him to go to Peru, where he will never see his wicked old mother again! Then he will be sorry, he will wish he were dead, but I shall not go to him, never, never, never!'

She spoke the last words with tremendous energy, and a low echo of her voice came back out of the open piano from the strings. She clenched her fist and shook it at an imaginary Lushington in space, and for a moment her face wore a look of Medean menace.

Margaret might have smiled, if she had not felt that the strange creature was really and truly suffering, in her own way, to the borders of distraction. Then, suddenly, the great frame was convulsed again and quivered from head to foot.

'I'm going to cry,' she announced, in rather shaky tones.

And she cried. She slipped from the piano-stool to the floor, upon her knees, and her heavy arms fell upon the keys with a crashing discord, and her face buried itself in the large depths of one bent elbow, quite regardless of damage to Paquin's masterpiece of a summer sleeve; and with huge sobs the tears welled up and overflowed, taking everything they found in their way, including paint, and washing all down between the ivory keys of Margaret's piano.

Margaret saw that there was nothing to be done. At first she tried to soothe her as best she could, standing over her, and laying a hand gently on her shoulder; but Madame Bonanni shook it off with a sort of convulsive shudder, as a big carthorse gets rid of a fly that has settled on a part of his back inaccessible to his tail. Then Margaret desisted, knowing that the fit must go on to its natural end, and that it was hopeless to try and stop it sooner. Women are very practical with each other in crying matters, but it is bad for us men if we treat them in the same sensible way under the identical circumstances. Margaret sat down again in her chair, and instead of taking up her work, she leaned forward towards the weeping woman, to be ready with a word of sympathy as soon as it could be of any use. She watched the heavy head, the strong and coarse dark hair, the large animal construction of the neck and shoulders, the massive hands, discoloured now with straining upon themselves; nothing escaped her, as she quietly waited for the sobbing to cease; and though she felt the peasant nature there, close to her, in all its rugged strength, yet she felt, too, that with certain differences of outward refinement, it was not unlike her own. Her own hair, for instance, was much finer; but then, fair hair is generally finer than dark. Her own hands were smaller than Madame Bonanni's; but then, they had never been used to manual labour when she had been a girl. And as for the rest of her, she knew that Madame Bonanni had been reckoned a beauty in her day, such a beauty that very great and even royal personages indeed had done extremely foolish things to please her; and that very beauty had been in part the cause of those very tears the poor woman was shedding now. Margaret was quite sensible enough to admit that she herself, after a quarter of a century of stage life, might turn into very much the same type of woman. While waiting to be sympathetic at the right moment, therefore, she studied Madame Bonanni's appearance with profound and melancholy interest. She had never had such a good chance.

The convulsive sobbing grew regular, then more slow, then merely intermittent, and then it stopped altogether. But before she lifted her face from the hollow of her elbow, Madame Bonanni felt about for something with her other hand; and Margaret, being a woman, knew that she wanted her handkerchief before showing her face, and picked it up and gave it to her. A man would probably have taken the groping fingers and pressed them, or kissed them, probably supposing that to be what was wanted, and thereby much retarding the progress of events.

Madame Bonanni pushed up the handkerchief between her face and her elbow and moved it about, with a vague idea of equalising her colour in one general tint, then blew her nose, and then sprang to her feet at once, with that wonderful elasticity which was always so surprising in her sudden movements. Moreover, she got up turning her face away from Margaret, and made for the nearest mirror.

'Lord!' she exclaimed, laconically, as she looked at herself and realised the full extent of the damage done.

'Wouldn't you like to wash your face?' asked Margaret, following her at a discreet distance.

'My dear,' answered Madame Bonanni, in a perfectly matter-of-fact tone, 'it's awful, of course, but there's nothing else to be done!'

'Come into my dressing-room.'

'If I were at home, I should take a bath and dress over a--a--a----' One last most unexpected sob half choked her and then made her cough, till she stamped her foot with anger.

'Bah!' she cried with contempt when she got her breath. 'If I had often made myself look like such a monster, I should have been a perfectly good woman! The men would have run from me like mice from a barn on fire! Have you got any of that Vienna liquid soap, my dear!'

Margaret had the liquid soap, as it chanced, and in a few moments she was busily occupied in helping Madame Bonanni to restore her appearance. Though long, the process was only partially successful, from the latter's own point of view. Having washed away all that had been, she produced a gold box from the bag she wore at her side. The box was divided into three compartments containing respectively rouge, white powder and a miniature puff for applying both, which she proceeded to do abundantly, sitting at Margaret's toilet-table and talking while she worked. She had made more confusion in the small dressing-room in five minutes than Margaret could have made in dressing twice over. Paint-stained towels strewed the floor, chairs were upset, soap and water was splashed everywhere. Now she started afresh, by rubbing plentiful daubs of rouge into her dark cheeks.

'But why do you put on so much?' Margaret asked in wonder.

'My dear, I'm an actress,' said Madame Bonanni. 'I'm not ashamed of my profession! If I didn't paint, people would say I was trying to pass myself off for a lady! Besides, now that I have cried, nothing but powder will hide it. Look at my nose, my dear--just look at my nose! Little Miss Donne'--she turned upon Margaret with sudden, tragic energy--'don't ever let that wretched boy know that I cried about him! Eh? Never! Promise you won't!'

'No, indeed! You may trust me. Why should I tell?'

'But it doesn't matter. Tell him if you like. I don't care. My life is over now, and there is no reason why I should care about anything, is there?'

'What do you mean by saying that your life is over?' Margaret asked.

Madame Bonanni's head fell upon the edge of the table and she looked at herself in the glass for some moments before she answered.

'I have left the stage,' she said, very quietly.

'Left the stage? For good?' Margaret was amazed.

'Yes. I was not going to have any farewells or last appearances. Those things are only done to make money. Schreiermeyer was very nice about it. He agreed to cancel the rest of my engagements in a friendly way.'

'But why? Why have you done it?' asked Margaret, still bewildered by the news.

Madame Bonanni had done one cheek and half the other. She leaned back in the comfortable chair before the glass and looked at herself again, not at all at the effect of her work, but at her eyes, as if she were searching for something.

'There is not room for you and me,' she said, presently.

'I don't understand,' Margaret answered. 'Not room? Where?'

'On the stage. I have been the great lyric soprano a long time. Next month you will be the great lyric soprano--there is not room----'

'Nonsense!' Margaret broke in. 'I shall never be what you are----'

'Not what I was, perhaps, because this is another age. Taste and teaching and the art itself--all have changed. But you are young, fresh, untouched, unheard--all, you have it all, as I had once. You are not the artist I am, but you will be one day, and meanwhile you have all I have no more. If I had stayed on the stage, we should have been rivals next season. They would have said: "Cordova has a better voice, but Bonanni is still the greater artist." Do you see?'

'Yes. And why should you not be pleased at that?' asked Margaret. 'Or why should not I be quite satisfied, and more than satisfied?'

'I wasn't thinking of us,' said Madame Bonanni, looking up to Margaret's face with an expression that was almost beautiful, in spite of the daubs of paint and the disarranged hair. 'I was thinking of him.'

Margaret began to guess, and her lip quivered a moment, for she was touched.

'Yes,' she said. 'I think I see.'

'He loves you,' said Madame Bonanni, still looking at her. 'I have guessed it. It is very hard for me to get him to like me a little, and he would not forgive me if the really good critics said I was a better artist than you. That would be one thing more against me, my dear, and he has so many things against me already! So I have given it up. Why should I go on singing, now? He does not care any more. When he has once heard you he will never want to come again and sit in the middle of the theatre all alone in the audience just to hear me, as he often did. Then I sang my best. I never sang as I have sung for him, when I have caught sight of his face in the audience. No, not for kings.

I used to go and look through the curtain before it went up, if I thought he was there. And it was just to hear me that he came, just for the artistic pleasure! He never came to my dressing-room, for that destroyed the illusion. But now he will go and hear you, and it would make him very bitter against me if any one said I sang better. Do you understand?'

'Yes. I understand.'

Margaret bent her head a little and looked down, wondering and puzzled, yet believing.

'At least I can do that for him.' Madame Bonanni sighed, looking into the glass again. 'I cannot undo my life, but I need not seem to him to be a hindrance in yours.'

It was impossible to receive such a confidence without being deeply touched, and Margaret's own voice shook a little as she answered.

'There have not been many mothers like you since the world began,' she said.

'I will tell you!' The singer turned half round in her chair with one of her sudden movements. 'If I had known that I was going to be so fond of him--and oh, my dear, if I could have guessed that he would care so much!--I would have led a different life! I would have left the stage if I could not. Oh, don't think it is so easy to be good! But it's possible! One can--one could, if one only knew--for the sake of some one whom one loves very dearly!'

'Of course it is!' answered Margaret, with all the heavenly self-confidence of untried virtue.

Madame Bonanni looked at her with a peculiar expression. There was a little pity in the look, and great doubt, a shade of amusement, perhaps, and a great longing envy through it all.

'Of course?' she repeated, in a thoughtful way. 'Did you mean "of course it is possible--and easy," my dear? The tone of your voice made me think that was what you meant. Yes--you meant that, and you have a right to mean it, but you don't know. That's the great difference--you don't know! You haven't begun as I did. You're a lady, a real lady, brought up amongst ladies from your childhood. But that's not what will keep you good! It's not your refinement, nor your good manners, nor your white hands that never milked a cow, or swept a stable, or hoed the weeds out from between the vines in summer. That was my work till I was seventeen. And my mother was a good woman, my dear, just as good as yours, though she was only a peasant of Provence. How do I know it? If she had not been good, my father would have killed her, of course. That was our custom. And he was good, in his way, too, and kind. He always told me that if I went wrong he would shoot me--and when the English artist came and lodged in our house for the summer and made love to me, my father explained everything to him also. So poor Goodyear saw that he must marry me, and we were married, before I was eighteen. He took me away to Paris, and tried to make a lady of me, and he had me taught to sing, because he loved my voice. Do you see? That was how it all happened--and still I was good, as good as you are! Yes--"of course," as you say! It was easy enough!'

'He died young, didn't he?' Margaret asked quietly.

She had seated herself on the corner of the toilet-table to listen, while Madame Bonanni leaned back in the low chair and looked at herself, sometimes absently, sometimes with pity.

'Yes,' she answered. 'He died very soon and left me nothing but Tommy and my voice. Poor Goodyear! He painted very badly, he never sold anything, and his father starved him because he had married me. It was far better that he should die of pneumonia than of hunger, for that would certainly have been the end of it.'

'And you went on the stage at once?' Margaret asked, wishing to hear more.

Madame Bonanni shrugged her shoulders and leaned forward to the looking-glass.

'I had a fortune in my throat,' she said, daubing rouge on the cheek that was only half done. 'I had been well taught in those years, and there were plenty of managers only too anxious to offer me their protection--managers and other people, too. What could I do?'

She shrugged her shoulders again, and laughed a little harshly as she gave a half-shy glance at Margaret. The latter was not a child, but a grown woman of two-and-twenty. She answered gravely.

'With your voice and talent, I don't see why you needed any protection, as you call it.'

Madame Bonanni laughed again.

'No? You don't see? All the better, little Miss Donne, all the better for you that you have never been made to see, and perhaps you never will now. I hope not. But I tell you that in Paris, or in London, or Berlin, or Petersburg you may have the voice and talent of Malibran, Grisi and Patti all in one, but if you are not "protected" you will never get any further than leading chorus-girl, and perhaps not so far!'

'No one has protected me,' said Margaret, 'and I've got a good engagement.'

The prima donna stared at her for a moment in surprise, and then went on making up her face. The girl had talent, genius, perhaps, but she must be oddly simple if she did not realise that she owed her engagement altogether to the woman who was talking to her. Was Margaret going to take that position from the first? Madame Bonanni wondered. Was she going to deliberately ignore that she had been taken up bodily, as it were, and carried through the short cut to celebrity? Or was it just the simple, stupid, innocent vanity that so often goes with great gifts, making their possessors quite sure that they can never owe the least part of their success to any help received from any one else? Whatever it might be, Madame Bonanni was not the woman to remind Margaret of what had happened. She only smiled a little and put on more powder.

'I'm not defending my life, my dear,' she said, quietly, after a little pause. 'Of what use would that be, now that the best part of it is over--or the worst part? I'm not even asking for your sympathy, am I?' Her voice was suddenly bitter. 'I only care for one human being in the world--I think I never cared for any other, since he was born! Does that make my life worse? It does, doesn't it? In the name of heaven, child,' she broke out fiercely and angrily, without the least warning, 'was no woman ever flattered into playing at love? Not even by a King? Am I the only living woman that has been carried off her feet by royalty? It wasn't only the King, of course--I don't pretend it was--there were others. But that's what Tom will never forgive me--the money and the jewels! What could I do? Throw them in his face, scream outraged virtue and cry that he was offending me, when he had nothing more to ask, and I was half drunk with pride and vanity and amusement, because he was really in love? Tell some great lady, your duchess, your princess, to do that sort of thing--if you think she will! Don't ask it of a Provence girl who has milked the cows and hoed the vines, and then suddenly has half Europe at her feet, and a King into the bargain! There was only one thing in the world that could have saved me then--it would have been to know that Tom would never forgive me. And he was only a little boy--how could I guess?'

She looked up almost wildly into Margaret's eyes, and then bent down, resting her forehead upon her hands, on the edge of the table.

'Don't be afraid,' she said, 'I'm not going to cry again--never again, I think! It's over and finished, with the other things!'

She remained in the same position nearly a minute, and then sat up quite straight before the glass, as if nothing had happened, and powdered her cheeks again.

Margaret sat still on the corner of the table, not at all sure of what she had better say or do. She only hoped that Madame Bonanni would not ask her whether she cared for Lushington and would marry him, supposing that his scruples could be overcome, and she had a strong suspicion that it was to ask this that Madame Bonanni had come to see her. It would be rather hard to answer, Margaret knew, and she turned over words and expressions in her mind.

She might have spared herself the trouble, for nothing could have been further from her companion's thoughts just then. The dramatic moment had passed and Margaret had scarcely noticed it, beyond being very much surprised at the news it had brought her of the great singer's retiring from the stage. Perhaps, too, Margaret was a little inclined to doubt whether Madame Bonanni would abide by her resolution in the future, though she was perfectly in earnest at present.

'I shall be at your first night,' said the prima donna, finishing her operations at last, and carefully shutting her little gold box. 'If you have a dress rehearsal, I'll be at that, too.'

'Thank you,' Margaret answered. 'Yes--there is to be a dress rehearsal on Sunday. Schreiermeyer insists on it for me. He's afraid I shall have stage fright because I'm so cool now, I suppose.'

She laughed, contentedly and perfectly sure of herself.

'The only thing I don't like is being brought on in the sack to sing that last scene.'

'Eh?' Madame Bonanni stared in surprise.

'The sack,' Margaret repeated. 'The last scene. Don't you know?'

'I know--but it's always left out. Nobody has sung that for years. It's a chorus-girl who is brought on in the bag, and when Rigoletto sees her face he screams and the curtain goes down. You don't mean to say that Schreiermeyer wants you to do the whole scene?

'Yes. We've rehearsed it ever so often. I thought it was strange, too. He says that if it does not please people at the dress rehearsal, we can leave it out on the real night.'

'I never heard of anything so ridiculous in my life!' Madame Bonanni was evidently displeased.

She had once done the 'sack' scene herself to satisfy the caprice of a foreign sovereign who wished to see the effect of it, and she had a vivid and disagreeable recollection of being half dragged, half carried, inside a brown canvas bag, and then put down rather roughly; and then, of not knowing at what part of the stage she was, while she listened to Rigoletto s voice; and of the strong, dusty smell of the canvas, that choked her, so that she wanted to cough and sneeze when Rigoletto tore open the bag and let her head out; and then, of having to sing in a very uncomfortable position; and, altogether, of a most disagreeable quarter of an hour just at the very time when she should have been getting her wig and paint off in her dressing-room. Moreover, the scene was a failure, as it always has been wherever it has been tried. She told Margaret this.

'At all events,' she concluded, 'you won't have to do it on the real night.'

They were in the larger room again. But for the decided damage done to her sleeve by her tears, Madame Bonanni had restored her outward appearance tolerably well. She stood at the corner of the piano, resting one hand upon it.

'I'm sorry for you, my dear,' she said cheerfully, because I've given you so much trouble, but I'm glad I cried as much as I wanted to. It's horribly bad for the voice and complexion, but nothing really refreshes one so much. I felt as if my heart were going to break when I got here.'

'And now?' Margaret smiled, standing beside the elderly woman and idly turning over the music on the desk of the instrument.

'I suppose it has broken,' Madame Bonanni answered. 'At all events, I don't feel it any more. No--really--I don't! He may go to Peru, if he likes--I hope he will, the ungrateful little beast! I'll never think of him again! When you have made your début, I'm going to live in the country. There's plenty to do there! Bonanni shall milk cows again and hoe the furrows between the vines this summer! Bonanni shall go back to Provence and be an old peasant woman, where she was once a peasant girl, and married the English painter. Do you think I've forgotten the language, or the songs?'

One instant's pause, and the singer's great voice broke out in the small room with a volume of sound so tremendous that it seemed as if it would rend the walls and the ceiling. It was an ancient Provençal song that she sang, in long-drawn cadences with strange falls and wild intervals, the natural music of an ancient, gifted people. It was very short, for she only sang one stanza of it, and in less than a minute it was finished and she was silent again. But her big dark eyes, still swollen and bloodshot, were looking out to a distance far beyond the green trees she saw through the open window.

Margaret, who had listened, repeated the wild melody very softly, and sounded each note of it without the words, as if she wished to remember it always; and a nearer sight came back to the elder woman's eyes as she listened to the true notes that never faltered, and were as pure as sounding silver, and as smooth as velvet and as rich as gold. It was a little thing, but one of those little things that only a born great singer could have done faultlessly at the first attempt; and Madame Bonanni listened with rare delight. Then she laughed, as happily as if she had no heartaches in the world.

'Little Miss Donne, little Miss Donne!' she cried, shaking a fat finger, 'you will turn many heads before long! You shall come to my cottage in the autumn, when we have the vintage, and there you will find old Bonanni looking after the work in a ragged straw hat, with no paint on her cheeks. And in the evening we will sit upon the door-step together, and you shall tell me how the heads turned round and round, and I will teach you all the old songs of Provence. Will you come?'

'Indeed, I will,' Margaret answered, smiling. 'I would cross Europe to see you--you have been so good to me. Do you know? I want you to forgive me for what I said in the dressing-room about my engagement. I remember how you looked when I said it, and now I know that you did not understand. Of course I owe it all to you--but that isn't what you meant by--"protection"?'

The prima donna's expression changed again, and grew hard and almost sullen.

'Never mind that,' she said, roughly. 'I wasn't thinking of that. I didn't notice what you said.'

She turned her back to Margaret, walked to the window and stood there looking out while she put on her gloves. But Margaret was humble, in spite of the rudeness.

'I'm sorry,' she said, following a little way. 'I'm very sorry--I----'

Madame Bonanni did not even turn her head to listen. Margaret did not try to say anything more, but broke off and waited patiently. Then the elder woman turned quickly and fiercely, buttoning the last button of her glove.

'If my own son has done much worse to me, why should I care what any one else can do?' she asked.

But Margaret was obstinate in her humility and would not be put off. She took one of Madame Bonanni's hands and made her look at her.

'I would not say or do anything that could hurt you for all the world,' said Margaret, very earnestly. 'I won't let you go away thinking that I could, and angry with me. Don't you believe me?'

There was no resisting the tone and the look, and Madame Bonanni was not able to be angry long. Her large mouth widened slowly in a bright smile, and the next moment she threw her arms round Margaret and kissed her on both cheeks.

'Bah!' she cried, 'I didn't think I could still be so fond of anybody, since that wretched boy of mine broke my heart! It's ridiculous, but I really believe there's nothing I wouldn't do for you, child!'

She was heartily in earnest, though she little guessed what she was going to do for Margaret within a few days. But Margaret, who was really grateful, was nevertheless glad that there was apparently nothing more that Madame Bonanni could do. She was not quite sure that the great singer's retirement would prove final; and on cool reflection she found it hard to believe that the motive for it was the one the latter alleged, and which had so touched her at first that it had brought tears to her eyes. The Anglo-Saxon woman could not help looking at the Latin woman with a little apprehension and a good deal of scepticism.

CHAPTER XX

The stage was set for the introduction to the first act of *Rigoletto*, the curtain was down, the lights were already up in the house and a good many people were in their seats or standing about and chatting quietly. It was a hot afternoon in July, and high up in the gallery the summer sunshine streamed through an open window full upon the blazing lights of the central chandelier, a straight, square beam of yellow gold thrown across a white fire, and clearly seen through it.

It was still afternoon when the dress rehearsal began, but the night would have come when it ended. There is always a pleasant latitude about dress rehearsals, even when the piece is old and there is no new stage machinery to be tried. While the play or the opera is actually going on, everything works quickly as in a real performance, but between the acts, or even between one scene and another, there is a tendency on the part of the actors and the invited public to treat the whole affair as a party of pleasure. Doors of communication are opened which would otherwise be shut, people wander about the house, looking for their friends, and if there is plenty of room they change seats now and then. Many of the people are extremely shabby, others are preternaturally smart; if it is in the daytime everybody wears street clothes and the women rarely take off their hats. It is only at the evening dress rehearsals of important new pieces at the great Paris theatres that the house presents its usual appearance, but then there have been already three or four real dress rehearsals at which the necessary work has been done.

The theatre at which Margaret was making her début was a large one in a Belgian city, a big modern house, to all appearance, and really fitted with the usual modern machinery which has completely changed the working of the stage since electricity was introduced. But the building itself was old and was full of queer nooks at the back, and passages and shafts long disused; and it had two stage entrances, one of which was now kept locked, while the other had the usual swinging doors guarded by a sharp-eyed doorkeeper who knew and remembered several thousand faces of actors, singers, authors, painters, and carpenters, and of other privileged persons from princes and bankers to dressmakers' girls who had, or had once had, the right to enter by the stage door. The two entrances were on opposite sides of the building. The one no longer in use led out to a dark, vaulted passage or alley wide enough for a carriage to enter; and formerly the carriages of the leading singers had driven up by that way, entering at one end and going out at the other, but the side that had formerly led to the square before the theatre was now built up, and contained a small shop having a back door in the dark alley, and only the other exit remained, and it opened upon an unfrequented street behind the theatre.

The dressing-rooms had been disposed with respect to this old entrance, and their position had never been changed. It had been convenient for the prima donna to be able to reach her carriage after the performance without crossing the stage; whereas, as things were now arranged, she had a long distance to go. The new stage door had been made within the last ten years, so that every one who had known the theatre longer than that was well aware of the existence of the old one, though few people knew that it could still be opened on emergency, as in case of fire, and that it was also used for bringing in the unusually big boxes in which some of the great singers sent their dresses. The dressing-rooms opened upon a wide but ill-lighted corridor which led from the stage near the back on the left; the last dressing-room was the largest and was always the prima donna's. Just beyond it a door closed the end of the passage, leading to the doorkeeper's former vestibule, which was now never lighted, and beyond that a short flight of steps led down to the locked outer door, on the level of the street. In the same corridor there were of course other dressing-rooms which were not all used in Rigoletto, an opera which has only two principal women's parts; whereas in the Huguenots, for instance, the rooms would all have been full, there would have been a number of maids about and more lights. In Rigoletto, too, the contralto does not even come to the theatre to dress until the opera is more than half over, as she is only on in the third act. The Contessa and Giovanna do not count, as they have so little to do.

This short explanation of the topography of the building is necessary in order to understand clearly what happened on that memorable afternoon and evening.

Margaret Donne was in her dressing-room, quite unaware that anything was going to occur beyond the first great ordeal of singing to a full house, a matter which was of itself enough to fill the day and to bring even Margaret's solid nerves to a state of tension which she had not anticipated. The bravest and coolest men have felt their hearts beating faster just before facing cold steel or going into battle, and almost all of them have felt something else too, which has nothing to do with the heart, and which I can only compare to what many women suffer from when there is going to be a thunderstorm--an indescribable physical restlessness and bodily irritation which make it irksome to stay long in one position and impossible to think consecutively and reasonably about ordinary matters. There is no sport like fighting with real weapons, with the certainty that life itself is depending at every instant on one's own hand and eye. No other game of skill or hazard can compare with that. It is chess, played for life and death, with an element of chance which chess has not; your foot may slip, your eye may be dazzled by a ray of light or a sudden reflection, or if you are not a first-rate player you may miscalculate your distance by four inches, which, in steel, is exactly enough; or if the weapons are fire-arms you may aim a little too high or too low, or the other man may, and that little will mean the difference between time and eternity.

But in the scale of emotion and excitement the theatre comes next to fighting, whether you be the author of the play or opera to be given for the first time before the greatest and most critical audience in the world, or the actor, or actress, or singer, who has not yet been heard or seen and of whom wonders are expected on the great night.

Margaret had not believed it true, though she had often heard it, and now she was amazed at the strangeness of the physical sensation which came over her and grew till it was almost intolerable. It was not fright, for she longed for the moment of appearing; it was not ordinary nervousness, for she felt that she was as steady as a rock, and now and then, when she tried a few notes, to 'limber' her voice, it was steady, too, and exactly what it always was. Yet she felt as if some tremendous, unseen shape of strength had hold of her and were pressing her to itself; and then again, she was sure that she was going to see something unreal in her brightly-lighted, whitewashed dressing-room, and that if she did see it, she should be frightened. But she saw nothing; nothing but the dresses she was to wear, the handsome court gown of the second act, the limp purple silk tights, the doublet, long cloak and spurred boots of the third, all laid out carefully in their newness, on the small sofa and the chairs. She saw Madame Bonanni's cadaverous maid, too, standing motionless and ready if wanted, and looking at her with a sort of inscrutable curiosity; for the retired prima donna had insisted upon doing Margaret the signal service of passing on to her one of the most accomplished theatrical dressers in Europe. A woman who had made Madame Bonanni look like Juliet or Lucia could make Margarita da Cordova look a goddess from Olympus; and she did, from the theatrical point of view. But Margaret was not yet used to seeing herself in the glass when her face was made up, beautifully though it was done, and she kept away from the two mirrors as much as she could while she slowly paced the well-worn carpet, moving her shoulders now and then, and her arms, as if to make sure that she was at ease in her stage clothes.

There was no one in the room but she and the maid. She had particularly asked Schreiermeyer not to come and see her till the end of the second act, and Madame Bonanni stayed away of her own accord, rather to Margaret's surprise, but greatly to her relief. At the last minute Mrs. Rushmore had refused to come at all, and had stayed in France, in a state of excitement and almost terror which made her very unlike herself, and would have rendered her a most disturbing companion. She could not see it, she said. The daughter of her old friend should always be welcome in her house, but Mrs. Rushmore could not face the theatre, to see Margaret come on in the last scene booted and spurred like a man. That was more than she could bear. You might say what you liked, but she would never see Margaret on the stage, never, never! And so she would keep her old illusions about the girl, and it would be easier to welcome her when she came on a visit. Margaret must have a chaperon of course, but she must hire one of those respectable-looking stage mothers who are always to be had when young actresses need them. It would have broken her old friend's heart to see her daughter chaperoned by a 'stage mother,' but it could not be helped. That much protection was necessary. She had burst into a very painful fit of crying when Margaret had left her, and had really suffered more than at any time since the death of the departed Mr. Rushmore.

Logotheti had given no sign of life, and Margaret had neither seen him nor heard from him since the eventful day when she had last spoken to him in his own house. He would not even come this evening, she was sure. He had either given her up altogether, or he had amused himself by obeying her to the letter; in which case he would not present himself till after the real performance, which was to take place on the next day but one. He might have written a note, or sent a telegram, she thought; but on the whole she cared very little. If she thought of any one but herself at that moment she thought of

Lushington and wished she might see him again between the acts. He had called in the afternoon, and had been very quiet and sympathetic. She had feared that even at the last he would make a scene and entreat her to change her mind, and give up the idea of the stage, at any cost. But instead, he now seemed resigned to her future career, talked cheerfully and predicted unbounded success.

She had received very many letters and telegrams from other friends, and some of them lay in a heap on the dressing-table. The greater part were from people who had known her at Mrs. Rushmore's, and who did not look upon her attempt as anything more than the caprice of a gifted amateur. Society always finds it hard to believe that one of its own can leave it and turn professional.

It was like Margaret to prefer solitude just then. People who trust themselves would generally rather be alone just before a great event in their lives, and Margaret trusted herself a good deal more than she trusted any one else. Nevertheless, she began to feel that unless something happened soon, the nameless, indescribable pressure she felt would become unbearable, and as she walked the shabby carpet, her step accented itself to a little tramp, like a marching step. The cadaverous maid looked on with curiosity and said nothing. In her long career she had never dressed a débutante, and she had heard that débutantes sometimes behaved oddly before going on. Besides, she knew something which Margaret did not know; for when she had come down to the theatre in the morning with the luggage, she had met Madame Bonanni in the dressing-room, and her late mistress had given her a piece of information and some very precise instructions.

A moment came when Margaret felt that she could no longer bear the close atmosphere of the small room and the curious eyes of the cadaverous maid, watching her as she walked up and down. Madame Bonanni would have made the woman go out or even stand with her face to the wall, but Margaret had not yet lost that aristocratic sense of consideration for servants which Plato ascribes to pride. Instead of turning the maid out, Margaret suddenly opened the door wide and stood on the threshold, breathing with relief the not very sweet air that came down the corridor from the stage. It came laden with a compound odour of ropes, dusty scenery, mouldy flour paste and cotton velvet furniture, the whole very hot and far from aromatic, but at that moment as refreshing as a sea-breeze to the impatient singer. The smell had already acquired associations for her during the long weeks of rehearsal, and she liked it; for it meant the stage, and music, and the sound of her own beautiful voice, high and clear above the rest. Lushington might think of her when spring violets were near him, Logotheti might associate with her the intoxicating perfumes of the East, but Margaret's favourite scent was already that strange compound of smells which meets the nostrils nowhere in the world except behind the scenes. I have often wondered why the strong draught that comes from the back when the curtain is up does not blow the smell into the house, to the great annoyance of the audience; but it does not. Perhaps, like everything else behind the curtain, it is not real, after all; or perhaps it has a very high specific gravity, and would stay behind even if all the air passed out, preferring the vacuum which nature abhors--nothing would seem too absurd to account for the phenomenon.

It did not occur to Margaret to wonder that there should be a draught at all, at the end of a closed corridor. She stood on the threshold, resting one hand on the door-post and looking towards the stage. In the distance she could see it, somewhere in the neighbourhood of what is technically described as L 3, where a group of courtiers and court ladies were standing ready to go on in the Introduction. The border lights were up already, Margaret could see that, and just then she heard the warning signal to be ready to raise the curtain, and the first distant notes of the orchestra reached her ears. She breathed a sigh of relief. The long-wished-for ordeal had begun at last, and the tension of her nerves relaxed. The sensation was strangely delicious and quite new to her; the quiet and solitude of the dressing-room would not be disagreeable now, nor the steady gaze of the sallow-faced maid.

She turned half round to step back, and in so doing faced the end of the corridor. She had not the slightest idea of what was beyond the door she saw there, and which she had not noticed before, but she saw that it was now not quite shut, and that it moved slowly on its hinges as if it had been more open until that moment. So far as she knew there was no reason why it should be closed, but a little natural curiosity moved her to go and see what there was on the other side of it. It was not three steps from her own door, yet when she reached it, it was tightly closed, and when she took hold of the handle of the latch it resisted the effort she made to open it, though she had not heard the key turn in the lock. This seemed strange, but being under the influence of a much stronger excitement than she herself realised, she turned back without thinking seriously of it, being willing to believe that her sight had deceived her, where the light was so dim, and that the door had not been really open at all. Her eyes met those of the maid, who had evidently come to the threshold of the dressing-room to watch her.

'I thought that door was open,' she said, as if in answer to a question.

The woman said nothing, but passed her quickly and went and tried the lock herself. Though she was so very thin, she was strong, as bony people often are. She tried the handle with both hands, turned it, though with much difficulty, and pulled suddenly with all her might. The door yielded a little at first--not more than half an inch perhaps--but then it closed itself again with a strength far greater than she could resist. She shrugged her shoulders as she desisted and came back.

'It is a disused door,' she said. 'It will not open.'

Her tone was so indifferent that Margaret paid little attention to the words, and turned away to listen to the music which reached her from the stage. The curtain was up now, and the courtiers were dancing, up stage; she could see a few of them pass and repass; then she heard the little round of applause that greeted the Duke's appearance as he went forward to begin his scene with Borsa. He had many friends in the invited audience, and was moreover one of the popular light tenors of the day. Doubtless, the elderly woman of the world who worshipped him was there in her glory, in a stage-box, ready to split her gloves when he should sing 'La donna è mobile.' Margaret knew that the wholesale upholsterer who admired the contralto was not far off, for she had seen a man bringing in flowers for her, and no one else would have sent them to her for a mere dress rehearsal.

Margaret was so well used to the opera that the time passed quickly after the Duke had begun his scene.

The silent maid approached her with a hare's-foot and a saucer, to put a finishing touch on her face, to which she submitted with indifference, listening all the time to the music that came to her through the open door. There was time yet, but she was not impatient any more; the opera had begun and she was a part of it already, before she had set her foot upon the stage, before she had seen, for the first time, the full house before her, instead of the yawning emptiness. It would be dark when she went on, for Gilda's first entrance is in the night scene in the courtyard, but it would not be empty, and perhaps it would not be silent either. It was quite likely that a little encouraging applause for the young débutante would be heard.

Margaret smiled to herself as she thought of that. She would make them applaud her in real earnest before the curtain went down, not by way of good-natured encouragement, but whether they would or not. She was very sure of herself, and the cadaverous maid watched her with curiosity and admiration, wondering very much whether such pride might not go before a fall, and end in a violent stage fright. But then, the object of the dress rehearsal was to guard against the consequences of such a misfortune. If Margaret could not sing a note at first, it would not matter to-day, but it would certainly matter a good deal the day after to-morrow.

When the end of the Introduction was near, Margaret turned back into the room and sat down before the toilet-table to wait. She heard her maid shut the door, and the loud music of the full orchestra and chorus immediately sounded very faint and far away. When she looked round, she saw that the maid had gone out and that she was quite alone.

In ten minutes the scenery would be changed; five minutes after that, and her career would have definitely begun. She folded her whitened hands, leaned back thoughtfully and looked into her own eyes reflected in the mirror. The world knows very little about the great moments in artists' lives. It sees the young prima donna step upon the stage for the first time, smiling in the paint that perhaps hides her deadly pallor. She is so pretty, so fresh, so ready to sing! Perhaps she looks even beautiful; at all events, she is radiant, and looks perfectly happy. The world easily fancies that she has just left her nearest and dearest, her mother, her sisters, in the flies; that they have come with her to the boundary of the Play-King's Kingdom, and are waiting to lead her back to real life when she shall have finished her part in the pretty illusion.

The reality is different. Sometimes it is a sad and poor reality, rarely it is tragic; most often it is sordid, uninteresting, matter-of-fact, possibly vulgar; it is almost surely very much simpler than romantic people would wish it to be. As likely as not, the young prima donna is all alone just before going on, as Margaret was, looking at herself in the glass--this last, for one thing, is a certainty; and she is either badly frightened or very calm, for there is no such thing as being 'only a little' frightened the first time. That condition sometimes comes afterwards and may last through life. But pity those whose courage fails them the first time, for there is no more awful sensation for a man or woman in perfect health than to stand alone before a great audience, and suddenly to forget words, music, everything, and to see the faces of the people in the house turned upside down, and the chandelier swinging round like a wind mill while all the other lights tumble into it, and to notice with horror that the big stage is pitching and rolling like the most miserable little steamer that ever went to sea; and to feel that if one cannot remember one's part, one's head will certainly fly off at the neck and join the hideous dance of jumbled heads and lights and stalls and boxes in the general chaos.

Margaret, however, deserved no pity on that afternoon, for she was not in the least afraid of anything, except that the courtiers who were to carry her off at the end of her first scene might be clumsy, or that the sack in the last act would be dusty inside and make her sneeze. But as for that, she was willing that the ending should be a failure, as Madame Bonanni said it must be, for she did not mean to do it again if she could possibly help it.

She was not afraid, but she was not so very calm as she fancied she was, for afterwards, even on that very evening, she found it impossible to remember anything that happened from the moment when the sallow maid entered the dressing-room again, closely followed by the call-boy, who knocked on the open door and spoke her stage name, until she found herself well out on the stage, in Rigoletto's arms, uttering the girlish cry which begins Gilda's part. The three notes, not very high, not very loud, were drowned in the applause that roared at her from the house.

It was so loud, so unexpected, that she was startled for a moment, and remained with one arm on the barytone's shoulder looking rather shyly across the lowered footlights and over the director's head. He had already laid down his baton to wait.

'You must acknowledge that, and I must begin over again,' said the barytone, so loud that Margaret fancied every one must hear him.

He moved back a little when he had spoken and left her in the middle of the stage. She drew herself up, bent her head, smiled, and made a little courtesy, all as naturally as if she had never done anything else. Thereupon the clapping grew louder for one instant, and then ceased as suddenly as it had begun. The director raised his baton and looked at her, Rigoletto came forward once more calling to her, and she fell into his arms again with her little cry. There was no sound from the house now, and the silence was so intense that she could easily fancy herself at an ordinary rehearsal, with only a dozen or fifteen people looking on out of the darkness.

But she was thinking of nothing now. She was out of the world, in the Play-King's palace, herself a part, and a principal part, of an illusion, an imaginary personage in one of the dreams that great old Verdi had dreamt long ago, in his early manhood. Her lips parted and her matchless voice floated out of its own accord, filling the darkened air; she moved, but she did not know it, though every motion had been studied for weeks; she sung as few have ever sung, but it was to her as if some one else were singing while she listened and made no effort.

The duet is long, as Margaret had often thought when studying it, but now she was almost startled because it seemed to her so soon that she found herself once more embracing Rigoletto and uttering a very high note at the same time. Very vaguely she wondered whether the far-off person who had been singing for her had not left out something, and if so, why there had been no hitch. Then came the thunder of applause again, not in greeting now, but in praise of her, long-drawn, tremendous, rising and bursting and falling, like the breakers on an ocean beach.

'Brava! brava!' yelled Rigoletto in her ear; but she could hardly hear him for the noise.

She pressed his hand almost affectionately as she courtesied to the audience. If she could have thought at all, she would have remembered how Madame Bonanni had once told her that in moments of great success everybody embraces everybody else on the stage. But she could not think of anything. She was not frightened, but she was dazed; she felt the tide of triumph rising round her heart, and upwards towards her throat, like something real that was going to choke her with delight. The time while she had been singing had seemed short; the seconds during which the applause lasted seemed very long, but the roar sounded sweeter than anything had ever sounded to her before that day.

It ceased presently, and Margaret heard from the house that deep-drawn breath just after the applause ended, which tells that an audience is in haste for more and is anticipating interest or pleasure. The conductor's baton rose again and Margaret sang her little scene with the maid, and the few bars of soliloquy that follow, and presently she was launched in the great duet with the Duke, who had stolen forward to throw himself and his high note at her feet with such an air of real devotion, that the elderly woman of the world who admired him felt herself turning green with jealousy in the gloom of her box, and almost cried out at him.

He took his full share of the tremendous applause that broke out at the end, almost before the lovers had sung the last note of their parts, but the public made it clear enough that most of it was for Margaret, by yelling out, 'Brava, la Cordova!' again and again. The tenor was led off through the house by the maid at last, and Margaret was left to sing 'Caro nome' alone. Whatever may be said of Rigoletto as a composition--and out of Italy it was looked upon as a failure at first--it is certainly an opera which of all others gives a lyric soprano a chance of showing what she can do at her first appearance.

By this time Margaret was beyond the possibility of failure; she had at first sung almost unconsciously, under the influence of a glorious excitement like a beautiful dream, but she was now thoroughly aware of what she was doing and sang the intricate music of the aria with a judgment, a discrimination and a perfectly controlled taste which appealed to the real critics much more than all that had gone before. But the applause, though loud, was short, and hardly delayed Margaret's exit ten seconds. A moment later she was seen on the terrace with her lamp.

Madame Bonanni had listened with profound attention to every note that Margaret sang. She was quietly dressed in a costume of very dark stuff, she wore a veil, and few people would have recognised the dark, pale face of the middle-aged woman now that it was no longer painted. She leaned back in her box alone, watching the stage and calling up a vision of herself, from long ago, singing for the first time in the same house. For she had made her début in that very theatre, as many great singers have done. It was all changed, the house, the decorations, the stage entrance, but those same walls were standing which had echoed to her young voice, the same roof was overhead, and all her artist's lifetime was gone by.

As Margaret disappeared at last, softly repeating her lover's name, while the conspirators began to fill the stage, the door of the box opened quietly, and Lushington came and sat down close behind his mother.

'Well?' she said, only half turning her head, for she knew it was he. 'What do you think?'

'You know what I think, mother,' he answered.

'You did not want her to do it.'

'I've changed my mind,' said Lushington. 'It's the real thing. It would be a sin to keep it off the stage.'

Madame Bonanni nodded thoughtfully, but said nothing. A knock was heard at the door of the box. Lushington got up and opened, and the dark figure of the cadaverous maid appeared in the dim light. Before she had spoken, Madame Bonanni was close to her.

'They are in the chorus,' said the maid in a low voice, 'and there is some one behind the door, waiting. I think it will be now.'

That was all Lushington heard, but it was quite enough to awaken his curiosity. Who was in the chorus? Behind which door was some one waiting? What was to happen 'now'?

Madame Bonanni reflected a moment before she answered.

'They won't try it now,' she said, at last, very confidently.

The maid shrugged her thin shoulders, as if to say that she declined to take any responsibility in the matter, and did not otherwise care much.

'Do exactly as I told you,' Madame Bonanni said. 'If anything goes wrong, it will be my fault, not yours.'

'Very good, Madame,' answered the maid.

She went away, and Madame Bonanni returned to her seat in the front of the box, without any apparent intention of explaining matters to Lushington.

'What is happening?' he asked after a few moments. 'Can I be of any use?'

'Not yet,' answered his mother. 'But you may be, by and by. I shall want you to take a message to her.'

'To Miss Donne? When?'

'Have you ever been behind in this theatre? Do you know your way about?'

'Yes. What am I to do?'

Madame Bonanni did not answer at once. She was scrutinising the faces of the courtiers on the darkened stage, and wishing very much that there were more light.

'Schreiermeyer is doing things handsomely,' Lushington observed. 'He has really given us a good allowance of conspirators.'

'There are four more than usual,' said Madame Bonanni, who had counted the chorus.

'They make a very good show,' Lushington observed indifferently. 'But I did not think they made much noise in the Introduction, when they were expected to.'

'Perhaps,' suggested Madame Bonanni, 'the four supernumeraries are dummies, put on to fill up.'

Just then the chorus was explaining at great length, as choruses in operas often do, that it was absolutely necessary not to make the least noise, while Rigoletto stood at the foot of the ladder, pretending neither to hear them nor to know, in the supposed total darkness, that his eyes were bandaged.

'Have you seen Logotheti?' asked Lushington.

'Not yet, but I shall certainly see him before it's over. I'm sure that he is somewhere in the house.'

'He came over from Paris in his motor car,' Lushington said.

'I know he did.'

There was no reason why she should not know that Logotheti had come in his car, but Lushington thought she seemed annoyed that the words should have slipped out. Her eyes were still fixed intently on the stage.

She rose to her feet suddenly, as if she had seen something that startled her.

'Wait for me!' she said almost sharply, as she passed her son.

She was gone in an instant, and Lushington leaned back in his seat, indifferent to what was going on, since Margaret had disappeared from the stage. As for his mother's unexpected departure, he never was surprised at anything she did, and whatever she did, she generally did without warning, with a rush, as if some one's life depended on it. He fancied that her practised eye had noticed something that did not please her in the stage management, and that she had hurried away to give her opinion.

But she had only gone behind to meet Margaret as she was carried off the stage with a handkerchief tied over her mouth. She knew very nearly at what point to wait, and the four big men in costume who came off almost at a run, carrying Margaret between them, nearly ran into Madame Bonanni, whom they certainly did not expect to find there.

When she was in the way, in a narrow place, it was quite hopeless to try and pass her. The four men, still carrying Margaret, stopped, but looked bewildered, as if they did not know what to do, and did not set her down.

Madame Bonanni sprang at them and almost took her bodily from their arms, tearing the handkerchief from her mouth just in time to let her utter the cry for help which is heard from behind the scenes. It was answered instantly by the courtiers shout of triumph, in which the four men who had carried off Gilda did not join. Margaret gave one more cry, and instantly Madame Bonanni led her quickly away towards her dressing-room, a little shaken and in a very bad temper with the men who had carried her.

'I knew they would be clumsy!' she said.

'So did I,' answered her friend. 'That is why I came round to meet you.'

They entered the dim corridor together, and an instant later they both heard the sharp click of a door hastily closed at the other end. It was not the door of Margaret's dressing-room, for that was wide open and the light from within fell across the dark paved floor, nor was it the door of the contralto's room, for that was ajar when they passed it. She had not come in to dress yet.

'That door does not shut well,' Margaret said, indifferently.

'No,' answered Madame Bonanni, in a rather preoccupied tone. 'Where is your maid?'

The cadaverous maid came up very quickly from behind, overtaking them with Margaret's grey linen duster.

'They did not carry Mademoiselle out at the usual fly,' she said. 'I was waiting there.'

'They were abominably clumsy,' Margaret said, still very much annoyed. 'They almost hurt me, and somebody had the impertinence to double-knot the handkerchief after I had arranged it! I'll send for Schreiermeyer at once, I think! If I hadn't solid nerves a thing like that might ruin my début!'

The maid smiled discreetly. The dress rehearsal for Margaret's début was not half over yet, but she had already the dominating tone of the successful prima donna, and talked of sending at once for the redoubtable manager, as if she were talking about scolding the callboy. And the maid knew very well that if sent for Schreiermeyer would come and behave with relative meekness, because he had a prospective share in the fortune which was in the Cordova's throat.

But Madame Bonanni was in favour of temporising.

'Don't send for him, my dear,' she said. 'Getting angry is very bad for the voice, and your duet with Rigoletto in the next act is always trying.'

They were in the dressing-room now, all three women, and the door was shut.

'Is it all right?' Margaret asked, sitting down and looking into the glass. 'Am I doing well?'

'You don't need me to tell you that! You are magnificent! Divine! No one ever began so well as you, not even I, my dear, not even I myself!'

This was said with great emphasis. Nothing, perhaps, could have surprised Madame Bonanni more than that any one should sing better at the beginning than she had sung herself; but having once admitted the fact she was quite willing that Margaret should know it, and be made happy.

'You're the best friend that ever was!' cried Margaret, springing up; and for the first time in their acquaintance she threw her arms round the elder woman's neck and kissed her--hitherto the attack, if I may call it so, had always come from Madame Bonanni, and had been sustained by Margaret.

'Yes,' said Madame Bonanni, 'I'm your best friend now, but in a couple of days you will have your choice of the whole world! Now dress, for I'm going away, and though it's only a rehearsal, it's of no use to keep people waiting.'

Margaret looked at her and for the first time realised the change in her appearance, the quiet colours of her dress, the absence of paint on her cheeks, the moderation of the hat. Yet on that very morning Margaret had seen her still in all her glory when she had arrived from Paris.

One woman always knows when another notices her dress. Women have a sixth sense for clothes.

'Yes, my dear,' Madame Bonanni said, as soon as she was aware that Margaret had seen the change, 'I did not wish to come to your début looking like an advertisement of my former greatness, so I put on this. Tom likes it. He thinks that I look almost like a human being in it!'

'That's complimentary of him!' laughed Margaret.

'Oh, he wouldn't say such a thing, but I see it is just what he thinks. Perhaps I'll send him to you with a message, by and by, before you get into your sack, while the storm is going on. If I do, it will be because it s very important, and whatever he says comes directly from me.'

'Very well,' Margaret said quietly. 'I shall always take your advice, though I hate that last scene.'

'I'm beginning to think that it may be more effective than we thought,' answered Madame Bonanni, with a little laugh. 'Good-bye, my dear.'

'Won't you come and dine with me afterwards?' asked Margaret, who had begun to change her dress. 'There will only be Madame De Rosa. You know she could not get here in time for the rehearsal, but she is coming before nine o'clock.'

'No, dear. I cannot dine with you to-night. I've made an engagement I can't break. But do you mean to say that anything could keep De Rosa in Paris this afternoon?' Madame Bonanni was very much surprised, for she knew that the excellent teacher almost worshipped her pupil.

'Yes,' said Margaret. 'She wrote me that Monsieur Logotheti had some papers for her to sign to-day before a notary, and that somehow if she did not stay and sign them she would lose most of what she has.'

'That's ingenious!' exclaimed Madame Bonanni, with a laugh.

'Ingenious?' Margaret did not understand. 'Do you mean that Madame De Rosa has invented the story?'

'No, no!' cried the other. 'I mean it was ingenious of fate, you know--to make such a thing happen just to-day.'

'Oh, very!' assented Margaret carelessly, and rather wishing that Madame Bonanni would go away, for though she was turning into a professional artist at an almost alarming rate, she was not yet hardened in regard to little things and preferred to be alone with her maid while she was dressing.

But Madame Bonanni had no intention of staying, and now went away rather abruptly, after nodding to her old maid, unseen by Margaret, as if there were some understanding between them, for the woman answered the signal with an unmistakable look of intelligence.

In the corridor Madame Bonanni met the contralto taking a temporary leave of the wholesale upholsterer at the door of her dressing-room, a black-browed, bony young Italian woman with the face of a Medea, whose boast it was that with her voice and figure she could pass for a man when she pleased.

Madame Bonanni greeted her and stopped a moment.

'Please do not think I have only just come to the theatre,' said the Italian. 'I have been listening to her in the house, though I have heard her so often at rehearsals.'

'Well?' asked the elder woman. 'What do you think of it?'

'It is the voice of an angel--and then, she is handsome, too! But----'

'But what?'

'She is a statue,' answered the contralto in a tone of mingled pity and contempt. 'She has no heart.'

'They say that of most lyric sopranos,' laughed Madame Bonanni.

'I never heard it said of you! You have a heart as big as the world!' The Italian made a circle of her two arms, to convey an idea of the size of the prima donna's heart, while the wholesale upholsterer, who had a good eye, compared the measurement with that lady's waist. 'You bring the tears to my eyes when you sing,' continued the contralto, 'but Cordova is different. She only makes me hate her because she has such a splendid voice!'

'Don't hate her, my dear,' said Madame Bonanni gently. 'She's a friend of mine. And as for the heart, child, it's like a loaf of bread! You must break it to get anything out of it, and if you never break it at all it dries up into a sort of little wooden cannon-ball! Cordova will break hers, some day, and then you will all say that she is a great artist!'

Thereupon Madame Bonanni kissed the contralto affectionately, as she kissed most people, nodded and smiled to the wholesale upholsterer, and went on her way to cross the stage and get back to her box.

She found Lushington there when she opened the door, looking as if he had not moved since she had left him. He rose as she entered, and then sat down beside her.

'Have you any money with you?' she asked, suddenly.

'Yes. How much do you want?'

'I don't want any for myself. Tom, do something for me. Go out and buy the biggest woman's cloak you can find. The shops are all open still. Get something that will come down to my feet, and cover me up entirely. We are nearly of the same height, and you can measure it on yourself.'

'All right,' said Lushington, who was well used to his mother's caprices.

'And, Tom,' she called, as he was going to the door, 'get a closed carriage and bring it to the stage entrance when you come back. And be quick, my darling child! You must be back in half-an-hour, or you won't hear the duet.'

'It won't take half an hour to buy a cloak,' answered Lushington.

'Oh, I forgot--it must have a hood that will quite cover my head--I mean without my hat, of course!'

'Very well--a big hood. I understand. Anything else?'

'No. Now run, sweet child!'

Lushington went out to do the errand, and Madame Bonanni drew back into the shadow of the box, for the lights were up in the house between the acts. She sat quite still, leaning forward and resting her chin on her hand, and her elbow on her knee, thinking.

There was a knock at the door; she sprang to her feet and opened, and found a shabby woman, who looked like a rather slatternly servant, standing outside with the box-opener, who had shown her where to find the prima donna. The shabby woman gave her a dingy piece of paper folded and addressed hurriedly in pencil, in Logotheti's familiar handwriting. She spread out the half-sheet and read the contents twice over, looked hard at the messenger and then looked at the note again.

'Who gave you this? Who sent you?' she asked.

'You are Madame Bonanni, are you not?' inquired the woman, instead of answering.

'Of course I am! I want to know who sent you to me.'

'The note is for you, Madame, is it not?' asked the woman, by way of reply.

'Yes, certainly! Can't you answer my question?' Madame Bonanni was beginning to be angry.

'I will take the answer to the note, if there is one,' answered the other, coolly.

Madame Bonanni was on the point of flying into a rage, but she apparently thought better of it. The contents of the note might be true after all. She read it again.

Dear lady (it said), I am the victim of the most absurd and annoying mistake. I have been arrested for Schirmer, the betting man who murdered his mother-in-law and escaped from Paris yesterday. They will not let me communicate with any one till tomorrow morning and I have had great trouble in getting this line to you. For heaven's sake bring Schreiermeyer and anybody else you can find, to identify me, as soon as possible. I am locked up in a cell in the police station of the Third Arrondissement.----

Yours ever,
C. LOGOTHETI.

Madame Bonanni looked at the woman again.

'Did you see the gentleman?' she asked.

'What gentleman?'

'The gentleman who is in prison!'

'What prison?' asked the woman with dogged stupidity.

'You re a perfect idiot!' cried Madame Bonanni, and she slammed the door of the box in the woman's face, and bolted it inside.

She sat down and read the note a fourth time. There was no doubt as to its being really from Logotheti. She laughed to herself.

'More ingenious than ever!' she said, half aloud.

A timid knock at the door of the box. She rose with evident annoyance, and opened again, to meet the respectable old box-opener, a grey-haired woman of fifty-five.

'Please, Madame, is the woman to go away? She seems to be waiting for something.'

'Tell her to go to all the devils!' answered Madame Bonanni, furious. 'No--don't!' she cried. 'Where is she? Come here, you!' she called, seeing the woman at a little distance. 'Do you know what you are doing? You are trying to help Schirmer, the murderer, to escape. If you are not careful you will be in prison yourself before morning! That is the answer! Now go, and take care that you are not caught!'

The woman, who was certainly not over-intelligent, stared hard at Madame Bonanni for a moment, and then turned, with a cry of terror, and fled along the circular passage.

'You should not let in such suspicious-looking people,' said Madame Bonanni to the box-opener in a severe tone.

The poor soul began an apology, but Madame Bonanni did not stop to listen, and entered the box again, shutting the door behind her.

The curtain went up before Lushington came back, but the prima donna did not look at the stage and scarcely heard the tenor's lament, the chorus and the rest. She seemed quite lost in her thoughts. Then Lushington appeared with a big dark cloak on his arm.

'Will this do, mother?' he asked.

She stood up and made him put it over her. It had a hood, as she had wished, which quite covered her head and would cover her face, too, if she wished not to be recognised.

'It's just what I wanted,' she said. 'Hang it on the hook by the door, and sit down. Gilda will be on in a minute.'

Lushington obeyed, and if he wondered a little at first why his mother should want a big cloak on a suffocating evening in July, he soon forgot all about it in listening to Margaret's duet with Rigoletto. His mother sat perfectly motionless in her seat, her eyes closed, following every note.

At the end of the short act, the applause became almost riotous, and if Margaret had appeared before the curtain she would have had an ovation. But in the first place, it was only a rehearsal, after all, and secondly there was no one to call her back after she had gone to her dressing-room to dress for the last act. She heard the distant roar, however, and felt the tide of triumph rising still higher round her heart. If she had been used to her cadaverous maid, too, she would have seen that the woman's manner was growing more deferential each time she saw her. Success was certain, now, a great and memorable success, which would be proclaimed throughout the world in a very few days. The new star was rising fast, and it was the sallow-faced maid's business to serve stars and no others.

For the first scene of the last act Gilda puts on a gown over her man's riding-dress; and when Rigoletto sends her off, she has only to drop the skirt, draw on the long boots and throw her riding-cloak round her to come on for the last scene. Of course the prima donna is obliged to come back to her dressing-room to make even this slight change.

Madame Bonanni was speaking earnestly to Lushington in an undertone during the interval before the last act, and as he listened to what she said his face became very grave, and his lips set themselves together in a look which his mother knew well enough.

The act proceeded, and Margaret's complete triumph became more and more a matter of certainty. She sang with infinite grace and tenderness that part in the quartet which is intended to express the operatic broken heart, while the Duke, the professional murderer, and Maddalena are laughing and talking inside the inn. That sort of thing does not appeal much to our modern taste, but Margaret did what she could to make it touching, and was rewarded with round upon round of applause.

Lushington rose quietly at this point, slipped on his thin overcoat, took his hat and the big cloak he had bought, nodded to his mother and left the box. A few moments later she rose and followed him.

In due time Margaret reappeared in her man's dress, but almost completely wrapped in the traditional riding mantle. Rigoletto is off when Gilda comes on alone at this point, outside the inn, and the stage gradually darkens while the storm rises. When the trio is over and Gilda enters the ruined inn, the darkness is such, even behind the scenes, that one may easily lose one's way and it is hard to recognise any one.

Margaret disappeared, and hurried off, expecting to meet her maid with the sack ready for the final scene. To her surprise a man was standing waiting for her. She could not see his face at all, but she knew it was Lushington who whispered in her ear as he wrapped her in the big cloak he carried. He spoke fast and decidedly.

'That is why the door at the end of the corridor is open to-night,' he concluded. 'I give you my word that it s true. Now come with me.'

Margaret had told Lushington not very long ago that he always acted like a gentleman and sometimes like a hero, and she had meant it. After all, the opera was over now, and it was only a rehearsal. If there was no sack scene, no one would be surprised, and there was no time to hesitate not an instant.

She slipped her arm through Lushington's, and drawing the hood almost over her eyes with her free hand and the cloak completely round her, she went where he led her. Certainly in all the history of the opera no prima donna ever left the stage and the theatre in such a hurry after her first appearance.

One minute had hardly elapsed in all after she had disappeared into the ruined inn, before she found herself driving at a smart pace in a closed carriage, with Lushington sitting bolt upright beside her like a policeman in charge of his prisoner. It was not yet quite dark when the brougham stopped at the door of Margaret's hotel, and the porter who opened the carriage looked curiously at her riding boot and spurred heel as she got out under the covered way. She and Lushington had not exchanged a word during the short drive.

He went up in the lift with her and saw her to the door of her apartment. Then he stood still, with his hat off, holding out his hand to say good-bye.

'No,' said Margaret, 'come in. I don't care what the people think!'

He followed her into her sitting-room, and she shut the door, and turned up the electric light. When he saw her standing in the full glare of the lamps, she had thrown back her hood; she wore a wig with short tangled hair as part of her man's disguise, and her face was heavily powdered over the paint in order to produce the ghastly pallor which indicates a broken heart on the stage. The heavily-blackened lashes made her eyes seem very dark, while her lips were still a deep crimson. She held her head high, and a little thrown back, and there was something wild and almost fantastic about her looks as she stood there, that made Lushington think of one of Hoffmann's tales. She held out her whitened hand to him; and when he took it he felt the chalk on it, and it was no longer to him the hand of Margaret Donne, but the hand of the Cordova, the great soprano.

'It's of no use,' she said. 'Something always brings us together. I believe it's our fate. Thank you for what you've just done. Thank you--Tom, with all my heart!'

And suddenly the voice was Margaret's, and rang true and kind. For had he not saved her, and her career, too, perhaps? She could not but be grateful, and forget her other triumphant self for a moment. There was no knowing where that mad Greek might have taken her if she had gone near the door in the corridor again; it would have been somewhere out of Europe, to some lawless Eastern country whence she could never have got back to civilisation again.

'You must thank my mother,' Lushington answered quietly. 'It was she who found out the danger and told me what to do. But I'm glad you're safe from that brute!'

He pressed the handsome, chalked hand in his own and then to his lips when he had spoken, in a very un-English way; for, after all, he was the son of Madame Bonanni, the French singer, and only half an Anglo-Saxon.

* * * * *

The last thing Madame Bonanni remembered, before a strangely sweet and delicious perfume had overpowered her senses, was that she had congratulated herself on not having believed that Logotheti was really in prison, arrested by a mistake. How hugely ingenious he had been, she thought, in trying to get poor Margaret's best friends out of the way! But at that point, while she felt herself being carried along in the sack as swiftly and lightly as if she had been a mere child, she suddenly fell asleep.

She never had any idea how long she was unconscious, but she afterwards calculated that it must have been between twenty minutes and half an hour, and she came to herself just as she felt that she was being laid in a comfortable position on a luxuriously cushioned sofa.

She heard heavy retreating footsteps, and then she felt that a hand was undoing the mouth of the sack above her head.

'Dearest lady,' said a deep voice, with a sort of oily, anticipative gentleness in it, 'can you forgive me my little stratagem?'

The voice spoke very softly, as if the speaker were not at all sure that she was awake; but when she heard it, Madame Bonanni started, for it was certainly not the voice of Constantine Logotheti, though it was strangely familiar to her.

The sack was drawn down from her face quickly and skilfully. At the same time some slight sound from the door of the room made the man look half round.

In the softly lighted room, against the pale silk hangings, Madame Bonanni saw a tremendous profile over a huge fair beard that was half grey, and one large and rather watery blue eye behind a single eyeglass with a broad black riband. Before the possessor of these features turned to look at her, she uttered a loud exclamation of amazement. Logotheti was really in prison, after all.

Instantly the watery blue eyes met her own. Then the eyeglass dropped from its place, the jaw fell, with a wag of the fair beard, and a look of stony astonishment and blank disappointment came into all the great features, while Madame Bonanni broke into a peal of perfectly uncontrollable laughter.

And with the big-hearted woman's laugh ends the first part of this history.

THE END

CPSIA information can be obtained
at www.ICGtesting.com
Printed in the USA
BVHW031007041020
590250BV00001B/74